# Sorrow's Blade

## Umbra Lance : Book One

HANNAH A. FINCH

Copyright © 2026 Hannah A. Finch

All rights reserved.

No part of this publication may be reproduced, distributed, or transmitted in any form or by any means, including photocopying, recordings, or other electronic or mechanical methods, without the prior written permission of the publisher. For permission requests email: contact@hannahafinchwriter.com

The story and incidents portrayed in this production are fictitious.

Cover illustration by Ellie – Ei__zy

Edited by Kayleigh – Enchanted Edits

ISBN 978-1-7642493-1-7 (pbk.)

*To my brother 'Gerald' i.e. Josh.*
*Thank you for listening to hours of my ramblings,*
*for being my first reader, and my main supporter through the years.*

# MONTHS AND SEASONS OF UMBRA LANCE

# KINGDOMS OF UMBRA LANCE

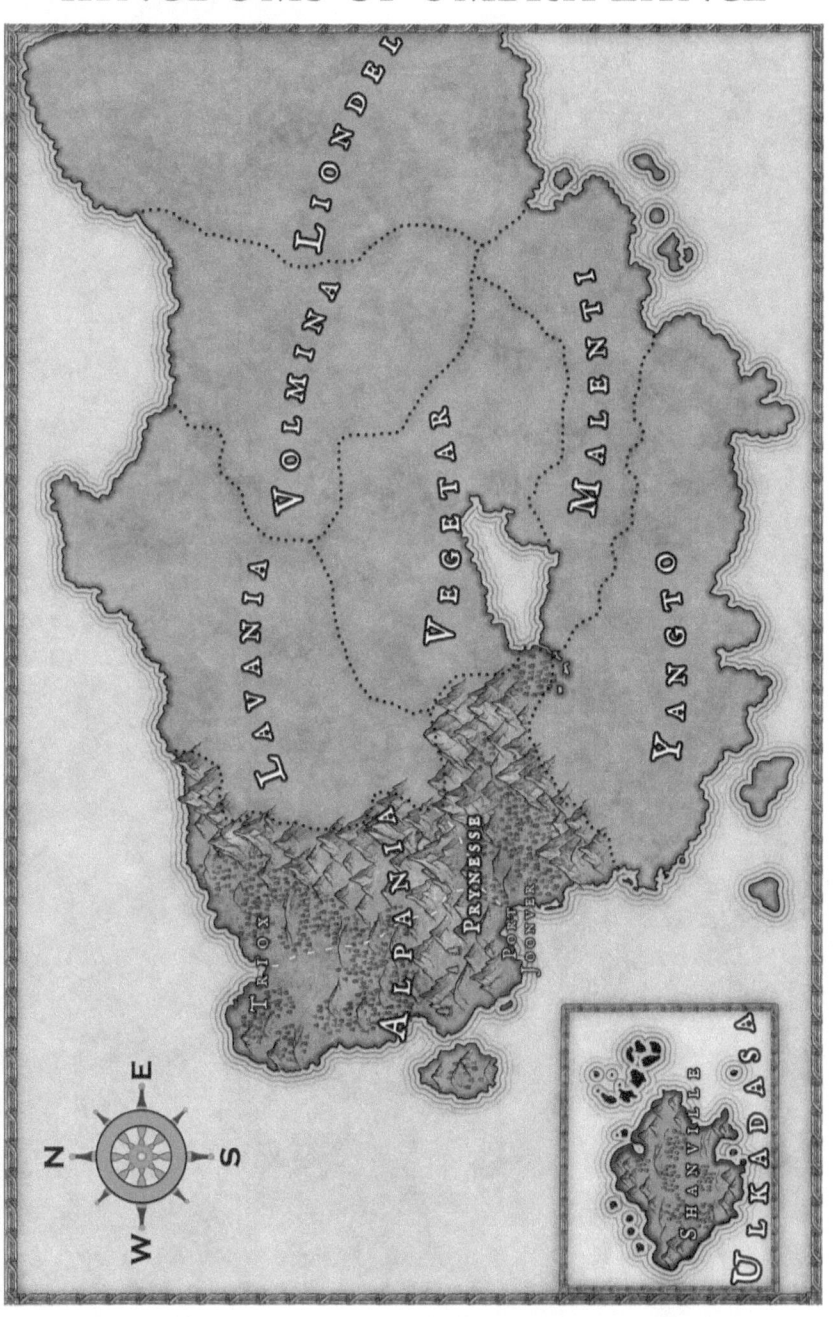

# CHAPTER ONE

*Life is full of decisions; some we make in a split second, and others we mull over until it feels like the most significant moment in our lives. In the end, these decisions produce our ambitions, our loves, our fears, and our losses; they make us into who we are. Decisions also lead to regret; things we wish we had done and things that we would rather forget had ever happened. We never know what the right choice is until we've already dived in and made a decision. Sometimes we never find out what the right choice was. Once made, however, it's too late to take it all back, it affects the path we've chosen. I have never been afraid of adventure and the unknown; I yearn for it, and I concede I will chase it to the bitter end, an end that may well destroy me.*

—*Ahzya Xion*

### Brielle 1407

#### TRI PEAKS TAVERN, TRIOX, ALPANIA

Ahzya Xion stood in the glow outside of a window of the Tri Peaks Tavern. Located in the city of Triox, a seaport on the northeastern coast of Alpania, the tavern was popular with the late evening crowd of drinkers and gamblers. Their shouts drifted down the street on the sea wind that whipped the outside of the tavern and caused its sign to constantly rock back and forth. Ahzya took a deep breath of fresh air before she plucked up her courage and pushed open the pine door. She winced as the door squeaked on its hinges that were rusted from the salt air and not maintained with oil.

Ahzya's knee-length, black leather boots barely made a sound as she stepped inside. The din of the tavern's patrons made her entrance barely noticeable except for the rush of fresh air that cut through the staleness of the room. She pulled the door roughly shut behind her, and the smell of alcohol and sweat permeated the room once more.

The incoherent buzz of laughter and banter between tables welcomed Ahzya into the tavern's hectic atmosphere. Friday night in Triox meant that many of the patrons' wallets were heavy with the coins collected from their week of labour. Many flocked to the tavern to pass the weekend in a drunken daze before returning to work on Monday with hangovers.

Lanterns lit up each table, illuminating the room with soft orange light. The first floor of the tavern had two large rooms, separated by a wide archway. Card games took place in the marginally quieter corners. Smoke hung in the air like a foreboding cloud over the gamblers. Gambling was a main attraction of the tavern, and bets were even being called over a dart match taking place on the left side.

The main demographic of the patrons of Tri Peaks Tavern was male, and flaring tempers made it a den of bar fights. There were a few women in the crowd, their eyes gleaming with a competitive nature and their alcohol, for the most part, better paced.

With all these characteristics, Ahzya Xion seemed a little out of place. Standing a little under five feet tall, she was dwarfed in size next to the rowdy crowd. Even at twenty-one years of age, many mistook her for a girl in her early teens. Ahzya believed what she lacked in height and muscle mass, she made up with dexterity and intelligence. She honed her cunningness with a dedication equal to the time spent mastering her blades. When living in Triox, one couldn't survive long without having some tenacity and skill.

Authorities classed Triox as the number one haven for crime, and they faced a challenge in keeping the offenders at bay. Assassins, thieves and thugs engaged in a diverse range of illegal occupations and congregated in and ultimately rule the area. This caused many scuffles between gangs, leagues and organisations, who all thought they were the best candidates to handle the power of leadership. A revisory committee had been founded, but it turned out to be a futile attempt by the royal family to crack down on the unruly citizens. The efforts of this committee usually ended in fights breaking out between the two sides in the street. Facing danger was part of the daily routine of the citizens of Triox, and many even craved the thrill of this uncertainty.

The area wasn't the most pleasant place on earth, but, as an orphan and runaway, Ahzya was used to such scenes. As a woman who seemed to attract adventure and chaos wherever she went, she enjoyed every adrenaline-pumping minute.

Ahzya pulled her hood down onto her neck, her grey-green eyes scanning the room, her view no longer hindered. Her chestnut hair curved shaggily in a top layer around her face and ears, while the layers underneath ran down the nape of her neck.

As Ahzya moved through the crowd, she crossed the path of a feisty dart match. The players were severely affected by alcohol, as the darts hit the wall more often than the dart board. This particular game was more a source of amusement for the betters rather than a subject of a lot of cash exchange. Catching one unusually wayward dart, Ahzya swiftly flicked it into the bullseye of the target. The original dart thrower squinted as the dart thudded into the board, before cheering proudly, wholly believing the result was due to his own talent.

Ahzya approached the bar bench where a denser crowd congregated and tried to catch the attention of the barkeeper. She sighed impatiently, as the barman's attention was wholly occupied with the thirsty men who were yelling for refills. Without hesitation, she drew a gold coin out of a pouch sewn into the lining of her jacket and tossed it casually into the air. The gold gleamed in the lantern light as it flipped through the air before returning to the palm of Ahzya's hand. The barman looked up from where he stood, his trained eye not missing the golden gleam. Even in the loud and packed room, gold always took first place in service, even minds heavily clouded by grog. The barman put aside the grubby cloth that he was using to wipe over a recently emptied tankard and then looked over Ahzya with a probing look. Several other greedy eyes of men at the bar also searched for signs of hidden gold.

"JP Dry, I hear he's got some sort of office here," Ahzya called, flipping the coin between her fingers with a calm fluidity.

The barman shrugged and picked up the cloth again. His eyes stayed fixed on the single gold coin, betraying his true intention. He knew the answer to Ahzya's question, but he wanted to make sure that she was only going to offer one of those precious gold coins.

"I coulda sworn the messenger said 'Tri Peaks Tavern'. I must have been mistaken."

Ahzya began to turn away, and the barman quickly switched his tune.

"Oi, missy," he called huskily. "In the back room."

Ahzya looked over her shoulder at him; her eyebrow raised inquiringly.

The barman motioned towards the back room with a nod of his head. The back room granted access to two office spaces, currently with closed doors, and a staircase to the second floor. The barman's nod tilted towards the right office. Ahzya flicked the coin to the barman; his eyes shone with greed at the easily earned shiny coin as he surveyed it. Ahzya let a smirk lift one side of her lips as she pushed towards the back of the room, knowing full well that the gold coin was counterfeit. Though convincing, it was a fake, cast by a talented con-artist who owed Ahzya more than a couple of favours.

Ahzya reached the entryway to the back room and flicked her hair off her face. She expertly let the dagger, which had been hidden in her sleeve, slip into her hand. Her fingers caressed the leather handle to ease her mind. She'd already planned a quick escape route by the time she'd taken two steps inside the tavern.

The message summoning her to Tri Peaks Tavern was left for her at her usual haunt on the other side of town, the Veritas Guild. It hadn't exactly come as a surprise, but it hadn't been overly informative either. Printed simply on a single piece of parchment and sealed with a cobra indented wax seal, the single line:

*Tri Peaks Tavern – 8pm – Job offer – JP Dry.*

Ahzya wasn't completely sure what would come from the invitation, though she had her expectations, and, in her profession, an escape route should always be in the plans.

With a flick of her wrist, the dagger disappeared. Ahzya noticed one of the patrons leaning against the wall next to the back door and quickly noted the clear eyes and lack of a flask or flagon in his hands. Though he seemed to be engrossed in the nearby card game, Ahzya saw the shift in his posture as she approached. Paying no mind to the man, she confidently reached out and she twisted the doorknob—she wasn't really one for knocking.

Ahzya's eyes took a moment to adjust to the much dimmer surroundings of the room. Two bulky men came to attention as she entered but remained standing with their arms crossed, watching her. Small batons hung at their hips, perfect for the crowded environment, which would be restrictive to any bigger weapons. Ahzya chuckled quietly and fixed an amused look on her face. She stepped further into the room; her arms lifted in feigned surprise.

"You've organised quite the welcoming party here, Mr Dry." Ahzya made no reaction as she heard the door shut firmly behind her, a small click following this action. This trapping move was undertaken by the 'undercover' guard who'd been standing watch at the door. "Do you always have your dogs intimidate your guests at the door? Or did you feel that you needed protection from an amiable guest like myself?"

A tall man stepped out of the shadows at the back of the room and surveyed her at a glance. JP Dry, Ahzya noted, as she returned his visual assessment with one of her own, had a powerful build. He wore black clothing that blended with the shadows flung by the one lantern in the room. A long-sleeved shirt, which was rolled up his forearms, defined his wide shoulders and toned arms. In the dimly lit room, he appeared to have an olive complexion. It was hard to see much else of his features, other than his hazel eyes and dark ash-toned hair. A single cobra insignia lay gleaming in silver on the left side of the vest he wore.

There were rumours, mainly spread by the young women of the district, that the rise of JP Dry was partially due to his charming countenance and captivatingly handsome features. Ahzya could see why there were rumours about his looks, though how charming a personality he had remained to be seen. Ahzya raised her gaze to meet JP's, observing an underlying dark gleam that stayed set in his eyes, even though he was now smiling broadly at her.

"Amiable you may be, but if your reputation is anything to go by, I should still keep a close eye on you," JP Dry said, sitting down behind a rugged wooden desk. "However…"

With a single wave of his hand, JP dismissed his two guards. They moved past Ahzya, knocking twice on the door. The door unlocked with a click, and the guards exited the room. As the door banged shut behind them, JP motioned for Ahzya to take a seat in front of the desk. Ahzya did so but couldn't help wishing the chair legs weren't so tall when her feet barely touched the wooden board floor.

JP retrieved two glass mugs and a bottle of amber-shaded liquid out of one of the desk drawers. The strong smell of whisky drifted out of the nozzle of the bottle as JP took the lid off. Ahzya wrinkled her nose but hid it behind her hand as she forced a cough.

"Drink?" JP asked, the bottle hovering over one of the glasses.

"I don't drink," Ahzya answered, shaking her head.

JP poured himself a glass and put the other back in the drawer. Ahzya noticed a wry smile appearing on JP's lips after she declined his offer.

"Business isn't advisable with a cloudy mind," Ahzya explained, allowing an annoyance to flash in her eyes as a defence. "Since it's one of my best assets, I prefer to keep my mind alert."

"Hmm." JP tilted his head for a moment, as if considering Ahzya's statement. He took a sip out of his glass, and then another bigger one. "A wise kid."

Ahzya let her annoyance simmer as she watched JP drink the alcohol. It was a show that he felt she was no threat to him at all, an underlying insult Ahzya couldn't ignore.

"I assume you had a reason for your message, other than longing for some dignified company, Mr Dry?" Ahzya asked, shifting her position on the seat.

"Straight to the point, aren't we?"

"While you seem to be at your leisure, no doubt under the impression that I have ample time to sit and enjoy chit chatting with you..." Ahzya paused, allowing her sentence to trail off unfinished, eyeing JP as he took another sip.

"Why would I assume that?"

"Your current manners—"

"My manners are lacking?"

"Despite it being no secret that most people consider your looks and manners to be...well, you know..."

"No, I'm afraid I'm not following. What about my looks?"

Ahzya felt like her insides were squirming from the awkwardness, yet she kept her disciplined posture still. JP was enjoying this far too much for Ahzya's liking. As he sat in his chair with a grin on his face, he looked as if he were a predator teasing its prey for pure entertainment. As his slightly shuttered eyes kept focused on her, he swirled the whisky in its glass. Ahzya's stubborn streak kicked into force. The meeting was proceeding like some sort of theatre lovers' flirtation rather than a business discussion, and she was determined to steer it back on track.

"Charming," Ahzya finished shortly. "Though from what I've witnessed, there's no substance to you so far. I could be doing much better things with my time than sitting in a dark room all evening."

"Am I keeping you from a romantic rendezvous? I'm jealous of the lucky guy."

Ahzya blinked across at JP and let silence fill the small room. JP looked disappointed that his prey didn't bite the bait further and sighed dejectedly.

"You're lucky that I happen to like people who get directly to the point, although I personally like to savour the process of newfound camaraderie," JP said, with a relaxed shrug.

*Camaraderie wouldn't be the word I'd use*—Ahzya kept her wry thoughts to herself.

"There's a difference between eagerness and an actual ability to undertake a job well. I have high hopes for you, though, that is why I thought of you when I devised my latest scheme," JP continued, straightening his back. "Upon properly achieving the task, you'll receive a considerable sum of money. Sound good?"

"Agreeing to something without context would be a foolish endeavour," Ahzya said, studying JP's face. "Money is all well and good, but it's no real incentive for me personally. A person in my...career path, has simpler ways of acquiring funds. In saying that, I'm always up for a new adventure."

JP smiled slyly and leant forward, setting down his glass on the desk.

"Oh, an adventure it will surely be," JP stated. "A small scheme set for scholars to enter into history books. By small scheme, I don't mean it won't be challenging, but I think you're more than capable."

JP left the statement hanging as if it were a hint for Ahzya to reply, even though he hadn't asked a question. Ahzya willed herself to remain still, not letting her impatience show. JP raised an eyebrow and drooped his shoulder slightly.

"You know you could help me add to the excitement a little."

"By this point, I really don't care whether you tell me or not," Ahzya lied, with a wave of her hand.

While she wasn't lying when she said she could acquire money easily, the fact was that she still wanted more. An opportunity that boasted a large payout would cover days' worth of her usual earnings. Another silent minute went by in which JP studied Ahzya while she viewed her short nails with disinterest.

"Your cooperation skills are lacking. You're a lone wolf usually, aren't you? You seem to have no conscience in recognising my wishes," JP reflected.

"Huh?" Ahzya responded distractedly.

"I find this quite disappointing."

"You should get used to it; life is full of disappointments."

"You needn't be the one to add to them."

"I'm helping you out, give you a big dose now, and you'll be prepared later on in life."

"You make me sound like a child."

"Hmm, how old are you exactly? I can't really tell by the way you're acting."

"I could ask you the same thing. You're being as stubborn as a child."

"I think you'll find the saying is 'stubborn as a mule'," Ahzya corrected.

"Is a mule similar to an ass? Because if so, I stand corrected, you stubborn ass," JP said pointedly, amused by his own wordplay.

"I'm not stubborn, I'm resolved."

"You're rather disrespectful. Shouldn't you be treating me, your boss, a bit better?"

"You're not my boss; you haven't even told me what you want to employ me to do."

"So, once I've employed you, you'll treat me with the respect I deserve?"

"Yes, the respect that you deserve…" Ahzya mused. "Which I doubt is much different from my current manner."

"Is that so?"

"Indeed, but we'll have to see. You could start by telling me what the job is," Ahzya said, crossing her arms. "Do you need a drum roll?"

JP didn't reply immediately and just pouted into his glass as he took a sip.

"…or would you prefer me to torture it out of you?"

JP's pout dropped and was replaced with a wide smile that barely showed his teeth. Ahzya realised too late, that she had fallen for the bait.

"A feisty inquisitor I have here. I knew you were deliciously intrigued! Lies suit you, my dear, but I'm a skilled adversary, you have a few years ahead of you before you can pull the wool over my eyes," JP gloated, savouring the victory.

Ahzya gritted her teeth in frustration, flexing her hand to release some tension. She had never been good at keeping her cool when she was a child, but she thought she'd outgrown it. Patience in the field was easy, patience in conversation less so.

"The assassination of King Mark," JP stated suddenly.

Ahzya froze, but no emotion showed on her face as she met JP's calculated gaze. His eyes reflected no hint of a joke, and the smile had disappeared from his face. He was apparently ready to do business; his previous teasing manner put to the side.

"You'll be the one undertaking the assassination," JP stated calmly.

It was a shock; the assassination of a king was not the kind of job Ahzya had expected. Assassination requests were few and far between, and usually people hired professional assassins, not people like her. Ahzya frowned and studied JP suspiciously.

"Why me?" Ahzya asked bluntly.

"I always keep my ear out for rising individuals that could serve me well in this dark underworld, and your reputation as a thief was particularly intriguing," JP said. "A 'silent mover', my connections said. With a skill set like that, there isn't much of a step up to be an assassin, is there?"

He said it with such a calm and matter-of-fact tone that a chill ran down Ahzya's spine.

"Besides, no-one would ever suspect a petite girl such as yourself to be an assassin," JP chuckled, relaxing in his seat again. "The castle will never guess that you will be a threat."

"A petite girl?" Ahzya sneered, her eyes flashing momentarily.

"Yes," JP answered, pulling a cigarette from his pocket.

JP's playful mood was back as he lit the cigarette and proceeded to breathe out a stream of smoke from his lungs.

"A petite girl, with training in the art of thievery. If the rumours are correct, you've got some wicked abilities," JP uttered, with a cheerful grin.

It was true. Ahzya was a thief, a criminal for years, and she was used to that way of life. She lived on her own, precarious in a business that could end in confinement or death. It hadn't always been like that. She'd led a carefree life and eventually found herself part of a family. However, the more innocently you dream of eternal happiness, the crueller it's ripped from you.

# CHAPTER TWO

### Six Years Earlier: Mew 1401

PORT SHANVILLE, ULKADASA

At fifteen, Ahzya spent her days playing in the local sea caves of a small fishing village, Shanville, in the country of Ulkadasa.

Cliffs and treacherous rocks that were hidden just under the surface, made up the shores of Ulkadasa. The water was freezing throughout most months of the year unless they experienced a rare heatwave that lasted a couple of weeks. Many of those born in the coastal ports and villages were fishermen and sailors. The children grew up learning the tricks of the trade, the best fishing spots and how to swim.

Ulkadasan trade centred on their successful fishing industry. The ever-growing population of fish inhabiting the coastal waters of the country were rare to other countries and inland Ulkadasa. The ocean was hazardous, and many of those working at sea ended up losing their lives there. Often those who went to sea died young, concerning many inland citizens, although this didn't reduce the demand for the fresh and delicious fish the coast provided. However, those who were taking the risk said they wouldn't change their jobs for the world. This left many of their children orphans, and many orphanages were established to care for these children. Nearly all the children from the orphanages, who knew better than anyone else the risk of going to sea, ended up following in their parents' footsteps and became sailors.

One morning in fumohora, Ahzya was dipping her feet in the rock pools. She watched a gathering of fishing boats in the ocean and squinted her eyes trying to identify which Shanville family the boats belonged to. Ahzya chewed on some fresh seaweed she'd already rinsed off, enjoying the salty snack as she hadn't bothered making a campfire or catching a more substantial meal that morning. She climbed further along the rocks and sat down, the breeze whipping long hair around her body. Ahzya kept her eyes on the horizon as she twisted her hair onto the top of her head and stabbed a stick through expertly, pinning it there.

On the horizon, a small, dark dot grew larger and soon developed the shape of a ship. It wasn't that of a fishing vessel, instead a huge three-masted ship made for travelling distant ocean waters. A flag fluttered at the top of one of the sails and it wasn't that of Ulkadasa. The Ulkadasan flag was a rich teal, a silver shield in the centre sporting within its confines the image of a water kelpie proudly rearing out of a wave. The flag on the approaching ship was a deep purple, and the image of snow-capped mountains swelled as the flag moved in the wind. An excitement zapped Ahzya to attention, and her bare feet slapped on the wet rocks as she began running along the fastest route to the port, where the foreign vessel was now headed.

The bay of Port Shanville was a wide inlet surrounded by the ever-present cliffs, yet boasted a depth that kept the bay floor and any sharpened rocks well beneath the surface. Port Shanville was created half by building into the cliffside and half by sturdy pontoons rigged to the cliffs, which boats then moored on to. To get down to the port area, you had to descend staircases carved into the rock cliffs. Apparently Ahzya wasn't the only one who noticed the arrival of the foreign ship as she joined curious villagers making their way down.

While the curiosity of the Shanville residents caused a hindrance to Ahzya, it provided a great funnel for information. For that day, Ahzya couldn't get close enough to see much with her own eyes, and so she settled for second-hand gossip.

The foreign ship hailed from a country called Alpania, a country to the east, past the islands of Corallia and beyond. It was an exploration vessel titled *Moonstruck,* and while on its latest expedition it had been separated from the rest of its fleet after it was damaged. The captain of the *Moonstruck,* upon seeing boats entering the bay, decided to stop for supplies before continuing its journey home.

The people from Alpania called themselves Alpanians. They used the same alphabet and basic language as the Ulkadasan people, but it was said the foreigners 'spoke funny'. It was soon relayed that the Alpanians found the locals' thick dialect, and Ulkadasan pronunciation of the shared alphabet, to be so different that it seemed like a completely separate language, even though the basic words were the same. Fortunately, the Alpanians had a soldier who possessed linguistic skills, and the captain covered the role of diplomat, so they quickly entered into discussions with the elders of Ulkadasa in the Shanville main hall. Discussions on the exchange of information and even a basic possibility of a trade agreement, kept the diplomats and elders busy for days.

While the officials talked politics and traded maps, the foreign sailors and soldiers freely explored the new surrounds and talked to the villagers. The newcomers brought with them new items to admire, and their deep-blue-coloured uniforms left the locals fascinated. The younger men of the ships even taught new games to the children and brought small treats for them.

Private Peter Lant was one of those sailors that quickly won over the curious Ahzya, and she followed him around for the next couple of days. Peter had the palest blond hair, almost cream coloured, and blue eyes. Alpanians were noticeably taller than Ulkadasans, and he was no exception. His time as a sailor had defined his muscles and despite only being twenty-two years old, through Ahzya's eyes he was like a storybook hero. Peter had a friendly manner and a face that was always ready to flash a smile.

One afternoon, Peter was sitting on a rock rewriting the orphan's names with how the Alpanians would write the Ulkadasan pronunciation.

All the kids were lined up and Ahzya joined out of curiosity. When it came around to Ahzya's turn, she stepped forward shyly.

"Ahzya Xion," Ahzya stated quietly.

"From the vocalisation, your first name is fairly simple to write," Peter mused.

Peter swept the dirt patch that he was writing it down in and rid it of the previous child's name. He then began to scrawl 'A-h-z-y-a' onto the ground with a stick.

"Your last name could have two spellings," Peter said. "Firstly…"

'S-h-i-o-n' formed on the ground, and then Peter wrote the second option of 'X-i-o-n'.

"The first syllable formed with the 'x' and 'i' of the second version is the same sound as 'she' and then you end both versions with the syllable 'on'," Peter explained, underlining each syllable.

Half of what he was talking about sounded like random babbling to Ahzya, but she nodded.

"How would you spell your name in Ulkadasan?" Peter asked.

Ahzya silently picked up a nearby short, thin stick and wrote the Ulkadasan spelling right next to Peter's interpretations. 'A-s-s-a' formed her first name and then she wrote her last name with a simple 'S-y-n'. She took a step back and grinned.

"I like the look of the Alpanian spelling of my name more," Ahzya complimented, looking at Peter's neatly printed writing with admiration. "The second version of my last name looks like a warrior's name."

Peter smiled at her. As the crowd of orphans dispersed at the sound of the orphanage's dinner bell, Ahzya lingered. Peter noticed and motioned for her to sit next to him.

"I can teach you how to write your name in this style if you wish."

Peter's suggestion led to them spending time rewriting the name Ahzya Xion over and over. With their friendly bond deepening, Ahzya eventually showed him the best coastal caves and the rock pools. Peter always listened to her speak of the ocean with utmost attention. One trip to the caves, Ahzya was staring out across the waves when she suddenly became melancholy. She'd spent the last few days in happy camaraderie with Peter, spoke more than she had for years, but soon he'd be leaving across that deep blue expanse and back out of sight.

"I don't remember much about my parents," Ahzya spoke softly. "Zac and River Syn. Miss Jaine said they crossed a kelpie and it dragged them into the sea in the middle of a storm. Of course, she also said she wouldn't have been surprised if I turned out to be a kelpie, since I had the nature of one. That's just ridiculous, if I were a kelpie, I would've returned to the sea long ago."

Ahzya ripped down the length of a piece of seaweed and sighed.

"Miss Jaine was always lying. My parents weren't dragged off by any kelpie. They found them tied together with a rope so they wouldn't lose each other. Dad must have anchored the rope to the boat, but it had smashed apart. With such preparation, they were too smart to fall for the tricks of some stupid sea beast."

Ahzya cleared her throat.

"I didn't have any other family, so our neighbour, Miss Jaine, took me in. She promised my parents, you see, but I lasted only a couple of weeks there after the funeral. Miss Jaine dressed me up real pretty and marched me down to the orphanage. That's what Jaine really wanted, me out of her care. Even though she was assigned as my guardian, I'd never gotten along with her, so I hardly acted like an angelic child. I cried a lot, like a baby, but I never let her see me!"

Ahzya stated this proudly, but the sympathetic smile Peter sent her showed he didn't believe in her bravado act.

"The orphanage turned out to be just as grey. Resources of the orphanage are spread thin, and the rooms are always packed beyond what seems possible. But then I found these caves," Ahzya said with a smile. "I find I can spend quite a few days and nights here, and the orphanage hardly even notices. It's glorious."

Peter listened to the story without interruption. He had a quiet and earnest side to him, allowing for a considerate flow of conversation, with pauses for just soaking in every moment. He and Ahzya got along without sharing more than a few words most days, but Ahzya felt comfortable sharing her random thoughts.

"No doubt they'll kick me out to find a job soon enough, I am fifteen after all. But I don't want to be a simple kitchen maid or babysitter. One day, I want to work on a ship," Ahzya said as she grinned and waved her hand to the ocean. "Not a fishing ship like my parents. I'd like to work on an exploration ship. I remember the odd trip with my father in the past; it was all about the adventure more than the fishing side that I liked."

Peter chuckled and skipped a rock into the ocean waves.

"So, something like the ship I came on?" Peter asked.

"Your ship is the king of all ships; I'd have to work hard to become part of its crew."

"It's a beautiful specimen, although we more commonly refer to her as the fleet's queen."

Ahzya went to a small rock pool in the corner of the cave and picked up a pointed stick. In this particular cave, the sea water still came in at high tide, and fish got captured in the pools. These fish made for great meals, and Ahzya usually had this instead of the sloppy porridge offered at the orphanage.

"Are you likely to be adopted?" Peter asked suddenly.

"No, not a chance. Adoptions are rare, and they usually look for younger children. Also, I'm not on the headmaster's good side," Ahzya answered with a casual laugh. "He'd probably send me to the back room if anyone actually came."

"What if someone went directly asking for you?" Peter asked thoughtfully.

"Well, I guess they'd be happy to have me off their hands in that case, but the headmaster is pretty stubborn," Ahzya answered with a frown. "Why?"

"Just curious," Peter said, standing up.

Several days later, Ahzya was sleeping in her rugged bed in the orphanage. The sea breeze made the wooden walls creak, yet Ahzya had long ago gotten used to the sound. Wrapped around her, adding warmth to the thin sheets, was a dark blue woollen cloak. Peter had given it to her as a gift and insisted that it would keep her warm against the cold sea wind. While the room was warm and several of the youngest girls snuggled into her like she was their hot water bottle, she didn't want to take it off.

A dark figure entered the room, the door's hinges creaking. Ahzya shared the room with only girls since the orphanage at least segregated the girls and boys for some sort of privacy. The figure tiptoed almost apologetically through the sleeping bodies and mattresses and headed straight for Ahzya's blue-clad body. They shook Ahzya awake and though her eyes were still blurry with sleep, Ahzya noticed the familiar uniform first.

"Peter?" Ahzya mumbled in a whisper.

"Shh," Peter's voice hushed her.

"What are you doing here?" Ahzya asked with sleepy confusion.

"Get up and pack a bag," Peter ordered in a quiet voice.

Peter kept glancing back at the door and hurried her along with a wave of his hand. When Ahzya took too long putting her few possessions in a bag, Peter just shoved them in. He threw the bag over one shoulder and guided Ahzya towards the door. Peter held her arm as they hurried through the halls, ducking into a room when a light lit the hall. The slow footsteps of the headmaster passed them by, and then they stepped into the hall again.

Ahzya's heart was pounding by the time they exited the front door, and she paused hesitantly. She had seen Peter talking with the headmaster earlier that day, on the orphanage's front steps. It had looked quite heated, but when she went to greet him, he'd disappeared. Now he seemed on edge and urgently turned when she stopped.

"What's happening?" Ahzya asked nervously.

"I guess this is a little strange," Peter mused, glancing towards the front door anxiously. "Oh, right, I never actually asked you what you wanted."

Ahzya switched feet, quickly becoming less scared as finally Peter looked her directly in the eyes.

"Would you like to come with me on the *Moonstruck*? I hadn't asked yet because I figured it's exactly what you wanted; you'd be going on an adventure," Peter whispered earnestly. "Dragging you out like this isn't the best way, so I'm sorry. Would you like to join my family?"

"Is that what you were talking to the headmaster about?" Ahzya asked with new understanding.

"Yep, your adoption," Peter answered. "I wanted to do it all officially, wave goodbye to this place with our heads held high."

"Wanted to?"

"He said that 'someone' had already spoken for you, which was an obvious lie. Then he said he couldn't give anyone from another country adoption papers for one of their children, since he couldn't be assured that they were going to a good home," Peter said with a sneer. "As if this place is even halfway decent! So, if he's going to be difficult, I figured we'd just have to take another approach."

"He'll know it was you and he'll go to your ship."

"Well, he will be too late by that time, we spent today stocking up on supplies. The *Moonstruck* will be leaving early this morning. As you've said, they barely notice when you're away at the sea caves, so he won't notice in time."

Ahzya felt the cold coastal mist make her face tingle and wrapped the cloak around her in a protective manner. Peter held out his hand, his eyes pleading. It would take one movement to change everything; she could choose to turn back or go with Peter. Ahzya smiled and put her small hand in Peter's large one.

"Then let's go," Ahzya spoke, her voice shaking.

Anything was better than the old orphanage, and it *was* the perfect chance for adventure.

## Present Day: Brielle 1407

### Seaport of Triox, Alpania

Ahzya slowly came out of her daydream and found herself again face to face with JP Dry. He was giving her a questioning glance, and Ahzya shook her head to clear her thoughts.

"What made you think that a thief would simply be able to turn assassin?" Ahzya questioned, her arms crossing.

"It was a natural state of progression; an assassin also needs to be silent and sneak into buildings unnoticed. The only addition is you enter to kill, and no matter how pretty you are, you can't convince me that you're so innocent as to have never killed anyone before. Not when you've lived in these parts for the past few years as I've heard," JP said with a wry smile.

Ahzya met JP's eyes but didn't give any response.

"So, will you take the job?" JP continued.

"It will be a challenge, but I'm not one to back down from challenges," Ahzya said, her voice steady and confident.

"Come on, how challenging can it be? As I've stated, I've already heard tales of you slipping through houses without detection or leaving a trace." JP shrugged.

"Sneaking through a target's house is a vast sight different from invading a fortress with a dedicated defence force," Ahzya replied with a scoffing sigh.

"And doesn't the castle play that to their advantage! Their enemies are deterred by the tall sturdy walls and number of foot soldiers, but the castle can rely too much on this deterring image and become complacent in their watch. They say only fools would attempt such a thing but allow these fools to slip in under their noses," JP mused, swirling the whisky in its glass.

Ahzya's confidence in her abilities was solid; however, despite JP's assurance, she was no fool. What JP stated wasn't a lie, castle soldiers may become complacent during times of peace; however, such a habit wasn't a characteristic of Alpanian guards. Drilled into them, from the time they put on their first training garb, was the mindset that your enemy is always at your neck, a threat lurking in every corner, both shadowed and well lit. In the cases of men born into military families this was implemented from birth. The Alpanian royal defence was not to be taken lightly.

"So, I'm to become this fool and inject myself into their system not to steal but to kill?" Ahzya asked, keeping her doubts to herself.

"In that aspect, yes, though no doubt you are relying on the fact you aren't a true fool."

"I know myself well enough, though isn't it more a case of *you* relying on that fact. After all, putting all your faith in a fool is akin to being a fool yourself."

"I'm confident in the basket I've put my eggs in, and, when this is all over, they will have been turned to gold. I know we both appreciate that currency."

"As long as you don't try to pay me in raw eggs painted with gold," Ahzya retorted.

"I have honour enough to boil them first," JP chuckled, leaning back in his chair. "You amuse me, and there are few things left in this world that can amuse me."

"Then perhaps you should have hired me as a clown instead of an assassin."

"A lost opportunity." JP sighed in disappointment. "Though we haven't sealed the deal yet…"

Ahzya slipped off the chair, her feet now on the floor once again. She reached out her right hand, hovering it over the desk within JP's reach.

"I'll do the assassination, but I'm afraid the service of clown is far too expensive for your wallet," Ahzya stated, tilting her head slightly.

JP sat up and nodded, dwarfing her hand with his own as he grasped it tightly.

"Very well, I may just have to work out another plan for obtaining that joy," JP stated lightly, as they firmly shook hands sealing the deal.

Despite the initial dark aura and serious job offer, Ahzya couldn't help but notice that their meeting had proceeded with a teasing manner. This fact just made everything feel that much stranger.

"Congratulations," JP said, his face showing how pleased he was. "I'm not known for my patience, too much of the business mindset on 'time is money' drilled into me, but if you must take time—"

"I'll get ready right away and depart directly for the castle," Ahzya interrupted. "Any particular method you prefer your assassins to use? Killing methods can send different messages depending on the motivation."

"You're talking like a seasoned killer," JP mused, studying her face before lifting himself out of the chair. "I have no specific message I wish to send, just do whatever makes you happy."

"Happy?" Ahzya mumbled incredulously.

"Gold makes you happy, right? Achieve this task, and you're well on your way to being a wealthy woman," JP said, giving her an unnerving smile.

JP moved around the desk; stood close to Ahzya, his body merely inches away from her. He didn't talk for what felt like a minute, although it was only a few seconds.

*He's so damn tall.*

"By the way, please don't get caught. There is a high possibility that you may be found out," JP warned her almost tenderly. "I'm worried it would be too much for you and you might call out my name. Of course, I'd have to intervene before that happened. The castle is far away, but you won't be completely unreachable, I do have contacts."

The whisky from earlier still hung on his breath, but Ahzya didn't flinch. Their eyes studied each others, neither one wishing to back down first. Finally, JP's gaze drifted down her slim jawline. Ahzya rolled her eyes at the uncomfortable tenseness that filtered into her limbs and turned, taking a step back. She hated the sly grin she felt JP giving upon her retreat.

Ahzya nodded her acknowledgement, pulling her hood over her head.

"If you're done with your cliché threats..." Ahzya trailed off. "I can assure you, your name won't pass my lips. Besides, I doubt JP Dry is your real name anyway."

JP shrugged casually and moved to the door. He rapped twice on the door and it unlocked. Ahzya brushed closer, pausing mid-stride as she crowded into his space this time. Ahzya kept her chin lowered, allowing her face to linger in shadows of it. JP raised an eyebrow, dipping to meet her conspiratorially.

"One more thing, Dry. Why do you have such an interest in assassinating King Mark?" Ahzya asked, her eyes watching him underneath her hood.

"Would it make you feel better if I had a self-justified reasoning for the assassination?" JP responded with his own question.

"There is a vast difference between justice and self-justification," Ahzya mused.

"I don't think our deal requires a moral debate. The simple answer is that this move is for power. That's usually why advisers and politicians scramble for higher roles," JP answered coldly.

"So, you stand to gain power from this experience?" Ahzya queried.

"Something like that. It's better for you if you don't pry," JP ordered. "All you need to know is that he is your target, and I am the one paying you."

"So, you don't have anything personal against the king?" Ahzya probed icily.

"I like to think that I've passed the point of trivial emotions, though in one way I also hate everyone and everything. As a businessman I have to use people as tools for my goals. My money and I are also merely a stepping stone for you and my men. We are bonded by money, not loyalty. You are tools that I will use to my advantage, and the king is just another block standing in my way."

"Continue with that kind of attitude, Dry, and you'll find yourself in serious trouble." Ahzya stretched her arms. "Bonds without trust tend to end with a knife in someone's back. Just so you know, my back is far too pretty to be scarred by a betrayer."

Ahzya straightened her back, and JP opened the door wide to let her exit. Several patrons eyed her as she passed on her way through the crowded tavern, but the glint of a blade deterred them from approaching. It was either the blade or JP's vigilant eyes that still watched her as she opened the front door.

Ahzya left the bustling tavern and took a deep breath of fresh air. She began walking till she was a safe distance away and then she rolled her shoulders. Her eyes darkened, and she flipped the blade in her grip. This may be a mission of power for JP Dry, but for Ahzya, this would be personal.

# CHAPTER THREE

### Six Years Earlier: Layzeth 1401

MAIN DECK, MOONSTRUCK, SEA OF GALES

Ahzya awoke in a small storage room, which Peter had made her bedroom. Due to her short frame, Ahzya only had to curl her body and lie on her side when she slept since the room was more like a large cupboard. Luckily, Peter had removed the shelving so she could stand when she needed to stretch her body. The room held only a pile of blankets and her belongings.

It had been two weeks since Peter smuggled her on board the exploration ship, *Moonstruck*, and she spent all day cooped up in her quarters. The only time she emerged was in the dead of night, when there were only the overnight crew stationed around the ship.

In the beginning, after being cooped up in the room for the day, Ahzya found by nightfall she was excited and energised to explore her limited outdoor playground. However, as the days went on, her exhaustion made getting up tougher. Peter could only smuggle her cold meals, and thus Ahzya's new diet consisted of biscuits and cheese. Ahzya left complaints about her energy levels unspoken, suspecting that Peter ate less in order to accommodate her meals out of his own rations. Sometimes, through an eyeball-sized hole in the door, Ahzya would be posted a surprise gift at random points during the day. Sometimes it was a stick of jerky or dried fruit and sometimes a round orb of coloured candy wrapped in wax paper. So far, she'd tasted three flavours: lemon, strawberry and orange. The tangy and sweet combination of the orange was her favourite. These little gifts did help revitalise her energies and she could still enjoy her nightly escapes.

In the quiet and pitch darkness of her bedroom, Ahzya roused herself so that she completely awakened. Ahzya slowly opened the door and peeked out to make sure none of the crew were milling around. Spotting no-one, she stepped outside and onto the slippery deck. Ahzya gathered her cloak around her body as the cold wind crept through her clothing.

Peter retrieved Ahzya a change of clothes after her arrival on the ship, and Ahzya had changed out of her faded dress. Her new clothes were an oversized pair of dark navy pants and navy shirt which she tied at her waist. Her feet were still bare since none of the boots fit, but she was used to it. She didn't mind, and the hem of her pants fell over them enough to shield them from the breeze when she stood still.

It was a chilled, overcast night, and the waves rocked the ship gently. The large white sails stretched high above the deck and billowed full in the wind. Ahzya glanced across at the second-in-command who stood, yawning, at the wheel of the ship. He looked like an intimidating man, with his large frame, but Ahzya found she could avoid him easily. She stepped gingerly along the deck; her eyes so used to the dark by now that she did not need a lamp to find her way around. Ahzya snuck her way to the stern of the ship and stood quietly observing her surrounds.

She stared up at the sky, through the clouds, looking for any sign of stars that might emerge from behind the dark blanket momentarily. Some nights it was so clear that she could make out many a constellation, including that of Telles the Seahorse, her personal favourite. Tonight, no such sight was beheld, even the horizon was blanketed in a fog. Ahzya drew in a deep breath and then let it out slowly.

"Night shift again?" Ahzya asked quietly.

Peter Lant stepped out of the shadows of the ship, his boots making no sound on the oak deck. His eyes had dark circles around them, but they were alert in scanning the ocean as he simply placed a hand on her shoulder.

"Mhm," Peter acknowledged. "The boys are starting to get suspicious of how eager I am to swap to night patrol. Nate doesn't seem to care though, since he's always willing to spare himself any loss to his beauty sleep."

Peter sighed, a stream of vapour pouring out of his mouth as he exhaled.

"Your perception skills are getting better," Peter complimented. "I decided to test you, considering it's a foggy night, but you still noticed my approach."

"People have some sort of misconception that it's hard to see things at night, but it's just about using what light there is and your other senses," Ahzya answered seriously. "You can see many things in the dark if you know how to look. At least, that's what my smart brother teaches me."

Peter smiled through the darkness, patted her shoulder, and continued his rounds. The water lapped at the side of the ship and the boat creaked as it rocked. The captain of the ship wanted to return to their home port in Alpania before the freezing weather of nixhora struck. There was only a month left until harsh storms would start assaulting the ocean, and the journey was already treacherous enough. Luckily, they'd already been on the home stretch when they happened across Ulkadasa, which meant the chance of getting home safely was more likely.

Peter informed Ahzya that the *Moonstruck* had already been sailing for nine months and the crew were keen to return home. Although it was first planned to be only half a year's expedition, a storm had dealt severe damage to the ship. It had taken weeks to fix a couple of the sail booms which had snapped. They also had several crucial diplomatic meetings, which, as with many political things, didn't proceed very fast.

Ahzya's eyes scanned the horizon, and she sighed. It would be a long month or so cooped up in that small storage room. Luckily the galley's oven was just through the wall, and it kept her quarters toasty warm. The nights were already growing biting cold, and soon she wouldn't be able to leave the room much at all.

A brief flash of light on the port side caught Ahzya's attention. Rather than look directly at the flash, Ahzya allowed her eyes to defocus. She waited and saw another faint reflection further to the right of where she thought she saw the first flash. Ahzya focused her eyes again and rechecked the area, making out the brief outline of a ship. It looked like a small boat, oars dipping in and out in strong, slow strokes, bringing the ship quietly skimming across the water.

Ahzya stayed still and felt her pulse quicken. A carved wooden front piece was at the bow of the ship, shaped into a skull and two swords. A chill ran down Ahzya's spine, and she backed up a little. It was the insignia of the Southern Pirates, a band of vicious pirates from the southern islands of Corallia. Though their name itself was hardly fear-inducing, the pirates were known for their bloodthirsty methods and silent attacks.

Ahzya spun around, intending to alert Peter of the new threat on the ship, and immediately bumped into something. The something turned out to be the captain of *Moonstruck*, Captain Ray.

Captain Ray, by the word of any crew who'd ever worked with him, was a great leader. His thoughtful and pleasant nature balanced his strict and serious leadership style. The sea breeze tousled his black hair, and his clothing fluttered. While his captain's uniform was a rich navy-blue and well-kept despite the constant days in the ocean weather, at this moment, he wore a simple tunic and pants which tucked into his soft-leather boots. The short sleeves on his tunic revealed a tattoo of the *Moonstruck* emblem on the bicep of his right arm.

Ahzya stumbled back a step and stood quietly, stuck between finding an explanation and not wanting to alert pirates or *Moonstruck* crew. Captain Ray didn't seem too surprised that a fifteen-year-old girl had just bumped into him. Instead, he just stood before her and looked down at her calmly with his blue eyes darkened by the night.

"I saw them," Captain Ray stated casually.

"What...what do you mean?" Ahzya managed to ask in a low tone.

"The pirates," Ray answered. "No-one can sneak up onto my ship without me knowing."

Ahzya averted her eyes. His words brought her a clarity on the situation; hinting to his already knowing who she was or at least that she'd been smuggled aboard, perhaps even since the beginning. Ray's eyes lifted from the guilty-looking stowaway and gazed across the waves.

"They've disappeared for now, no doubt they'll return in a moment. Southern Pirates have a habit of sending a scout out first and ambushing once they ascertain the risk. Nights like this are their preferred hunting ground. Their main ship will be sailing out of view, hidden by the fog," Ray explained, seemingly calm despite the threat.

Just then Peter came around the side of the ship and spotted Captain Ray. Peter came to attention and glanced at Ahzya in concern. He then started to mutter an explanation for why Ahzya was there, and Captain Ray raised his hand.

"Private Lant, stop standing there muttering and run and get the men up," Captain Ray ordered, his voice quiet but firm. "If you say that a band of vicious pirates are about to board the ship, that should get them up without too much grumbling."

Peter glanced across the waves but saluted.

"And for goodness' sake, tell them to be quiet. Get them to wait under the deck and only return with Nate and Craig. I'll speak to Johno at the wheel. I want to see those bastards' faces when they realise we're not a bunch of sitting ducks," Ray added.

Peter glanced at Ahzya and then jogged quietly to do the task. Captain Ray then returned his attention to Ahzya and placed one of his large hands on her shoulder.

"As for you, stay inside your room beside the galley," Captain Ray said, leading her in the direction of her bedroom. "There's about to be all hell let loose on the deck, we don't want to be dodging you."

"Okay," Ahzya answered, shaking slightly.

"Stay in here, and don't exit unless either myself or Private Lant come for you," Captain Ray said, patting her shoulder. "We'll knock seven times so you know it's us."

Captain Ray opened the door to the room, and Ahzya slipped inside. He then knelt so he could be eye level with her.

"Have you ever handled a blade before?" Captain Ray asked.

"Only to shuck oysters, fillet fish and other kitchen duties," Ahzya answered honestly.

"At least you won't hurt yourself," he mused, reaching for her right hand. "This is for your protection only if you find yourself in imminent danger."

Captain Ray held her hand gently with his left and then placed an object into her open palm. He folded Ahzya's fingers around the object.

"I doubt you'll have to use it. I captain quite a competent crew; a band of stupid pirates will be easy pickings," he said with a reassuring smile before ruffling her hair.

Ray then stood as his second-in-command approached, carrying Ray's sword and dagger. The second-in-command was an observant fellow and had noticed Peter's movements. He'd swapped with another crew member at the ship's wheel and busied himself assuring that his captain was properly armed. Ray observed Peter and two other crew members gather near the midship, their movement slowed due to sleepiness.

Ahzya gulped nervously and then opened her hand. Looking down, she saw what Ray had given to her earlier. Resting in the palm of her hand, with a handle of twisted green and blue leather, was a dagger.

Now armed, Ray rolled his shoulders. He met Ahzya's scared gaze, but gave a serious, reassuring nod and closed the door. The room went dark, a faint glow showing through the eyeball-sized hole in the door but not bright enough to cut through the pitch black. Ahzya began to take deep, irregular breaths and sat down, pulling a blanket comfortably over her knees.

From her small room, Ahzya could hear the quiet voice of Captain Ray addressing his men with a quick message. The men had moved from the midship when they saw Ray and the second-in-charge together, and they were now gathered right next to the storage room. Ahzya hugged her knees as Captain Ray's low voice spoke.

"We work as a team, watch each other's backs and under no circumstance should any man be left fighting alone," Captain Ray ordered. "The Southern Pirates play dirty; they focus on lone prey, so stay alert. Now everyone in your positions; I don't want to see anyone in the open."

Not wanting to raise too much suspicion, many of the *Moonstruck* crew remained underdeck, ready to flood the deck on signal. Captain Ray and a gathering of other crew, who were trained fighters, proceeded to set positions near the sides of the ship. The angle from the surface of the ocean, given the size of *Moonstruck*, made it possible for the crew to remain undetected by crouching low and navigating without light. It helped that the pirates approached in low rowboats, adding to the angle.

Therefore, when the pirates boarded from the port side of the boat moments later, the crew of *Moonstruck* were ready. The pirates used hooked ropes to grapple onto the railing of the ship, and climbed up one after the other. Upon reaching the railing they were surprised to be met with the sharp blades of defending sailors.

The pirates fell from the ropes, colliding with those behind them. The *Moonstruck* crew let out a loud battle cry as they cut the boarding ropes, and the pirates returned a throaty chant. Although surprise was on Captain Ray's side, the pirates managed to push onto the deck. A second and then a third pirate boat pulled aside on the starboard and port side, and the pirate's numbers soon outnumbered the defending crew.

Not about to be overpowered, Captain Ray's crew drew together, and there was only a moment's pause. The clanging of metal on metal sounded all over the ship. Not a man on board wasn't fighting. Blood covered the deck, adding a slickness to the wooden boards.

Meanwhile, Ahzya sat huddled in her small room, listening to the sound of battle outside. She gripped the dagger tightly in her fist, and with her other hand, she held her cloak around her. Every cry of pain made Ahzya cringe, and she wanted to cover her ears. Ahzya felt her muscles tensing up, and her heart beat wildly.

She was praying that Peter was still alright. Stuck in the storage room, she had no idea who was winning. Ulkadasan sailors often rumoured about the Southern Pirates. Sometimes all that was left behind from their attacks was an empty ship, covered in dark blood stains.

The Southern Pirates weren't the most skilled fighters, they were thugs and thieves, self-taught fighters mostly. They relied on numbers and surprise. However, this line of pirate's guild had highly skilled killers and marauders amongst them. These members were numbered amongst the rest of the pirate ship's crew, but they were notably more dangerous. They played a significant role in taking down ships when their ambush tactic was broken. While these skilled pirates cut their way through a ship's crew, the less skilled pirate crew would pick off stragglers or lone sailors by ganging up on them.

Ahzya wondered how many sailors were already dead or injured. Although she wanted to help desperately, Captain Ray had given her orders. Ahzya would be more of a hindrance than a help anyway. She'd been given a dagger, but she didn't know the first thing about wielding it.

Ahzya wasn't even sure what she'd do if a pirate opened the door. Would she even be able to use the dagger? The pirate would probably cut her down before she'd lift the blade.

So many negative and worried thoughts swirled in her head, and she felt like she was going to be sick. She'd always had a strong constitution, but just the idea of being abandoned on the ship and emerging to the dead bodies of Peter and the crew made her want to vomit. Ahzya jumped as a couple of familiar voices rang through the night suddenly outside her room.

"Nate! Watch your back. They're devils," a gruff voice called.

"I would watch my back, Craig, but I'm too busy watching out for yours, old man," a younger voice called, surprisingly jolly for the current situation.

"I'm more agile than you think, lad," the other returned. "Sing like a banshee, hit like a…"

"Tortoise…" the younger finished, laughing loudly at his joke.

"Could you two galahs join the fight? I know I look like I could tackle a whole army by myself, but you'll have to let me off today, I'm running on an empty stomach," a loud voice interrupted.

"Righto, Johno, righto," the younger called. "The quicker we get this finished, the sooner we'll all be able to fill our stomachs with JB's fine cuisine."

"The best you're gonna get, mate, is the leftover peelings from last night's meal," came a raspy young voice. "There's a wide choice, potato peel, carrot peel and even some onion peel for a change."

"JB, as fine as that sounds, I'd rather have that fruitcake you have hidden in the secret compartment in the pantry. It looks mighty moist and delectable to me."

"Hang on a sec...JB's been keeping a supply of fruitcake from us?" the gruff voice broke in.

"Well, you ate the previous lot before we had even left port!"

Suddenly the door flew open with a bang and Ahzya recoiled away from it. Nobody entered the small area, in fact, nobody even noticed that it was open. Ahzya leant forward quickly to shut it, and it was then that she surveyed the battle scene.

Soldiers, sailors, and pirates alike were fighting each other on the slippery deck, some battling one-on-one and others in groups. Some of the men lay motionless on the deck, and others were trying to avoid crushing and tripping on them. Dark blue uniforms were stained purple as blood drenched into the fabric. Ahzya met several glazed eyes, and pained groans echoed in her ears.

It was then that Ahzya caught a glimpse of Peter, through the multitude of razor-sharp swords. Peter was struggling in one-on-one combat with one pirate, who sported a wicked scar across one eye. The pirate had a captain's hat on his head, probably taken from the captain of a past pillaged ship. The pirate sported a heavier wielding sword than Peter, and its blade was already red with blood.

Peter was working hard to defend from the continuous blows. Peter's blade strokes were becoming slower, but the pirate just drove on. Peter's chest rose and fell with heavy breaths and his arm buckled under one of the blows.

Without another thought, Ahzya stepped forward, out of the sanctuary of the small room. Ahzya launched herself into the battle zone. Her little form ducked and slid past all the other battling figures without receiving so much as a mark. Ahzya had done this before when she had often escaped punishment from the headmaster.

Peter continued fighting against the pirate captain who had a hatefully cheerful grin plastered on his face. Peter's hands were sweaty, and his grip on his sword slipped. The sword went flying out of his hand and onto the deck with a clatter. Peter's eyes widened, and his jaw clenched as he glared stubbornly up at the pirate captain. The pirate captain stood victoriously above him, flipping his sword, wanting Peter to beg. Peter wasn't ready to die like a coward, and he spat at the pirate. The pirate sneered as he raised the sword and readied it for a sideways slash.

Suddenly the pirate's face twisted in agony, and he dropped his sword to the deck. He started to grope at his back, confusion evident in his eyes. The pirate began to turn around, but Peter acted quickly and brought his elbow up, smacking it into the pirate's jaw. A crack sounded as his jaw made contact and even Peter winced at the sound. The pirate's eyes glazed over, and his eyes rolled back. He stumbled to his knees and then fell face forward, unconscious, at Peter's feet.

Behind where the pirate had previously stood, Ahzya breathed heavily, wide-eyed. Her face was pale, droplets of blood on her face and clothes, but she sighed when she saw that Peter was alright. Her gaze then lowered to fix on the pirate, who lay before her blood-stained bare feet. Ahzya gripped the green and blue leather dagger firmly in her hand, and both were covered in sticky blood. The pirate's body sported multiple wounds to his lower back, where Ahzya had repeatedly stabbed until he fell.

Ahzya's mouth filled with a sour bile as she convulsed and began to choke on her own vomit. Peter leapt over the pirate's unconscious body and caught Ahzya by the shoulders as she slumped over. Combining with her already overloaded senses, she began to shiver at the memory of her flurry of wild stabs sinking into the pirate's flesh. The sounds of battle faded from her ears and her vision blurred to darkness.

# CHAPTER FOUR

CAPTAIN'S QUARTERS, MOONSTRUCK, SEA OF GALES

P eter Lant's face was the first thing Ahzya saw when she stirred the morning after the pirate attack. Peter sat back-to-front on a chair, his hair messy and dark circles under his eyes. He gave her a welcoming smile as their eyes met, and he stood up. He turned around to grab a pot of simmering brown liquid off a small stove in the corner of the room. A rich aroma drifted through Ahzya's senses, as she recognised the familiar smell of coffee. Peter began pouring some of the coffee into a mug, and Ahzya took this opportunity to study her surrounds.

The bed Ahzya was lying on wasn't even a bed, but a hammock. The hammock rocked with every slight movement Ahzya made, but she found it a relaxing rhythm.

Around the room, nails tacked detailed maps and charts to the walls. Several paintings of Alpanian ships hung tastefully in dark wooden frames. A telescope, charts and compass were splayed over a desk situated opposite the hammock. Several chests lined the far wall, and a pair of sheathed swords leant against the desk.

Peter turned back to Ahzya, the coffee in the mug steaming as he handed it to her. Ahzya took a sip of the dark liquid, noting that it held an especially sweet flavour to it. Peter had evidently added a generous dollop of honey. Whenever she'd snuck a cup while at the orphanage, honey wasn't an affordable addition; however, with her current cup, she was pleased with the way it cut through the bitterness. Ahzya let out a satisfied sigh and wrapped her hands around the warm mug.

"Thank you," Ahzya said with a smile.

"How are you feeling?" Peter asked, pouring another mug of coffee.

"I'm fine," Ahzya said, taking a sip of coffee. "Although, my clothes smell like I've taken a dip in a sewer."

Ahzya sniffed her top and sneered. Her clothing had obviously not avoided her bout of illness, and she felt herself growing exhausted from just the thought.

"Sorry about that. I tried cleaning it off," Peter said, with an apologetic smile. "Once you feel up to it, I'll prepare a tub of hot water, and you can clean up."

Ahzya nodded but a frown furrowed her brow.

"I take it we managed to defeat the pirates?" Ahzya asked quietly.

"Yeah, the men fought back and drove them off," Peter answered.

There was a moment's silence as Peter returned to his former position sitting backwards on the chair. He rested his cup of coffee on the back of the chair and gazed into the dark liquid.

"How many of the crew were killed?" Ahzya asked cautiously.

"A lot. The doctor is still tending to the injured," Peter said, his eyes darkening. "It wasn't as bad as it could have been."

"But they were your family, no matter how many we lost."

"Yeah." Peter's fingers thrummed on his coffee cup.

"You should get some rest. You look like hell."

"I can't sleep," Peter replied, shaking his head. "Besides, I'm back on duty soon."

"You have to work? Still, you should try," Ahzya pushed in concern. "Perhaps just a quick nap. I'll wake you up."

"You'd have to knock me out to give me any useful respite. Nightmares are the only things that come to me when I close my eyes to sleep."

Ahzya felt an unease at Peter's words. Before she could slip back into the memories from the night, she took a purposeful, large mouthful of coffee.

"While I appreciate your concern," Peter thanked, "we are down crew, and everyone is pulling their extra weight; I'm no exception. Even injured men are still undertaking some duties, so it's my job to help where possible, even if that means losing a few more hours sleep."

Ahzya fell silent. Peter's explanation made sense, despite her wish to make sure he was alright.

"Besides, the detained pirates need to be watched and tended to. So that's added to our already heavy workloads," Peter said, rolling his right shoulder.

Ahzya clenched her hands into fists and frowned.

"Why tend to them? They wouldn't have done that for us," Ahzya said with a sneer.

"No, they wouldn't have," Peter agreed. "However, we must do the right thing. If we just leave them to die or have their wounds infected, then we are no better than they have been."

"I guess you're right."

Despite her accepting words, Ahzya still couldn't understand why they would treat the captured pirates as guests. If she were in charge, she would let them go hungry and feel pain. They deserved nothing less.

Ahzya returned to her browse of the room and her eyes rested on a glass container on one of the shelves. The container was full of the round candies which Ahzya had sampled through the postal hole of her small room. Ahzya frowned and glanced at Peter with concern.

"What's with that look?" Peter asked raising his eyebrows.

"Those candies," Ahzya said pointing at the container.

"Ah yes, the captain's treasure stash. I have no idea where he buys them, but they're—"

"If they are Captain Ray's, did you steal them for me?" Ahzya asked.

Peter just proceeded to look between the candies and Ahzya.

"I've never taken any of the candies to you," Peter said in defence. "You've tried them?"

Just then Captain Ray opened the door to the room, making Ahzya jump. A bandage wrapped his right arm and it was set in a sling. Ray took off his hat with his left hand and placed it on the desk. If Peter had looked tired, Ray looked like a walking dead man. As captain of the ship, he had apparently not taken a moment's rest since the attack. Ray let out a long sigh and moved a chair over to the side of the hammock. He dropped into the seat and leant back with an exhausted groan.

"How are you feeling this morning, Miss Xion?" Captain Ray asked, running his left hand through his hair.

"I'm fine. How is your arm?" Ahzya answered politely.

"Fine, it's just a small graze, it should be healed in a couple of days," Captain Ray answered.

Captain Ray rested his left arm over his eyes, his posture slumped, and head hung backwards. His chest rose and fell slowly, patches of blood still stained his shirt.

"I'm sorry for disobeying your orders last night," Ahzya said apologetically. "I hope I didn't cause any trouble by doing so…or by passing out."

"Private Lant informed me of your mid-battle escapade," Ray said. "Don't worry about it. Your reason for disobedience was understandable."

Ahzya hung her head, and she copied Peter in gazing into their coffee mugs.

"I can't say I'm glad that you had to use that dagger, even if it wasn't because you were in imminent danger, but rather in the service of a member of my crew. So, while I'm not glad you were forced to…" Ray said, sitting up. "Thank you."

Ahzya looked up in surprise and met Ray's earnest gaze. There was a short silence, and Ray leant back in his chair once again.

"I hope my quarters aren't too messy," Captain Ray stated, looking around at all the papers that were in messy stacks everywhere.

"I haven't had time to fully enjoy it," Ahzya answered, following his gaze. "However, I hope you don't mind that I've taken over your cabin."

"I don't mind at all. I'm sorry there isn't a proper bed in here, but I like the hammock more," Captain Ray said.

Peter raised one eyebrow at this and shook his head.

"That's when you get any sleep, sir," Peter said. "I don't think I've ever seen this room without the lantern lit at night."

"Did you ever consider, Private, that I can't sleep without a nightlight?" Ray asked, his gaze steady on Peter.

"Er, I...well, sir, that makes—" Peter started mumbling a response.

"It's a joke. You need to lighten up, Private Lant," Ray said, shaking his head in disappointment. He sighed. "No, the piles of paperwork don't seem to disappear despite my late hours. I still need to write up the log and a report for the attack."

"How are you going to do that with your injured arm?" Ahzya asked, looking at the bandages.

"The pirate conveniently injured my right arm," Ray said, before lifting his left hand with a wave. "I write with my left. Even pirates won't let me get out of paperwork."

Ray chuckled, and Peter turned and poured yet another mug of coffee. Peter took a small spoon of honey and mixed it in. He then swivelled and reached to give it to Ray.

"Thank you, Private," Ray said, taking the offered beverage. "Can you pass the honey?"

"I added a spoon—" Peter informed him.

"The honey, Private," Ray interrupted firmly.

"Yes, sir," Peter said, as he grabbed the tub of sweet honey.

Ray took one spoon and then another and then yet another. He stirred it in and took a long sip, his eyes closing.

"Did you want some coffee with that honey?" Peter asked jokingly. "Sir."

Peter added the 'sir' almost as if he just realised he was talking to his commanding officer. Ray raised an eyebrow and took a thoughtful sip.

"Private, I won't make you walk the plank for saying something without saying 'sir' at the end of it," Captain Ray said, shaking his head.

"Yes, sir," Peter said.

Ray yawned and then placed the coffee onto a precarious pile of paper.

"Captain Ray, I have a confession," Ahzya spoke timidly. "I think I may have eaten some of your orb candies and, while I didn't know they were yours, I'm still sorry."

"Why are you apologising for that?" Captain Ray answered matter-of-factly. "I posted them to you so you could eat them. I'd be more concerned if you'd let them go to waste."

Ahzya smiled as Ray fit together all the puzzle pieces for her. She relaxed and started to swing the hammock gently.

"Actually, I've got something else to give you, Ahzya," Captain Ray said, reaching across his desk.

Ahzya sat up, for, like any young person, she loved presents. Captain Ray removed something from the drawer and handed it to Ahzya. Ahzya looked down and saw the familiar blue and green leather dagger in a sheath. Ahzya took the dagger out of the sheath and looked over the blade.

"That is now yours, just make sure you don't start cutting off your fingers," Captain Ray ordered.

Ahzya sheathed the blade and ran her finger along the twisted leather handle. The dagger and her cloak were now her most precious belongings. She'd never been given presents since entering the orphanage, as it was seen as favouritism, and the orphanage couldn't afford gifts for all the children.

"I'd better go and check on the men," Ray said, downing the rest of his coffee. "When you're ready to get up, there are some clothes you can look through in that chest. I'm sure you can make something out of them."

Ahzya nodded her head in appreciation, and Ray picked up his hat from the desk. He pulled it firmly onto his head, one of its three pointed corners facing forwards.

"Private Lant, you're on duty in five minutes, I want to see you on the deck by then," Ray ordered, his blue eyes serious.

"Yes, sir," Peter said, coming to attention.

Ray then tipped his hat to Ahzya and turned on his heel, exiting the door moments later.

"Better get on deck then, as they say, 'Better to be early than late'," Peter said.

"In Ulkadasa that saying goes a little different," Ahzya said, smiling.

"In Alpania too, but I don't think anyone who ever worked on a ship and especially not under Captain Ray would ever be heard saying the actual quote," Peter said. "I'll see you later."

Peter then left Ahzya alone in the still and quiet room.

Ahzya soon made herself busy, slipping awkwardly from the hammock. A pitcher of water and small washing basin allowed her to wash up. Peter had forgotten about drawing hot water for her, but Ahzya had forgone such luxuries before. She found a washcloth and did her best to wash her body of the foul odour that clung to her skin.

In the chest Ray had previously pointed out to her, Ahzya found several items of clothing that she could wear. One pair of pants actually fit her, once she'd rolled up the hem a bit, and she added a long, wide piece of blue faded fabric and a white shirt to the mix. Ahzya tucked the shirt into the pants at her waist and then she folded the material into a thick belt. The belt of fabric covered the top of the pants and wrapped around her waist so that the shirt didn't look quite so baggy.

Looking in a tall mirror, Ahzya was satisfied with her clothing, but when she looked at her hair, she winced. Knots littered her waist-length hair, and she had horrible split ends. Picking up a comb, Ahzya tried to brush out the knots. She winced and bit her lip as she tried to pull the comb through her hair. Ahzya soon gave up and sighed.

Running her hand over her hair, Ahzya turned to the hammock. Picking up her dagger, she slid the blade out of the sheath. Picking up a section of hair, Ahzya lifted the dagger, closed her eyes and sliced through the strands. Opening one eye cautiously, she brought her fist full of hair down and held it in front of her. Ahzya glanced up at her reflection in the mirror. Well, the shorter side of her hair didn't look horrible, and she could already feel the difference in weight. Ahzya continued to slice sections from the rest of her long strands. When she had finished to her satisfaction, her hair fell to mid-neck length. Ahzya shook her head like a dog and smiled at how strange it felt.

Ahzya combed through the short hair easily and picked up the hair that had fallen onto the floor. She then walked over to the door and pulled it open.

The captain's quarters were situated under the helm at the stern of the ship so that the captain could quickly get to the helm if required. There were two sets of stairs either side of the entrance into the captain's quarters, and the main deck stretched out in front of the door.

The crew had scrubbed the oak wood back to its natural wooden colour, removing any bloody evidence of the battle. The sun shone brightly on the deck, and despite it being late fumohora, the temperature was lovely.

As Ahzya walked barefoot to the side of the ship, she firmly grasped the cut hair in her hands. Ahzya rose onto tippy-toes and leant against the side. She lifted her hands casually over the edge and let the hair slip out of her fingers. She then watched as it disappeared into the water and got swept into the bow wave that followed behind the ship.

Ahzya then turned and walked down the deck, curious to see what the rest of the crew were doing. Several glanced at her as she passed, but they busily continued on their way. Peter was leaning over a chart, tracing an invisible line with one of his fingers. Another sailor joined him, and they began to talk seriously. Leaving him to his work, Ahzya continued towards the bow of the ship.

A couple of injured sailors were sitting on benches getting some sunlight, and Captain Ray was talking to them. The sailors were smiling, and Ahzya soon realised that Ray was doing his best to distract them from their pain. Ahzya walked over and stood by the railing watching Ray, as he checked on each sailor's health.

"Who's the new crew member, Cap?" one older soldier asked, his gruff voice sounding familiar.

Ray looked up, raising an eyebrow, and then noticed Ahzya. He smiled and beckoned her over with a wave of his hand.

"This is Ahzya Xion, she'll be a crew member for the trip to Alpania," Ray introduced.

"Ok, and what job does Ray have you labouring at, Ahzya?" an orange-haired sailor asked, his voice Ahzya recognised as the jokester that had been bantering outside her room during the battle.

Ahzya shrugged and looked at Captain Ray for guidance.

"Ahzya will be helping out in the kitchen with food preparation, Nate," Ray answered.

"Ok, Ahzya, do you know how to make delicious chocolate pudding?" the first soldier asked, with a wink. "It happens to be a favourite of mine."

"Don't listen to Craig, Ahzya. Everyone knows that sticky-date pudding is much better than chocolate," said a sailor with large muscles.

As Ahzya looked up at the sailor who had just spoken, she recognised him as the second-in-command. Now that he wasn't stood at a distance at the ship's helm as she usually saw him, he towered above her. Ahzya wasn't about to disagree with him. The red-haired sailor, Nate, laughed aloud and stood up.

"Ah, don't worry about Johno, Ahzya. He's really a big softy, show him a big smile, and he'll be eating out of your hand in no time," he said, giving a huge grin at the bulky man.

Johno came to full height next to Nate and looked down at him with a frown. Johno was indeed a fearsome figure to behold as his buff muscles were defined by the white singlet and navy shorts that he wore. He had a scar on the left-hand side of his neck and the other side sported a dragon tattoo. Since he was standing next to Nate, who had a thin stature and no muscle definition, Johno looked even more prominent. Johno's face broke into a big, beaming smile and he ruffled the smaller man's hair.

"A smile and maybe a piece of cake, and then I'll do whatever you want, kid," Johno said aside to Ahzya. "Of course, I do feel we are already friends, after spending so many night shifts together it's really no surprise."

"You knew too?" Ahzya's mouth opened slightly wider than usual.

"The captain spoke to me the night after we left Shanville. He said not to bother the small spirit that slunk around the ship at night since it was Private Lant's new pal," Johno explained jovially. "So, I just made sure you didn't fall overboard and left it at that."

"I just wish the rest of us crew had been informed," Nate piped in. "We were oblivious, and it almost gave me a heart attack when I saw a creature flash past me in the midst of battle and take down one of the most skilled brutes."

"I stabbed him in the back, I'd hardly call that a skilled take down," Ahzya doubted.

"They can't expect an honourable battle when they fight dirty too," Johno replied quickly. "Now, crewmate, I think it's time you go ask JB what's on for lunch."

"Make sure he adds something to the stew if he's making it. The last lot tasted like vegetables and water mixed in a gluggy mass," Nate said. "Tell him to add a bit of that salted fish I saw him picking up at Shanville, that should give it some flavour."

"Gee, Nate, if you're so knowledgeable on the subject maybe you should be the cook instead of poor JB. By the way you talk, anyone would think you're a culling chef," a sailor with a bandage around his head said.

"I think you mean culinary chef, but maybe I should become one, maybe I will," Nate said.

"You try telling JB that, he's sure to give you a taste of his mind," Craig, the older soldier, replied.

"I've tasted brain before and didn't find it to my liking."

The soldier groaned, and Johno rolled his eyes. Captain Ray shook his head and ordered Johno to take the wheel of the ship.

"Off you go, I told JB to go easy on you for the first day, so he'll probably have you peeling carrots or something like that," Ray said, looking down at Ahzya.

Ahzya nodded and saluted to the rest of the sailors. She turned to run down the deck to the galley, but Ray stopped her.

"I notice you cut your hair," Ray observed aloud.

"Yup," Ahzya replied proudly, shaking her hair.

"It suits you," Ray complimented scratching behind his ear. "Just, perhaps you might want to introduce yourself to Doc later. He's our resident barber and he'll help even it out for you."

Ahzya just nodded happily and skipped away to where a new acquaintance awaited her. As Nate and Captain Ray watched her go, Nate turned to Ray, his face surprisingly serious for a change.

"Sir, what will happen to Private Lant?" Nate asked, his brow furrowed.

"I can't know for sure," Ray said, watching as Ahzya jogged down the deck. "I guess that depends on what happens when we reach port."

"We all know that in the Sailors Code it states that no sailor should smuggle anything on board a ship, be that alcohol, animal or human."

"Glad you are up to date on the code," Ray said simply.

"However, the code also states to stand by your fellow sailor and be loyal in supporting them," Nate added seriously. "As far as we are concerned, Ahzya is now a crew member, and therefore we will support both her and Private Lant."

"You make a solid argument," Ray said, nodding. "I personally have no intention of bringing the subject up. However, if King Mark were to ask me about it directly, what do you think I'd do?"

"It would be your duty to tell him the truth and inform him of every detail."

"Exactly, I'm loyal to my king before anyone else. However, my crew are in my charge. I will take as much of the blame as he will, and somehow, we will work something out."

"You seem to be putting a lot on the line for our little shipmate," Nate mused.

"Ahzya saved one of my men, in my eyes she's earnt her spot on the ship," Ray answered.

"I guess so."

"Now Nate, I believe you're on duty," Ray stated, putting an end to the conversation.

# CHAPTER FIVE

### Plamm 1401

#### Moonstruck, Joonver Bay, Alpania

The following month saw storms push them off track, and several of their wounded sailors passed away. With their crew numbers diminished, they faced another setback when a virus started to spread through those left on board, suspected to have been brought on board by one of the captured pirates. Life at sea was not for the faint of heart, and Ahzya plunged into the busy and dangerous life.

Most days were spent cooking and cleaning in the galley, making sure the plates that the ill men used were separate from the rest. As she walked inside the ship's corridors, she had a face mask which Ray had insisted on them wearing. The mask was more to protect her from the stench of some of the strong medicines than prevent her from catching it. If Ahzya was going to catch the disease, she'd already well and truly been exposed. Thus, she tended to the less severe cases of illness, wiping their brows and administering warm broths. When she emerged onto deck for fresh air most evenings, she removed the mask and leant on the railing. She allowed her arms to fall on the other side, reaching for the surface of the ocean. She could almost imagine diving into the cold, salty embrace of the water, removing the clammy feeling that stuck to her skin.

All the crew were exhausted and working overtime to cover for those who were ill. Ahzya made sure she was no exception, working hard during the day and sometimes even at night. Although Ray insisted at first that she take his quarters, she refused. He needed the area and the comfortable place to rest when he could. Her room was small but warm, and she didn't mind spending her nights in the room. Ahzya didn't tell Ray that the storms caused water to seep through the door and soak her blankets and bedding.

Besides, there were side effects of having lived through the severity of the pirate attack, and nightmares plagued Ahzya's hours of rest. She became so exhausted some nights that she didn't even bother fighting the dream phantoms, only wishing that the end would be swift. Fortunately, the illness didn't plague her dream world too as Ahzya had often taken care of the other children at the orphanage and witnessed first-hand the effects of disease.

While the ship's illness incurred slow and laboured deaths to the weaker ones it claimed, the almost calm final breaths under warm blankets and with a watchful friend by their side seemed peaceful. Peaceful compared to the mutilated, gruesome imagery which sharp blades and senseless wrath painted.

Nearing the end of their crazy journey, things appeared calm. Peter's twenty-third birthday arrived, and Captain Ray broke into his candy supply and shared it with the entire crew until not even one sweet orb was left. The illness finished its onslaught and Ahzya sighed in relief.

Another week and the day finally arrived where they were to sail into the ship's home seaport, Port Joonver. Captain Ray barked orders to the sailors as he stood stationed at the helm of the ship. Sailors rushed around on the deck, pushing past each other, as Ahzya dried the breakfast plates. The sailors finished their last meal before arriving home, and they were all excited. The air buzzed with anticipatory movement as Ahzya hung up the dish towel and neatened the galley for the last time. She removed a plain white apron from around her neck and hung it up on a peg on the wall. Ahzya sadly smiled as she glanced around the area that had become her home over the month and a half at sea.

Ahzya's enthusiasm about reaching port was at an all-time low. She couldn't help feeling restless, despite the excitement of seeing what Alpania and Peter's hometown looked like. For the rest of the sailors, they were returning home. For her, it was like entering a stranger's house.

Nate dodged her as she exited the galley, and he grinned cheekily.

"Breakfast was great, Ahzya, you've taught JB a few things about cooking," Nate called.

"I doubt that's true, Nate, perhaps it is merely that your taste buds have died over the last month," Ahzya replied with equal enthusiasm.

"Perhaps so, but I hope not, 'cause I have my mother's cooking to return to, and I fully intend on tasting every spice in her beef stew," Nate returned with a wink.

Nate waved goodbye to her with a grin and Ahzya waved back. Ahzya then made her way towards her small room to grab her bag, which she had already packed, and sailors greeted her as she went. Ahzya called to them all by name and gave a friendly smile to each of them. Peter approached and had her small bag slung over one of his shoulders, and he carried his own in his left hand.

"Hey there, Ahzya, are you excited about hitting the town for the first time since you've gotten on this beauty?" Peter asked, handing her bag across to her.

"Yes," Ahzya said hesitantly. "Although I kind of feel like this ship is where I belong."

"Don't jest, Ahzya," Captain Ray drawled, approaching them as he inspected the deck. "Surely, you can't enjoy hanging around a bunch of bumbling sailors?"

"I must admit, you were all quite a handful, but I didn't mind," Ahzya joked.

Captain Ray smiled and ruffled her hair with his hand. He then turned and barked orders at a couple of sailors who were standing at the railing nearby. Ray also raised his eyebrows at Peter, and Peter dropped his bag by Ahzya's side.

"Look after that, will you?" Peter said, jogging to the mainsail.

"Captain, we're nearing the port," Johno bellowed from where he had taken position at the helm. "Awaiting your orders!"

Ray strode towards the stern and up a couple of steps towards the helm. Partway up the stairs, he turned back around.

"Haul up the royal and topgallant sails!" Ray ordered, his voice loud.

The crew under the foresail and mainsail began to haul on ropes that fell from the top of the five sails to the deck. The lines made the sails fold and be pulled up onto the yardarms.

Ahzya watched in awe as the crew moved quickly as a team so that the movement was smooth and systematic. While she had seen them manoeuvre the ship before, it never ceased to impress her. The wind was blowing from their port side, and Ahzya forgot their bags as she ran to the railing. She made sure that she wasn't in an area where the crew needed to move and paused to watch.

Ahzya turned to notice that Captain Ray had taken his position at the wheel. Johno dropped down the stairs, preparing to help with the next set of hauling.

The ship skimmed across the waves, but at another order to haul up sails, the boat began to reduce speed. Ahzya spotted the seaport in the distance and studied the town with increasing excitement.

The seaport they were approaching appeared busy with the hustle of the early morning fishing trade. Moored along the dock sat rows of fishing ships, and Ahzya could spot groups of young men bustling to bring in the morning's catch. The town stretched out for a bit before backing onto a mountain range covered in dense forest. The forest looked deep green, so rich and beautiful in the morning sunlight. Store owners rushed to claim the best fish for their shops, and fishermen hurried for the top prices for their catches.

"Haul down the jib!" Ray bellowed, the sailors moving on his words.

The sailors positioned at the bow hauled down the small sail called the jib so that it no longer fluttered freely in the breeze. Even as the sailors began to haul it in, Captain Ray shouted an order to the crew members gathered at the stern of the ship.

"Haul up the spanker!" Ray called.

The sailors pulled on the ropes, and the small sail at the stern unfolded and went taut.

"Brace yourselves!" Ray called. "Hard aport."

The crew braced themselves as Ray spun the wheel and they turned into the blustering breeze. The topsails began to lift, and another order signalled for all sails to be brought in. The ship moved slowly, losing speed as it was no longer gaining rhythm from the sails.

"Let go anchor!"

Several of the stronger crew hauled on the windlass, and the anchor, which was attached to a sturdy length of steel chain, was dropped into the bay water.

"Brail the spanker!"

The spanker was hauled in as the anchor did its job and the ship came to a complete stop. Ahzya could hear cheers from shore, and she realised they weren't that far away from the docks. Though they were anchored, there were still plenty of jobs to be done before they could row to shore. Still early morning, they'd be working until the afternoon. Celebrations would come when the crew were dismissed from their duties.

"Lay aloft and furl the sails!" Captain Ray yelled, a proud smile on his lips.

Sailors began climbing the rigging up to their assigned yardarms to fold and stow the sails against the yardarms in the correct manner. A mess of ropes were on deck and the rest of the crew began to coil them and hook them on designated positions on the side of the ship. Several smaller vessels were rowing out towards them, and Ahzya realised they were there to help unload. Well, a majority were there to help transport things onto the dock, while there were others who yelled greetings and waved at their loved ones on board.

The excitement on board continued to hum as final inspection and disembarkment from the ship began. The crew would be relieved of their duties later by an overnight team who were stationed to guard the exploration fleet. However, until then, they could hear their hometown celebrating but not participate. As they went about their work in a rhythmic system, the sailors sang a traditional sea chant.

*We've sailed home*

*From a long trip*

*My hair hasn't seen a comb*

*And it needs a snip*

*But my darlin'*

*She's a-waitin' for me*

*I can see her smiling*

*While staring at the sea*

*Almost home*

*Almost home*

*The ship is anchored*

*And we're coming home*

The morning quickly passed since, although they had been packed and prepared, there was still plenty of work to be done. When all the necessary supplies and new charts and documents had been shipped to shore, the deck was scrubbed and polished. Captain Ray wanted his ship to be in the best condition he'd ever seen it, and not one foot would step off until he was satisfied. Only the badly injured and still sick crew were allowed to leave, along with the few imprisoned pirates, who were escorted to shore with soldiers in a guarded boat.

Finally, Captain Ray addressed his crew with a message of thanks and congratulations. He kept it short, and by the time he said 'dismissed' several rowboats had moored beside them. Ray warned them to be orderly in their disembarkment, but excitement caused the moment to be pure chaos. Several sailors chose to swim when their fellow crew members took up the seats in the rowboats. Johno and Nate jeered from the sidelines, for they were seasoned sailors and patient enough to await the boats' return.

Ahzya hung back, well out of the way. She felt someone touch her shoulder, and she looked over. Peter grinned at her and called an insult to one young sailor who was doggy paddling his way to shore. Peter then beckoned for her to follow him and with a last glance at the scene, Ahzya followed.

Captain Ray joined them as they walked, and he had a small bag slung over his shoulder. Ahzya noticed that his eyes still scanned the deck, ropes and sails as if he was making sure everything was in place one last time. Ray looked exhausted and yet even in the final minutes of his time aboard he kept professional vigilance on the state of his ship.

"Are you returning home to family, Cap?" Ahzya asked curiously.

"Unfortunately, not tonight," Ray answered. "A captain's work is never done. Over the next few days, I have a report to give to King Mark, then I'll be going with Johno to the family of the sailors we lost, and with Craig to the soldiers' families."

Ahzya felt her chest tense and she bowed her head.

"Besides," Ray said, in a brighter tone, "my only family is my sister and her family, and they live days away. I will visit at some point, but not until I look less tired and ill. My sister is always telling me to take better care of myself, but my work and crew are more important."

"Don't worry about the captain, Ahzya. He is a frequent visitor to Nan's Kitchen, and the food from there could cure any illness," Peter assured her.

"Ah, they know my taste in coffee too," Ray added with a smile.

The final rowboat approached to take Peter, Johno, Nate, Ray and Ahzya to shore. Ahzya noticed that there were ten men already on the boat and they all wore dark purple half cloaks over one shoulder. Hats made of the same purple material adorned their heads, and they sported an embroidered mountain symbol, same as the Alpanian flag, on the side.

"We are members of the Fourth Regiment of the King's Army. Permission to come aboard," one of the men called out formally.

"Permission granted, you may climb aboard," Ray answered.

As the soldiers climbed onto the ship, they came to attention before Captain Ray and saluted. Ray saluted back and nodded his head to each one. Thus concluded the hand over to the night guard; officially ending the expedition.

Peter motioned for Ahzya to climb down the ropes provided and into the rowboat. Ahzya realised that Nate and Johno had already descended and now they sat patiently waiting for the other three.

"I'll leave her in your capable hands," Ray saluted and disembarked the ship.

### NAN'S KITCHEN, PORT JOONVER, ALPANIA

"I hear that they are holding a dance at Colonel Vernan's home tonight in celebration of the return of *Moonstruck*," a young woman cooed from across the room.

Soon after arriving on shore, Peter led Ahzya through the streets of Port Joonver where the ambience, after the bustle of the morning trade, had slowed to a gentle hum. As they walked, Ahzya was fascinated by the beautifully painted signs which proudly displayed names above the stores and buildings in the business sector of town. The Iron Bull appeared to be a blacksmith, X Marks the Spot was a cartographer's shop selling all manner of maps, of both the inland and ocean, and a cute café was titled Morning Dew.

Ahzya found the signs and names very odd. In Ulkadasa, cafés and trades buildings didn't have names, they just were what they were. If one wished to meet a friend or business associate at a specific place, one would simply use the owner's name or the building's location via proximity to town landmarks or the store's visual description. To give a building a name of its own seemed like something out of a fairy tale storybook.

The café turned restaurant Peter had led Ahzya to had a more straightforward name of: Nan's Kitchen. It had a homely feel, considering the fact the owner was trying to emulate the feeling of arriving home to a beloved grandma's home cooking. The quaint place was decorated with beautiful yet simple touches, with large windows that let in as much daylight as possible. The café attracted a large number of customers; the workers offered bright smiles and friendly greetings to each one.

Ahzya sat in the corner, her hands wrapped around a hot chocolate and several daintily plated sweet slices sat on the table. Two mouthfuls of the delicious morsels and Ahzya had felt that was enough. She wasn't used to such food; the sugary taste and soft texture quickly became sickening to her mouth.

Peter had left her with an assurance that he would be back soon. He had business to finish at the dock and also supplies to buy. His house had been uninhabited for months and he'd practically emptied the house of food supplies before leaving.

"Yes, the colonel may be holding a dance, but I doubt many of the sailors or soldiers will be there. Those with families will certainly have personal celebrations taking place, so only single, lonely sailors may be attending." An older lady was speaking now.

"Oh, I don't mind if they are single and lonely, in fact, I prefer them that way," the young woman returned with a prim laugh.

Ahzya sighed and gazed into the chocolatey depths of her mug. Despite the language barrier, Ahzya could still understand the essence of what the women were talking about. Understanding the contents of what was being said, however, didn't stop Ahzya from being confused over why other women were so obsessed with their constant talk of men. As far as she'd experienced, boys were horrible creatures who spat at you and called you names, for no justifiable reason. However, those on the ship had been acceptable and kind, and the only conclusion Ahzya came to was that the Shanville boys were different from other boys.

"Are you enjoying your meal, miss?" a serving girl asked, approaching her table.

The girl had a pointed chin and light brown eyes. Long auburn hair ran down to the waist of her short and slim figure. She looked to be eighteen or nineteen years of age, and she carried a tray with a bowl of pumpkin soup, a crusty bread roll and a glass of sweet orange juice.

"It's good, thank you," Ahzya returned politely, talking slowly so her pronunciation was as clear as what Peter had been teaching her.

"Do you mind if I sit and talk to you?" the girl said, waving a hand at the chair opposite Ahzya.

"I don't mind," Ahzya answered, offering a smile.

The café was busy and there were few spare seats, so offering the girl a seat at her table seemed the only considerate option.

"The town's abuzz with excitement over the *Moonstruck* returning after its long expedition," the girl said, taking a seat. "It was fun to see all the sailors arrive. Can you believe that some of them actually swam to shore?"

"I guess if I were at sea for that long I'd be willing to swim to shore too," Ahzya mused.

"Totally! Although I'd be more afraid of eels and whatever other slimy creatures lurk under the water," the girl said with a shiver.

Ahzya just nodded and took a sip of her hot chocolate. She was unused to making conversation, although the other girl was comfortably content to start a lively discussion with a stranger.

"When the rest of the fleet returned without *Moonstruck* everyone was so anxious. The fleet were separated from *Moonstruck* in a storm and they had no word on whether the ship had sunk or not. Everyone was trying to be positive though, so when *Moonstruck* was spotted entering the bay, we were so relieved," the server girl said, placing a hand over her heart. "You can't imagine how many days I cried thinking he'd— I mean *they'd* never return."

"A lot of them didn't," Ahzya mumbled into her mug.

"So, what relation are you to the sailor who was with you a short while ago?" the girl asked.

Ahzya paused and looked up at the girl. Peter had never really stated anything, but she had begun to think of him as a brother. He was far too young to be her adoptive father, and brother remained the only logical answer.

"He's my brother," Ahzya answered after a moment's pause. "He is a private."

"Peter Lant, right?" the girl asked casually. "I didn't know he had a sister."

Ahzya's heart skipped a beat and she intertwined her hands as she stuttered, "I-I'm adopted."

"Really?" the girl pressed.

"Y-Yes, very recently," Ahzya stumbled.

"So, his parents adopted you and you have come to visit because Peter has arrived back?" the girl said, smiling. "It must have been a long journey from where you live to here."

Ahzya merely nodded. Ahzya was aware that the calculations didn't add up. If *Moonstruck*'s return hadn't been certain and the message was only circulated that morning, there would be no way for her to be visiting town to greet Peter. Especially if what the girl said was correct, and Peter's family lived far away. Ahzya's lies were making no sense, and this girl asked way too many questions.

"That's amazing," the girl continued cheerfully, seemingly unaware of the contradictions. "You must be happy that he returned. I bet you missed him while he was gone."

Ahzya just nodded again and then spooned a sliver of slice into her mouth. The other girl watched her and then ate her own food.

"Mmm, this is delicious," the girl was talking again. "But that's grandma's cooking for you!"

Ahzya nodded again; things were starting to get a little awkward. She felt exhausted and despite her best efforts, concentrating on a conversation was hard.

"By the way, she isn't really my grandma, in fact, she's never married, but everyone calls her grandma around here anyway. I'm Naomi, by the way," the girl said, offering Ahzya her hand.

"Ahzya," Ahzya said, shaking the girl's hand for a moment.

"Oh, did you see King Mark at the docks today?" Naomi said, her eyes twinkling. "I guess it's his duty to check on the captain of a ship from His Majesty's fleet the moment he reaches the port, but still it was all so exciting."

Ahzya furrowed her brow and thought back to what had happened when they had reached the dock only an hour ago.

Sailors and townspeople cheered as the rowboat had drawn near the pier. There were many helping hands offered to lift them from the boat and questions were already being asked of Captain Ray. Ray waved them off with a slightly annoyed flourish of his hand, but it didn't seem to cause much of an effect.

The crowd only parted for a group of soldiers who walked along the pier keeping close formation. Captain Ray stepped forward to meet the soldiers and then knelt to one knee.

A tall man with broad shoulders stepped forward between the gatherings of soldiers and smiled down at Ray. The man's curly brown hair shifted in the breeze, and as he offered a hand to Ray, Ahzya noticed a signet ring on one of his fingers. The ring was golden, and Ahzya could barely make out the same mountain symbol that had been on the soldier's cloaks, engraved into the metal. A dark purple cloak, much like the soldiers' beside him, hung over his shoulders. Golden thread formed the same embroidered symbol, and golden chains cinched the cloak at the top of his tunic.

Ahzya had barely stepped foot on solid ground, when the man turned and looked directly at her. He frowned slightly and his blue eyes watched her with an air of suspicion. Peter stepped ashore beside her and also spotted the man looking their direction. Peter grabbed her shoulders and drew her close. Johno's form quickly covered the angle of view as he dragged Nate by the collar up onto the pier.

"Watch it, you giant bear!" Nate said, flailing comically. "You'll undo all my good efforts."

"You put in effort?" Johno replied in a doubt-laced tone.

"Of course, I'm an integral and important member of *Moonstruck*, people expect a certain level of class," Nate retorted proudly, straightening his clothes as Johno set him down. "They look to me as a symbol of courage and rugged handsomeness."

Johno scoffed, reaching to ruffle Nate's red curls till they sat messily spiralling in multiple directions. Peter chuckled and his hold on Ahzya's shoulders relaxed.

Ahzya ducked her head slightly, looking past Johno and Nate, to glanced back towards the richly dressed man, but he had moved his attention onto other things. Ahzya watched with a curious interest. After all, Captain Ray had never paid obeisance to anyone while on board *Moonstruck*. Now as Ahzya watched Ray bow deeply to this man, she figured that he must be someone important. As if to confirm this suspicion, Ray straightened from his bow and fell into a serious discussion with the noble man.

"Who is that man Captain Ray is talking to?" Ahzya asked, tilting her head towards Peter.

"King Mark Erinth, ruler and most powerful man in all Alpania," Peter said. "He is a man respected and honoured by all Alpanians."

Despite Peter's words, Ahzya couldn't seem to shake the nervous feeling in the pit of her stomach. It didn't help that, until they were out of view of King Mark, Johno, Nate, and Peter remained like a protective wall between them. Ahzya knew full well that Peter's actions of bringing her into the country could get him put in serious trouble. Ahzya knew this and had every intention of not letting him be found out, and if that meant avoiding the public eye, she'd willingly make that sacrifice.

"Are you going to be going to the dance tonight?" Naomi's voice broke through her thoughts.

"No," Ahzya answered bluntly.

All Ahzya wanted to do was disappear into a dark room, where the quietness of sleep could envelop her. Despite Naomi's friendly nature, she wasn't in the mood for any more conversation.

"Found a friend already?" a familiar male voice asked.

Peter approached the table; a grin spread across his handsome face. He came to a stop behind Ahzya and leant gently on the back of the chair. Ahzya glanced up at him and then across at Naomi. Naomi had a look on her face that encapsulated the energy of an enamoured puppy.

Naomi stood up in a shy manner and motioned for Peter to take a seat. She was trying to spit out some sort of flurry of words, however, her nerves got the better of her. Peter refused her politely and Naomi sat down again, her brown eyes staring at him.

"Don't allow me to interrupt the conversation you were having," Peter said kindly.

"Of course," Naomi managed to blurt out with a blush.

The table fell silent, and Peter looked between the two girls and decided to eat the leftover pieces of slice. When another awkward minute passed, Peter started shifting around. Naomi looked nervous and bit her lip before her eyes brightened with an idea.

"Hey, Ahzya, I'm going to the castle tomorrow, my father works there from time to time. He got permission to take me, and I was just wondering whether you would like to join me?" Naomi asked, looking inquiringly across at Ahzya. "You don't have to pay anything, and it will be great fun."

A visit to a castle did sound like fun. Ulkadasa didn't have castles, they had palaces. From what Peter had described, they were very differently designed, but Ahzya hadn't visited any of the Ulkadasan palaces either. Ahzya looked at Peter for his opinion.

"I guess I could let you go for the day. In fact, it will be quite convenient since I have sailor duties to deal with, and I also have to fill in paperwork for my pay. Then there is..." Peter said, beginning to count on his fingers.

Naomi giggled and Ahzya rolled her eyes at Peter with a smile.

"I guess so," Ahzya agreed shyly.

"Okay then, we could meet here and have breakfast, and then we could go with my father in the horse and cart. We can have a picnic lunch on the castle grounds, and then still be home by dinner," Naomi said. "I'm excited now! It is so much better going on an excursion with a friend rather than travelling by yourself. I'd better get back to work now, but I guess I'll be seeing you tomorrow."

"Okay," Ahzya said, with a slight smile.

Ahzya looked over at Peter, who had sat down in the now vacated seat, and realised that he was staring at her. Ahzya stared back at Peter, but he held her gaze, a smirk playing on his lips.

"Is something on my face?" Ahzya asked.

"You haven't been in this country for five minutes and you've already made a friend," Peter whispered, winking. "It took me twenty years to make even one friend!"

"Really?!" Ahzya asked, her eyes widening in surprise.

Peter threw his head back laughing like a little kid, which earned him a couple of strange looks from around the room. Peter didn't seem to mind the attention, but Ahzya sank into her chair.

"You're so gullible, Ahzya. No matter how antisocial you may think I am, I'm not that bad," Peter said, grinning across at her.

"Perhaps I should go and tell her I won't be able to go," Ahzya said, having second thoughts.

"No, it will be good," Peter said shaking his head. "Besides, I know Naomi's father, and he'll make sure everything is okay."

Ahzya just shrugged before standing up and pushing her chair back in. The bell on the door jingled as they exited and they were greeted with fresh air. Ahzya took a deep breath and savoured the scent as she walked alongside Peter as he led the way up the street. Peter led her back towards the port and finally onto the cobblestone street that ran parallel to the bay. Peter took Ahzya's hand and pulled her gently through the crowds of fishermen and townspeople, most of which were packing up shop. They walked away from the pier and made their way through the town. The bustling sound of the wharf died down the further they walked, and soon it was only a soft mumble in the air. It must have rained not long ago because mud off the street covered their boots.

"So, exactly how far away is our house from here?" Ahzya asked, stretching her arms.

"Not too far, just up this road a little further," Peter said.

"What about the supplies you mentioned earlier? Are they being delivered later?"

"No, I came home while you were at the café and got a fire started and dropped off supplies."

"You should have just brought me along with you," Ahzya said quietly.

"But then you wouldn't have met your new friend," Peter said with a cheerful laugh. "It's fine, we will be there in a minute."

Sure enough, as Ahzya and Peter rounded the gentle bend in the road, they came into sight of a gathering of wooden cottages. Ahzya took in a deep breath as she stared at them and smiled happily. The scene was almost like out of the storybooks Ahzya used to listen to one of the older girls at the orphanage read before bed each night. Like most of the other girls in the orphanage, she loved fairy tale stories, although Ahzya also adored adventure tales with ships and battles. She followed slowly behind Peter, who was heading towards the farthest cottage. Peter had her bag slung over his shoulder without much thought, and Ahzya was swinging her arms by her side.

They soon stopped in front of one small wooden cottages and Peter paused in front of the door. Peter lifted his right arm and felt above the door frame. A couple of seconds later, he had retrieved a key and was working on the lock on the door. With a click, the door unlocked and Peter pushed the door open. They entered into a kitchen with a small table, which had two chairs at it, and there was a brick fireplace with a fire cheerfully crackling in the grate. Ahzya gazed around curiously and reached up to brush her hair out of her eyes. She took a deep breath of the homely-scented air and could feel herself relaxing.

"Well, here we are. Home sweet home," Peter said, waving a hand around the room.

Ahzya smiled and dropped into one of the seats, exhaustion flooding her body.

"I don't know about you," Ahzya stated sleepily. "But I think an early night is in order."

Peter laughed. "I think I could sleep quite comfortably for a week straight."

Ahzya smiled because, for the first time in a matter of months, she could relax completely. If this was what home was supposed to feel like, then Ahzya had no complaints.

# CHAPTER SIX

PRIVATE LANT'S HOUSE, PORT JOONVER, ALPANIA

Early the next morning Ahzya woke up in the comfortable bed of Peter's room. Peter was sleeping on the couch in the living room until they sorted out a new bedroom. There was technically a bedroom free in the house, but Peter was using it for storage and it would take time to clean and organise.

Ahzya slid her legs off the edge of the bed and tiptoed across the cold floorboards. She glanced out the window to where the night's darkness still lingered. However, as she watched, rays of sunlight tried to shine through the low fog that surrounded the house, giving the world a grey glow. Ahzya spotted her reflection in the mirror and sighed. She wore a pair of Peter's old pyjamas which fit far too loose. The previous evening, after a hearty laugh at her expense, Peter decided that they needed to go shopping. Even though Ahzya knew she required new clothes, her conscience pricked at her for being a burden. She was sure that with his set wage, Peter didn't need extra expenses. With this in mind, Ahzya recalled he'd mentioned something about clothes in the attic. Ahzya tiptoed out the door of the room, but noise from the kitchen indicated Peter was already awake.

"Good morning," Ahzya said, entering the kitchen.

Leant with his hip against the bench, Peter watched a pot of coffee slowly begin to steam. His blond locks stuck flat on one side and severely mussed on the other. His eyes were still glazed with the grogginess of sleep.

"Good morning. Up already?" Peter asked, yawning.

"Yeah, I was just going to check the attic to see if I could find outfits that fit me," Ahzya answered. "It would be better than shopping for new ones."

"Alright, go right ahead. Call me if you need me," Peter said.

Ahzya turned to climb the stairs that led to the attic and found herself in a room filled with chests and other storage. Ahzya got to work on some of the trunks and found them filled with clothing and blankets. Stacked books took up room in several others, and Ahzya began to get distracted by one picture book.

"I forgot Mum left them here when they moved out," Peter said, his head appearing above the stairs that led to the attic.

"I thought usually children move out," Ahzya mused.

"I'm not a normal child," Peter said, grinning. "A healer told Mum that she needed clear mountain air after a bout of illness. I guess they just fell in love with their place up there, and I took over this place."

"How long ago was that?" Ahzya asked, lifting articles of clothing from the chests.

"Four years ago, I was eighteen at the time," Peter replied.

"Did it take long to adjust to the changes?"

"I was already spending months at sea; barely ever home," Peter replied. "You'll get used to it, Ahzya. It may be awkward and strange at first, but I think you'll come to love it here."

Peter had a way of reading into the real reason behind her questions. Ahzya knew nothing about this new country, and she knew no-one outside of Peter and the *Moonstruck* crew.

"That's why this outing with Naomi is a good idea," Peter said, sitting on one of the chests. "You'll adjust a lot quicker if you have friends here."

"I guess so," Ahzya agreed reluctantly. "She talks a lot though."

"Naomi Thatcher is a sociable chatterbox. She doesn't know what to do when she comes across those of us who are shyer and less talkative. When you don't say anything, she probably assumes you don't like what she said," Peter said with a laugh. "Just answer with more than yes or no, and you'll find she'll relax."

"You seem to know a lot about her," Ahzya said, raising an eyebrow.

"Us village kids used to play together, so we were childhood friends."

"Were?"

"As a member of an expedition crew you can't see people as much as you used to," Peter replied with a casual shrug. "Guess we just lost touch."

"Well, in that case, I think she believes you've forgotten her entirely," Ahzya said, pushing away the pile of clothes she'd collected.

"Really? Why?" Peter asked curiously.

"You didn't greet her at the café, and then we all just sat there awkwardly not talking," Ahzya said. "Wouldn't old friends usually have something to talk to each other about?"

"I guess so," Peter said, his brows dipping in concentration.

Ahzya felt convinced that Naomi had initially started a conversation with her because of her association with Peter. Ahzya didn't mind it too much, but it did make things awkward. However, perhaps she was wrong; Naomi might prove to be a close confidante yet.

Ahzya turned a dress in her hands and sighed. She'd grown so used to wearing pants and shirts, that the thought of wearing a dress was daunting. However, a trip to the castle required a touch of formality and a gown would provide that.

"Can you sew?" Ahzya asked Peter suddenly.

"I learnt a few stitching techniques on the ship, 'cause, believe it or not, the other boys on the ship don't offer to do your mending for you," Peter said, casually picking a book.

"I thought they'd all just jump at the chance to sew for everyone. It's such a thrilling hobby," Ahzya said sarcastically. "I never learnt personally."

Peter laughed and allowed his gaze to roam across the attic. Peter looked like he was struck with an idea and turned to pull a dusty chest from the edge of the room. It was an oak chest, ruggedly yet beautifully carved, with pictures of deer and forest creatures. Peter ran his hand gently across the top of the chest to remove the dust settled on the lid. Ahzya leant forward to look at the chest closer and smiled as she spotted an elf peeking from behind a tree.

"Who's the woodcarver in the family?" Ahzya asked, reaching forward to touch the carvings.

"That would be me. My father taught me when I was just a boy. It's my hobby. I do smaller carving work on the ship," Peter answered, smiling thoughtfully. "Only in my spare time though, not while I'm on duty."

"Captain Ray would probably correct you of that unwise decision," Ahzya replied, watching as Peter lifted the lid of the chest carefully.

Inside the chest, soft red silk lined the sides, protecting souvenirs from other countries, old sea charts and captains' logs. Peter picked up one of the logs and handed it to Ahzya. Ahzya reached to carefully take it from Peter and opened the cover gently.

"My grandfather was captain of a ship called *Northern Vice,* and those are some of the logs he wrote. He was the reason I became a sailor in the first place," Peter said, watching as Ahzya continued turning pages.

"It's so interesting," Ahzya stated quietly, her eyes scanning the uniform lines.

Peter smiled and nodded his head in agreement. Back into the chest, he moved aside a few charts. Peter found what he was looking for and lifted it delicately. Ahzya looked up from the log, which she'd continued flicking through, feeling the textures of the pages. Peter handed her a paper-covered package tied with a faded ribbon.

Peter motioned for her to open the package, and Ahzya fell to this task with enthusiasm. Once she had untied the ribbon and folded back the tissue paper, it revealed a dress made out of soft cotton. The design of the dress was simple, but elegant embroidery decorated the hem and collar. With vine designs and small, delicate leaves of bright green, the embroidered pattern stood bold against the light, sky-blue material. It was a smaller size than the previous dresses Ahzya had spotted and looked like it would fit her much better. Peter surveyed the awe on her face as Ahzya fingered the hem gently between her thumb and forefinger.

"It's from the island of Uo Uo, the cotton is picked on the island and hand woven," Peter said.

"And why would a sailor buy this?" Ahzya answered, frowning with confusion.

"I actually bought it for Mum, on my first expedition. However, I hadn't taken into account her measurements," Peter said, letting a grin break out on his face. "Let's just say it didn't fit very well when I got home. My mum said she was flattered, but…"

"I'm pretty sure it will fit me though," Ahzya said, returning the smile. "Are you sure I can use it?"

"Yes, it's for the best, it's well time we took it out of the dark depths of my attic."

### NAN'S KITCHEN, PORT JOONVER, ALPANIA

Naomi was waiting outside Nan's Kitchen, a warm dark blue coat wrapped around her body and a fawn-coloured soft woollen hat sat snugly on her head. Ahzya and Peter approached her, both with their sailor quality jackets and wool lined caps. They had matching grey gloves and scarves, and Ahzya waved a gloved hand as they approached.

Naomi waved back and smiled as they reached her on the sidewalk.

"It's a bit brisk this morning, isn't it?" Naomi asked, nervously.

"That's a tame description, Naomi, it's freezing. I predict it will snow soon," Peter replied, breathing out a stream of white mist.

Naomi's face brightened at Peter's cheerful greeting, and her eyes sparkled above her bright red cheeks. She rubbed her hands together and then motioned for them to follow her inside.

The atmosphere in the café had the group warmed both inside and out, as they ate a delicious breakfast. A fire crackled away in a fireplace at the back of the dining quarters. People flocked to the small café to escape the crisp morning, but 'grandma' and her staff were well prepared, and service was swift and friendly.

Ahzya had never seen so much breakfast in all her life. There were variations of egg, including scrambled, boiled, fried and spiced. The menu boasted freshly cooked bacon, sausage, tomato, toast, savoury and sweet muffins, fruit, cream and the list continued.

Peter made an effort to start a conversation this time, and he listened earnestly to Naomi's replies. Naomi relaxed slowly, and Ahzya soon found her reservations slip away. Once he had finished eating, Peter excused himself. He bid the girls a good day, and he made his way out to begin work at the dock. Naomi's father, Urban, arrived shortly after to journey with Naomi and Ahzya to the castle.

"There's plenty of blankets, so wrap yourselves up until we reach Prynesse or until the sun takes this chill out of the air," Urban said, standing comfortably in a short-sleeved tunic and shorts.

"Oh, Urban, haven't I told you many times before, you should wear a jacket so that we don't have to shiver at the sight of you," Naomi's mother scolded.

Naomi's mother had come to see them off, and Ahzya noticed a baby bump protruding from the folds of her cloak. Even in warm clothes, she rubbed her arms to warm them up.

"I've packed your lunch, girls, and make sure you don't get lost in the castle. Be on your best behaviour, Naomi, and don't go anywhere you shouldn't go," Naomi's mother said.

"Of course, Mother. I'm old enough to know all of that. Thank you for making the picnic," Naomi said, kissing her mum on the cheek. "You'll have to excuse us if we are cutting it close to nightfall. There is much to see at the castle. We might be lucky enough to see King Mark or the royal family."

"Have fun, dear," her mother said, patting her on the cheek.

"And if any of those young knights start trying to get your attention, tell them that they'll have to deal with me first," Urban stated, firmly.

"Dad, that's not going to happen," Naomi said, rolling her eyes.

Ahzya had already climbed onto the seat of the cart and snuggled under the blankets. She watched the family's friendly banter quietly. Naomi sent her a sympathetic smile as she climbed in beside her.

"My family can be overwhelming sometimes," Naomi whispered.

"I think it's nice," Ahzya answered, offering a shy smile.

Urban climbed into the driving seat and settled down with the reins.

"Are we ready to go, girls?" Urban asked.

"More than ready, let's get moving," Naomi said, hooking her arm in Ahzya's.

The cart shook as it made its way along the muddy ground, and Ahzya could feel every bump. It had been many years since Ahzya had been on a cart ride, and although Naomi relaxed in her seat, Ahzya couldn't help but feel jittery. She soon settled into the movement, and the fascinating surrounds drew her curious gaze.

They entered the forest, and the fog hung around the trunks like grey blankets. It gave off a different feel than town and droplets fell from the leaves above. Naomi explained in a whisper, as if not to disturb the peaceful quiet of the forest, that a lot of forest animals had started hibernation for nixhora.

"I think there will be snow today," Urban stated. "My leg is troubling me again."

"Your leg is always troubling you," Naomi replied in annoyance.

"It feels different when snow is coming," Urban explained. "The truth is, usually it is already snowing by this time of year, yet people are still complaining about the cold. I mean it is nixhora; they seem to forget how seasons work!"

"Peter said that it felt like it would snow too," Ahzya offered softly.

"Peter is a smart young man," Urban said with confidence. "I've always said the *Moonstruck* crew have sensible heads on their shoulders."

The trip through the forest stretched on for ages, and Ahzya felt sleepy under the warm blankets. Even as she yawned for the tenth time, they slowly emerged out of the trees. The trees may have let up, but in its place was a city of houses and shops. All the buildings were situated close together, and Naomi pointed out some newly built structures.

"This is Prynesse. It seems to grow in size every time I visit," Naomi stated. "In the warmer months, there are always new houses and shops being built."

"You said you've never been to Prynesse, Ahzya?" Urban asked, looking sideways at her.

"Never," Ahzya confirmed. "I spent a lot of time in an orphanage; we didn't learn much outside of how to do chores."

To cover for her limited knowledge, Peter and Ahzya devised a cover story. An uneducated and uninformed orphan wasn't strange, and her recent adoption wouldn't have given much time for further education.

"That's nothing to be ashamed of," Urban encouraged. "That just means we have the joy of sharing everything with you for the first time. No doubt, Naomi will love to inform you all about it on your visit."

Naomi hugged Ahzya's arm and nodded her head enthusiastically.

"For now, though, I can flex my insider knowledge," Urban boasted with a grin. "Prynesse is considered a prime location. It's next to the main castle where the royal family lives and is an easy ride to the main port of Alpania, Port Joonver. Joonver Bay moors a lot of the King's Fleet and Prynesse houses a major section of our military force. Where the army is, there too will be merchants. Prynesse has developed quickly over time, they've even begun to build a wall around the city of Prynesse as an extra security measure. For now, we can easily enter up until the main castle's outer rampart."

Urban quietened as he focused on manoeuvring the cart through Prynesse. People darted in front of the cart as if it was an everyday occurrence, but Ahzya tensed up in fear that they'd roll over someone. Naomi began to excitedly point out different stores, and Ahzya soaked in the information with utmost curiosity. The road became cobblestone, and the cart began to rock less. Everything was in incredible condition, appearing in vivid colour, and Ahzya couldn't help feeling mesmerised.

With her eyes gazing at things on the same level as the cart, Ahzya barely noticed the enormous rampart until they were only a few streets away. Her eyes widened on spotting the thick stone walls and looming towers. Prynesse and its castle were nestled in a mountain range, and the undulation of the land made the rampart look menacingly tall. Soldiers in gleaming armour patrolled the top of the wall, watching villagers and carts as they entered the castle walls. The gates themselves were made of thick steel bars, and the stone archway had ornate statues of winged deities guarding the entrance. Ahzya took a deep breath in awe.

# CHAPTER SEVEN

MAIN GATE, CASTLE PRYNESSE, ALPANIA

Soldiers and officials interacted energetically around the castle gate, and Urban moved the cart slowly through the crowd. Soldiers checked every person and vehicle entering for the correct identification documents. As they approached, Urban pre-emptively drew papers from his pockets.

"How are you today, Urban?" one of the soldiers greeted them.

"Freezing my fingers off. What about you, Terrence?" Urban answered cheerfully.

"I'm akin to an ice block," the soldier, Terrence, returned. "But don't tell the captain that, he'll order I march double time around the grounds to warm up."

Urban chuckled along with the soldier, and Terrence turned to look at the two girls.

"Seems you have a few strange looking wares there," Terrence teased.

"Where did you say your captain was?" Urban returned, stretching his neck as he feigned a search. "My girls are too precious to even offer to royalty, let alone, be called wares."

"Sit down, Urb," Terrence soothed with a laugh. "Here to tour the castle, precious ladies?"

Naomi nodded cheerfully, but Ahzya just watched the soldier with idle curiosity.

"First time visiting?" Terrence asked.

"I've been here a few times, but it is Ahzya's first time at the castle," Naomi replied.

"Well, in that case, I'll run over a few ground rules. I'm going to give you visitor passes; they are to hang visible around your wrists at all times. This allows the castle guards to know you've been authorised access and you won't have to explain all your movements," Terrence explained, handing them both solid bracelets with a 'v' stamped into the metal.

"With this pass you can enter the throne room, just don't approach any of the royalty or nobles or wander the rest of the inner castle. You have free rein of the outer-castle grounds. The lake has a walking track around it, which, while not great for swimming in this weather, is still a worthwhile trek. Avoid the barracks and training grounds to the right, some of the kids are still learning how to use their bows and take some pretty wayward shots. Other than that, have a good time, and don't get into any trouble or we'll have to escort you to the dungeons, and you'll spend the night with the creatures down there," Terrence finished with a joke.

Terrence then waved them on, and they passed through the short entrance tunnel that ran through the deep fortification. The tunnel opened into a cleared area, and a paved road led straight, until it circled around a simple garden. A set of stairs allowed access from the road to the main entrance to the inner castle.

The cleared grounds between the inner castle and outer rampart harboured several buildings and fenced areas. Assigned to one area of the open castle grounds, the stables and yards housed the livestock and animals for the castle's army and food needs. The barracks and recreational halls for the knights and soldiers lined the right wall. Castle Prynesse was the primary training headquarters for young men who wanted to become knights, horsemen and archers for the Alpanian army. Attached to this area was the blacksmith and armourer area, which was always busy crafting new weapons or fixing armour. The blacksmiths doubled as farriers, and several horses stood waiting to be reshod.

Ahzya spotted a group of young soldiers sparring with wooden figures. An older soldier was calling orders, and each of the young men reacted, hitting their targets in rhythm. Their movements were trained into them from day one, so that it would become second nature when they eventually faced their foes in battle.

Ahzya wished she could have watched for longer, but they turned left down a track that led in the opposite direction. They approached a large building, where horses rotated and switched with fresh steeds. Several horse handlers called greetings to Urban, and Ahzya sat up straight, the blankets sliding off her shoulders.

"What exactly do you do here at the castle, Urban?" Ahzya asked, staring at the horses.

"I'm a horse trainer," Urban replied with a smile.

"Why do you live so far away from your work?" Ahzya queried.

"The castle breeds horses near to Port Joonver, so most of my work is undertaken there. By the time the horses reach the castle, they're broken in and their initial training completed. From the moment they arrive here, they are then trained with heavy armour or for speed, depending on what the end goal is for that particular horse," Urban explained enthusiastically.

Ahzya let out an indistinct breathy sound in awe.

"Don't encourage him by asking more, or your ears will start bleeding from all the information he'll give you," Naomi said with a sigh.

"Come now, Naomi, don't be rude," Urban said, glancing at her.

"I am interested though," Ahzya assured.

"Like horses, do you?" Urban asked.

"Yup, they're the ships of the land," Ahzya said.

"What are carriages and wagons then?" Urban relaxed the reins.

"They're cargo ships. You still need horses to pull them."

"What about oxen? A lot of folks use them instead of horses. Especially for farm work."

"Hmm," Ahzya pondered the question for a moment. "I suppose they'd be the rowboats?"

Urban laughed heartily. "So, any wishes for a steed of your own in the future?"

"I want a horse of my own, but I also want to sail. One day I'll get a position as a sailor on a ship like the *Moonstruck*," Ahzya explained, smiling across at him.

"Well, I wish you all the best with your future endeavours," Urban said with a chuckle.

"You're a strange one, Ahzya," Naomi said with a frown. "Most girls I know don't want to work on ships. Especially not expedition ships where they're at sea for months."

"Why not? In Ulkadas…" Ahzya trailed off.

"Hmm?" Naomi asked, tilting her head and giving an encouraging nod for Ahzya to continue.

"Nothing," Ahzya replied quickly.

The cart moved through the open stable and halted at the back where men unloaded other wagons. Urban jumped down from the seat and began conversing with several other stable hands. Ahzya noticed Naomi slip to the ground and she followed slowly.

Soldiers and horse handlers roamed everywhere and horses' hooves clicked on the stone floors. The stables smelt terrible, but Ahzya could overlook it for the sake of being able to see the horses.

"Come with me, Ahzya!" Naomi called, grabbing onto her arm. "Let's get out of here and explore somewhere more interesting."

Ahzya allowed herself to be dragged away, but she let her gaze linger on the stable for just a moment longer. Urban was calling something after them, but Naomi was well on her way.

"Shouldn't we wait for your father?" Ahzya asked hesitantly.

"Oh, he'll only stay in the stables or the equestrian areas for his work. Considerably uninteresting compared to where we're going. You'll be fine with me," Naomi assured her.

Ahzya's boots fell onto the soft green grass as they exited the stable and came in view of fenced areas where the horses could run freely. As they faced the castle, on their left was a large lake, its cloudy water connecting with a wooden walkway built along the shore. Ahzya didn't have long to admire any of that, as Naomi rushed towards the main entrance to the inner castle.

Two soldiers stood stationed at the main entrance, which remained propped open. They didn't seem to pay much attention to Ahzya and Naomi as they entered, other than glancing at their wrists to ensure the visitor's band was attached. Naomi slowed down once they went inside, and Ahzya finally had a moment to breathe and admire her surrounds.

The main doors led into a wide hallway that ran vertically to the small entryway room. The hall stretch on, and the walls were lit up with torches. Another hall stretched out in front of them, but this one was shorter, and it had a set of doors at the end. The double doors were made out of the same dark wood as the main door and had silver handles on each one. Along each of the halls were archways and doors that led to many other rooms.

"Where should we explore first?" Naomi asked, turning excitedly.

"Are you sure we can just walk around? Won't we get in the way?" Ahzya asked nervously.

"Of course not, people visit the castle every day!" Naomi said dismissively. "We can visit the throne room first. You'll see it has a really pretty balcony overlooking where King Mark often holds court. Then there's the general hall, where court ladies gather to play instruments and sew and gossip."

Naomi began walking straight down the hallway, and Ahzya followed with less certainty.

They entered through the large doors, and Ahzya's eyes widened at the site of the marble columns and reddish mahogany floorboards. Courtiers and women dressed in long gowns and draped with fine jewellery barely looked their way as they glided through the room. A sense of formality hung in the air and she straightened her back as they stepped further into the room. Large stained-glass windows ran along the right wall, and the images created by the glass depicted epic battles and royal scenes. At the back of the room, on a raised platform, were four thrones. The two in the middle were tall and intricately formed out of silver. Set in the headpiece were several jewels, and the backs had built-in bright red velvet cushions. The other two which sat either side of the golden thrones were smaller and slightly set back. They were also made of silver but only had one jewel in the headpiece and the cushions were deep blue.

"They are wonderful, aren't they?" Naomi whispered beside her.

"They are beautiful," Ahzya breathed in agreement. "But why are there four of them?"

Naomi glanced sideways at Ahzya; her puzzlement obvious.

"I really didn't learn much at the orphanage," Ahzya reminded.

"Oh, sorry, I'd forgotten. Let's see," Naomi apologised, pausing to point to each throne on the dais as she continued to explain. "The middle right is where King Mark sits, with his wife, Queen Maria on his left. Their daughters are seated at the silver thrones. Princess Anna is at King Mark's right-hand where the chosen heir always sits, and Princess Cleo is in the other one."

"So, Anna is the older daughter?" Ahzya asked, trying to figure out the royal family.

"Yes, she's the older twin," Naomi confirmed with a nod.

"Twins?" Ahzya echoed. "So the eldest, Anna, becomes the heir?"

"Yes, though not yet officially, since they both have a right to ascend the throne. Princess Anna is the first born and has always been the more popular twin. She garnered a lot of support from the noble families, so they predict she'll ascend to the throne upon King Mark's abdication or death," Naomi explained with obvious admiration. "I know less about Princess Cleo, as I've barely heard anything about her. Anna is always hosting gatherings for nobles to congregate at and socialise, but I think Cleo prefers to stay out of the public eye. I have heard nobles call her The Raven, though I doubt the nickname is merited. Ravens are considered bad omens, but as far I know, there's no enmity between Cleo and the influential Alpanian dignitaries."

Ahzya nodded, even though she couldn't quite figure out the details of the family. Since Ulkadasa was ruled by a government rather than one ruler or king, the fundamentals of the royal family proved to be a confusing lesson. Ulkadasa was originally ruled by an emperor and his family line; they'd even built many of the rich palaces of the country. However, a coup removed the emperor's powers and replaced it with an elected committee made up of army generals and advisers, and it had continued that way for a hundred years. Ahzya decided that if she were going to continue living in Alpania, she'd better study up on monarchical society.

"Come with me, we can get a better view from the balcony," Naomi said, moving towards a spiralling staircase on the left of the room.

Ahzya shifted her inspection from the dais towards the second floor. On the level above, a wide balcony bordered the throne room. The railing was polished wood; the vertical bars carved into a twisted and braided pattern. Two large candle chandeliers hung from the ceiling, with ropes running to secure at the columns. Ahzya assumed the chandeliers were lowered to the ground to have the candles lit every day and extinguished at night. Ahzya didn't envy the castle staff for the work required for such extravagance.

"Come along, Ahzya," Naomi called from halfway up the staircase.

Ahzya didn't move immediately, but when people turned to look, as Naomi repeatedly called to her, she slowly walked over. She let her hand glide over the polished and smooth rail. She stepped to the side as several ladies descended the stairs. When they smiled kindly at her, Ahzya returned a shy one of her own. Their air of grace and genteel manners were infectious, so Ahzya perfected her posture and tried to mimic the lady's charisma. This didn't prevent her from skipping up the last couple of steps.

Naomi beckoned her over to the railing with enthusiasm, urging Ahzya to make haste. Awareness of the change of atmosphere finally dawned on Ahzya, as her curiosity drew her to the rails. The entire throne room had fallen silent and only a few voices drifted up from below. Ahzya peeked over, mimicking others in the balcony area.

She noticed the military presence first: soldiers with neatly presented uniforms and golden symbols gleamed on the top of their shoulders. Their eyes constantly scanned the room, and Ahzya also noted the swords and daggers at their waists.

Observing the room further, Ahzya caught sight of a familiar face and realised why everyone was making such a fuss. Walking towards the thrones was the king himself, King Mark Erinth.

He wore a different outfit from the port, and this time he wore a golden crown on his brown hair. Golden buttons gleamed on his tunic, and the glamorous elegance set him apart from all others in attendance. Those around him bowed or curtsied as he made his way to his throne and sat down. A maid brought forward a goblet on a tray, but King Mark just waved her away. Once he sat, the room's veil of silence lifted, and everyone returned to their previous conversations and avocations.

The two soldiers stationed themselves either side of the throne, about two steps back.

King Mark's brow furrowed as an official proffered a stack of parchment to him. He flipped through them and then addressed the official in a firm tone. The official replied with equal confidence, and Mark appeared to accept the explanation. The king handed the pages back with a nod of his head, and the official left the court looking very pleased with himself.

"I'm ready to move on," Naomi sighed beside her.

Naomi grew bored quickly, whereas Ahzya was fascinated by the movements of those in the castle. Ahzya remained leaning against the rails, gazing at the scene below.

"Ahzya, let's go," Naomi said, raising her tone.

"I want to stay here a little longer," Ahzya replied quietly.

"They are just undertaking the day's meetings," Naomi replied.

"You can go on without me if you wish," Ahzya said, her stubborn streak showing its face.

"Ahzya," Naomi warned, crossing her arms. "I don't want to waste time on trifles when there's scope for more exciting engagements elsewhere. We came together, so you need to come with me."

Several ladies glanced their way and raised their eyebrows. Apparently, their small argument was attracting some curious ears. Ahzya turned back to survey the room below, leaning her chin on the balcony railing.

As if sensing the uneasy presence from the balcony, King Mark turned to glance up at them. His mouth moved as he continued his conversation with a new nobleman, but his eyes wandered. When they made eye contact, Mark's brow furrowed and then transitioned into a raised eyebrow. He held up a hand to pause his current consultation and swivelled towards the guard to his right. He leant his elbow on the armrest and brushed his upper lip with his right hand. The movement concealed his lips, but his jaw movement hinted at his questioning his armed escort. The guard and a few surrounding officials weren't exactly discreet when they all turned to look at Ahzya.

Ahzya felt her muscles tense as she remembered his suspicious glance at her at the port. With a moment's hesitation, she stepped back and rushed along the balcony. Within seconds she disappeared down into a hall and out of sight of the group. Naomi called after her, but Ahzya ducked past several groups of people and didn't stop to wait for her companion to catch up.

Ahzya slowed to a walk but continued through the endless halls. She began to feel nervous, realising she had no idea where she was going. Ahzya didn't even know where she had come from. With a sigh, she stopped and tried to backtrack but soon became even further lost in the identical halls. Ahzya searched around, now earnestly looking for a way back. Castle staff passed her, but her embarrassment and shyness prevented her from asking them anything.

Over the next half hour, she managed to find the kitchen, a giant ballroom and several bedrooms with fine furnishings. None of which yielded the appearance of her abandoned guide. Ahzya couldn't help but regret her words to Naomi. A little voice in her head told her that Naomi had still been acting rather selfishly, but Ahzya felt she should have complied to her wishes, especially since she was the one who had invited her in the first place.

Just as Ahzya was beginning to give up ever finding her way back, she spotted a spiralling staircase in what she guessed was a corner of the castle. A sudden idea came to mind as she remembered the tall towers that she had spotted when they were entering Prynesse Castle. With renewed courage and energy, Ahzya began jogging up the staircase. Her boots made soft thuds on the wood, and she continued past several doorways on her way up. She was about to pass yet another, but a fresh breeze tempted her outside. She exited the tower and found herself on the outer wall, high above the grounds below. The clouds above were dark and dense, yet there was still a soft grey glow of light illuminating the world below the clouds.

Her body radiated heat, and her thick cloak and scarf felt suffocating after her run through the castle. The brisk air was a welcomed relief, and she loosened the scarf around her neck. Although there still didn't seem to be anyone around, Ahzya felt relaxed by no longer being confined in the endless stone walls.

A sudden cough almost scared her out of her skin, and she jumped at the abrupt sound. Ahzya glanced around trying to spot where the cough had come from. The first thing she noticed was a pair of legs, dressed in dark pants and tall black boots which had a brown trim on the top of them. The curve of the wall hid the rest of the person, and Ahzya casually leant back trying to see them in more detail. Ahzya heard a rough cough again, and she frowned with concern. The chesty and harsh cough left the person gasping for air. Pushing her cautious nature aside, Ahzya walked towards the sound.

The person was revealed to be a young soldier, who was leaning with his back to the wall. He wore a light blue jacket, which Ahzya had seen the training recruits wearing earlier. His ash blond hair was cut short for convenience and one of his hands rested over his face.

Ahzya frowned when she noticed a blood stain on the collar of his jacket. His arms were patchy blue with bruises and specks of blood seeped from scratches.

"Are you okay?" Ahzya asked as she arrived beside the soldier.

The trainee's arm dropped from his face, startled by Ahzya's seemingly sudden appearance. With his arm removed from its position, Ahzya was shocked to find that his face was also beaten. He'd obviously tried to wipe away the blood from a split in his lip, as the red smeared right across his mouth and chin. His nose took on a crooked slant, though it looked to be a past injury, not a current one. One eye was bright red and the eyelid had already begun to swell.

"You're hurt," Ahzya exclaimed, looking over the wounds.

"Just a little, but I'm fine," the trainee replied.

"I'll go fetch some help for you," Ahzya said, turning to find help.

"No, please don't," the trainee pleaded hurriedly.

He grabbed onto her arm as she turned, and she glanced back to find his grey-green eyes held a desperate gleam to them. Even with his eye bruised and lip split, the young trainee seemed more concerned about being seen than about his injuries.

"You have to get that seen to," Ahzya insisted firmly.

"I'm fine," the trainee repeated, sitting up straight.

Ahzya glanced at his wounds and her brow dipped. Without further hesitation, she drew a clean handkerchief from her pocket. A puddle of water had settled in a dip in the top of the castle wall, which had gathered after the recent rain. Dipping the handkerchief in the cold water, she wrung it out slightly before kneeling next to the trainee.

"You don't have to do that," the trainee said, raising his hands.

"Look, do you want to be able to see out of that eye?" Ahzya said sternly. "If we don't put something cool on it, it will swell and close over."

The trainee huffed a breath of air through his nose at her firm attitude but allowed her to tend to his wounds. Ahzya held the cold handkerchief to his already bruising eye and brushed her thumb soothingly along his jaw when he clenched it. She unwrapped her scarf from around her neck and also dipped it in the water.

"Hey, you'll catch a co—" the trainee started to object.

"Hush," Ahzya said, cutting him off. "I live on the coast; I've dealt with the cold before."

The trainee chuckled and leant against the wall again with a groaning sigh. Ahzya wiped the blood from his lip and face.

"You seem to have done this before," the trainee said, watching her movements.

"The boys back home always got into fights, and I was the one who had to patch them up at the end of the day when they ran home with their tails between their legs," Ahzya said, her voice indicating her annoyance.

"I didn't know boys could have tails. Where exactly did you grow up?" the trainee joked.

Ahzya rolled her eyes and pressed the dampened scarf along his jaw.

"Hold that on there. I'll refresh the handkerchief," Ahzya instructed.

The soldier followed her directions obediently, and Ahzya turned away from him. Ahzya was curious as to how the soldier got injured but guessed that the soldier would just avoid the question.

"Your accent is cute," the trainee complimented.

"Is it that noticeable?" Ahzya asked wincing.

"It's about as obvious as a punch to the face," the trainee teased.

"Well, you'd know all about that, wouldn't you," Ahzya mumbled.

The trainee scoffed, flipping the scarf to the cooler side.

"I think we should introduce ourselves," the soldier chirped. "I'm Cole, and I am currently a trainee soldier."

Ahzya turned around and approached with the cool handkerchief in hand.

"I'm Ahzya, and I'm currently the personal healer for a certain trainee soldier," Ahzya replied. "Although in my spare time, I enjoy touring strange castles and getting lost."

Cole chuckled, but winced and moved his hand to his chest. Ahzya wouldn't have been surprised if he had several bruised ribs, which would be very painful for him. His hands were scratched and bleeding too. At the discovery of each wound, Ahzya added fuel to fiery anger brewing in her mind. As she sat down next to him, studying his battered face, she seethed at the brutality of Cole's assailant.

"Why would anyone do this?" Ahzya whispered, and Cole turned to look at her.

"Really, Ahzya, it is fine," Cole assured, although his face grew paler even as they spoke.

Ahzya opened her mouth to speak again, but Cole doubled over and coughed forcefully. His whole body shook with the convulsions and Ahzya leapt forward, patting him gently on the back. As his fit subsided, Ahzya rubbed her hand in a firm circular motion, hoping it brought comfort. When Cole's coughing stopped, he slumped against the wall, taking in large gasps of air.

"Cole..." Ahzya started in concern.

"What are you slacking off up here for?" a loud male voice called from the direction of the tower. "You aren't skipping on your duties, are you?"

While the words took on the form of a scolding, instead of malice the voice utilised a jovial, teasing modulation. A soldier leaned his tall body onto the frame of the archway of the tower. Instead of a trainee uniform, his appeared to be more similar to the one King Mark's guards wore. Cole scrambled to his feet, and although he winced, a smile spread across his face, concealing it instantly.

"Brother!" Cole called, limping lightly.

"Cole," the older soldier gritted out tensely. "What the hell happened to you?"

"Just a scuffle with my friends. It was all in good fun," Cole replied, grinning up at his brother.

"Adapting to the soldier life, I see, I just hope you left them looking worse," his brother said, ruffling the younger's hair. "Don't make a habit of it, or I'll have to start making trouble for your opponents. Can't have you coming home to our dear mother looking like this all the time. Come on, we don't want to be late to lunch, and you'd better clean up a bit so that Mum won't have a fit."

"Give me a minute, I'll catch up to you," Cole answered.

His brother barely glanced in Ahzya's direction before he marched away. Cole winced as he limped back over. He smiled down at where she still sat against the wall, and he offered his right hand. Although it was evident that he was offering her a lift up from the ground, Ahzya thought it best not to accept that offer.

Ahzya stood, brushing the dust from her dress, and shook Cole's hand. She feigned ignorance so that she would not cause further injury to him, but Ahzya noticed a pained expression spread across his features despite her thoughtfulness. Being denied the act of a simple gentlemanly task apparently hurt Cole's pride, but he valiantly shook it off.

"Thank you for helping me," Cole said, flashing her a dimpled smile that sent a surge of adoration through her system.

Ahzya returned his smile giddily, but shook her head, as she felt she hadn't truly helped him much at all. Wounds still painfully marred his skin, although the bleeding and swelling had stopped.

"It's really no problem," Ahzya assured. "I hope your bruises fade soon."

"I dunno, it adds to my tough exterior," Cole joked. "However, with you and my brother warning me to not make a habit of it, I'll try my best not to repeat the experience."

"Just take care of yourself."

"With you being my personal healer, I'll just look for you if I get hurt. You'll visit again?"

Cole stuck his hands deep into his pockets, and his eyes gently pleaded with her. Ahzya tilted her head sideways and he mirrored the movement, an eyebrow quirked ever so slightly in question.

"Of course, I will," Ahzya assured, "but if you are ever in Port Joonver, come visit me too."

"Deal, I feel that's a fair exchange."

He chuckled and started moving away, walking backwards as to keep her in sight for as long as he could before he got to the tower.

"Let's be friends, Ahzya," Cole called back to her.

"That's a given. I don't go offer my healer services to anyone less qualified than a friend!" Ahzya replied before muttering to herself. "Peter will think I'm a social butterfly with the way I've made two friends in as many days."

Cole waved to her as he entered the tower and the door closed behind him. Ahzya sighed and hugged her arms. With the heat of her earlier exercise fully dissipated, she registered the chill reddening her exposed skin. She bent to pick up her scarf and wrapped it around her neck despite the dampened fibres. Luckily the scarf was black, otherwise, Ahzya was pretty sure she'd be able to see Cole's blood on it.

Ahzya spun around, looking for another item, and then checked her pockets when she couldn't find it. With a frown, she looked around once more before giving a resigned smile. Cole wasn't just a trainee soldier, but also a handkerchief thief.

# CHAPTER EIGHT

PETER LANT'S HOUSE, PORT JOONVER, ALPANIA

Peter tapped Ahzya on the shoulder gently and sent her a look that indicated his concern. Ahzya shrugged and offered a slim smile in response. It had been an interesting day, to say the least. Although Peter had prepared a simple, delicious meal, Ahzya didn't feel like eating.

Naomi had followed Ahzya home and proceeded to invited herself to dinner. She had enough of an appetite to make up for Ahzya's lack of one. Not only did Naomi have a taste for food but also conversation. She had hardly stopped talking to Peter since her arrival, and Peter sat listening to her constant rambling with exceptional patience. Ahzya admired Peter's ability to look intently interested, even if his mind was a million miles away. However, this ability also left Naomi feeling as if she had to make the conversation, a nervous habit that kicked into full swing around the quiet duo she found herself dining with.

"Ahzya is a speedy sprite though," Naomi stated, sending a smile her way. "When she got lost, I barely knew in which direction she'd disappeared."

"I'm sure Ahzya didn't purposely get lost," Peter said calmly.

"Oh, I'm not complaining. It was a little disappointing that we didn't get to see the general hall; however, when Ahzya returned we had our picnic by the lake, which felt exhilarating with the cool breeze," Naomi replied enthusiastically. "Ahzya seemed to enjoy our tour of the grounds more too."

Ahzya did smile at that comment. The grand lake, with the fresh breeze sending ripples over the surface, did much in calming Ahzya of her nerves. The floating boardwalk reminded her of the pontoon piers of Port Shanville, and the trek cemented a sense of familiarity in a day of new experiences.

"There will be plenty of opportunities to return and explore the rest of the castle," Peter encouraged. "I'll have to join the fun next time."

"You should definitely come with us," Naomi said sweetly. "I'd enjoy that a lot."

Naomi quietened and her neck, cheeks and ears took on a rouge complexion. Ahzya fidgeted in her seat and poked at the potato on her plate with her fork. Her eyes felt heavy and the warmth from the fireplace was like a blanket. Peter cleared his throat and focused on the meal with renewed enthusiasm.

"Actually, King Mark took a particular interest in Ahzya," Naomi stated suddenly, her gaze flicking between the other two. "It was a bit weird, really. He started asking me all sorts of questions about her."

Peter looked up at this and Ahzya frowned at her plate.

"Why would he be interested in knowing more about me?" Ahzya asked quietly.

"I have no idea," Naomi mused, her brow furrowing as she recollected the memory. "Once you ran off, King Mark summoned me to meet with him. I was honoured at first, but I felt like I was some sort of informant. He wanted to know what you were doing here, and who your family was. He also asked if I thought your manners were strange or foreign. Running from royalty is strange, perhaps, but I didn't think it warranted such questions, given that you're so young."

"And what did you tell him?" Peter asked, his tone level.

Ahzya glanced across at Peter, looking for assurance even though her stomach made a flip. King Mark couldn't have realised her true origin, or Ahzya hoped that that was the case.

"I just told him that Ahzya was touring the castle with me. Then only what Ahzya told me: That she was visiting from your parents' place as their adopted daughter," Naomi answered. "I told him that I didn't know much else since we'd only met in Nan's Kitchen on the day *Moonstruck* came to port. Should I not have said even that?"

"No, it's fine. I was just wondering," Peter said with a wane smile.

Peter stood to take his plate to a basin and began washing it slowly. Ahzya pushed her full plate away from her and leant against the back of her chair heavily. Ahzya caught Naomi watching her.

"You're really quiet and cute, Ahzya," Naomi said softly. "I was surprised when you scampered off like a jackrabbit. I told King Mark that, although your manners need polishing, you're just shy. So don't worry too much about what happened."

Naomi hadn't said anything wrong, or anything that King Mark couldn't have found out through his other channels. Yet Ahzya felt uneasy, and her leg bounced under the table. Peter crossed the room and picked up Naomi's empty plate. To her credit, Naomi noticed the change in mood, so she rose from her seat.

"Well, I had best get home," Naomi said, awkwardly smoothing her dress. "But thank you so much for dinner. I hope you have a good evening."

"You too, Naomi," Peter answered quietly. "Get home safely."

"Bye, Ahzya, thank you for coming with me today," Naomi said. "Don't get lost without me!"

Naomi giggled at her friendly jest and then went to the door, where her coat and scarf hung on one of the hooks. She donned her warm clothing and waved goodbye. A flurry of snow blew through the door, and Peter swiftly shut it behind Naomi with a shiver. Ahzya raised an eyebrow at Peter as he sighed deeply.

"Well..." Peter trailed off. "That was an experience."

"No kidding," Ahzya replied with a tired smile.

"I say we get dressed in the most comfortable clothes we can find, forget the rest of the dishes and then you can tell me your edition of the day," Peter said, grinning across at her.

"That sounds amazing," Ahzya answered, picking up her plate.

Peter was by the window and yawned loudly, his gaze lazily staring through the dark. Ahzya was about to say something further when Peter's muscles tensed. He grasped the windowsill so tightly that his knuckles turned white. Peter swivelled to look at Ahzya, his eyes showing the apparent fear that gripped his body.

"Ahzya, go to your room immediately," Peter ordered, his hand gentle on her shoulder, pressing her to move.

"What's wrong?" Ahzya asked, gazing up at Peter.

"Everything's going to be okay, alright?" Peter said, pausing to look at her thoughtfully.

"Why wouldn't it? What's outside?" Ahzya asked rapidly.

"It seems King Mark has decided to call upon us in the middle of the night," Peter answered.

Ahzya realised immediately and ducked through the door as Peter held it open. He glanced at her and then proceeded to smile as naturally as he could muster. Despite his efforts, Ahzya wasn't assured, and she bit her lip nervously.

"Go to your room, and I'll come and get you when it's all clear," Peter instructed.

Ahzya turned and walked through the hallway to her room. Peter closed the hall door once he saw her enter her bedroom. Ahzya, however, had no intention of staying there waiting and tiptoed back. Her feet made little sound, yet she felt like her steps thudded.

"Good evening, Private Lant," a familiar voice said through the door.

"Good evening, sir," Peter returned solemnly. "I wasn't expecting visitors so late in the evening."

"Yes, it was short notice for me too," Captain Ray's voice replied.

"I'm sorry to interrupt your plans for the evening, gentlemen. I have come to talk to you both about a serious matter; serious enough to postpone any other plans," a calm voice said.

Ahzya guessed the identity of the unfamiliar voice as that of King Mark. Ahzya doubted that the king called on the two sailors simply because of their recent return from an expedition. Although a meeting with Captain Ray was understandable, Peter was a different matter. A meeting with Peter could only mean trouble.

"Can I get you a drink before we begin, Your Majesty?" Peter asked politely.

"No, we are fine," King Mark answered for both men. "If you don't mind, I'd like to immediately get down to the matter at hand."

"Of course, Your Majesty, please take a seat," Peter said.

Ahzya pushed against the door lightly, pressing her ear against the chilled wood. The conversation became fainter, but she could still make out most of what they were saying.

"It has come to my attention, that a certain ship's crew have hidden a significant matter from me," King Mark was talking. "Rather than jump to conclusions, I decided to investigate further."

"How can we help?" Captain Ray asked, his tone level.

"I heard that a vessel in the Royal Fleet was used to break the rules and regulations established by my forefathers," King Mark stated. "Private Lant, would you be kind enough to recite Rule 34 from the Sailor's Code for us?"

There was a brief pause; Ahzya strained to hear the conversation.

"Rule 34 of the Sailor's Code states the following, all cargo on board a ship must be inspected and reported to the king, including but not limited to; imported supplies, any maps or charts produced and gold," Peter replied clearly.

"And Rule 36, Private?" King Mark said.

"Rule 36 states that no sailor is authorised to smuggle anything on board a ship, be that alcohol, animal or human. If a sailor wishes to bring any of the mentioned on board, then he must seek authorisation by an official or the king."

"Correct, now the crew in question have broken both of these regulations. Not only have they brought an unauthorised person on board one of my fleet, but they have also failed to report this person's presence to me upon reaching port."

None of the men spoke. Ahzya almost began to think that perhaps something had happened to them. She was in shock herself. King Mark suspected them; he'd arrived to deal with the matter.

"Now upon hearing this, is there anything you wish to report to me, Private Lant?"

Ahzya held her breath. As a moment passed without Peter's voice answering, Ahzya's eyes widened. They had been found out. If Peter tried to hide her origin at this point, it would be a blatant lie. To smuggle someone on board was one thing, lying to the ruler of your country was a whole other story.

"If you don't mind me saying, Your Majesty, you're being strangely cryptic," Peter said. "Do you wish for me to cite the consequences of smuggling as well? If the person or item is discovered in the sailor's care or household, then punishment must be dealt to the sailor. This punishment would consist of work without pay and in a serious case, say when the sailor tries to deceive those in charge, then there would be time spent in prison."

Ahzya couldn't help but feel nauseous. She knew the risk and punishment was severe, but to think that Peter could go to prison. The cramping in her stomach tightened and her hands shook.

"The smuggled personage would be shipped back to where they came from. On this the regulations are quite clear," King Mark continued seriously from what Peter had cited.

"A rather broad regulation, I'd say," Peter returned, as Ahzya gritted her teeth and closed her eyes.

"I'm not about to debate the circumstantial details to the code of ethics that have been in place for years," King Mark replied in exasperation. "I'm here to get a straight answer and clear up what exactly has happened, and why it wasn't reported to me. Now, I'll ask you again, Private Lant. Do you have anything to report to me?"

"Any answer I may give requires discussion and explanation. While you demand an explanation, what you really want is an answer that fits in the box you're already demanding; which I won't be giving, Your Majesty," Peter replied firmly.

"Very well," King Mark's voice was sharp. "What about you, Captain Ray? Do you have anything you wish to report to me?"

There was a lull in conversation, and even though Ahzya was not in the room, she felt the tension in the air. Ahzya would have given anything just to wake up and find that this was all just a bad dream. Everything felt very real, too real, and her heart sank.

"Peter..." Captain Ray's voice said quietly.

This was the first time that Ahzya had heard Ray use Peter's first name by itself. His voice held the most apologetic tone, and though Ahzya couldn't see him, her eyes stung.

"Your report, Captain Ray," King Mark interrupted.

"On our journey, we acquired a new crew member at Ulkadasa—" Ray began.

"Did you know this 'crew member' before you set sail?" King Mark interrupted.

"Not at first, no," Ray answered truthfully.

"And if I were to search this house, I would find that person living here?" King Mark asked.

"I believe so, Your Majesty," Ray answered, his voice strained.

"Had this new 'crewmate' been in your reports; had the proper steps been taken, this situation may have been negotiated. However, I value honesty. Rather, as king, I rely on it. I can't allow the sailors on board my ships to be liars," King Mark spoke firmly.

"As you are aware, Your Majesty, I've yet to complete my written report. As for Private Lant, he's just trying to protect his family."

It almost broke Ahzya's heart to hear the raw emotion in Ray's voice. Although he was a resilient man and excellent captain, he had a humanity and compassion to him too. Ahzya witnessed it often when they were on board the *Moonstruck*. Ray cared for his injured crew with an attitude and kind-heartedness that Ahzya admired. Although he had put on a brave front when multiple crew members passed away, Ahzya could see that he was hurting. His duty and job held him to a professional and reliable standard; his heart was one of gold.

"I understand his wish to protect this girl, no doubt you've all become quite attached during your journey back, but I have to protect this country. There are reasons we have procedures in place. Now that there is an attachment, what I may be forced to do will hurt her and you even more." King Mark's voice was cold compared to the captain's tone.

"Your Majesty, we were months travel away from our home port with no official on board, since the king's official died when we were separated from the rest of the fleet. The captain and Johno had to play the role of diplomat and official in Ulkadasa, but they don't have the authority to accept passengers without the king's representative, due to possible conflicts of interest with crew members. Of course, I considered returning here and filling out the proper paperwork, but if we had left her there, it would have been half a year at least before we could return. By then, she would have been syphoned off into the workforce and difficult to find, despite any paperwork we'd filled out here," Peter spoke up, trying to keep his emotions in check. "Even then the plan would rely on Your Majesty to even send *Moonstruck* on another expedition to Ulkadasa."

"So that justifies trying to deceive me on this matter? This way, there is no way she'll ever be able to be a citizen of Alpania, and it leaves your station in my fleet in peril. Can't you understand?"

Ahzya massaged the centre point of her collar bone as her arms and chest began to shudder. She couldn't sit by and allow both men to suffer on her behalf. She knew that not only would Peter be subject to punishment but Captain Ray as well, since he wouldn't let Peter take the blame alone.

Peter's recited words from earlier suddenly came to her mind.

*If the person or item is discovered in the sailor's care or household, then punishment must be dealt to the sailor.*

It all suddenly came together, and Ahzya pushed away from the door. If she wasn't discovered in the house, then they would have no reason to punish Peter. If Ahzya became merely a ghost, with no connection to either Peter or the crew of *Moonstruck,* then there would be no need for this matter to go on further.

It was the only thing she could do for them, and there was no other choice but to leave her new life behind. Her life in Alpania with Peter had barely just begun, and already there was a threat. Either way, she wouldn't be able to stay here. She could choose whether to be shipped back to Ulkadasa or to run and be free in Alpania on her own. With both choices, she'd separate from Peter and his home at Port Joonver.

Ahzya didn't listen to another word from the room. If she was going to do this, then she had already wasted enough time.

Ahzya pulled on another pair of clothes and wrapped her cloak around her body as well as the scarf. She shoved a few belongings into a bag as well as the few coins she had saved from her trip to the castle. Even as she packed, she began to feel overwhelmed. Ahzya shook her head roughly and took a deep breath. She wouldn't cry; she wouldn't be a coward.

Barely a few minutes later and Ahzya tiptoed back into the hall. There were only two exits from the building, and the front door wasn't an option unless she wanted the men to see her. The back door was all there was, and Ahzya yanked it open. She glanced back to make sure none of the men had heard her and then stepped outside into the flurrying snowy night.

Ahzya ran, the snow covering over her footsteps clearing any evidence of her existence there. She didn't look back, not even a glance. Ahzya swore never to return and believed that it was for the best of every person involved. She had lived most of her life alone, and she would do it again. As Ahzya ran, cool tears began to drip down her cheeks, freezing partway down, and she muffled her sobbing. After all, it had never been that she wanted to be alone, but sometimes life was an unfair master.

# CHAPTER NINE

## Present Day: Tealle 1407

DEEP IN THE MOUNTAINS OF ALPANIA

Ahzya Xion woke up with a jolt to find herself lying under a canopy of pine trees. She rolled over and sighed. Dreams of her time on board *Moonstruck* and the subsequent few days with Peter in Port Joonver had filled her nights since she'd accepted the task of assassinating King Mark. Truthfully it had been years since she had truly dwelt long on it. It was hard to erase the consequences of that time entirely from her mind; it had become a form of obsession. However, she focused on what that meant for her future actions rather than the actual memories. Ahzya hit the ground with her fist to shake the memories that came again as she lay there.

Ahzya sat up on the blanket she had been lying on and reached for her backpack. Taking a bottle out of the bag, she undid the stopper and took a large mouthful of water. Water dribbled onto her chin, and she wiped it off with her sleeve. She stretched her leg muscles and rolled her shoulders before moving to a crouching position.

The only thing to do about her wandering mind was to start doing something. Ahzya tightly rolled up the blanket and shoved it into her bag. Grabbing the saddle which she had been using as a pillow, Ahzya walked over to where a palomino mare stood.

"It seems we'll be making an early start, Reggad," Ahzya said, brushing the mare's back with her hand. "You'd better warm up those muscles of yours."

The look the mare gave her in reply seemed to show the creature's annoyance at such an early start. Perhaps it was all Ahzya's imagination.

"Listen, I know you hate early journeys, but I can't sleep nowadays so we may as well travel."

The mare let out a low rumble and shook her mane gently. Ahzya smiled as she threw the saddle blanket onto Reggad's back. She ran her hand smoothly along the palomino's muzzle and rested her forehead on the mare's neck.

Reggad was her pride and joy. Her passion for horses hadn't faded in the last six years; however, her handling of them had improved. Ahzya could almost sense what Reggad was feeling and saying with her movements. That or Ahzya was prone to a little craziness, and hours spent alone with a lack of other companionship left her looking for it in her horse.

Ahzya had worked for a year doing odd jobs at a lumberyard, which involved long hours and physical exhaustion. The work was tiring but seeing the money build up slowly gave Ahzya a sense of pride. She had one goal with the work, and that was to earn enough money to buy a horse. The money wouldn't be from her thieving ways but hard, honest work.

Reggad, a young filly when they had first met, connected with Ahzya right away. Reggad was a beautiful, healthy horse and loved to run. She reminded Ahzya of a sense of freedom. Reggad's owner wasn't going to let her go for a small price, which meant that Ahzya ended up after hours at a tavern.

The tavern work was some of the worst work Ahzya had ever experienced, and she was fortunate she had been in many similar environments before that point. Having lived several years on her own in Alpania, she had had her fair share of flirty drunkards and bar fights.

Ahzya sighed into the scratchy, coarse mane and then stepped back as Reggad whinnied quietly. Ahzya pet Reggad's nose affectionately again and then bent to pick up the saddle.

Ahzya swung the saddle up and then reached for the girth. Reggad stood quietly and merely bent her head in search of an early meal. Ahzya cinched the girth strap and picked up her backpack.

Ahzya didn't carry anything more than what fit in a backpack and found she rarely needed anything else. When on a thieving run, she usually packed Reggad with large saddlebags. However, this trip she wouldn't be taking anything back with her and the saddlebags just meant extra weight.

A dense fog covered the mountain range, and Ahzya tried to regain feeling in her fingers as she rubbed them together. Ahzya donned a pair of thick, warm, woollen gloves after cinching the saddle, because it was harder to do so while wearing gloves. Further in the mountain range, snow coated the earth in a thick blanket, but as they neared the coast, and rode onto the lower ranges, the snow disappeared. It was still frosty cold, but it didn't hold the same terrain struggles as snow posed.

She knew Prynesse wasn't much further, but had chosen to camp for the night rather than reach there the previous evening. Ahzya grew nervous about returning to the castle and Prynesse. She had risked visits to the outskirts of Prynesse since running away, but several years had passed since her last. A lot of things had changed since then, making Ahzya's previous visits feel vaguely distant; a lifetime ago. Even then, Ahzya never visited Port Joonver. Ghosts from her past lurked in that town, and although searches for her had ceased, there was a risk that people may still recognise her.

Ahzya's eyes felt heavy, and the gentle sound of hoof beats were slowly lulling her to sleep. Reggad let out a low rumble from her throat and quivered her body.

Reggad always did that when she could feel Ahzya slipping in the saddle. It was like a personal waking mechanism, and Ahzya came to attention immediately.

They were about to cross a stream, and the sound of the bubbling water was notably relaxing. However, with the cold weather, Ahzya could be assured that the water would be freezing.

"It would probably do me some good, it would wake me up at least," Ahzya said, stretching.

Reggad merely let out another rumble in response and began wading into the water. Ahzya kicked her feet from the stirrups and rested her feet on the saddle. She also kept an eye on the depth of the water. If the water turned out to be too deep, then she would have to dismount anyway. Luckily this didn't seem to be the case, and they reached the other side with Ahzya still sitting dry in the saddle. Ahzya bent and patted Reggad's neck a couple of times and scratched her forehead affectionately.

"Without you, I'd get lost, wouldn't I, Reggad?" Ahzya crooned.

Reggad let out a friendly whinny as if agreeing with Ahzya, and Ahzya couldn't help but smile. There was little in her life that could make her laugh and smile anymore. She had thought her first fifteen years were tough, but it hadn't even compared to her life after Port Joonver. Reggad was one of the only sparks that kept her human.

Girls at the orphanage had always made the life of a thief out to be romantic and thrilling. A thief went on adventures wherever they went and had enough gold to buy several castles and could well afford maids to take care of their chores. Ahzya now knew better than to believe this romanticised version of a thief's life. Many thieves were greedy and ruthless and didn't give a damn about anyone else. How could you care when you take what isn't yours and leave despair and loss wherever you go?

Ahzya had never considered herself a sheltered child, but she could hardly believe what the last six years had taught her. Her childhood innocence was shattered and disappeared with any other of her youthful dreams. In this world, there was much the fifteen-year-old version of herself would have never thought existed. Ahzya had lived in a dream world by the sea and imagined herself a strong, independent orphan who was ready for the adventures outside Shanville. She'd been ruthlessly incorrect, and the outside world held as much filth as it did beauty.

A melodic hum began to filter through the trees, and Reggad's ears pricked to attention at the sound. As they journeyed forward, the hum became clear enough to make out words. Ahzya recognised the tune as that of an old love ballad. The male voice was low and full of emotion as it retold a story of a lifetime of love:

*Day o' old*
*Hazy, floral scented memories*
*Lovers' promises bold*
*True, confessions o' youth*
*Day o' old*
*Charms an' secrets unknown t' known*
*The days when I loved you*
*Longed to be in your arms*
*Day o' old*
*Gone, a lifetime now memories*
*Yet by ye side I'll stay*
*Loyal to youthful love*

They were heading straight for the area the song was coming from, and Ahzya didn't change her course. She bent in the saddle to duck under some low hanging branches and kept her eye out for the forest bard.

*Day o' old*
*Lost oot here, wi' a broken cart*
*Pitiful bloke I am*
*No market will I see*
*Day o' old*

*The market will be long gone*
*Life is so damn unfair*
*Drag me sorry ass home*

The song swept off course from the original, and Ahzya raised an eyebrow at the annoyed tone. She emerged from the pines on a scene of chaos. Crates of produce were stacked on the ground, and another box scattered across the clearing.

"Why did that damn idiot have to go and break his leg?" a male voice grumbled.

Ahzya looked to her left to see a man lying on his back on the ground. A horse was grazing nearby, and a cart was untethered and abandoned near to the man. Ahzya noticed that there was a hole in the base of the cart, and she raised an eyebrow.

"Perhaps you could break his other leg as punishment," Ahzya spoke aloud.

The man sat up startled and looked across at her. Ahzya brought Reggad to a stop and glanced down at him. She leaned forward and rested her forearm on the pommel of the saddle. The man was middle-aged and pretty average looking for an Alpanian. He got over his surprise rather quickly and smiled halfheartedly, shaking his head.

"No, probably no' the best thing to do, 'specially since he's me son-in-law," the man answered, standing up swiftly.

"All the more reason," Ahzya responded without blinking. "However, if I can be of service to you at this moment, I'd be open to helping you out."

"I don't know how much help you can be," the man admitted. "I'm a fruit an' vegetable pedlar in Prynesse, but the bottom o' me cart broke."

Ahzya dismounted and went over to examine the damage. There was a sizeable breakage, undoubtedly caused by weak timber and water damage. Ahzya turned to look at the amount of produce the man had to sell and then calculated their options.

"I'm going to Prynesse too," Ahzya spoke carefully. "If we utilise the area around the break, I could sit in the back of the cart and make sure none of the crates slide and fall through. That way you should still be able to make it to town in good time. Once in town, you can find somewhere to repair your cart and be able to pay for it with the money you earn."

The man nodded solemnly and surveyed the option carefully.

"I don't see why we canna give it a try," the man agreed. "And we can hope and pray that the rest o' it don't break in the meantime."

They worked together to put the crates back in the cart, distributing the weight evenly. Ahzya unsaddled Reggad and tethered her to the side of the cart. Ahzya then climbed into the back along with the crates and braced herself above the broken boards.

"What is a young lass like you doing travelling by yerself through these woods?" the man asked, clicking his tongue at his horse.

"I have business in Prynesse and decided to have an early start," Ahzya answered.

"Just for the day?" the man asked further.

"I wish," Ahzya responded. "I'll need longer than that, but I'm not sure how long."

"Where are you travelling from?"

"Up north."

The man appeared to get the hint that she wasn't open to discussing such personal questions and a couple of minutes passed in silence.

"I'm Noah Eagal," the man stated.

"Catherine Torpay, it is a pleasure to meet you," Ahzya answered in a friendly tone.

Catherine Torpay was one of a few aliases that Ahzya had. 'Ahzya Xion' had become non-existent other than in the underground world, and, even then, only a few people knew her real name. Instead, those who hired her used her underworld nickname and title, Trickster. Most of the time an information guild, the Veritas Guild, handed the request to Ahzya as a middleman. Some people even believed that Trickster was merely a myth, a thief created from drunken tales spun at bars.

Ahzya rested lazily for most of the journey, the rock of the cart turned out to be oddly comfortable. The hole in the cart prevented any sleep from actually taking over, but the temptation was there. Although Noah barely spoke, he hummed different tunes as the sun began to splay its rays through the canopy of leaves. Some of the songs Ahzya knew, and she joined in with the melodic hum.

It was mid-morning by the time they reached the last mountain and gazed across Prynesse, the castle and its grounds. Ahzya sat up and felt the oddest sense of nostalgia. She eyed the tall stone walls and rows of neat houses and dotting of shops. The surrounding forest sat oddly peaceful next to the bustling city. It was like seeing an old friend; it was familiar yet bizarre and new.

Noah was eager to get into the city and set up his cart for morning trade. Ahzya wasn't about to stop him and took the chance to reacquaint herself with the layout of the city. The cart first trundled through the outer gate to Prynesse. Construction of the outer wall around the city had been completed while Ahzya had been away. It was a little different from Castle Prynesse's rampart as housing was built as a part of the wall, the entrances only accessible from the city side. There was no inspection or pass required to enter the city unless the country fell into war, in which case more soldiers could be stationed there and the gate closed. The city had continued to expand, becoming barely recognisable from the six years earlier. Ahzya had visited a little over two years prior, so it wasn't quite as disorientating, but she still felt a sense of awe as they passed through the wall.

Children still manoeuvred their games around the wagons, carriages and horses. Castle soldiers could be seen in their purple uniforms; however, regular soldiers, with much less flashy uniforms, were stationed all around the town to actually keep the peace. Sailors were also taking a day trip from Port Joonver and merchants from neighbouring countries travelled even further to come do their business with the city.

The town square was already alive with a market-like atmosphere, and people were calling from every corner. It seemed they thought that whoever could out yell their competition would draw more customers. Ahzya wasn't so sure that this was true and would have much rather shopped at a store in a quiet corner of the square.

Noah positioned the cart as best he could amongst the throng of vendors and villagers. Which was no easy feat, especially when other shop owners yelled at them saying they had already claimed that area.

Ahzya wasted no time in helping him unload and set up his stall. Noah, grateful for the help, managed to set up in half the time it usually took him. Not only did she help him set up, but even as she did so, she sold the produce. A friendly smile to some passing off duty soldiers sold several pears as a lunch treat. Soon enough Noah's store was open and selling enough goods to cover the time they had lost to the broken cart.

"I appreciate all ye help!" Noah said gratefully. "I owe ya more than a favour or two. If ever ya need somethin', let me know."

"Well, there is one thing you could help me with..." Ahzya said, pausing to show a reluctance to ask.

"Name it," Noah said with a smile.

Noah could provide her the perfect opportunity; Ahzya couldn't stop the happy thrill that ran through her nerves at everything going to plan.

# CHAPTER TEN

MAIN MARKETPLACE, PRYNESSE, ALPANIA

"Hello, what can I serve you today?" Ahzya Xion asked as a maid from the castle approached.

While working for Noah, Ahzya gathered information on King Mark's social movements and activities. Ahzya found that many of the soldiers and maids from the castle felt comfortable talking about casual castle happenings with the friendly vegetable man. She soon discovered that King Mark had a very busy schedule and was in constant contact with the city officials. While his meetings meant there were many opportunities where she could approach him, Ahzya also noted the soldiers that uniformly surrounded him. His bodyguards were always attentive at his side, as were another dozen officials and curious onlookers.

Any smart person would instantly realise that any attack on the king, while he was outside the castle, would be futile. Ahzya wasn't a rash decision maker, and therefore the planning stage was equally important as the execution. As a thief, she took weeks scoping the area and observing the target's movements and general patterns. With this in mind, Ahzya began forming a new plan in her head. As the maid approached, Ahzya gave one of the most charming smiles she could manage. Phase one of the plan began.

"Morning!" the maid said, dimples appearing in her cheeks. "How are you today, Catherine?"

"As well as can be expected, Lesley," Ahzya responded. "Here for lunch or castle duties?"

"A bit of both, I hope," the maid answered. "Madam Hill wants me back as quickly as possible. If Queen Maria hadn't specifically requested a meal that requires ingredients from outside the castle, I wouldn't have been allowed out. We're so short-handed right now, I barely get a chance to breathe."

"Why is the castle so understaffed?" Noah piped in to the conversation.

"A few of the maids have caught some sort of flu, it's left them bedridden. Usually, they'd have to work through it, but one of them collapsed in front of Her Majesty, so Madam Hill was forced to make them rest," Lesley said with a tired shake of her head. "Then, one of the youngest maids disappeared a couple of weeks ago. Madam Uran says she ran off with her man, and we all had to endure her lecture about the ridiculous standards she wants us to adhere to."

"Sounds like hell," Ahzya empathised.

"Sounds like a perfect opportunity to me, Cath," Noah said from behind her.

Noah had been calling her Cath ever since she had begun working for him, and the name became her nickname for most of their customers too. Ahzya didn't mind the name. It was short and convenient. Catherine had always sounded like that of a lady of the high court, and that certainly didn't suit her overall personality.

"Opportunity?" Lesley asked, frowning with confusion.

"Cath, who I really wouldna mind stayin' with me, has had her eye on a position at the castle since she came to town. Unfortunately, there didn't seem to be any positions open. Poor Cath was heartbroken and had to settle for working for ol' me," Noah answered on Ahzya's behalf.

"Heartbroken is a strong word. I was a little disappointed when I wasn't even allowed to see the head maid," Ahzya said with a shrug.

"Ah, security has been heightened recently, so that's probably why," Lesley said her lips pursing in thought. "It might be different if I recommend you. You should come to the castle after your work today and I'll meet you at the gate. I'll talk to Madam Hill; I'm sure she'll welcome the help."

Ahzya bowed her head in thanks and flashed a smile. Noah and Ahzya quickly gathered the castle's supplies together. Although the castle grew many of their own vegetables and fruit, Noah brought delicacies from deep within the mountains. It appeared that the queen had a taste for the mushrooms that Noah sold, and the head cook often sent a maid to collect them.

"You may wish to try and tidy up before you come to the castle, Catherine," Lesley said, putting the mushrooms into a basket. "Madam Hill will ignore you if you turn up with dirt on your hands or messy hair, even if you have the best references ever."

"I shall try my best to look presentable," Ahzya answered, giving an adorable smile. "Thank you so much, Lesley, you've been a big help."

"No problem at all, and I wish you the best of luck. Now I must excuse myself, or I'll get my ear yelled off," Lesley said. "Something you have to look forward to."

Lesley laughed good-naturedly and winked. Ahzya waved to her as she left and busied herself on other tasks. Trying to dress up would be more of a problem than Lesley could have imagined. Ahzya's pack consisted of breeches, tunics and bedding. Other than having her hair regularly trimmed, her hand was the only brush or comb she used, and perfume was something that only lavish people used. Ahzya supposed she could have a dip in the hidden stream next to where she'd camped. She could buy a bar of soap easily enough, but that still left her with a clothing issue.

"Hey, Cath, I see your admirer approaching," Noah said, interrupting her thoughts.

Ahzya turned to Noah, raising an eyebrow, and Noah nodded his head towards the crowd. Ahzya looked across the square searching for the familiar face and spotted a shock of red hair only metres away. Ahzya plastered a smile on her face as a young man approached.

"Good morning, Mr Customer," Ahzya greeted with a friendly tone.

"Good morning, Cath," the young man answered with a beaming smile. "You know you could use my name for once."

Ahzya shrugged and turned to give a customer their purchase, bidding them goodbye by name.

"How are you today, Ethan?" Noah asked the man with a smirk.

"Other than being constantly ignored by Cath, I'm doing quite well," the young man said, his blue eyes bright and happy.

"In town for personal time or business?" Noah continued the friendly conversation.

"Business this time. I got put on supply duty with Cassik for the *Moonstruck*," Ethan replied.

Ahzya's head swung up at the mention of *Moonstruck*, and Ethan noticed. He smiled across at her and then continued proudly.

"Captain Ray sent us personally," Ethan boasted, leaning on the stall.

Ahzya hid her nervousness at hearing the familiar name. She had continued to overhear the name for years, but even the mention of it still filled her with a pang of regret and sorrow.

"Should you really be addressing the commander of the King's Fleet under the title of captain?" Noah asked, moving around the stall.

"Everyone else may call him Commander Ray; however, he'd punch any of the crew if he heard us call him that," Ethan replied with a chuckle. "He prefers us not to be so formal; we are all friends on board *Moonstruck*."

Ahzya's curiosity surged, but the threat of being recognised caused her to hesitate. Luckily Noah asked more than enough questions.

"Is your uncle Nate still causing mayhem?" Noah asked.

"Yup," Ethan answered with a roll of his eyes.

Ahzya softly chuckled as she put lettuce in a basket. When was Nate not getting into trouble? That was the real question they should be asking. Ahzya could see the resemblance between Ethan and Nate now that she thought about it. They both had the same titian-coloured, curly hair and sea blue eyes. Not to mention they were both sociable and irritating in a comedic fashion to boot.

"So, just like yourself?" Ahzya said aloud.

"Ah, she speaks!" Ethan said, faking surprise.

"Only when the conversation is interesting enough," Ahzya replied slyly.

"Well, since you seem to be interested in the *Moonstruck* and Captain Ray, then I'll share some secret information with you," Ethan said, leaning forward towards her.

He beckoned towards her to come closer as if about to whisper to her like children always did. Ahzya raised an eyebrow, but her curiosity overcame any suspicion she may have had about his actions. She leant into the stall, turning her right ear towards Ethan as if to hear better.

"I have been entrusted with a message from the castle summoning Captain Ray to dine with King Mark and Her Majesty tonight," Ethan whispered.

"Really? Does Captain Ray dine with the king regularly?" Ahzya asked, leaning forward.

"Not regularly, but often enough," Ethan answered, enjoying the attention he received in return. "The cap is the commander of the King's Fleet, but they've also been friends for decades. However, the message seemed to be more of a business manner than usual. If it's just a friendly dinner, then King Mark usually sees Captain Ray himself. This time it was all official with a messenger and everything."

"How fancy," Ahzya stated, drawing away with a smile.

"Indeed!"

Ethan hovered at the stand a moment longer until a male voice started calling his name from a few stalls away. He sighed and smiled across at Ahzya.

"Well, I had best go and deliver the message," Ethan said.

"Yes, it sounds a perilous and important task," Ahzya replied, taking a moment to smile back.

Ethan threw back his head in a laugh, but then leant across to whisper, "Not even kelpies could steal it from my safe hands. I'll see you later!"

"You may not if Cath gets a job at the castle like she hopes," Noah informed.

Ethan paused and glanced at Ahzya to see if this was true. Ahzya did not attempt to confirm or deny the fact, and the man calling for Ethan was getting impatient.

"Well then, I wish you the best with that, although I hope you don't get any work there," Ethan said hurriedly. "I'd hate to miss our lengthy conversations."

Ahzya thought she'd caught a slight tone of sarcasm in his last statement, but he turned and disappeared by the time she looked up. His actions over the last few days had already informed her that he'd developed some sort of crush on her. It was cute and light-hearted.

Ahzya couldn't help but feel sorry for him. After all, she wasn't an easy target. As young as she was, Ahzya had already loved, and she doubted she'd ever be able to feel that way again. She'd become unrecognisable even to herself when she'd lost that love, she was almost scared of what would happen if she faced similar heartbreak again. Perhaps one day, when she was no longer in search of revenge, then perhaps she'd have time to consider it. By then Ethan would be married; Ahzya wouldn't even be a memory.

### CASTLE PRYNESSE, ALPANIA

Ahzya ran her hand over the white-laced apron, which covered the black uniform dress, and then readjusted the frilled headband that kept her short hair away from her face. Black stockings and a pair of low-heeled shoes finished off the outfit. Ahzya had visited Madam Hill with Lesley, and the moment she stated her business, Hill had hired her without much questioning.

"Thank the heavens, I'm glad Lesley brought you," Madam Hill prattled, her skirts bustling around her. "Blaire went and eloped. It seems she had been seeing one of the soldiers behind our backs, though not even her roommate knew of any attachment between them."

Ahzya exchanged a look with Lesley, who rolled her eyes at Hill's back.

"And that's a bad thing?" Ahzya asked, noting the annoyance in Hill's voice.

"My word, yes! Engaging in flirtatious interactions is strictly frowned upon and highly discouraged. Minds are easily led astray and distracted with romance, and negligence soon follows. We work as representatives of the castle, to do such things would bring down the reputation of Castle Prynesse," Madam Hill said, before pointing warningly at Ahzya. "So, you be warned, no wasting time with men while employed here at the castle, or there will be serious consequences."

Ahzya bowed her head respectfully, although quietly she thought that the rule was ridiculous. At least for her, she could safely say that was not going to be a problem. Romance wasn't something that she was seeking during her time at the castle.

Ahzya was the second youngest maid and as she was introduced to the others, she bowed respectfully. The youngest maid was barely sixteen, Hill explained, and this was her first job. Madam Hill continued to complain about the lack of young ladies wishing to work as castle maids and that replacements were hard to come by.

"Now Her Majesty, Queen Maria, is hosting her birthday celebrations in barely two weeks, so there will be lots of work and long hours for everyone," Madam Hill said to all the maids gathered. "The guest rooms must be aired and cleaned spotless. There will be an inspection of the rooms next week, and then they will be cleaned again before the guests arrive. Daily tasks will go as usual; Catherine, you will be helping Mrs Youn in the kitchen and waiting on the main table."

Ahzya nodded and continued standing in the row of maids as Hill proceeded to tell everyone their duties. Ahzya wasn't thrilled about her own position, a kitchen hand wasn't conducive to scouting out the castle's inhabitants' movements. However, she thought better than to speak up, she'd figure out something later. Madam Hill was respectful yet firm, and when one of the older maids sneered at the job that she was given, Hill soon corrected her attitude with a stern glare.

"We must all pull our weight here, and if you have any complaints..." Madam Hill said, pausing to look at the disgruntled maid directly, "keep them to yourself. None of us wish to hear your whining."

Madam Hill looked along the row of maids and inspected their uniforms closely. She came to Ahzya and gazed over her newest employee's slim figure and gave a nod of satisfaction. Ahzya gave an inner sigh of relief, for she had been trying on varying sized uniforms for a while and had finally found one that fit her well. Hill specifically directed Ahzya on how she should look and as she studied Ahzya's face she made a dissatisfied 'tsk' sound with her tongue.

"Catherine, Catherine," Hill sing-songed her name, "if you are going to be a maid at the castle, you must try to keep up an appearance that is both professional and beautiful."

Hill motioned for another maid to bring her a chestnut-coloured box with silver latches. Ahzya glanced down at her clothes, trying to spot a fault. Others may have taken offence at Hill's statement but Ahzya, who knew nothing of vanity, or fashion, supposed she knew what she was talking about.

"What you need is a touch of makeup, my dear. I possess an artistic flair, so I'll have you looking presentable in no time," Hill said, opening the box to reveal lines of varying makeup merchandise.

Ahzya hid a sneer, for she thought makeup was a waste of time. She kept this opinion to herself, as such a statement might not have been taken well by the other ladies in the room. After all, Ahzya didn't think any less of the court ladies or maids who did choose to wear such products. Even her best friend was talented with a makeup brush, and she admired these skills and the results on her friend. However, for Ahzya, it never posed much of an attraction.

"Makeup is part of the uniform here at the castle," Hill continued talking. "If you don't know how to apply it, then you shall learn. I shall teach you each morning until it becomes second nature."

"Is it essential though?" Ahzya asked, her eyes widening at the sight of seemingly endless products and brushes that Hill removed from the box.

"Of course, as I stated earlier, as maids, your presentation reflects on the castle. If the maids are untidy, then what kind of place would that make the castle?" Hill said, shaking her head. "You may be thinking that no-one will take notice of us anyway, but believe me, the visitors to the castle have hawk-like eyes. They will spot a stain and assume the staff lack professionalism."

"I'd rather not attract any attention," Ahzya muttered quietly.

"Then you'd be very different from the last maid. I hear she even tried to instigate a meeting with His Majesty the day before she eloped," Hill gossiped loudly.

Ahzya turned her head to glance at the window; the outside world faded away. She almost forgot that she wasn't supposed to be letting her own opinions show. With a slight shake of her head to organise her thoughts, she gave a bright smile. With that, she quickly settled back into the friendly, polite and charming act of Catherine Torpay.

"Very well, you are too kind to teach me all this," Ahzya stated. "I'm just so new to it all."

"Don't worry about that, sweety. You'll get used to it," Hill stated, her face lighting up with enjoyment. "Now we'll just have to do some testers to see what suits you the best."

Ahzya groaned inwardly but lifted her face with fake enthusiasm. It was going to be harder than she thought, especially if she had to go through this torture every morning. However, from here she had endless possibilities, one of which was to make King Mark suffer.

# CHAPTER ELEVEN

### KITCHEN, CASTLE PRYNESSE, ALPANIA

"Take this to the dining table and place it next to the gravy," Mrs Youn ordered, placing a tray of steaming hot sliced beef on the bench. "Also make sure that the punch bowl is set up. Her Majesty always asks for a glass when she enters the dining room."

Ahzya reached for the tray of glistening meat, and her hands met with searing hot metal. With a silent curse, she dropped the tray back onto the bench. One of the other kitchen maids put a silver dome over the tray and placed some serving utensils by it. Ahzya winced and collected a thick cloth from nearby. Mrs Youn barely glanced in her direction as Ahzya laid the cloth along one arm and proceeded to balance the beef tray on top of it. She picked up the serving utensils that went with the tray in her other hand.

Mrs Youn, the head cook, was an older lady, who still retained the swift movements and sharp tongue of her youth. While her tongue was sharp, it showed her wit rather than being harsh. She welcomed Ahzya's help gladly, and Ahzya found her to be overall good-natured. Youn ran her kitchen with firm organisation, yet was happy and quick to clarify any instructions she gave with utmost patience.

Ahzya's experience as a waitress was useful, yet not quite suited for the atmosphere of a castle rather than a tavern. The glassware proved to be a more fragile material than the wooden flagons they used at the tavern, and her nerves prickled anxiously whenever she handled them. Ahzya gratefully passed the day without making any major mistakes, and Youn even teased her for working a bit too hard for her first day.

"You're supposed to relish the status of a new hire for as long as possible," Youn had said, as Ahzya finished her tasks with dedicated swiftness. "You can slack off a little and everyone will just assume it's because you're still learning."

With the dinner serving in full swing, Youn's brow furrowed and her skirt swished around her as she bustled around the kitchen unloading delectable morsels from their practical pots into fancy serving dishes. Ahzya set off for the dining hall, which luckily wasn't too far from the kitchen area. She carried the tray carefully up a spiralling staircase and down a long corridor. Several guards watched her pass, looking longingly at the tray with hungry gazes. Although Ahzya was hungry herself, she knew better than to eat any of the food she'd been tempted with since her kitchen duty had started.

Ahzya leant back on a door and pushed it open, squeezing through the gap carefully. Hoping that the door wouldn't close on the tray as she went through, she was relieved to see it had survived. Ahzya smiled at another maid as she walked past on her way back to the kitchen. The other maid offered a weak half smile and continued on her way. Morale appeared low amongst the maids and the more she worked, the more Ahzya noticed it. Dark corners seemed shadowed with whispers of the staff, and Madam Hill was always hovering nearby.

"Catherine," Madam Hill addressed her directly.

*Speak of the devil.*

"Yes, Madam Hill, how can I help?"

"The table has only been set for two," Hill stated pointedly.

Still balancing the tray on her arm, Ahzya's eyes flickered to the table. Although she hadn't been in charge of setting up the plating, thanks to Ethan's information earlier, Ahzya knew there would be a third addition. Still, the extravagance and sheer amount of food prepared for the party of three left Ahzya in awe. The kitchen cooked enough food to feed an army.

"We are expecting Commander Ray for dinner, but it seems not everyone got the memo. Just because you are new, Catherine, doesn't mean you can be complacent," Hill chided her.

Ahzya's reaction remained neutral as she noticed the youngest maid flinch. The maid twisted a napkin in her hands and looked down at the ground, her blonde braid slipping over a shoulder. She looked like she wished to melt into the floor. Despite assigning them their roles that morning, it appeared Madam Hill had mixed up their responsibilities.

"I'm sorry," Ahzya said with a low curtsy. "I suppose I was too focused on which fork went where; I promise I'll set another place right now. Should I sit him at an end or on the side?"

"Sit him opposite from Her Majesty and then prepare the punch glasses," Hill said hurriedly. "Now remember, King Mark dislikes fruit pieces in his punch, so make sure you just have liquid in the glass for him. I've never served Commander Ray punch before, so you may have to ask him what he prefers. Don't just assume. Assumptions never got anyone very far in life."

Ahzya curtsied and Hill left the room, leaving her to do the tasks to the best of her abilities. Ahzya felt a pair of eyes watching her and turned to find the younger maid cautiously hovering. When their eyes met, the maid smiled genuinely but apologetically. Ahzya nodded her head and returned to the kitchen to retrieve the special glasses for the punch.

The punch glasses came in a unique velvet-lined box, and the top had grapes carved into the wood. Ahzya ran a finger over the smooth wood and couldn't help but admire the workmanship. It reminded her of the chests in Peter's attic, which made her brow furrow. She had always wondered how Peter was; after all, that was the whole reason why she left. He was probably married by now. Ahzya cringed a little as she thought of the possibility of Naomi hanging from Peter's arm as his wife. She'd developed a tinge of bitterness in her heart for the other girl's talent in conversations, especially when it came to giving information to King Mark. She was beyond the point of rebuking herself for her unfair blame on the innocent extrovert.

"Catherine, you should hurry with those glasses," Mrs Youn said gently. "The guest will be arriving soon, and guests tend to be parched for refreshments."

Ahzya nodded, turning with the box in hand. Her feet ached in the pinching black shoes she'd been given to wear. They had belonged to the runaway maid, and since they hired Ahzya on short notice, there wasn't enough time to customise a pair of shoes for her. If she could wear her soft-soled leather boots, Ahzya would be happy to gallivant around the castle with enough food to feed all of Prynesse. The ruffles on her arms and neck scratched her, and the headpiece shifted to unusual angles.

Ahzya yawned as she leant to push through the dining room doors with force.

"Careful!" a male voice warned moments too late.

Ahzya collided with a male figure, and she lost her balance. With a quick movement, she held the box of glasses against her chest, praying to the heavens that she wouldn't fall and break them all into tiny gleaming shards. Ahzya noticed a male hand reached out to steady her, but she avoided it by taking a step back. Within a moment, she regained a steady footing and let out a quick sigh of relief.

"I'm incredibly sor—" Ahzya began to apologise.

The friendly smile, which Ahzya was about to give, froze. She experienced an incredible sense of déjà vu. Before her, stood a middle-aged sailor, a captain's hat tipped forward slightly on his brow. Piercing blue eyes watched her with a spark indicating amusement and a smile played on his lips.

Captain Ray had hardly changed from six years earlier. Although his hair had grown longer and greyed and wrinkles creased his forehead and around his eyes, he may as well have stepped out of a portal from the past. He still stood to a height that towered over Ahzya.

As for Ahzya, she was glad of the tediously applied makeup. She felt as though she had also barely changed from the awkward young girl who had collided with him on the deck of *Moonstruck*. Ahzya hoped that the makeup and her more feminine figure were enough not to spark a familiarity in Ray's mind.

"Sorry?" Ray finished the sentence for her.

"Yeah, I'm sorry," Ahzya said with a chuckle.

"Don't sweat it, I shouldn't have been standing just inside the door," Ray said with a broad smile.

"Thank you, sir," Ahzya said, remembering her manners. "We weren't aware of your arrival."

"Eh, I only had paperwork to do back at the ship. Honestly, the invitation was an excuse to avoid that and have a delicious dinner instead," Ray answered with a friendly and casual tone.

Ahzya had prepared herself to see Ray after talking with Ethan that morning and finding that she was on dinner duty. Ahzya hadn't expected to actually hold a conversation with him and had, in fact, held hopes of avoiding him during his visit.

"Seems like a real spread," Ray said, waving a hand towards the table.

"A bit over the top if you ask me," Ahzya answered quietly before biting her lip. "Sorry, I... that comment was out of line."

"Honesty isn't something you should have to apologise for," Ray said, walking to the table. "Are you a new employee?"

"Yes, only recently hired," Ahzya answered.

"Enjoying the work?" Ray continued the conversation.

"It requires long hours, but the work is fairly straightforward," Ahzya replied, wanting to keep the tone casually friendly.

Ray sat down in one of the red velvet seats and removed his captain's hat. He placed the tricorne hat on the table as Ahzya moved to clear the glasses from their box. The crystal glasses reflected the light from the lanterns around the room and also the giant chandelier that hung above the table.

"Can I get you some punch while you are waiting?" Ahzya asked, holding a glass up to the light.

"No, thank you," Ray answered, leaning back in his chair. "However, if I could trouble you for a glass of water, it would be very much welcomed."

Ahzya curtsied and turned to a prepared porcelain jug. Several other maids filed into the room, curtsying at the sight of Captain Ray at the table. The maids stood on either side of the room and tucked their hands behind their backs.

Moments later a woman entered the room, her honey blonde hair gleaming and a silver crown sitting on the top of her head prominently. A lady-in-waiting followed closely behind her, her brunette hair twisted in a bun at the nape of her neck. Both glided into the room with a grace that Ahzya doubted she could ever accomplish. As Queen Maria entered the room, the rest of the maids lowered their heads and curtsied close to the floor. Ray stood quickly from the chair, and it scraped on the wooden floorboards. The queen kindly smiled as Ray bowed, and she approached and offered her right hand. Ray lifted the hand to his lips and then beamed at the woman as he straightened.

"Commander Ray, you arrived early," Maria greeted cheerfully.

"Good evening, Your Majesty. I came early since I didn't have anything important to attend to back at the port," Captain Ray answered, interlocking his hands behind his back.

"I see, finished all that paperwork, then?" the queen asked, her voice holding a tone of doubt.

"I'd be lying if I told you I have; it can always wait another day," Ray answered with a chuckle.

"You and my husband run by the same rule, I see. 'Paperwork can always wait for tomorrow; it will only gather dust. Dust was never fatal, I think,' is what he says."

"No wonder your husband and I are good friends, Your Majesty."

"Please, Commander, call me Maria. Formality is not welcomed amongst friends. I feel as though we are at odds when you speak so."

"Then you must call me Ray, everyone else does," Ray answered.

"Hello, Ray."

"Hello, Maria."

Satisfied, Maria turned to Ahzya, her smile still crinkling the skin around her eyes. "I'll have my punch now, and have you offered one to Commander Ray yet?"

"Yes, I have, Your Majesty," Ahzya stated carefully with a low curtsy.

Maria merely nodded in satisfaction and approached her chair. Ray quickly moved to pull out her seat, and Maria sat down.

"Mark should be here soon," Maria stated. "He had a meeting with a messenger which has taken much longer than I would have expected."

"I'm sure it's something of royal importance, which we will no doubt never hear about."

"Well, you may," Queen Maria said. "I am likely to receive a watered-down version or nothing at all. However, I do prefer talk of weddings and fellow countries' news rather than the usual castle business that he finds interesting."

Ahzya placed the glass of punch in front of Queen Maria and only managed to get back to her designated spot before King Mark entered the room. The king's presence brought an intimidating aura to the room, and Ahzya schooled the spike of anxiety that tried to tense her muscles. Mark shuffled his hand through his hair, leaving it fluffed. He greeted Ray as one would a friend, hugging him with a few pats on the back. Mark then stooped to kiss Maria's brow, slipping a hand along her shoulders.

Ahzya spun immediately to pour the drinks, the joyous atmosphere irking her unreasonably. Mark's strange warmth of manners painted a very different one from the icy impression he'd left on her at Peter's house. She served King Mark his drink as he took a seat; he didn't say anything.

Dinner passed with friendly conversation and jokes. Ahzya stayed at attention, topping up glasses as they were emptied and continually filling their plates with delicious food until they waved her away.

NORTHERN HALLWAYS, CASTLE PRYNESSE, ALPANIA

Ahzya went up two sets of steps and down several lengthy corridors, all while carrying a tray packed with a hot jug of coffee, a smaller jug of milk, several cups, a jar of honey and two spoons.

When Ahzya had offered to take the two men some coffee Mrs Youn had considered it an inspired idea. Ahzya's nosiness fuelled her kindness, she wanted to know why the king required a meeting with Captain Ray. It wasn't too strange a concept considering Ray was the commander of the King's Fleet. Yet it still piqued her interest, and what better excuse than coffee did she have for interrupting the meeting.

"They're scrawled like the ramblings of a child," King Mark declared from inside the room. "However, when it mentioned an assassination attempt, I thought I should get a second opinion."

"We should treat it as serious even if the letters are barely legible," Ray's voice stated. "You said there was a previous warning before this one, correct? Perhaps we should delay Maria's birthday celebrations while we research the seriousness or plausibility of this note."

"Maria has been planning the party for a year, we aren't going to make a last-minute cancellation," Mark stated seriously.

"But if it could offer a chance for this assassin to strike, then I'm sure no-one will think the worst of you for calling it off," Ray explained. "With news of Prince Ivan's assassination, we should take this seriously, especially since the assassin wasn't caught in Lavania."

"Cleo is investigating for King Eugene, and they suspect the assassin fled across the border into Alpania. Even so, this may be someone running off news of the Lavanians' crown prince's death and using it as a way to threaten us. If we cancel Maria's birthday celebrations, that may be exactly what the person who wrote this note wanted to happen. If I give in to fear, then the author of the note would have won."

"The note may be a genuinely concerned individual trying to warn us before it is too late."

"If they were truly concerned, they would tell us who it is and the details of the threat. This is no more than ramblings of how someone wants me dead. I have received threat letters before, and they've resulted in nothing. Just because this one includes the word assassination doesn't mean it is any different."

"You called me in today for a second opinion, and I have informed you of my stance. We shouldn't dismiss the threat so lightly."

"Alright, I agree. I won't be postponing or cancelling Maria's celebrations, but I shall increase the number of guards and take extra precautions."

"Very well. I would like to request I be allowed to stay here at the castle until all possible leads have been explored," Captain Ray stated.

"You needn't go that far for me," King Mark said. "I know you sleep better in your hammock on your ship than anywhere else."

"That may be true, but right now I'm more concerned about your situation and apparent blasé response to it all."

# CHAPTER TWELVE

KING MARK'S OFFICE, CASTLE PRYNESSE, ALPANIA

Inside the room fell silent, and Ahzya settled her nerves and took a deep breath. It took her courage to recover from the overload of information discovered through her eavesdropping. Ahzya felt the container of water as she straightened to enter the room. The once hot jug of water had cooled a little, which was the work of the cool night air. Ahzya shrugged as the water should still be hot enough, and if not, it would provide her a quick escape plan.

Ahzya knocked on the door sharply, while balancing the tray on her left arm.

"Enter!" King Mark's voice called through the door.

Ahzya opened the door and entered, curtsying as she walked in and caught King Mark's eye.

"I brought some coffee for you. Her Majesty thought you could use the sustenance," Ahzya lied.

"Thank you," King Mark said with a nod of thanks.

"I apologise if I interrupted," Ahzya apologised.

"Not at all, just finished up, so you had great timing," he answered in a friendly tone. "I hope you brought plenty of honey, my friend here has more honey than coffee."

"I was told to bring a pot," Ahzya stated, lifting up the container of rich honey.

"I've visited too often, Mark, they've memorised my eating and drinking habits," Ray stated, with a shake of his head. "Perhaps one day I'll shake things up by asking for it to be slightly different. That will throw a spanner in the works."

Mark chuckled, and Ray joined in the laugh. Ahzya busied herself to preparing the two cups and spooning in several scoops of honey, making sure that one had a lot more.

"How is work, Ray?" Mark asked. "My fleet functioning in perfect order?"

"The fleet is thriving, though they have a little too much time on their hands if the lengthy reports they keep sending me is anything to go by. I try to avoid paperwork most days and then find I have a whole day of it waiting when I get back," Captain Ray answered. "I wish I could just pass that duty onto someone else."

"Don't we all. Unfortunately, it's our jobs as leaders to fulfil that duty ourselves," Mark agreed.

"Well, when we eventually retire, I will never touch a report again," Ray stated.

The men fell silent for a moment, and Ahzya poured the rich coffee into their cups carefully. She was about to excuse herself when King Mark spoke again.

"How is Sergeant Lant nowadays?" King Mark asked, his tone casual.

"You are still concerned about him?" Ray asked in surprise.

"To tell you the truth, he has continually made excuses as to why he can't come and dine at the castle," King Mark answered.

"He's a busy man, with caring for his parents to also doing his duties on board *Moonstruck*," Ray answered. "His workaholic nature is the reason he gained his promotion, though we are constantly assured that promotion isn't his motivation. He's like a pendulum, always in motion."

"Well yes, I understand that, but for every week you're in port for the past five years?" Mark sighed. "That's how long I've been inviting him."

"I don't think Peter is the kind of person to hold grudges," Ray said calmly. "However..."

Ray's voice trailed off, as if he wasn't sure that he should continue with what he was saying.

"However?" King Mark pressed, cautiously. "You think I was in the wrong that night?"

"No..." Ray answered in a drawn out, unsure tone.

"That's the strangest 'yes' I've ever heard from you."

"We did rock up, unannounced, to his house in the middle of the night," Ray began to reason. "He went on the defensive, and you weren't exactly serene waters yourself."

"Perhaps I was a little hasty in my anger and didn't present myself in the most open and understanding light. However, Ray, Peter broke regulations and—"

"Allegedly," Ray interrupted.

Mark sighed in exasperation and his eyebrow quirked as he peered at his friend unamused.

"We spooked a young girl so much she decided to flee into a snowstorm—" Ray reasoned.

"Allegedly."

Ray hummed noncommittally. "When Peter isn't undertaking his duties, we both know that he spends his time looking for his sister."

It appeared the jug did indeed keep the coffee hot and Ahzya hissed as her hands shook and liquid spilled over the edge of the cup she'd been moving. She quickly put it down, and both men glanced up for only a moment.

"I'm sure she is long gone by now," Mark said, shaking his head. "Even if she is still in the country, she'd be twenty by now, correct?"

"Yes, twenty-one, I believe," Ray said.

"I'm just concerned that things won't be how he imagines, even if he does find her."

"Peter won't concentrate on anything else until he has an inkling that she is okay," Ray answered. "Or an explanation of what exactly happened after that night."

"She disappeared like a ghost," Mark said. "If I hadn't seen her with my own eyes then I might doubt she even existed."

"No word ever came despite the posters?"

"Not even one, but we certainly put enough effort into discovering where she went," Mark said. "However, we both know her chance of survival was low. That snowstorm wreaked havoc, and she had nothing more than a few coins. Even the most experienced survivors would have struggled with those circumstances, and she was only fifteen."

The men turned their attention once more to Ahzya, who was animatedly mopping up the spilled coffee. She turned to them with an apologetic look and curtsied.

"I'm incredibly sorry, Your Majesty, it seems my clumsiness got the better of me," Ahzya stated, with a nervous smile. "Please enjoy your coffee, I'll excuse myself."

"Very well," King Mark said dismissively.

Ray watched her leave and Ahzya hoped that her strange actions hadn't attracted his attention too much. The last thing Ahzya needed right now was to have attention drawn to her, especially when it seemed they had been warned about her presence. It was strange that the news or information had travelled so fast, and hopefully, the next few days would deliver no further information. Suspicious and thoroughly shaken, Ahzya returned dutifully to collect their empty cups, but excused herself quickly and didn't dawdle any longer by the office.

## Maid's Quarters, Castle Prynesse, Alpania

Ahzya was beyond exhausted, and her limbs felt like they were heavyweights. Her eyes were already closing as she shuffled through the hall to her living quarters. Ahzya shared her room with the youngest maid and having roomed with many assorted characters during her teen years, it didn't bother her. With both of them waking early and working till late at night, her morning routine wouldn't change much.

Ahzya stretched her back, and her neck cracked as she rolled it. Crawling into bed without even bothering to wash her face or tend to her short hair was her next goal. Her uniform needed to be presentable for the next day, otherwise she would have been tempted to just jump under the covers as she was.

The door was ajar as she paused in front of the faint orange glow streaming from the doorway. Her thief instincts kicked in reflexively and before she realised it, she was squeezing through the gap with no sound.

The small room had barely enough space for the two beds that ran along opposite walls. One square bedside table separated the two thin cots, and the two girls would be sharing the one closet. Luckily neither of them had many clothes, and Ahzya preferred to leave her clothing in her bag anyway. The only light source in the room, a lantern, sat on the bedside table.

Beside the cot on the left-hand side of the room, was the young maid, who Ahzya recalled was named Noelle. Noelle knelt beside the bed in her nightwear, and her shoulders were shaking. Ahzya realised the young maid was sobbing into her arms and she crossed over to her side without much thought. With one hand she reached out and laid it gently on the girl's back.

Noelle shuddered in surprise but didn't turn to look at Ahzya. Rubbing the girl gently on the back, Ahzya used her other hand to draw blonde tendrils of hair away from the girl's face.

"What's wrong, Noelle?" Ahzya asked gently.

"Madam Hill found out that I was the one who hadn't set the table correctly. She got mad that you'd taken the blame for me and said I needed to face punishment," Noelle sobbed uncontrollably. "She also said that if I do anything like this in the future, I'll be fired on the spot."

*A rather harsh punishment for such a simple mistake.* Ahzya continued to pat Noelle's back gently, and the girl slowly calmed down.

"I swear I wasn't even informed about Commander Ray's visit." Noelle's voice broke.

"No doubt Hill thought she'd informed us in the morning, she doesn't seem to have the best memory," Ahzya said wryly. "I'm sorry if I caused further problems by covering for you that time."

Noelle sat up quickly and urgently looked directly at Ahzya.

"Oh no, it's not your fault, I should have paid more attention, or made sure I clarified how many would be dining, but instead I made a silly mistake," Noelle said earnestly.

Ahzya barely listened to her words as she sat in stunned silence, studying Noelle's face carefully. Despite Noelle's bloodshot brown eyes, brimming with tears and puffy from those already fallen down her cheeks, something else made Ahzya's blood freeze. Running over her top cheekbone was a bruise slowly turning blue. One side of her mouth was swollen slightly, and a small wound split her top lip. Ahzya reached out instinctively to run her fingers gently on the bruises.

"Are you okay?" Ahzya whispered, looking at the bruises with transfixed horror.

"It hurts like hell, but I'll be fine," the maid answered truthfully.

"You should put a cool cloth on your eye," Ahzya said, standing up. "It will help reduce the swelling and bruises and also ease the pain."

Noelle blew her nose into her nightgown and then continued to sniffle. Ahzya quickly retrieved handkerchiefs from her pack and carried them to a basin of water near the door. She dropped two next to the porcelain container and the other she handed to Noelle. Noelle blew her nose roughly and then continued to twist it tightly in her hands.

Ahzya dipped one of the handkerchiefs into the cold water, but as she reached for the other, she paused. She picked up the cream cloth and ran her finger gently over an embroidered symbol in one of the corners. Ahzya's eyes softened, as she surveyed the handkerchief with a rare fondness.

"Catherine?" Noelle called, interrupting Ahzya's thoughts.

Ahzya folded the handkerchief and tucked it into the pocket of her maid's uniform.

"Sorry, did you say something, Noelle?" Ahzya asked, turning with a soft smile.

"I was just saying that it doesn't matter as long as it doesn't swell," Noelle stated carefully. "It's getting late, and we shouldn't stay up any later. Besides, Madam Hill is a professional and has dealt with our bruises with makeup in the past. That is the good thing about makeup as the dress code; you never have to worry about blemishes or bruises."

"That doesn't seem right," Ahzya replied, her expression darkening again. "The brazenness to beat a maid and then cover it up with makeup."

"Oh, Madam Hill doesn't hit any of us," Noelle stated with a shake of her head.

"I don't think I quite understand."

"Madam Hill gets annoyed, that is for certain. However, Madam Uran is the wicked witch sent to punish us," Noelle explained. "I guess you haven't had the displeasure of meeting her yet, but when you do, you'll understand what I mean."

Ahzya felt sure she'd have a few things to say and do to this Madam Uran if she ever witnessed her hitting any of the maids. Abuse of any kind was something that Ahzya couldn't tolerate, especially when it was in a professional environment.

"Have you dealt with bruises before?" Noelle asked quietly.

"I grew up around boys, and they have a tendency of getting hurt," Ahzya said with a smile. "Black eyes seemed to be something they purposely went out to get."

Noelle chuckled lightly; then winced as Ahzya pressed the cool handkerchief onto her cheek.

"This feels rather nostalgic actually," Ahzya said, tilting her head sideways. "I used to have a friend who was always coming to me with a split lip and bruised face."

"Why would someone want that to happen to them?" Noelle asked, shaking her head.

"With him, it wasn't willingly or purposefully received," Ahzya answered, her eyes narrowed.

"You say 'was' though, so he mustn't be getting beaten now," Noelle said, forcibly trying to lighten the mood.

Ahzya glanced down and gave a resigned smile that didn't reach her eyes.

"That's true, I haven't had to tend to his wounds for a couple of years," Ahzya answered.

Ahzya shook her head of a painful reality that she just hoped she could forget. Forgetting, however, would bring just as much pain, and when she was honest with herself, she didn't want to forget. To forget would ruin the good memories, the memories of happy days when she had been able to overlook the fact that she was a runaway and living a life that no-one would be proud of.

She began untying her uniform, letting it drop to the floor around her ankles. Her sleepwear wasn't a cute nightgown like Noelle's; instead, she had a soft pair of old breeches and loose-fitting tunic. Ahzya heard Noelle move onto her cot as it creaked and she paused to glance over her shoulder. Noelle's face was peaceful, as if Ahzya had been able to ease her pain. With a quick movement, Ahzya bent and pulled the handkerchief from the pocket of her uniform.

"Thank you for everything, Catherine," Noelle muttered sleepily. "You're incredibly nice."

"Hush and get some sleep," Ahzya said softly.

Ahzya ran her finger once more over the handkerchief before turning to blow out the lantern with a single breath. As she dove under the covers to prevent from freezing in the cold room, Ahzya still clung to the handkerchief. Her forefinger continued to feel the threads of the embroidery. With every swipe, she memorised the ridges of the threads and shape. The swirling curvature of the letter 'C'. The embroidered letter engraved into her mind and touch even as the clutches of sleep swept over her.

# CHAPTER THIRTEEN

DINING HALL, CASTLE PRYNESSE, ALPANIA

Ahzya stood at attention at the far end of the dining hall, waiting while King Mark and Queen Maria ate their meal. Ahzya's dinner duties consisted of removing plates from the table once emptied and refilling their glasses. The royal couple conversed quietly during the lunch. Their conversations contained nothing of importance, just socialite news and the latest correspondence from family members. Maria commented on members of the nobility who expressed how much they missed the presence of their eldest daughter, Princess Anna, at events. Both princesses had been out of the kingdom for some time but were expected to travel back shortly before the birthday ball.

Mealtimes provided Ahzya with an excellent opportunity to gain information about the king's planned movements during the following days. Ahzya was stationed in the kitchen the rest of the time, and it left her with little time for snooping, except at night.

Messengers occasionally interrupted the meals with news from around the kingdom. Maria usually sighed quietly when any messenger entered. She looked annoyed at the interruption in her limited time with her husband. Ahzya felt sympathy for her, but even in the annoyed gaze of the queen Ahzya noticed the underlying adoration.

It was on one such day when they were just finishing their meal when a soldier entered. It was good news, because if the soldier's smile on delivering the message hadn't given it away, King Mark's pleasure on hearing the news left no doubt on the matter. Mark turned and quietly told Maria, who unlike her usual resigned smile, beamed with joy.

"Catherine, fetch Madam Hill and Mrs Youn for me. We are to receive a special guest for dinner, and I wish to go over the menu and other details with them," Queen Maria addressed Ahzya.

Ahzya curtsied respectfully, before heading to the kitchen to find the head cook.

The castle life became further buzzed with energy as maids and chefs rapidly called out orders. One of the main lavish guest rooms, other than the one that Ray was now staying in, had to be cleaned spotless. Ahzya thought this was overkill, after all, the castle was already being prepared for the queen's party and was as spotless as could be. However, the castle staff were known for their small details, and fresh towels and scented candles were taken to the room, along with a bottle of wine and some specially acquired chocolates. The linen and blankets also had to be changed, supposedly the guest preferred the colour green over the rich red that already adorned the four-poster bed.

If all this had to be prepared for one guest, Ahzya hated the thought of how much would have to be spent in both time and resources to prepare for the party guests. To Ahzya it seemed half the country were going to be attending in a week's time, the guest list had already been shared with the staff and the queen requested individual touches for each family that was to stay at the castle.

It was early evening when the acclaimed guest arrived, and unlike most castle guests, Mark and Maria actually went to greet them at the main door. A crowd of attendants and castle occupants gathered at the meeting place just inside the castle's main doors. Ahzya made an excuse to leave the kitchen for a while and hung back. She was both curious and reserved to see who had created such fuss.

While avoiding asking questions which may have drawn attention to her lacking knowledge on the esteemed members of the Alpanian high class, Ahzya accumulated a little information on the guest. The guest was male, that much was sure, and rumours said he was one of the king's best friends, even closer than Commander Ray, though this point was debated. The guest also came with credentials, including being a former commander in the Royal Mounted Forces. A more recent promotion assigned him an influential role overseeing a district in the kingdom. Rumours said his work there was miraculous, though Ahzya had never heard of which area they spoke, nor the damn bloke's name.

Ahzya haunted the throne room, knowing they'd probably make their way there eventually. Dinner was already prepared and waiting to be brought to the table, and Ahzya had offered to act as a scout to announce when the party neared the dining room. Ahzya wasn't the only one lingering in the area for a glimpse of the elusive official. To avoid the main crowded area, Ahzya waited in a shadowed servant's access corridor. She flipped a butter knife as the guest took longer than she expected to appear. Ahzya yawned, fighting the temptation to give up on her inquisitive quest and consequences be damned if the dinner service arrived a little early to the tables. In fact, she was about to do just that when the group entered through the giant doors and filed in, talking enthusiastically. Her eyes finally registered and studied the newcomer, but the task left her stationary in an icy shock. Ahzya found the figure all too familiar.

The black uniform and silver cobra insignia were enough to identify the guest. The grin and quick, cheerful replies in his cool tone of voice put Ahzya on full alert.

*The hell.*

Ahzya took several cautious steps back, planning a hasty retreat from the room. The movement didn't go unnoticed, and Ahzya met the gaze of JP Dry moments before she could escape fully into the dark, narrow corridor. What Ahzya didn't like was the sly smirk and the gleam in his eyes when he immediately recognised her.

With time to walk the corridors to the kitchen to start the delivery of dinner, Ahzya reorganised her thoughts and came to a calmer understanding. Certainly, it came as a shock that JP had suddenly arrived at the doorstep of the castle as a highly revered guest, but as far as she knew his end wish was the same. He'd mentioned that he stood to gain power from the assassination, so his position did make sense in that aspect. If he knew what was good for him, he'd ignore her completely, act as a perfect stranger, which they pretty much were anyway. He knew she had a job to do and interfering with that would be against his better interest.

JP Dry sat in the seat for honoured guests, the right-hand seat, next to King Mark who was at the head of the table. Ray sat opposite to him, Queen Maria at the foot of the table, and several high-ranking military officers and advisers, along with their wives, filled the rest of the positions at the lengthy table.

They'd barely taken a seat at the table when King Mark stood to make a toast. Ahzya stood at attention behind one of the advisers, ready to serve when signalled, and had to take an extra step back as chairs grated as everyone stood once again.

"To my dear friend, Jonathan Dryen, to your health and happiness," King Mark said, raising his goblet of wine and nodding his head to JP.

Everyone else raised their glasses and heartily agreed with several grunts and 'Hear, hear!'s. Everyone took drinks and smiled at each other in turn, laughing until Mark sat again. Again, the grating of chairs echoed through the room.

"I fully intend on keeping my health, and will savour this fine meal set before me, to keep my strength up," Jonathan said heartily, gaining several smiles and nods as response. "Unless, of course, it's poisoned."

Ahzya felt a muscle in her neck twitch and kept her eyes focused on the roast in the centre of the table. Everyone at the table paused, Mark planted his goblet down more heavily than intended.

"I'm joking, gosh, you have enough security around here that I figure you still employ a praegustator to test every dish," Jonathan chuckled, slapping Mark on the shoulder.

Mark let the palpable tension linger for a moment and then his face broke into a grin; the edge in the air dispersed almost immediately.

"Oh no, we had to let him go late last year: found out he was eating half our rations," Mark jested.

"Ah, too bad," Jonathan replied just as quick.

"Just make sure you don't choke on your food, Jon, and chew well," Ray cut in across the table.

Jonathan switched his gaze to Ray, who gave him a curt smile in reply, and Ahzya swore she saw a momentary fire in Ray's eyes. Ray wasn't known for liking endless prattle, and Jonathan had that in the bucket loads. Jonathan didn't seem to recognise Ray's annoyance and inclined his head in respectful acknowledgement, though his smirk didn't falter.

"Look at you, finding fun ways of telling me to shut up already. Your concern for my health is touching, Captain, it reminds me of old times." Jonathan spoke up and his tone suddenly changed. "Speaking of old times, have I ever told the story of how His Majesty got stuck down a well when he was but a young man?"

The table fell into a chaos of tales and conversation and dinner was served and maintained until each guest had eaten their fill. The table was so rowdy that Ahzya could barely hear herself think, let alone garner any crucial information from the buzz of voices.

Ahzya's quiet and observant nature had been a survival method over the last six years. She had to learn from those around her so she could start to blend in as an Alpanian. Her Ulkadasan speech patterns and language knowledge were both a hindrance and a help in allowing her to communicate effectively. Everything was substantially the same words, and if Ahzya had known how to spell, it would have looked exactly the same for a majority of the vocabulary. However, since all Ahzya knew was phonically understood, the Ulkadasan pronunciation of the alphabet and subsequent words was so extremely different that it took Ahzya a great amount of concentration to understand the Alpanian pronunciation and then copy it. All of this was before throwing the slang used by many rural villagers into the mix. She had a whole new appreciation for Ray and Johno who'd undertaken the meetings in Ulkadasa during the *Moonstruck*'s visit.

Ahzya still used her native dialect when she was alone with Reggad or when she drank heavily, which she didn't do often and always only when she was deep in the forest away from any human ear. After all, for fifteen years that's how she'd communicated. Alpanian had become second nature, but she translated it all from Ulkadasan in her mind. Her Ulkadasan language helped her relax, since nearly every part of her Alpanian identity felt fake.

Thus, Ahzya often found herself focusing on people's tones and vocal indicators and found herself growing annoyed when people spoke at the same time. Even now, she understood everything said despite background noise, but after long exposure, it felt overstimulating.

At one point, Ahzya left the dining room to go and fetch more refreshments and platters of fresh fruit. The cool, dark stone corridors provided a sweet tranquil relief from the overload of sound. Ahzya took her time, the guests were too busy to notice if the refreshments took ten minutes to arrive instead of five.

Descending a spiral staircase, Ahzya took the chance to practice moving quietly in her heels. It had taken her a while to get used to the shoes, and even longer to figure out how to null the effect of the wooden heels that clattered on every flooring type in the castle. Musing on the day's happenings as well as how little she'd managed to plan, Ahzya almost turned the last bend in the staircase to interrupt a conversation between Lesley and one of the other maids, Merida. Ahzya caught herself last second and quickly retracted her steps out of sight.

"Are you sure you don't need to lie down?" Lesley's clear voice asked.

"I'm fine. Besides, I've noticed Uran watching me when I disappear and I just know I'm going to get in trouble," the older maid's voice replied.

"Nothing will please that monster. We could do God's work perfectly and she'd still find some fault in it."

Ahzya leant on the banister, eavesdropping was a simple and effective way of learning things. Merida's troubles were of little consequence to Ahzya in the greater realm of things, but should a bit of leverage or help be garnered from the situation, it couldn't hurt.

"Oh Les, she's going to start getting suspicious soon."

"Suspicious? It's a miracle not all of us are sick with the amount of work they have us doing," Lesley proclaimed. "We work late nights, early mornings; our families barely get to see us."

"That's not what I mean, Les." Merida paused. "She'll find out that I'm... I'm pregnant."

Lesley let out an excited squeal that made Ahzya almost jump.

"Hush, Les," Merida ordered, clamping her hand over her friend's mouth.

"Hush? Why wouldn't I be excited? You're going to be a mum, that's awesome news!" Lesley said, removing her friend's hand. "Thomas must be thrilled."

"Oh, he is, and so am I. But if the Madam Monster finds out— You know how she feels about us allowing our personal lives to effect work.

Especially when it comes to relationships. She's warned us that we can't get pregnant."

"Good grief, Merida, you're married! It's not like she can expect you to abstain," Lesley stated incredulously.

"Oh stars, watch your tongue, saying such embarrassing things," Merida rebuked, lowering her voice. "I have no intention of allowing her to ruin my marriage like that. However, she has the power to fire me. We need my pay cheque, Lesley, you know how Thomas is struggling to heal after the injury," Merida replied earnestly. "Once Thomas is properly healed, he can return to work, and I can quit and be a mum and maybe even have the household somewhat together for the baby's arrival."

"I understand, I do, but you can't overstress yourself. It's not good for you... or baby."

"I just need to keep this job for a few more months. I shouldn't start showing too much until then and if you help me, I'm sure we can keep it from her for as long as necessary."

"Don't you worry about a thing," Lesley assured, giving Merida a hug.

"But what if she hits me, Les? Like last time? I barely survived after the loss of my first—" Merida's voice broke.

"You've fallen pregnant before?"

"Yes, I was only a couple of months, when I got hit—it was just an accident, but..." Merida's voice was enough to show evidence of tears, "I was still that blessed child's mum."

"Oh, Merida..."

"I can't risk the safety of my child like that again. I'll leave as soon as I can, but until then," Merida said suddenly, seeming to rally herself.

"If she even dares to touch you, I'll kill her!"

"Les!"

"Oh, you know it's just talk, I don't have the guts, but if she so much as lays a finger on you, quit. I'll give you my entire pay cheque if I need to!"

"Oh, hush... We've been away for too long, we'd better get back before we actually get in trouble," Merida said, detaching herself from Lesley. "Thank you."

The two maids hurried off and Ahzya rounded the last turn in the stairs. Her brow furrowed as she mulled over her colleagues' conversation. Despite only being in the castle for a short time, it hadn't taken long to notice the abuse especially at the hands of the Madam 'Monster' Uran. Ahzya couldn't risk drawing attention to herself, so stepping in just wasn't an option. She had to fly under the radar and so far, she'd managed to achieve that. However, perhaps one more body could be added to the death toll before she left, a certain monster needed to be hunted.

Meanwhile her other prey was acting like a young kid with JP Dry, or rather, Jonathan Dryen. It seemed their friendship went back quite far, though King Mark was, from what Ahzya knew, more than a decade older than Jonathan. They'd met when Jonathan was a mere recruit, soldier in training, and his skills had left the recently crowned young king on his behind after a duel. Jonathan then became a bodyguard and rose in the ranks, not from his friendship with the king, though that didn't hurt, but due to his tactical mind and leadership skills.

Jonathan held no qualms when it came to talking casually with King Mark, and to Ahzya's surprise the other guests at the table didn't appear disgusted or shocked by the lack of decorum shown by him. They laughed at all his jokes and quirky tales, which there seemed no end to. If one more person asked him to elaborate on some childhood memory or noble ball's exploits, Ahzya was about to show them how dangerous a spoon could become in the hands of an expert.

Luckily, Jonathan ignored Ahzya's movements, neither made eye contact or indicated any sign of acknowledgement, even as she served him more wine later in the meal.

The royals and their guests had already been at the table for three hours. Dinner had come and gone, as had dessert, tea and coffee prepared and poured, then the stronger liquor had been requested from the king's personal cabinet, which only served to heighten the chatty mood of the group. Ahzya volunteered to stay on attending the group while most of the other maids went to complete their day's chores and head to their respective rooms or homes for some well earnt rest. Only the king's and queen's personal attendants remained at attention by the door, though Ahzya thought one of them had fallen asleep standing up.

Ahzya's saviour finally came in the form of Ray, who stood from his seat and picked up his hat. The attending staff shifted their postures, looking at him as a sign of hope. King Mark and the rest of the table silenced their conversations and turned their attention to Ray.

"As pleasant an evening as this has been, I believe I should get some rest, I have paperwork I have to be awake for in the morning," Ray said, placing the hat on his head.

"Indeed, we should probably all adjourn for the evening, it's gotten quite late," King Mark said, standing up from his seat too. "Thank you all for an enjoyable evening."

The rest of the party followed in standing from their seats, some less steadily than others. The guests bid their 'good evenings' and filed from the room, at the same point Ray slipped out too. This left Their Majesties and Jonathan as the only ones of the group in the dining room.

"I guess I should go unpack a few things and get my beauty sleep. It's been a long day of travel and conversation," Jonathan said.

"Madeline will show you to the room that we've prepared for you," Maria offered, smiling sweetly at her guest.

The queen's personal attendant stepped forward, and Ahzya felt as though everything was being wrapped up nicely.

"Actually, if it doesn't displease you, I'd like to request to be accompanied to my room by an alternative gorgeous attendant," Jonathan said, with a graceful bow.

"Who do you request?" Maria asked, with a raised eyebrow.

Ahzya felt a twist of dread and prepared herself for what she already guessed was coming. Sure enough, Jonathan turned directly towards Ahzya and gave her a winning smile.

"This beauty has intrigued me all evening. May I be so bold as to ask for your name?" Jonathan asked, looking directly in Ahzya's eyes and ending it with a wink.

Ahzya stood blinking for a moment, trying to find some sense of a reply. He acted as a stranger; however, he also directly drew the attention of the others in the room. Ahzya saw Maria roll her eyes and Mark chuckled with a shake of his head.

"You are too forward for your own good, Jonathan. This is—" King Mark began, resting a hand on his friend's shoulder.

"No, no, don't tell me. Let me guess," Jonathan said, his hand stroking his chin. "Something classy, I am sure. I'm going to guess, Catherine?"

"Are you telepathic, Jonathan? This is a new talent that we've discovered," Mark said, smiling.

"I have many talents you don't know about, Mark," Jonathan said proudly. "I'm sure I could surprise you with many more things about me."

*Oh, I know my own share of things that would surprise His Majesty about you.*

"However, in this case I must confess," Jonathan continued disappointedly. "I'm afraid I cheated this time. Miss Madeline—" Jonathan indicated the queen's attendant "—noticed my interest in Miss Catherine and, upon my further request, thoughtfully informed me of her name."

"Ah, and thus the truth is revealed. However, I've always admired your ways of finding out everything you want to know," Mark stated, leaning his hand on his chin while resting his elbow now on Jonathan.

"I thank you for your compliment, my liege. If it pleases you, may I steal Miss Catherine for a moment? I would be honoured if you could escort me on a tour around the castle," Jonathan said, addressing the last statement towards Ahzya. "Or perhaps, considering the hour, to my room."

Jonathan bowed politely, causing Mark's resting post to collapse, and Maria instead claimed the now free arm of her husband.

"Catherine, can you please escort Mr Dryen to his room, then you may be dismissed for the night," Queen Maria addressed Catherine in her sweet tone.

"Of course, Your Majesty," Ahzya responded with a low curtsy. "I would be honoured to escort you, sir." Ahzya added a curtsy for Jonathan too.

"Good evening, Jonathan," Maria bid goodbye, and Mark merely nodded his head to Jonathan.

Ahzya fixed a smile to her lips.

"Come, Master Dryen, we can tour part of the castle along the way. I know a few prime locations I can show you."

"Indeed? You have me entranced," Jonathan said, offering his arm to her.

Ahzya accepted the offered arm uncertainly, which won her an amused smile from Jonathan and a glimpse of a sympathetic one from

Her Majesty out of the corner of her eye. Ahzya lowered her voice as they walked through the double doors out of the room. She let the smile fade, and she instead fixed Jonathan with a simmering glare.

"Oh yes, I was thinking we could start with the gallows," Ahzya murmured. "Or where the perfect spot for the gallows would be, should our dear king be so inclined. Then I thought our next point of call could be to the dungeons."

"Sounds delightful."

"If you are *very* lucky," Ahzya said, leaning closer. "I might even show you the torture chamber. But I don't think they have one of those either."

"How disappointing, I was looking forward to seeing the spiked chamber or such," Jonathan replied, pouting disappointedly.

"Oh, don't worry, Master Dryen, I'm sure they could arrange one for you. You're the king's '*dear friend*' after all."

# CHAPTER FOURTEEN

EASTERN CORRIDORS, CASTLE PRYNESSE, ALPANIA

Ahzya unlinked arms with Jonathan once they'd strolled far enough away, highly tempted to disappear and leave him to find the room on his own. The comforting idea of Jonathan getting lost in the endless passageways was short lived, when the realisation that he'd grown up in the castle slowly dawned on her. Ahzya may have all passageways mapped out in her mind, but Jonathan moved as one would in his own home and no doubt knew all the secret passages and routes.

"I understand your frustration at my drawing attention. However, I was highly curious at how fast you work. Can you blame me for wanting to speak to you?" Jonathan said, easily keeping up with Ahzya's quick strides.

"I can and will blame you," Ahzya replied quickly.

"It was either this, sneak into your room, or summon you to my own, and I figured you'd dislike any rumours of midnight rendezvous with me. So, I went with a second option, where people will merely see a rambunctious flirt such as myself hitting on you."

"I'd rather option three."

Jonathan raised an eyebrow.

"Where we don't interact, you remain curious, but I get your job done," Ahzya offered.

"I hate feeling curious," Jonathan dismissed with a shake of his head. "I just have to know. Though I can assure you, with the way you're acting you'll come out of this just fine. No-one will accuse you of leading me on with the offhanded way you reluctantly escorted me tonight. You're still just a pure maiden in all their eyes."

"What a great comfort that is," Ahzya retorted sarcastically.

"I have to admit though, I would never have imagined you'd take the maid approach. You didn't seem the cleaning and serving type."

"Must I remind you, that you barely know me, JP," Ahzya replied. "I have a talent for acting, it helps get the job done. You also seem to hold a gift for acting, so it shouldn't be too difficult for you to ignore me from this point forward."

"Ah, but I'm beginning to have fun," Jonathan drawled. "Who knew my favourite little assassin would be living under the same roof as me. I look forward to observing you work over the following days."

"I do not require a watchdog," Ahzya retorted, gritting her teeth. "I am no-ones *little* anything, least of all yours. The only thing you should worry about with living under the same roof as me, is waking up to find an appendage missing after your abundance of words draws too much attention."

"Oooh, scary. I like all my appendages; would be a pity to lose them," was Jonathan's jolly reply.

"Why are you here, JP?" Ahzya asked directly.

"Do you suffer from short-term memory loss? You are showing me to my room, that's why I'm here. We aren't lost, are we?"

"I meant at the castle."

"Oh, well, you may not have heard, but Her Majesty, Queen Maria, is having a big birthday ball, and considering I'm a friend, I was invited."

"And yet all the other guests are not arriving for a few days, so what brings you so early?"

Jonathan was silent for a moment and Ahzya felt the urge to turn and look at him but resisted.

"You want to know the truth?" he asked slowly and thoughtfully.

"If that's even a possibility for you, I'd appreciate it."

Another pause.

"I was bored, and since you're here instead of in Triox, I didn't even have a beautiful woman to call upon and spend a relaxed evening with."

Ahzya glanced over her shoulder with an annoyed sarcastic smile and all Jonathan did was wink back. Ahzya finally came to a halt in front of an engraved door, bringing her heels together. She bowed to Jonathan and waved towards the door.

"Your room, Master Dryen," Ahzya said. "Sleep well, sir, and, if I may, I'll leave you with one more word of advice. You said you just do the hiring. This may be a new twist for me, but trust that I know what I'm doing and stay the hell out of my way."

Jonathan bowed with a flourish of his hand.

"I make no promises. I'm a gambler," Jonathan said smiling, "and from what I see, I'm holding all the cards, and I'll play them as I please."

Ahzya and Jonathan shared a sizzling glare before Ahzya turned on her heel and strode away. She kept her posture straight as she didn't hear Jonathan enter his room and could feel him continue to watch her.

"Good night, Catherine! Sweet dreams!" Jonathan called out to her as she rounded the corner.

### KITCHEN, CASTLE PRYNESSE, ALPANIA

Erring on the side of caution, Ahzya sought out Mrs Youn and the maid, Merida, early the next morning. She spoke to Youn alone first, approaching her as she was busy kneading dough on a wooden bench sprinkled with a dusting of flour.

"So, you wish to exchange duties with Merida?" Youn asked, the dough twisting in her hands.

"Yes," Ahzya answered simply.

"You've been a splendid help," Youn answered, her brows furrowed. "Can I know the reason why you don't want to help in the kitchen?"

"It's not that I don't love the work here," Ahzya assured quickly. "Rather, it's because I admire and trust you, that I believe this is the best option."

"You're confusing me."

"You've said before that the kitchen is your realm, correct?"

"I'd like to see someone try to barge into my kitchen and take charge," Youn said, her red cheeks puffing. "The Madams have tried to muscle into my business, telling me what to do. My kitchen, my rules; I don't care to have them sticking their powdered noses around my pots and pans."

"Exactly," Ahzya said, smiling. "I need this to be a safe spot for Merida. I know you're a sensible woman, and she can't be going around doing strenuous chores and getting stressed."

Youn looked up to meet Ahzya's eyes, the secret understanding quickly settled in.

"Well, isn't that grand," Youn said, a sparkle in her eyes. "I'll take care of the young lady Merida. You mind yourself though, you'll be in their realm out there. My kitchen will always be a haven for you. I've got a lot of big knives."

It then took only minutes to offer to take Merida's tasks of preparing the guest rooms, including washing and carrying around heavy bedding. In exchange Merida would be on kitchen and dinner duties, a much less strenuous task. Ahzya didn't let on that she knew that Merida was pregnant, but after a moment's indecision, Merida quickly agreed to the swap.

Ahzya thus managed to avoid Jonathan Dryen all day, though her own muscles were starting to ache from the wringing of heavy sheets and carrying blankets back and forth. It had occurred to Ahzya as the queen's birthday drew closer that King Mark's daily patterns became random and unorganised. Planning out an attack was made a lot harder this way. There were places he frequented, but these places were also crowded or he was under a close escort. Ahzya was forced to conclude that perhaps it was best to postpone her mission until things went back to normal. Despite Commander Ray's words that the party would be an assassin's prime opportunity to attack, Ahzya was convinced only a fool would want to take on such a task. There were too many people roaming around in the preparation phase, let alone when the main event took place. Too many eyes would be watching.

Ahzya's new duties allowed her to further map out the castle, see the guest lists for the upcoming party, as well as have quiet moments alone. The northern wing accommodated the staff lodgings as well as a multitude of storage rooms. This wing was barely ever visited by anyone but the staff. There were central passageways connecting the eastern and western wings of the castle, so as to simply bypass the northern wing altogether. In the centre of the castle were dining rooms, the war council room, as well as two ballrooms, one bigger than the other.

After lugging a heavy basket of freshly aired bedding to Commander Ray's room, Ahzya set it down at the foot of the bed. She moved over to the heavy draperies over the windows and pulled them back. Sunlight flooded into the room and Ahzya took a second to soak in the bright afternoon rays. She hoped the light could dissipate the exhausted ache from her bones. She'd barely slept since arriving at the castle. The beds were rough, and unlike the guest rooms' silky bedding, the staff's were stuffy and the woollen blankets scratched awfully. The only respite she'd claimed were a few hours before dawn when she'd given up sleeping in the cramped quarters and climbed onto the roof. Lying on the cool shingles, with the stars winking down at her, she gained a small reprieve as sleep swept over her.

Ahzya rolled her shoulders and her neck before turning to the bare bed. When she'd arrived at the room early in the morning, the smooth bedspread made it quite obvious that Ray hadn't slept in it. However, her duties were to change every bedding and clean every room, so off the covers had come. Captain Ray kept his living space clean, though Ahzya noticed the pile of papers on his desk and couldn't help a reminiscent smile from appearing.

Forgetting the covers for a moment, Ahzya crossed over to the desk to browse the papers. There were ship logs, maps, supply reports and other ship documents splayed across the oak wood. One piece of paper caught Ahzya's attention and she picked it up, squinting at the words on the page. She mouthed the letters, which were all written messily and unevenly.

Over the last two years, Ahzya had begun to learn the written Alpanian language; however, most of it still made as much sense to her as squiggles on a page. A friend was trying to teach her, but her mind wandered and other tasks kept her from her studies. Her writing was worse than that of the author of the note she held in her hands and the mess of letters almost made more sense to her. Although she couldn't confirm her suspicions that the note was the assassination warning letter that Captain Ray and King Mark had talked about, the childlike writing did match with the description. Ahzya felt a sense of familiarity about the letter, unfortunately, that was all she managed to garner from the letter.

"Can I help you?" Commander Ray's voice broke through Ahzya's concentration.

Ahzya dropped the letter on the desk and spun to face him. She hooked her arms behind her and curtsied.

"Sir," Ahzya said, keeping her head lowered.

"Are you a spy or something? Here to steal our plans and sell it to our enemies?" Commander Ray asked, entering the room and crossing over to the desk.

"If I'm an information spy, I'd be horrible at it."

"Oh?"

"I can't read, well, I can read very little. Though my writing is even worse."

"And what did your curiosity garner you from this document?" Captain Ray asked, picking up the letter and shaking it in front of her.

"Very little, I'm trying my best to learn to read, sir, and I saw that letter and thought it could be good practice," Ahzya said, semi-truthfully.

"Doesn't the castle have a library?"

"I get what you are hinting at, sir, I only thought the writing looked simpler than the king's fancy books. Is it a personal letter of yours? From a son or nephew?"

"You think the author is male? Even though you can't read?"

"Well, I guess, it could be a female writer, but the letters seem to be cut off bluntly, like how I'd imagine a boy would write. Of course, that's not substantial evidence, I just assumed it was."

"Intriguing, and that's all you saw in the letter?"

"Yes, sir, I only looked at it for a minute, and I'm afraid I had very little luck at anything beyond guessing at the author's identity."

Ray was silent and added the letter to a stack of papers before putting even more books on top.

"You won't tell Madam Uran about this will you? She doesn't like us snooping and, in her eyes, educating ourselves should be low on our priority list," Ahzya begged urgently.

"Well, there's no harm done, so I don't know why I'd go around talking about it. Just make sure you don't snoop into people's personal correspondence, and I'll look past it this time," Ray answered, putting his hat on the back of the chair.

"I'm sure your son or nephew is honoured you keep his letters," Ahzya said relaxing her stance.

"Yes, my nephew is slowly improving his writing, with a bit of practice he'll be doing better in no time. Just keep practising, on actual books, mind you, and I'm sure you'll get there too."

"Thank you, sir," Ahzya said, smiling. "I'll finish cleaning your room so you can work in peace."

Ahzya couldn't help watching Commander Ray carefully as she meticulously cleaned and made the bed. They were both silent, and Ray sat at his desk the entire time. He picked up several books and then put them down, then he began writing in a notebook for several minutes before also giving up on that task. With a stretch, he retrieved his hat from the back of the seat and put it on his head. Leaning back in the chair, his backside moved to the edge of the seat, he tipped the hat forward over his eyes.

*So that's where he's been sleeping.*

Captain Ray began breathing heavily from sleep as Ahzya fluffed the pillows and smoothed the top cover. Ahzya matched his breathing and felt almost calmed by the action. She'd done it often on the *Moonstruck* and it had turned into a form of relief over the weeks at sea. There was something in the rhythm and the soft sound, along with memories of the sea air and ship movements, that caused a homesick ache to etch its way into her heart.

Before leaving the room, Ahzya crossed to the window and quietly closed the drapes. Darkness enveloped the room and Ahzya stole one more look at Ray before closing the door behind her.

# CHAPTER FIFTEEN

FRONT ENTRANCE, CASTLE PRYNESSE, ALPANIA

A carriage trundled up to the front steps to the castle and Ahzya approached with a male servant. The male servant collected a step hooked to the back of the carriage and placed it on the ground before the door. He then opened the carriage and bowed as Ahzya lowered herself into a low curtsy.

Due to being short-staffed, several extra tasks were assigned to Ahzya as the birthday event drew ever closer. Being set on greeting and escort duty cut into her chore time horrendously, considering their guests arrived at sudden intervals throughout the day. Ahzya grew to suspect they only arrived right as she organised some semblance of a battle plan and work rhythm.

A girl leapt from the carriage skipping the step completely. Her brunette curls fell around her face as she planted her feet firmly on the ground.

"Miss Kola! Be careful; slow down," a lady's voice called out.

The governess didn't yell, for that would disgrace herself; however, her tone was firm, a desperation in her voice.

Kola, it seemed, had no intention of slowing down. Now free from the cage of travel, she began to run up the castle steps. Ahzya noticed the small jolt as Kola tripped on one of the stone slabs. With swift, instinctual movement, Ahzya skipped two steps and hooked an arm around the girl's waist. Kola squealed as she was stopped mid-fall and lifted up to the next step, steadying her stance immediately. Ahzya released Kola and retreated a little. A calm couple, Prince Tobias, King Mark's younger brother, and his wife, Lady Eleanor, exited the carriage, followed by a flustered looking governess who emerged seconds later.

"Miss Kola, wait for me, running isn't ladylike," the governess said.

"I'm not a lady, I'm a girl. I'll be a lady when I get older," Kola replied, without so much as a glance in the governess's direction.

"You won't become a lady unless you learn what I teach you," the governess threatened, moving forward with short strides and straightening her skirts at the same time.

Ahzya smirked and lowered her head to hide it, thus looking down at the young rebel. Kola met her gaze directly, her eyebrow quirked and a mischievous grin revealed a row of baby teeth.

"Are you a lady?" Kola asked directly.

"No, young miss," Ahzya replied, shaking her head, before saying in a whisper, "Not in your governess's meaning of the word at least."

"Miss Kola, this young woman is a maid. You will have several of your own when you grow up, they will help you dress and make your meals—" the governess began to explain.

"So, she's like you then!" Kola interrupted with enthusiasm.

The governess looked flabbergasted at being lowered to a maid's level. Kola giggled with pleasure and then shook her head at her governess.

"I know what maids are, Miss Harmony," Kola said, rolling her head. "My parents *are* royalty."

Ahzya's orders were to direct the prince and his family to their rooms, while the manservant took care of their luggage. Ahzya would then escort the guests to the throne room to meet with King Mark and Queen Maria before dinner. With the governess about to have kittens, and Kola's parents distracted by a conversation between themselves, Ahzya thought it best to do her duty.

"If you follow me, I will show you to your ro—"

"Princess Kola!" Jonathan's familiar voice echoed out along the stone walls. "Her Majesty of the land of fairies and mermaids, may I welcome you to this land and offer you a sweet peace offering."

Kola squealed with joy and skipped up the last few steps, throwing herself into a hug with Jonathan. He swung her into the air, ruffling her skirts, which caused her governess to gasp. Jonathan rested the girl on his left hip and dangled a curved candy before her cornflower blue eyes.

"Thank you, Jonny!" The girl grinned at him with unrestrained joy.

"Jonathan Dryen, it's been too long," Prince Tobias called, finally distracted from his wife and paying attention to the rest of the group.

"Your Royal Highness," Jonathan said respectfully, bowing as much as he could with the little rebel on his hip.

"How have you been?" Tobias walked up the steps with long strides and slapped Jonathan on the shoulder in a friendly manner.

"I've been perfectly well. We have much to talk about, but we'll have plenty of time to catch up at dinner," Jonathan replied, with a smile. "Before then, let's get you settled in to your rooms."

Jonathan turned to Ahzya, who followed not too closely behind the royal couple.

"Catherine, please show our guests to their rooms and unpack their bags," Jonathan offered.

*If you hadn't arrived, we'd already be doing just that.*

"Of course, sir." Ahzya curtsied and crossed the landing to lead them into the castle.

"Do you know that maid, Jonny?" Kola asked curiously.

"That's correct, you're pretty cluey," Jonathan answered, tapping Kola on the nose. "She's my favourite, so I'm trying to befriend her."

"She doesn't want to be your friend?"

Jonathan must have shaken his head, because Ahzya heard Kola give a horrified gasp.

"Why not? Did you break her doll like you did to my Mr Rabbit?" Kola whispered.

"Shh, that was an accident, and I fixed Mr Rabbit better than ever," Jonathan defended himself in a hushed tone.

"Better? One ear's still wonky and his right eye's bigger than the left!"

"I thought you'd accepted my candy bribe, that means you can't punish me for that anymore, so put away that pout quick."

"You have a point."

### PRINCE TOBIAS' GUEST ROOM, CASTLE PRYNESSE, ALPANIA

Nothing could have prepared Ahzya for the absolute chaos that would follow the smallest guest's arrival for the queen's birthday celebrations. Ahzya directed the manservant to put the luggage by a set of drawers in the main bedroom and then dismissed him to his other duties, she could only imagine his list was similar to hers. Ahzya picked up the smaller pieces of luggage, which she double-checked were Kola's, before exiting the main bedroom.

The royal's guest 'room' was more akin to a house within the castle. The main bedroom connected to the living area, where a small office area furnished a desk for business or writing letters. There was a sitting area with comfortable lounges for entertaining personal guests and a large fireplace to warm the space and adjoining rooms. On the opposite side of the main area was another bedroom, this one specifically set up for the young rebel. The castle staff prepared several dolls and toys in preparation for her arrival. When laying out the toys earlier, Ahzya imagined a spoiled yet polite young royal, but at the appearance of Kola, Ahzya knew that her imagination had fallen short.

Ahzya set Kola's bags down on the sickly pink cover set of a fourposter bed. She unlatched the bags and opened them to reveal the perfectly organised rows of dresses and stockings and other undergarments. Ahzya turned to the set of drawers in the room and laid them out in accordance to their kind. She removed a carefully wrapped gown from the luggage and hung it up to allow gravity to do as much ironing out that it could, though the maids would press the gown and return it before the birthday ball anyway.

A scream from the governess's room quickly drew Ahzya's attention and she left her post to check on what had happened. The governess's room had a door into Kola's room for easy access, and it also joined onto the main room via another door. Ahzya pulled open the door and raised her eyebrows when she spotted the governess standing on the bed still screaming.

"What's wrong, miss?" Ahzya asked in confusion.

The governess turned to Ahzya, her face shifting from fright to rage in a split second.

"There is a rat in my room!" the governess screeched. "No doubt this is a result of poor staffing arrangements! Such vermin shouldn't be allowed to roam noble grounds such as Prynesse Castle!"

Ahzya gazed around the room, trying to find the offending creature, and Kola appeared beside her, peering around her legs. The governess's room was smaller than the other rooms and usually went unused when there were no young children staying there.

"Where did you see him? Did you see where he went?" Kola asked.

"It leapt at me from the dresser near the doorway, and no, I didn't see where it went. I was far too busy fearing for my health and well-being," the governess huffed.

Ahzya stepped into the room and Kola followed without much caution. Ahzya reached for the door handle and closed it behind them.

"Don't trap it in here with us!" the governess said in shock.

Ahzya remained silent, keeping alert to any sound or movement around the room. If a rat had somehow made its way into the room, then Ahzya could only imagine the chaos there would be if she didn't find it. Trapping it in the room would seal its fate once she found its current hiding spot.

Staying still, Ahzya scanned the floor gradually and finally spotted the perpetrator near the bed. Unfortunately, Ahzya wasn't the only one to spot it in that moment, as the governess let out another scream, leapt off the bed, and sprinted for the door. If the yelling hadn't jarred her, Ahzya may have laughed at the sight of the governess hitching up her skirts and losing all ladylike dignity to leave the room as fast as she could. The door closed with a bang, and Ahzya winced at the sharp sound. With a sigh, Ahzya spotted the governess's sewing basket, complete with knitting needles, sitting by the bed. She moved forward quietly and picked up one of the needles, flipping it between her fingers.

Kola watched her closely, smiling the whole time. It seemed the fear that gripped the governess didn't cross over to her underling. Ahzya looked back to where the rat was making its way across the floor. Ahzya frowned, as it wasn't acting very rat-like. Sure, it looked just as rat as any other, but it moved so leisurely that it didn't seem concerned with any of the chaos happening elsewhere around the room. It was then that everything clicked into place and, with a last second glance in Kola's direction, Ahzya flung the knitting needle like a dart through the room. The rat was dead, pierced through one of its beady eyes, before it could take another breath.

It was then that Kola let out a little gasp, staring at the dead rat with shocked horror. Ahzya bent over the twitching body and drew the knitting needle out of the corpse with a swift movement. Wiping off any rat from the needle, Ahzya tossed it back across to the sewing basket. Turning to Kola, Ahzya saw the quivering lip and tilted her head to the side.

"So, are you going to confess, or should I go and confess for you?" Ahzya asked.

"What do you mean?" Kola asked cautiously.

"You smuggled your former pet rat here to scare the governess, did you not?"

"You knew? Why did you have to kill him?" Kola asked, her lip quivering again.

"Because rats make horrible pets, and there was a lesson to be learnt on why you shouldn't bring such pets into an environment that will get them killed," Ahzya answered, crossing her arms.

Kola let several quivering tears roll down her cheeks and Ahzya felt a slight pang of regret. Ahzya sighed and knelt to Kola's level, reaching out to pat her brown curls. Kola sobbed quietly and Ahzya used her sleeve to dab as more tears followed the others.

"I'm sorry, young miss," Ahzya apologised honestly.

Kola looked up with red eyes and met Ahzya's gaze bravely. To Ahzya's surprise, Kola shook her head making the curls dance.

"I caused troub... but I didn't fink... dat... Jonny would die," Kola said between sobs.

"Jonny?" Ahzya asked in amusement. "You named your rat Jonny? After Jonathan Dryen?"

"Yup, and I sent him to his death," Kola said, nodding again.

Ahzya couldn't help feeling a little less bad, perhaps even a touch satisfied, about murdering the pet rat after Kola's revelation.

"Well, I'm sorry, and if there's anything I can do to make it up to you, let me know," Ahzya said, wiping the last tears as Kola stopped crying.

"Okay," Kola sniffled.

"Alright, if you're okay, I'm going to show your governess that we've caught the rat, and then go bury him in the courtyard," Ahzya said, turning to pick up the poor rodent.

Kola held onto Ahzya's skirt as they walked across to the door. Ahzya opened it with the hand not holding the rat corpse and waved Kola through in front of her. The governess awaited them in the living area, having calmed herself, and she held her head high as she turned to address them.

"We've caught the rat, miss," Ahzya said, before the governess could say anything. "I apologise for such an incident and guarantee that it won't happen again."

As she delivered her apology, Ahzya lifted up the rat for full view and inspection by the governess. The governess gasped and took several cautious steps back.

"Get rid of that thing!" the governess ordered. "I will be reporting this incident to Prince Tobias. I assure you, he shall not find this as amusing as you seem to. I'll make sure he brings it up with King Mark, so that this never happens again. I'll make sure of it!"

Ahzya curtsied low but made no move to defend herself or explain the situation. As far as Ahzya was concerned, she would get in trouble, but there was little likelihood that she'd be fired, especially not on the orders of a mere governess. To Ahzya's surprise, Kola stepped forward and stood firmly in front of Ahzya.

"You will do no such thing," Kola said firmly.

"Miss Kola, this is not something for you to concern yoursel—" the governess started calmly.

"I've come to confess," Kola interrupted, reverently.

Kola folded her hands in front of her abdomen and bowed her head. The governess seemed cautious of Kola's sudden act but motioned for her to continue.

"I was the one that put Jon— the rat in your room."

"What? Why would you do that?"

"Because I don't like you," Kola answered bluntly. "I thought it would be funny to see you get scared, but then you began to blame Cath. If you're going to report anyone, report me."

"Your parents won't care! They let you run wild; they'll probably find it funny!" the governess said, exasperatedly.

"I know," Kola said, with a sweet yet mischievous smile.

"What's going on here?" Lady Eleanor asked from the doorway.

Ahzya hid the rat quickly behind her back and curtsied, bowing her head. Kola, seconds after her confident rebellion, hid behind Ahzya, as her mother appeared in the room.

From what Ahzya had observed of Lady Eleanor, she was a beautiful woman, very much in love with her husband, and not afraid to show it. As Lady Eleanor glided across the room now, however, Ahzya saw the motherly furrowed brow and the authoritative presence of a noble.

"Kola, care to explain?" Lady Eleanor asked, directly looking to her daughter for an explanation.

"With all due respect, my lady, your daughter released a rat on me. She is a rebellious and devious child. I've never worked with such a disobedient charge, and I'm afraid I must request my leave," the governess spoke up in frustration.

Lady Eleanor met the governess's annoyance in a calm manner, trying to glance at her daughter around Ahzya's skirts at one point, and viewed the guilty retreat as confirmation. She took a moment to assess the situation, before nodding her head to the governess.

"I'm sorry and sad to hear that you feel that way, I will arrange a severance fee to be paid to you once we return home, and then you may take your leave," Lady Eleanor apologised.

"Oh no, my lady, I will not be staying. I've had enough. I will return home tomorrow morning, and I shall drop by the royal residence to collect my pay once you've returned," the governess answered, shaking her head at Lady Eleanor's plan.

"I ask that you stay on until then, please. Kola shall improve on her behaviour, and we will pay you extra. We can't allow her to be by herself for the queen's birthday celebrations."

"I'm sorry, my lady," the governess said, with a curtsy. "I must pack my things."

The governess rushed to her room and closed the door behind her. Lady Eleanor watched her go and let out a tense sigh.

"Kola," Lady Eleanor said, her tone enough to warn her daughter of what was coming.

"I'm sorry, Mama," Kola said, moving out from her hiding place.

"Why did you have to push her over the edge at this point of the trip?" Lady Eleanor asked. "What are we going to do now? I know you don't want to attend tea parties with me, and there's no way your father will want you hanging around while the men catch up."

Kola looked at her feet and Lady Eleanor watched her daughter as she pondered what to do next. Kola suddenly looked up with a bright expression.

"Don't worry, Mama, I know the perfect person to look after me while you enjoy your time here," Kola said happily.

"Who would that be?" Lady Eleanor asked doubtfully.

"Cath, here," Kola said pointing at Ahzya with enthusiasm.

*Pardon?*

"Cath said that she would do anything I ask her to," Kola said.

"Why is that?" Lady Eleanor said, glancing up to study Ahzya.

"Because she needs to make up for killing Jonny," Kola answered straight away.

Lady Eleanor raised an eyebrow in shock and question at Ahzya. Obviously, Kola's nickname for Jonathan was familiar to Eleanor. Ahzya mouthed the words 'the rat' and a light of realisation showed in Eleanor's eyes.

"Catherine, I know this is a lot to ask, but do you mind caring for Kola over this week?" Lady Eleanor asked earnestly.

"I have my other duties, my lady," Ahzya began to explain.

"Don't worry, I'll speak to Mark and sort all that out," Lady Eleanor said with a smile.

Ahzya paused and considered her options. Kola was looking at her expectantly, her eyes beseeching her like a puppy, but Lady Eleanor seemed happy to give her a moment to think it through.

"I miss Jonny," Kola whispered under her breath.

Ahzya sighed and forced the sweetest smile she could muster.

"I'd be honoured to look after Kola during your visit," Ahzya said with a curtsy.

"Thank you, Cather—"

Kola danced and let out a whoop of joy, grabbing Ahzya's hand. Lady Eleanor laughed and laid her hands on her daughter's shoulders to calm her down.

"I'll discuss it with Mark before dinner. You go and finish the rest of your duties for today, and you can start looking after our little lady in the morning," Lady Eleanor explained.

"I'll follow your orders, my lady," Ahzya answered, with a curtsy.

Ahzya carefully backed towards the door, the rat still hidden behind her back in one hand.

"Make sure to give Jonny a proper funeral," Kola called after her.

Ahzya exited the room and couldn't make it to the castle wall fast enough, before tossing Jonny unceremoniously over the wall and into some bushes below.

*What's with creatures called 'Jonny' messing up my plans? Rest in peace, rat, I hope a bird comes and gouges out your other eye and you feel it in rat hell.*

# CHAPTER SIXTEEN

PRINCE TOBIAS' GUEST ROOM, CASTLE PRYNESSE, ALPANIA

"Can you read me a bedtime story, Cath?" Kola asked her, holding up a book.

A new day dawned and Ahzya spent the day with Kola, surprisingly enough passing the hours by enjoyably. Kola flourished under Ahzya's set of simple rules, and it seemed Kola had become quite attached. Though Ahzya was firm, Kola found it easy to learn her new boundaries, and the rest of the time was actually good company.

"Not tonight," Ahzya said reluctantly.

"Please," Kola begged. "I promise to go straight to bed after."

"I'd rather just tell the story out loud rather than read it," Ahzya answered, holding the book uselessly in her hands.

Learning to read was a whole different aspect to embarrassing herself in front of Kola, who already read far better than Ahzya could.

"*The Princess and the Pea*," Kola said, tipping her head to one side. "It's one of my favourites."

"Ah, right," Ahzya said with a little uncertainty. "I'm not super familiar with it."

"You can just read it," Kola said again, tapping the book.

"It's so much better if I just make it up from the beginning," Ahzya said, trying to convince the young girl. "I promise."

Kola looked at her for a moment before smiling happily.

"Okay," Kola said, nodding her head of curls.

Kola settled down on the bed, and Ahzya lifted the blankets to cover her legs to her waist. Ahzya then took up position on the edge of the bed.

"Once upon a time, in a land with waterfalls and rolling mountains, there lived a princess," Ahzya began, pausing to look at Kola.

She had Kola's complete attention, as she hugged a pillow to her chest.

"The princess was beautiful, but also selfish and proud. One day she was greeting villagers in her large throne room. One villager brought her his best cow, which gave creamy milk, another brought her a basket full of roses and yet another brought chocolate from a faraway kingdom."

Kola's eyes gleamed excitedly. Ahzya already knew that she had a taste for chocolate.

"As she gratefully accepted these gifts, an old woman approached with a small basket. Peas, already harvested from their shells, filled the basket. The princess hated peas, and she sneered at the gift and threw the basket away in disgust. The peas bounced and scattered across the marble floor."

Kola crinkled her nose since she hated peas and beans, a fact Ahzya had already observed from dinner the night before.

"Little did the princess know, but the old woman was a witch!"

Kola gasped, and Ahzya couldn't help smirking.

"So, while the princess crawled onto her feather-stuffed mattress that night, wearing her silk gown, the witch cast a spell on the discarded peas. The peas suddenly came to life and started bouncing on the princess's bed!"

Kola's eyes widened and Ahzya leaned forward, holding onto Kola's ankle through the blanket.

"The princess was horrified and scared all at the same time. 'Oh, tell us, princess, how can we a-peas you?' 'We'll make your skin turn green like ours, that'll teach you.' The peas just teased her all night, and she couldn't sleep a wink. The next day the old woman came to the princess again, and this time the princess accepted her gift with scared gratitude. The princess always ate her peas, and she never had to deal with cruel peas again. However, there is a rumour that if little children don't eat their peas, the whispers of the peas' voices keep them awake all night. And that is the tale of the princess and the peas."

Kola looked terrified, and Ahzya noticed her eyes filling with tears.

"I promise I'll eat my peas from now on," Kola sobbed. "I don't want the peas to attack me."

"Don't worry, I'll protect you from them tonight," Ahzya said, patting her head.

Kola seemed satisfied with that response, but Ahzya had already noticed a figure watching from the open doorway and tilted her head to confirm her suspicions. Sure enough, upon her movement, Jonathan stepped in to the room.

"Unless, of course, your name is Jonny, then the peas will always haunt and attack you with fiery vengeance," Ahzya continued, standing up to finish tucking Kola in.

"You're a horrible storyteller," Jonathan stated with a chuckle.

"I thought it was actually good, though a little scary," Kola defended.

"Thanks, little rebel," Ahzya said, offering up a smile.

"That's a truly sad revelation," Jonathan mused, "if you actually consider *that* a good story."

Jonathan stood close beside Ahzya and grinned at her with an additional wink. Ahzya crinkled her nose at him and then patted Kola on the head.

"Bid the young miss good night, sir, so that she may go journey to the land of dreams," Ahzya said, taking a step back to allow him room.

"We can't leave her with that sad, horrible story as the last thing. She'll have nightmares," Jonathan complained, shaking his head. "Instead, how about a story as told by the one and only Jonny Dryen?"

Kola sat up again at this proposal and her row of teeth glinted in the gentle lantern glow that illuminated the room. Ahzya sighed and pulled across a chair for Jonathan. It seemed she was outvoted.

"Once upon a time," Jonathan began his tale.

"I think I've heard this one before," Ahzya said, sitting at the end of the bed.

"Me too," Kola whispered back with a giggle.

"There was a very beautiful woman with short brown hair and the most stunning green eyes ever seen by man. She was feisty, strong-willed, and yet the cutest lady to grace the halls of the castle she lived in," Jonathan said, gazing across at Ahzya as he spun the story.

"She sounds just like you, Cath," Kola whispered, thoroughly enjoying herself.

"Impossible, can't be," Ahzya bantered back.

"Many a person would assume that she was the princess of the castle, but alas, she was a mere maid. Cursed to a life of cleaning and cooking, the little joy she found was nightly strolls along the castle walls, when the moon was at its highest and not a soul was there to disturb her."

"It's definitely you," Kola said with a confident nod.

Ahzya put her finger to her lips in a hushing action and shot a glare at Jonathan.

"One day a prince came to visit the castle," Jonathan continued with another wink at Ahzya.

"My father?" Kola asked in confusion.

Jonathan shook his head.

"This prince was handsome and insanely mischievous but charming in every way. His name? Jonny," Jonathan said confidently.

For the second time is as many days, Ahzya mouthed 'the rat' and Kola smirked and nodded her head in understanding of the inside joke.

"He fell in love with the beautiful maid at first sight and made it his mission to try and get to know her. However, no matter how hard he tried, the maid ignored him as she hurried around to do all her chores."

Kola shook her head sadly, disappointed that Prince Jonny couldn't garner the attention of his one true love due to things like dishes and washing.

"Secretly, the maid had noticed the prince and was madly in love with his charms as well."

Kola looked confused, but if Jonathan noticed he didn't pause the story to explain.

"But alas, she was but a poor maid, how could she ever be in a relationship with a prince? And so, they both spent their days in the sad loneliness of mere dreams. That is until one day, the prince entered into a room, his mind in turmoil with what his heart was feeling. He didn't notice the maid enter into the same room, and in a moment they both looked up and were utterly surprised to see each other."

"How convenient," Ahzya mused aloud.

"The prince didn't want to miss the chance, so he reached out and caught the maid's hand. 'I love you!' the prince claimed. He looked at her in complete and utter admiration and the maid felt her heart flutter. With a graceful movement, she held onto the prince and—" Jonathan was completely enthralled in his own delirious story and Ahzya could only imagine the sickly-sweet ending he was about to spin.

"And so, the maid pulled him close..." Ahzya interrupted, continuing with the story's tone.

Jonathan stopped, looking intrigued at where Ahzya was going to go with his tale.

"And using her knitting needles that she had at hand, stabbed him right in the eye socket," Ahzya said, jumping up from her chair and acting out the scene, even lunging towards Jonathan. "The needles pierced through the skull and hit the soft, mushy brain of the prince, and he was killed. The maid then left the castle and lived happily ever after."

With the tale now over, in its abrupt way, Ahzya tilted her head in a smile at the shocked Jonathan. She retreated back to the safe distance of the end of the bed.

"Well, I stand by my statement: you are a terrible storyteller," Jonathan said, shaking his head in disappointment. "Now there is no chance of Kola getting sweet dreams tonight."

"Actually, I witnessed the ending of the story yesterday. It *was* certainly shocking to behold such a sight at the time, but I slept just fine. Besides, the maid wouldn't have been happy with a rat. Unless the rat was cursed and his true form was that of a handsome human prince," Kola explained thoughtfully.

"You two confuse me to no end," Jonathan resigned, throwing his hands in the air. "But, the bright side of Catherine's storytelling is that I got to draw close to her for a moment during the attack. My heart was almost beating out of my chest. If I were to be stabbed through the eye by anyone, I would want it to be you, my love."

"Don't tempt me," Ahzya muttered.

Jonathan winked at Ahzya yet again. Ahzya quickly got up at that and shooed Jonathan from the room. She pushed most of her weight into his back as he went.

"You should get that eye of yours checked out. It keeps closing on its own," Ahzya hissed at him. "If you wish, I could try and dig out whatever's flown into it...with a knife."

"Joke's on you, I'd look dashing with an eyepatch," Jonathan bantered, glancing back over his shoulder for her reaction.

Ahzya shut the door in his smug face. She returned to tuck Kola into her covers and pointed a finger at her meaningfully.

"You go to sleep now, you've had two stories," Ahzya ordered.

"Yes, Cath," Kola murmured obediently. "Good night."

"Good night, little rebel," Ahzya whispered back, collecting the lantern from the bedside.

Ahzya slipped out the door, the lantern splaying its last flickering light into the room.

Jonathan was waiting on one of the big leather sofas in the room and Ahzya sat down on the arm of a chair opposite. Ahzya's brow furrowed as Jonathan grinned across at her, his form slouched comfortably into the brown cushions.

"You know you can drop the act. I'm not fooled by your over-attachment, and there's no-one around for you to deceive, so stop before you make a fool of yourself," Ahzya said with a sigh.

"You don't enjoy my attention?" Jonathan asked, his grin disappearing. "I felt sure you were enjoying my advances; I even spotted a blush at one point."

"I'm not a teenage girl who blushes at such things, nor am I a woman vying for your attention either. But you are well aware of that already and obviously find pleasure in annoying me nonetheless," Ahzya denied.

"You have made this trip to the castle especially amusing, I will say that," Jonathan admitted, stretching his limbs out. "Besides, how do you know I don't choose a pretty maid to flirt with each time I'm here?"

"The looks your actions garner me from my fellow castle staff, as well as more distinguished guests, are evidence enough that you don't stoop to such levels of interaction usually. Though you may court a variance of ladies, as far as I've heard, you've only ever been a gentleman, far from the teasing pursuit you've taken this time around."

"You do bring out the rascal side of me. Although, I would argue that's because you don't join in on any normal conversation and only ever react when I step on that temper of yours," Jonathan reasoned. "In fact, from the beginning you've only ever been cold towards me, which again I may argue, garners you further attention considering everyone else adores me."

Ahzya chuckled, splayed her fingers through her hair and tilted her head sideways at Jonathan.

"So, it's technically my fault?" Ahzya asked.

"I'm not going to point fingers, but had you acted like an overly adoring fan when I'd arrived, instead of glaring at my back at dinner, I would have probably ignored you," Jonathan answered with a shrug.

"Oh, to turn back time!" Ahzya cried in exasperation.

"If it's any consolation, after this mission is done, we'll go our separate ways and you'll probably never see me again," Jonathan consoled, watching Ahzya closely.

"Indeed, there shall be celebrations in the street on that day," Ahzya jested. "However, may I ask that you drop your antics and actually allow me to finish my work?"

"I won't make any promises. Besides, I doubt you plan on actually accomplishing your task until after the ball either way," Jonathan answered. "As I say, Cath, you amuse me, and I intend to enjoy our time together while I can."

"Promise you'll tone it down when we're alone around Kola. You don't need to involve her in your amusement."

"Very well, I can do that."

Ahzya nodded and shifted off the arm of the chair. Ahzya went to check on Kola one last time, and was satisfied to see her slightly flushed cheeks and slowed breathing. The day had been long, and Ahzya felt a yawn forming as she saw Kola's eyelashes flutter in her sleep. Jonathan got up quietly and left the room, and Ahzya felt herself relax even more.

ROYAL GARDENS, CASTLE PRYNESSE, ALPANIA

Ahzya was playing with Kola in the courtyard, an exercise that exhausted the rebel and also allowed Ahzya time to train. To pass time in a helpful manner, Ahzya trained her flexibility and strength by climbing the trees and army-crawling across the grassy area. The royal gardens were unlike the regular courtyard, where staff and visitors would congregate in and pass through on their way to other areas. The royal gardens were kept specifically for the royal family, and most of the time they were too busy to fully appreciate the grounds. This meant Ahzya and Kola were quite at their leisure to climb trees, tussle on the grass and accomplish all sorts of rambunctious and fun exercises. Ahzya wore her maid uniform without all the petticoats and extra ruffles and wore a pair of riding pants underneath. When they were safely in the courtyard, she had cinched the skirt up with several buckles and donned some gloves to protect her hands while climbing.

Kola had been hesitant at first, for although far from fully trained in the ways of a lady, her upbringing had not allowed for tree climbing and such endeavours. Upon seeing Ahzya swiftly scale up a tree with the ease of a monkey, Kola became intrigued. Ahzya showed her how to grip onto branches and position her feet to help with climbing. Flushed cheeks and laughter replaced the usually quiet exploration of the castle and they even sat happily on a large tree branch enjoying some baked goods they'd scored earlier from the kitchen.

"I wish I could grow up quickly and be like you, Cath," Kola mused, pastry flakes on her lips.

"Why is that?" Ahzya answered, switching her focus to the girl.

"People ignore you when you're little," Kola said, her gaze lowering. "Even if they spend time with you, they're always looking for someone to pass you off to. When you're grown up, you get to choose where you go and who you talk to."

Ahzya silently reached out to tuck one of Kola's stray brown ringlets behind her ear.

"No-one's ever wanted me to be anywhere," Kola whispered. "I'm only there because of Mama and Dad. Even Jonny and my cousins leave me when they have something better to do."

"When you go home, I'll be left behind. Does that mean you hate spending time with me now?" Ahzya asked, continuing to play with Kola's hair.

"No! I love you!" Kola proclaimed defensively.

"It's the same for your family and Jonny. They love spending time with you, even if they can't always be with you. So, don't rush to grow up, little rebel. You see, when you grow up, different monsters come to steal your time, and you lose moments doing things you love."

"Was the man talking to Jonny this morning a time-stealing monster?"

"What man?"

"A scary soldier," Kola answered, keenly lifting her head. "I wanted to say hello to Jonny, but the soldier saw me first. He smiled, but it was like how I imagine those evil ghosts smile in Jonny's stories. My spine tingled, like when I see a snake."

"That must have been scary," Ahzya sympathised as Kola shivered. "Don't worry, if you see the scary soldier again, find me and I'll protect you, even if I need to use a hundred knitting needles."

The lush green carpet of grass soon became a mat for Ahzya to stretch out on. Kola lay on her back staring up at the clouds that passed lazily overhead. Ahzya was relieved to find that despite a week of not being able to stretch due to castle work, her flexibility had not completely left her. Ahzya curled backwards, arching her back, and placed her hands right next to her feet.

"I'm afraid you'll snap in half," Kola said, biting into a red apple.

Ahzya chuckled before kicking up her legs and balancing as to complete several push ups with her legs straight in the air. Ahzya then somersaulted a few times before falling beside Kola to join in the cloud spotting.

"That one looks like a rabbit," Ahzya said with utmost relaxation.

"Really? Where? Which one?" Kola asked, searching the sky.

Ahzya pointed up at the rabbit-shaped cotton ball, and Kola let out small sound indicating her awe. This triggered Kola into pointing at the different clouds and trying to come up with things they looked like. Ahzya soon became distracted, however, as she noticed they were joined by King Mark, who was alone. He didn't interrupt their time and just stood under an archway that separated the garden from the circling hallway. Ahzya didn't move to fix her appearance, nor did she interrupt Kola's cloud watching. It wasn't like they were doing anything particularly wrong, even if her outfit was a little strange.

"That one looks like a big pot of stew," Ahzya mused, pointing out another cloud to Kola.

"IT DOES!" Kola said excitedly. "What kind of stew? Do you think it's a chicken stew?"

"Only the best stews can become clouds," Ahzya confirmed.

"Chicken stew is the best! I'm proud of you, stew!"

There was a quiet chuckle from the archway, a sound that even brought out a smile of her own. It was almost nice, just lying there, knowing that the country's leader was also taking a break from his own duties. It made the moment of downtime just a little more relaxing; almost justified.

"Mark!" a voice called out from further down the hallway from where the king stood.

Mark quickly hushed the newcomer and out of curiosity the figure joined him at the archway. Of course, Ahzya already knew who it was before they even appeared. Jonathan's voice had become almost too familiar to Ahzya.

"What are those two ladies doing?" Jonathan mused in a tone that was quiet, but Ahzya could still hear enough to understand.

"Cloud spotting," Mark answered simply. "A pastime even I used to enjoy."

"Nostalgia kicking in, Your Majesty?" Jonathan asked cheerfully.

"Recently more and more," Mark answered with a sigh.

Jonathan and Mark watched as Ahzya continued to play with Kola. Ahzya saw no need to change the course of their day simply because the two men had appeared. If Kola wanted to continue making flower chains and watching the movement of clouds, then that's what they'd continue to do. At one point, Jonathan spoke again after letting out a long pent-up sigh.

"I fear she is hiding a dark secret," Jonathan murmured.

Ahzya's ears strained to hear what they were saying, she'd trained herself to ignore other sounds. It came in helpful when on stealth jobs. Hearing approaching footsteps or far off conversations had saved her skin on several occasions.

"Indeed?" Mark asked semi-curiously before his tone took on a hint of sarcasm. "Do you think she's the assassin?"

"No, no," Jonathan quickly denied. "I fear something much more sinister."

"This is a serious claim. Then what, may I ask, is the accusation?"

"I regret to suggest that she may be a..." Jonathan paused, as if gathering his courage.

"A what exactly?" Mark pressed, highly invested by this point.

"A witch, Your Majesty, an enchantress. She has my heart under a spell. Her delicate fingers may as well be holding the fate of my entire life."

"You only like her because she's one of the only women that hasn't fallen for you at first sight or being informed of your remarkably elevated status," Mark stated, his tone light-hearted.

"True, but she does have a unique charm about her."

"Do you mean the ability to insult you to your face?"

"It's a unique quality," Jonathan answered without missing a beat. "Not many people consider me in the same regard that she does."

Mark chuckled in amusement, but his relaxed manner soon disappeared at the appearance of a small group of advisers. Ahzya turned to watch the group and noticed Mark tense up as he greeted them formally and started talking immediately of casual business greetings and undertakings. Ahzya stood up and claimed Kola's hand as they moved to be out of sight of the group. Ahzya didn't feel like having the judgement of officials and advisers against her right at that moment. Unfortunately, the appearance of the group had spoiled any of the peaceful and relaxed ambience the area had held.

"Perhaps we should take this to my study," King Mark suggested after the initial conversation came to a close.

"An excellent idea, Your Majesty," an advisers said with enthusiasm.

The adviser continued to babble annoyingly, bowing continuously to King Mark even as they walked. He was short and pudgy and for some reason reminded Ahzya of a piglet.

"His Majesty is so kind to allow us to escort you. I was indeed honoured, Your Majesty, to receive an invitation to the queen's birthday ball. My wife was overjoyed when I showed her, and do you know what I told her? I said: 'Never in our lives will we ever meet someone with such grace and kindness as His Majesty, King Mark. It is such an honour to serve him, in our own little ways.' She agreed with me completely..." the adviser prattled.

They turned a corner of the hallway and passed by the column that Ahzya and Kola were hiding behind. Mark visibly sighed, though no sound escaped from him, and he turned to Jonathan. Jonathan was showing the annoyance that Mark himself obviously felt and was glaring at the adviser.

"Surely he isn't much of an adviser or diplomat. People would get annoyed by just spending a minute in the same company as him," Jonathan muttered to Mark.

"I don't disagree with you there, but he was in the service of my father, and it would upset him should I demote him from my staff," Mark answered in a whisper of resignation. "So, I don't really know how to deal with him."

"Simple," Jonathan replied, his eyes sparking mischievously.

Mark watched as Jonathan motioned to one of his bodyguards with a flick of his wrist.

"Kill him," Jonathan stated, loud enough for the whole entourage to hear him.

Everyone froze in the hallway and looked at Jonathan queerly. Ahzya leant hard against the stone wall and watched on curiously to see the reactions of the party. They looked utterly confused and slightly horrified, especially the prattling adviser.

"Just kidding," Jonathan chuckled, breaking out in a huge grin. "Just keeping you on your toes."

The entourage good-naturedly laughed along with him and the adviser joined in, complimenting Jonathan on his sense of humour. Ahzya just shook her head.

*JP Dry really could get away with anything.*

# CHAPTER SEVENTEEN

MAID'S WING, CASTLE PRYNESSE, ALPANIA

Ahzya should have expected the repercussions from her sudden promotion to royal babysitter, but nothing prepared her for the berating served to her several days after her change of position. She had just finished tucking Kola into bed and telling her another tale, this time about pirates and the hero who defeated them with his mighty magical sword.

Ahzya was incredibly hungry, of course she didn't eat with the royals, and before and after the meal she was with Kola. This left little to no room for food, and often the kitchen had been cleaned and tidied so no meal would be found there. Some of the staff began to look at Ahzya differently too. They suspected she was trying to shirk her difficult responsibilities by trading jobs and becoming a temporary governess to make a name for herself amongst the nobles. Fortunately, Mrs Youn wouldn't allow such gossip in her kitchen and Lesley, Merida, and Noelle all still greeted her happily when they passed each other during the day.

Ahzya had already come to the decision to leave the castle and go hunting, have a meal, and then return. It was unlikely that she'd be missed, other than by Noelle, and she already planned on informing her before she snuck out. The other option was Prynesse tavern, but Ahzya didn't feel like fighting the crowds and a night hunt would give her a much-needed respite and time alone.

Ahzya entered the staff wing of the castle, specifically that of the female maids, and she noticed several lanterns giving off light further up the hallway at a bend. Having traversed the hallways many times at night already, Ahzya knew something was wrong or at least out of place. Flexing her fingers in preparation for any trouble, Ahzya kept her walking pace the same. Turning the corner, Ahzya was ambushed by Madam Hill and Madam Uran, who had obviously been waiting for her to return from her duties.

"Catherine, we need to have word with you," Madam Hill said, her back straight and her gaze steady.

"It's late," Ahzya said. "Can't this wait till morn—?"

"No, your behaviour has gone unchecked for too long," Madam Uran cut in, her hawklike nose casting a shadow onto her cheek.

"May I ask what behaviour has offended you?"

"Taking the innocent act, are you?" Uran sneered. "It's no mystery that your actions recently have been nothing but rambunctious and appalling. Your intentions are rather clear. You seemed unhappy with your assigned kitchen tasks and swapped with another maid. From there you squirmed your way into the employment of her ladyship, Lady Eleanor. All while toying with the attention of Jonathan Dryen like a seductress."

"You should blame the incompetence of Kola's governess for that change of employment. She was so busy being self-absorbed that she couldn't sympathise with her charge who merely wished for affection and friendship. I didn't wish for this role, but if it means the little rebel doesn't have to wallow in odious lessons of status and decorum all week long, I don't dislike it," Ahzya replied, her tone even and her gaze meeting Madam Uran's steadily. "As for the seduction of Master Dryen, I have never encouraged his ridiculous flirtation. I am well aware of my status and I'm not delusional. If I were vain, I might even be flattered that you think I have the wiles to seduce him, but I truly don't—"

"Liar!" Madam Uran again cut in. "You are a witch, Catherine, your words are empty and you mean to deceive us. We will not let your behaviour slide. You aren't the first maid to try and elevate her status by courting a—"

"Courting!" Ahzya almost snorted at the thought. "You must believe me; this is not a courtship. Even if Jonathan Dryen were interested in me, which he isn't, thank goodness, I am not inclined to accept such a proposal. He doesn't really fit my vision of an ideal man."

"Bite your tongue! How dare you speak ill of Jonathan Dryen. He is a gentleman. Yes, he may not be of noble birth, but his manners have earnt him the position he holds today. A maid like you could never dream to be held in the same regard that he is. Why, the royal family adore him, and dare I say the entire country does too."

"You're all charmed by him, I won't argue that, and he is an incredibly smart man. However, just because you all hold him in such high esteem does not mean that *I* am head over heels for him," Ahzya argued out of frustration, barely managing to keep her tone calm. "If anything, this should assure you that I am the very last person you should be scared of seducing your precious official."

"We do not believe you," Madam Hill finally spoke again.

"Then that is your choice, it doesn't rule out the truth of my words," Ahzya replied.

Ahzya could tell by Madam Uran's stance that she was far from being finished with her berating. Her cheeks were flushed, her hands were busy kneading together and her lips were going white from being pursed together.

Ahzya could already feel the knot of hunger growing tighter and considered bolting from the hallway to escape the onslaught. However, she needed to somehow smooth things over and leave relations somewhat connected, merely so she could keep her job at the castle.

Even though she had started babysitting Kola, her overall position was still firmly in the hands of the castle management.

Madam Uran started winding up for a new ramble, when Ahzya spotted a shadow at the end of the hallway opposite from where she had come from. Considering the amount of light from the two lanterns that Uran and Hill had set down, the shadow was only faint, but the object casting the shadow moved, drawing Ahzya's attention. It disappeared as Ahzya watched.

*It seems we have an eavesdropper.*

"You must realise that your attitude..." Madam Uran began.

It was then that the suspected eavesdropper decided to step out of their position and saunter around the corner. The tall boots made of soft leather made no sound, and the shadows did little to hide who the eavesdropper was. Ahzya was surprised to see who it was, as the captain's hat unmistakably identified the newcomer. Though why Commander Ray was snooping around the staff wing of the castle so late at night was a mystery.

"Good evening, ladies," Ray said, his voice causing Uran to stop her speech and turn in shock. "Isn't it too late for the knitting group to be having a gathering?"

"Commander Ray, what brings you here?" Madam Hill asked as the ladies all curtsied.

"I'm taking care of the nightly rounds while His Majesty is otherwise engaged with guests," Ray answered with a smile. "It's a lovely night for it, so I don't mind the task."

"The night is quite agreeable," Madam Hill replied politely.

"I do hope you aren't punishing this poor maid too harshly on such a pleasant night," Ray said, raising his eyebrows at Ahzya.

"No, no, sir, just going over a few things," Uran replied, stuttering slightly. "How did you guess that Catherine was being corrected, sir?"

"Why else would the two head maids be looming over a lone employee in the maid's quarters? I just figured that must have been the case, especially considering your own sleeping quarters are located in a separate area," Ray said with a shrug.

"How perceptive," Hill admired.

"Perceptiveness is important, especially on nightly inspection rounds."

Ray didn't leave, instead he just stood with them quietly. If he felt affected by the awkward silence that followed, he definitely didn't show it. He gazed around at the endless stone as if it held all the intricacies of a flower garden. Ahzya hid a smile, but she was grateful that Ray stayed. It was almost as if he was hinting that it was time to break the group up. Fortunately for her, the madams realised Ray wasn't going to leave and instead took leave themselves.

"Just keep in mind what we said, Catherine, don't make us have to use further disciplinary actions," Madam Hill said before she curtsied and walked away.

"So, what truly brings you here, sir?" Ahzya asked, relaxing her stance and looking across at him.

"I'm honestly just on my rounds," Ray answered. "Though I will admit that I came up here because I saw Jonathan Dryen snooping at the corner. Whatever you were talking about, it seems it drew his attention."

"Master Dryen was watching us?" Ahzya asked curiously.

"Seems so, when he saw me approaching, he left the way I'd come."

There was a pause as Ahzya frowned and then shook her head to clear her mind.

"May I hear what exactly you were discussing?" Ray asked, watching her closely.

"Nothing of consequence," Ahzya replied with a shrug.

"You weren't caught snooping through another guest's correspondence?"

"No, sir. I don't tend to repeat my mistakes."

"As in the mistake of snooping through people's correspondence or mistake of getting caught?"

"The latter," Ahzya said with a chuckle.

Commander Ray pointed a warning finger at her before tipping his hat and leaving without so much as a goodbye.

Ahzya felt marginally less tired than before, and the adrenaline from the conversation with Hill and Uran left her blood pulsing. A night hunt would be the perfect outlet of frustration as well as scoring her some food. As she changed out of her uniform, she realised she'd been given the morning off from her babysitting duties due to the royal party and certain guests going on a picnic outside the castle. With that in mind she packed a few extra supplies, with the idea of sleeping in the forest and visiting Noah in the morning.

MORNING MARKET, PRYNESSE, ALPANIA

A wild rabbit had made a tasty meal for dinner that night, or by then early morning, and having experienced the thrill of a hunt, Ahzya was a lot happier by the time she entered the marketplace in search of Noah. Several scratches marred her arms, but having tended to them with a few herbs of the area, she left them on display to the fresh air.

Ahzya even greeted several of the sellers, who she'd met when she was working with Noah, with a cheery hello and a quick banter. An acquaintance with the local marketplace dwellers also made finding Noah's spot for the day easier. The marketplace was never organised; whoever came first got first pick of the positioning. This made business in the area competitive and interesting, because everyone had the chance to set up in a prime spot; however, it made it difficult to find a specific loyal vendor.

Ahzya zoned out the loud calling of the vendors and focused on the delicious scents that drifted in the morning air. It was a mix of sweet fruit, earthy vegetables, baked goods and smoke from the contained fire pits that cooked several food options around the market. Everyone still had plenty of produce, and the hum was loud and constant. The sun warmed the area in the most comforting way, meaning joyful customers and wallets were more readily at hand to make purchases.

Ahzya wove her way through the market, dodging baskets and slow-walking groups. Horses, other than the vendor owners, were banned from the area, making it easier for pedestrians to manoeuvre their way around. There was the odd rider who thought they'd be smart and ride in, but the thick crowd and berating from said crowd soon kicked them out of the area. The only horses that the crowd parted for were those of the city guards patrolling the marketplace to make sure people and vendors were kept in line and operating legally.

Not just anyone could set up shop in the market, each vendor had a written agreement with the country, which was signed by King Mark himself. These papers had to be presented upon request, but since the guards knew the regular owners well, only fresh faces were usually asked.

The first thing Ahzya saw when she finally happened across Noah's stall was Reggad. Reggad was a smart horse, and while Noah's back was turned, tending to a customer, the mare stretched out her neck and snagged one of the carrots from the wooden bench.

*It seems Reggad has paid a little too much attention to my work.*

Ahzya smirked as she approached Reggad, and the mare immediately sensed her presence and looked up. Reggad let out a loud whinny that scared one of the ladies nearby and expressed every bit of joy the mare felt.

"Hello, my girl, sorry about not seeing you for so long," Ahzya said, pouting her lips at Reggad.

Reggad let out another neigh and shook her mane. Ahzya moved close and scratched the mare's nose and ears, before stroking her nose affectionately. Reggad flared her nostrils and bent her neck, nudging Ahzya gently and letting out a low nickering and sigh.

"Don't worry, it's only going to be a short while and then we can go exploring again, just the two of us," Ahzya whispered, resting her head on Reggad's forehead. "We'll even go on a long trip, somewhere new."

Reggad just seemed happy to see her mistress again and looked almost dejected when Ahzya reluctantly pulled away to greet Noah.

"Well, hello there, Cath girl. Long time no see," Noah called across at her as he packaged up an order. "'Twas beginning to think the castle had murdered ye an' hidden ye in their catacombs."

"I've dodged all their tries so far. How goes business?" Ahzya replied, genuinely happy to talk to the farmer again.

"Very good, I'm missing me right-hand woman though," Noah answered, turning to give the package to the customer and bid them a good day.

While he was distracted, Ahzya felt Reggad nibbling on her jacket and pet her nose to show the mare that she hadn't been forgotten.

"I'm starting to miss the work myself," Ahzya replied once Noah had a break in customers.

"Ah, the maid's life not it's all cracked up to be, ey?" Noah asked with a chuckle.

"Considering I wake the same hour I did when I worked for you, but don't see my pillow until midnight, with no breaks, I'm thinking I may have been conned. However, I've got this morning off, so I can't complain too much, especially since the queen's birthday is tomorrow and everyone else is probably run off their feet."

"With the amount of food an' other supplies they've been sending up to the castle, you'd think the whole country were attending," Noah said, shaking his head at the thought. "But if there's going to be a big party for anyone, I guess it should be for Her Majesty, she's a wonderful queen after all. Graceful, charming, thoughtful, an' caring, an' not above coming to visit us commoners in our own homes from time to time."

"I do hope she has a great night. I hear her daughters are going to be arriving for it too," Ahzya mused, boosting herself to sit on Reggad's hitching post. "They thought they weren't going to make it, but a messenger came in last night with the news that they'd hope to arrive in the morning. I've never seen Her Majesty look so happy to hear from a messenger at the dinner table."

"No doubt, they're late due to the funeral. Heartbreakin' news about the passing of the Lavanian prince. The assassination of a royal is always terrifyin', the country must be in turmoil. Due to their friendship, Cleo must be feelin' it keenly," Noah said, shaking his head sadly.

Ahzya felt a shiver of fear, but for a whole other reason. It was eerie how often she'd heard talk of assassinations since she'd accepted her latest job.

"Sounds like it'll be a good night though," Noah said. "Princesses Cleo an' Anna will enjoy catchin' up with everyone too, 'specially since they've been out of the country for six months now."

"Really? Why have they been gone for so long?"

"Cleo often travels, she became friends with the heirs of our neighbouring countries, strengthening the alliance, an' it seems she felt Anna should accompany her this time," Noah explained, before giving a chuckle. "Anna may be considered the castle's diplomat here, but Cleo has so many connections with other countries that she's by far our best ambassador. I don't think our own country realises it. Her efforts an' connections have opened up a world of trade."

"It's probably because they're unofficial agreements that the nobles don't acknowledge the work she's doing, especially since all they seem to see and deal in is paper."

"I'd watch who ye said that around, 'specially since ye employer at the castle wouldn't appreciate such talk," Noah warned with a raised eyebrow. "But between yeself an' me, I can't disagree."

"Don't worry, I'll keep our revolution a sec—"

"Cath! You've returned!" a familiar cheery voice yelled all of a sudden nearby.

Ahzya turned her head to see Ethan run, dodging several small children, to where they were. His red hair was a mess, but he was obviously on ship business as he wore his navy uniform. His wide grin greeted her with absolute joy and his eyes sparkled with happiness.

"Mister customer," Ahzya acknowledged with a nod of her head.

"Ethan! Calm yeself down, an' tell me how ye family is," Noah said, leaning on his own stand as he watched the young man come to a bounding stop.

"All good, Noah, nothing to report," Ethan replied hurriedly. "Do you have the day off, Cath? You're not in your maid uniform."

Having been suitably dismissed, Noah shrugged at Ahzya and then turned to attend to a couple of elderly ladies who were browsing his produce.

"Only this morning, I have to return in a little while," Ahzya replied.

"Aw, too bad, I was going to suggest we go to lunch together," Ethan replied, his energy depleting somewhat.

"Sorry," Ahzya apologised. "What brings you to town?"

"Just running a few errands, I also had a message to deliver to Captain Ray, but they wouldn't let me in to deliver it myself. I had to hand it to one of the guards, who gave it to one of the staff. Man, security has never been so tight."

"I guess with all the important nobles arriving they don't want anyone suspicious slipping through. It's annoying, but I can understand it."

"Well yeah, but I'm hardly a stranger, I'm even in uniform. I don't look the least bit suspicious," Ethan said, holding out his arms to show off his uniform and giving a charming smile.

"Exactly, you're so thin that even if you did try anything, they could just snap you in half."

"Ouch." Ethan winced, letting his arms drop. "I'm working on bulking up. Just you wait, I'll be flexing muscles of a warrior in no time."

"I'm sure," Ahzya assured with a chuckle.

"You're such a tease," Ethan sighed.

"I thought you'd enjoy one of my quips, for old times' sake. Besides, you're hardly weak if you go around hauling lines and sails all day."

Ethan cheered up quickly at her assurance and joined her in sitting on the hitching post.

"Don't you have more errands to tend to?" Ahzya asked, with a raised eyebrow.

"Nope, I can stay until you have to go back," Ethan replied, petting Reggad on the neck.

The mare let out a sigh as Ethan petted her neck, and Ahzya realised that Ethan must have been befriending Reggad while Ahzya had been away at the castle. Usually, Reggad was wary of strangers and kept her distance as she'd been trained to by Ahzya.

"MAKE WAY! Their Majesties, the King and Queen, are passing through!" a young boy yelled.

The boy was in a palace uniform, and he ran ahead of a larger group that could be just seen at the end of the marketplace area. While the message was meant to clear a path, calmly and in an orderly fashion, the call attracted more chaos than order. Crowds of people seemed to appear out of nowhere around them, causing a mass to gather in the marketplace, making it difficult to even clear a path. The royal party were collecting a few fresh products on their way to their picnic. Ahzya was sure that it was more out of novelty rather than that they actually needed to go through the marketplace. A maid could have easily fetched what they required and delivered it to the party before they left or at the picnic area itself.

Of course, with security heightened and the party being of elevated status, there was a circle of bodyguards around them, and anyone that didn't move out of the way was soon forced to. Luckily the crowd, though dense, did seem to move at the last second, and only a few people were roughly pushed away.

As the party moved, they stopped at several vendors to purchase items, though most vendors gave them it as a gift.

"For Your Majesty, Queen Maria, consider it an early birthday gift," they said, with bows.

Thus, another reason why the royal party came through themselves, their supplies ended up costing them next to nothing.

Ahzya sat up to scan who was in the group as they stopped at the stall next to Noah's. King Mark and Queen Maria led the party of course, with Prince Tobias and Lady Eleanor following closely behind. Several other relatives also spoke with Their Majesties, and the group was in a jolly mood. Ahzya then smiled when she spotted the curls of Kola's head, beside the figure of Commander Ray, though she quickly became less pleased when she spotted Jonathan with them.

"So, they are your employers, hey?" Ethan said, leaning closer to be heard over the crowd.

"That would be them," Ahzya turned to reply and focus on their conversation.

"They seem to be quite a big deal," Ethan mused, looking past her.

"It would appear so. Comes as quite the surprise to me," Ahzya replied with joking sarcasm.

Ethan threw back his head and laughed, the sound swept into the drone of the mass of people that bustled around them.

"Catherine?" Jonathan's voice broke through the hum of everything else.

Ahzya turned to see the royals paused at Noah's stall and Jonathan looking directly at her with his hazel eyes. Upon seeing that it was in fact Ahzya, Jonathan ducked through the bodyguard circle and approached. Ahzya could see him glance at Ethan a few times and a friendly smile formed on his lips. As Ahzya had noted in previous encounters, any friendliness he displayed via his smile, didn't show in his gaze.

Ahzya tensed. Her interactions with Jonathan had become regular while she babysat Kola. When they were around the young rebel, Jonathan was fairly relaxed; however, he tended to act unpredictably around others. The whole situation put Ahzya on edge. Ethan noticed the change and for the first time since meeting him, Ahzya saw his expression darken.

"I was looking for you this morning, Catherine. You should have informed me of your plans to travel to the marketplace, I would have happily escorted you on your walk," Jonathan said, moving closer to converse with her.

"Why would she make considerations for you, and inform you of her personal plans anyway?" Ethan piped up beside her.

Jonathan turned to size Ethan up, the friendly smile slowly dropping before being replaced by another forced one.

"I'm an esteemed guest of the castle, I was sure she'd be willing to hear my request," Jonathan replied smoothly. "It's only natural I'd expect as much."

"Ah, I think he's mistaken the position of maid for that of a servant," Ethan returned, angling it more as an offhanded whisper to Ahzya. "Imagine being so conceited that you try to forcefully interrupt someone's free time. It's no wonder you sought out some friends to help release the tension of having to put up with such company while working."

"I have nothing against Cath seeing her friends. I merely missed her presence. She's rather cute and I got used to having her around," Jonathan said, his tone even and his eyes watching Ethan's movements closely. "Cath, I am concerned by this lamb you've befriended... he appears more wolfish with every passing moment."

"This guy needs his eyes checked," Ethan taunted before gritting his teeth. "He seems to be mistaking a loyal guard dog for a wolf, or was it a lamb?"

"I thought loyalty went hand in hand with honesty," Jonathan scoffed. "Never mind that, at least *I'm* only here to express my feelings for your master honestly and openly. I'll love and protect your master well, so go find a squirrel to chase, pup."

"Master Dryen," Ahzya seethed, slipping from the hitching post. "You should stop."

# CHAPTER EIGHTEEN

MORNING MARKET, PRYNESSE, ALPANIA

Ahzya's ears were flushed and her teeth gritted. The attention of the marketplace had quickly turned to the three of them, even the royal party stopped their conversation. Several were frowning, Queen Maria was looking at King Mark for advice, and her husband looked as lost on the situation as everyone else. Of course, the crowd beyond the small grouping only filled with questions about what was happening and still held quite a loud volume.

"I apologise for being so forward," Jonathan offered, though Ahzya felt no truth to the words.

Ahzya's temper simmered, especially when she spotted Kola peeking through the bodyguard circle. If this was his way of toning things down and not acting out his ridiculous theatre performances in front of Kola, then he was doing a horrible job.

"Your apology is noted," Ahzya replied shortly, as she felt the veins in her neck pulse.

"As way of apology, I would like to bestow you a gift," Jonathan said.

Ahzya wished she could reach out and punch that fake smile from his face, but she clenched her fists by her side instead.

"No need—"

"Wait here," Jonathan interrupted, disappearing across the way.

If Ahzya had wanted to run away from Uran and Hill the night before, at this point she was ready to sail right back to Ulkadasa. She felt the eyes of those around them boring holes into her, but similar to the night's interaction, she couldn't really afford to make a break for it.

Jonathan emerged back into the area with a red rose held in his fingers. As he approached, he bowed and held the flower out to her. Ahzya tried not to snatch the rose from his hand, putting on a fake smile of her own.

"Thank you. Have a good day, sir." Ahzya curtsied and began to turn away.

"I'm not finished with my apology," Jonathan stated, quickly grabbing onto her hand.

"Can't you see, sir, you are forgiven. Let's just leave this behind us," Ahzya lied urgently.

Jonathan lowered his voice and a mischievous smirk graced his lips. "Just go along with me."

At his whisper, Ahzya knew the last thing she was going to do was act in the little play he was setting up. She really didn't want to witness the scene he aimed to orchestrate.

"I would be honoured if you would attend Queen Maria's birthday ball tomorrow night by my side," Jonathan asked loudly, bowing his head respectfully. "Don't worry about your dress, I shall attend to your every need in preparation."

Ahzya could only blink at such an absurd proposal, while the crowd murmured at such a romantic gesture. Several men whistled, and Ahzya didn't even dare to look at the royal party. Jonathan looked up again and sent her a wink, this time an almost satisfied gleam to his eye.

*He can't be serious.*

"No way in hell," Ahzya said under her breath.

"Pardon?" Jonathan asked, still smiling. "It's so noisy."

Ahzya took a deep breath and stood tall, her chin lifted.

"No... sir," Ahzya said loudly. "I will not give you that honour. Definitely not."

A dreadful silence followed. Jonathan barely changed his manner, Ahzya assumed out of shock. The crowd began whispering, all with negative remarks about Ahzya.

"Why did she refuse such a gentleman?"

"Who does she think she is?"

"He can take me instead. His attentions are lost on that girl."

Ahzya felt welded to the spot, cringing at the sneers. It reminded her too much of her days as a street urchin. This time she may be wearing clean and well-kept clothes, and she had money, but the comments took her back to days in grubby clothes and a corpse-like frame.

Ahzya's left arm jolted her suddenly, yanking her from Jonathan's loosened grasp. Ahzya barely kept her balance as she was dragged away, almost bumping into several bystanders. Ethan pulled her along, his own body cutting a path through the masses. Recovering from the sudden shock, Ahzya quickly sustained a better footing. They raced through the streets, curious faces and vendors passing by as flashes. Ethan led the way through alleyways until the crowds had thinned so much that they were barely seeing any other human. Several stray dogs joined in the run, finding their exercise to be highly entertaining, compared to looking for food scraps.

With space enough for them to run, Ahzya caught up to Ethan and began running beside him, though his hand still held tightly to her own.

"So, how far are we fleeing?" Ahzya asked, her breathing slightly irregular from the impact on the street.

"However far you need to recover," Ethan replied, glancing at her.

"Port Joonver?" Ahzya replied as a semi-query.

"Will it take you that long to recover?" Ethan asked, his voice slightly concerned.

"Nope, I just feel like seeing the sea, and if we are going to run anywhere, that's where I'd choose," Ahzya said with a breathy laugh.

"Sounds like a plan, though it will take us a couple of hours to walk and run there."

"I can always use the excuse of you kidnapping me to explain why I'm back late, and I'm not sure whether they'll be expecting me back anyway," Ahzya replied, although she hated to think about what she'd face when she actually did return to the castle. "Hopefully I still have a job."

"I wouldn't worry too much," Ethan replied, slowing their pace as they came to the edge of the city. "From the look on King Mark's face, he was more sympathetic than outraged by the situation."

"Is that so?" Ahzya asked, regulating her breathing so she could recover quickly.

"From what I could guess, yeah. Cap looked mad; his glare almost stopped my heart. I don't know whether he was angry with me or Jonathan, the situation, or his morning coffee."

Ahzya chuckled and stretched her arms as Ethan released her hand almost apologetically.

"His morning coffee?" Ahzya asked with amusement.

"Yeah, get his coffee wrong and he's mad for the rest of the morning," Ethan explained. "This is coming from a person who's lived on a ship with him, so I'd know."

"Some people wouldn't understand his taste in coffee, or rather, honey," Ahzya replied knowingly.

"Oh, so you know about his honey obsession?"

"I've witnessed it on occasion."

"Midshipman Ethan," a firm voice interrupted their discussion.

"Speak of the devil," Ethan whispered, stopping and turning.

Ethan saluted and Ahzya glanced back to see Commander Ray riding towards them on a dapple mare. He reined his horse in and glanced down at the runaway pair with a raised eyebrow.

"Where do you think you are going?" Ray asked his midshipman.

"Just escorting this lovely lady to Port Joonver, Cap," Ethan answered, motioning a hand towards Ahzya.

"I signalled you to remove her from the situation, not the entire city," Ray said, shaking his head.

Ahzya looked confused and glanced to Ethan.

"At first, I was confused when you sent the signal, Cap," Ethan replied with a smile.

"Perhaps you should study up on all the different signals then, and report to me when I officially return to the ship," Ray answered sternly.

"I remember the signals perfectly, I just never expected you to ever signal me to abandon ship," Ethan explained himself quickly.

"Understandable, I only ever use it in social situations on land. You'll know now for the future."

"Yes, Cap," Ethan said with a firm nod.

Ray then turned his attention to Ahzya, who, having garnered a foothold on the situation, bowed her head.

"Chin up. You tend to get yourself in trouble, don't you," Ray stated with a smile. "I'll take you to Port Joonver, if you wish, though I hope you intend on returning to your duties at day's end."

"I do," Ahzya responded.

"Ethan, you return to help Cassik and then return to the ship with him," Ray ordered.

"Sure, Cap," Ethan said with a nod. "I'll see you later, Cath."

Ethan waved goodbye and began to jog back into the city. Ray offered his hand to help her climb onto the back of the mare. With the help of Ray and her own athletic capabilities, Ahzya leapt up and held onto the back of the saddle.

"Comfortable? I can't say I usually ride with a passenger. I don't ride at all," Ray said, looking over his shoulder.

"I ride bareback often, so I'm perfectly comfortable," Ahzya answered, shifting her seat slightly.

They stayed silent as Ray urged the mare into a trot, and Ahzya quickly assessed and adjusted to the horse's rhythm. Ray was clearly not totally accustomed to travel via horse, as Ahzya saw he kept his legs tensed and his grip tight. The horse sensed her rider's inexperience, but being of good breed and trained by castle staff, she adapted to her rider's abilities.

Ahzya felt grateful for Ray's intervening in the earlier incident, but considering many found her actions disagreeable, she didn't know whether to thank him or just remain grateful at heart.

"Jonathan Dryen can be incredibly brash in his ways," Ray said, his head remaining facing forward. "He is smart when he actually takes the time to think things through, but unfortunately you've witnessed one of his less... bright moments."

"You don't have to defend him, sir," Ahzya replied.

"I know, it's just, believe it or not, when he was younger, well I was younger too, we were actually pretty good friends," Ray spoke seriously. "Ah, what the heck, we still are friends, but he's been through some things in the last two years, and it's warped his whole outlook. He's become increasingly impulsive and sarcastic."

"Is sarcasm a bad thing?" Ahzya asked out of curiosity.

"Sarcasm itself isn't inherently bad; I can see the amusement in it. However, while a sarcastic man may be amusing, there can come a point where joke and truth become blurred. It's like when a man says something unkind and then plays it off as a joke. Who's to know the man's true intentions and nature? I prefer a man to speak the truth and not have hidden meaning in his words."

"So, you want me to go easy on Mr Dryen?" Ahzya asked doubtfully.

"No, you were well in your rights to refuse him. Probably did him good," Ray answered with a chuckle. "But from the way you looked at that flower he gave you, it seemed you were going to tear it apart and feed it to him, if you hadn't kept your temper in check."

"The truth of the matter is, I'd rather be plucking out Mr Dryen's eyeballs and crushing them under my boot," Ahzya vented, making a stomping action.

Ray let out another hearty chuckle.

"Well, whether you do or do not end up going to the ball with Jonathan—"

"Believe me, I won't," Ahzya interrupted him.

"It might not be totally under your control. Either way, I hope you keep your stubbornness. He has to learn one way that most women have morals and won't just fall for his tricks or social manipulations."

"I guess, if my job comes to depend on it, I'll have to attend with him. I hope it won't diminish my good morals and values in your eyes."

"Never. Anyone who can remember my coffee taste and makes a good cup can't be truly virtueless. In the same way, a woman who can see through the flirtatious screen of Jonathan can't be totally immoral."

"I have no idea why you hold me in such high regard. Considering you caught me browsing your personal correspondence not so long ago."

"My sister, she's like you, a total firecracker," Ray said thoughtfully. "I'm older than her, but she always found a way to boss me around. I didn't appreciate her opinions at first, but, when my family moved away, she convinced me to stay here. She seemed to know that my heart belonged on the ocean, and though the loneliness got to me at first, she wrote, and eventually her son wrote too. It's the only paperwork I actually enjoy."

Ahzya smiled as she remembered Ray's hatred for paperwork and yet, when she'd seen him writing letters to his sister on *Moonstruck,* he'd always held a soft look on his face.

"This one time, my sister was quite fond of this merchant, she was still young, but he seemed earnest in his wish to court her. My sister is quick to care and extremely loyal, to the point that when warning signs started to appear, she kept them to herself and disregarded them. However, he was caught courting another woman in Prynesse and word got back to us and my sister. So, naturally, I thought I'd be a good big brother and go show him whose family he messed with," Ray recalled.

"You thought? So, you didn't?" Ahzya asked, watching Ray's back.

"Nope, when I got to his place, the guy I met with had a crooked nose and a black eye. Supposedly, my sister had already paid him a visit, and he was incredibly apologetic," Ray explained with another chuckle. "What about you? Any family?"

"Not really, sir. My parents passed away when I was a child, sometimes I wonder if the faces I remember are truly theirs or something my imagination made up of them," Ahzya pondered. "I guess I learnt to make my family into a broader range of things over time. My horse, the people I met along the way, but I definitely don't have such fun memories like yours."

"Well, I'm sorry to hear about your parents, I'm sure they'd be proud of you. You're a castle maid, and have won over the king's niece. I'd call that something to be proud of."

Ahzya was silent, but a frown brought her eyebrows down. She was sure her parents wouldn't be proud of the life she'd made for herself. No parent could be proud of a thief, especially one that no longer did it just to survive. Ahzya's entire character had become what she'd been forced to live. A liar and schemer, as shameful as it was to admit, she'd gotten pretty good at it. The mind games and adrenaline were a natural part of her day to day, normal life almost felt empty without it.

"Well, how long will you need in Port Joonver? I can take you back with me once you're finished, and I'll check on my ship while you do what you have to do," Captain Ray spoke up.

"Just an hour, my parents were sailors so, when I need to relax, I like being by the water. All my fondest memories happened on or near the sea," Ahzya replied honestly. "Besides, I have to return to face the music, see if insulting our esteemed guest has earnt me some kind of torturous punishment."

"Alright, an hour it'll be," Ray said, before they fell silent once more.

The hour in the port was just what Ahzya needed. The salt air and the sound of the waves, the ships manoeuvring the bay, their white sails floating above the waves, everything was beautiful to her. She avoided the town as best she could, skirting the main congested areas. Ahzya wasn't ready to walk familiar streets, and she'd already had enough nostalgia from talking with Ray.

When Ahzya did finally make her way to the meeting spot with Ray, her eyes had brightened and her cheeks held a healthy pink glow.

### Maid's Quarters, Castle Prynesse, Alpania

Ahzya stood at attention as Madam Uran stood across from her with her arms crossed and brow furrowed. She was yet to sight Madam Hill, but considering the bustle of new guests arriving, that wasn't surprising.

"I was appalled to hear of the way you treated Master Dryen this morning." Madam Uran spoke, her tone tight and authoritative.

"You heard about that?" Ahzya asked, already knowing the answer.

"Heard about it? Oh yes, it's all the town and castle have been talking about. You should know that your reputation has taken quite the spike. Many consider your actions to be deplorable."

"And the rest, what do they think?"

"Some of the soldiers have the nerve to find it hilarious. I found several of them laughing over it on their lunch break. Though with their manners, I know they don't know anything about correct etiquette or the ways of the upper class."

Ahzya gave a small smile at the thought of the soldiers gathering around to jeer at the misfortune of their former fellow soldier, but soon let it fade at Madam Uran's raised eyebrow.

"You find that amusing, do you?" Madam Uran asked, pursing her lips.

"A little— No, Madam," Ahzya answered, bowing her head.

"You obviously don't hold any care for your own reputation; however, to drag Master Dryen into your web was a mistake."

"My web?" Ahzya asked incredulously.

"Oh, don't play innocent," Uran scoffed. "This castle has eyes and ears everywhere. It's well known that you and Master Dryen spend time alone, conversing plenty when you think no-one is watching. Though you do have a talent for not being close enough for your conversations to be understood, but from what I've heard, Master Dryen always seems in high spirits."

Ahzya let out an inner sigh and made note to be extra careful to not speak of her true plans, not when Uran's spies were obviously lurking around.

"I must hereby tell you to call off this fling you are having and stop pursuing Master Dryen."

"I was the one who turned him down just this morning, remember?"

"No doubt a ploy to test his feelings, and string him along some more. One moment you're cosying up to him, and the next you act as though you are thinking of his status and the gap between his and your own, causing him to see that you are *genuine* and don't want to court him for his wealth."

"I have not been 'cosying up' with Mr Dryen and I don't ever intend to," Ahzya said firmly back.

"You are a liar, and I see you have no intention of owning up to your wrongdoings," Madam Uran said, her face growing red. "I hereby forbid you from ever—"

"Uran, unfortunately I must stop you from making her take such a vow," Madam Hill interrupted from the doorway. "It seems we have a problem."

"What do you mean, Hill?" Uran said with a frustrated tone.

"Master Dryen is still expressly wishing for Catherine to escort him to the dance," Madam Hill explained, crossing her arms. "Should she refuse, then he swears he won't be attending. Do you realise the problem we face if you forbid her from seeing him?"

"I don't believe it!" Madam Uran said, taken aback. "Are we going to let this seductress have her own way?"

Ahzya clenched her jaw. She would like nothing better than to see this woman slapped for her rudeness. However, Ahzya had already promised herself that she would do nothing to be fired right at this moment. Uran was on the verge of doing so already, and she'd been prepared to beg.

"Now Catherine, you *will* escort Master Dryen to the dance, and you *will* do your absolute best to act in a civilised manner. You will not cause problems that may cast a shadow on his or the castle's reputation," Hill said, looking down at her haughtily.

"Then, come morning you shall return to your duties, and this whole fiasco will be forgotten, just as Jonathan Dryen will forget you," Uran said, turning her face away as if disgusted.

Ahzya simply curtsied. There were a lot of words that Ahzya wished to defend herself with. A majority of them would shock the ladies to hear. Her blood was boiling from the damage to her pride, and she took several deep breaths.

"Good, we will help you prepare tomorrow," Hill said, her demeanour changing. "It's a rare occasion that Master Dryen goes to the dance escorting a young lady. We are secretly very curious about the effect you are having on him."

"I am having no intentional effect of any kind on him, I assure you. However, if I were to speculate as to his reasoning..." Ahzya mused, tapping her chin, "perhaps he finds me a little cute."

Uran huffed. Ahzya decided not to take the situation too seriously. Uran was set against her, no matter how she defended herself, and soon she'd be leaving the castle anyway. She'd just be wasting time trying to convince and win them over.

"I agree with you, Uran. He must have some strange tastes to fall for me, when he is surrounded by so many beautiful ladies of refined and noble backgrounds," Ahzya mused.

"You will watch your tongue, Catherine," Uran said. "You are lucky to have his attention."

"I agree, I agree," Ahzya said, nodding furiously.

"Do not patronise me, Catherine."

"Obviously, I should ensure he enjoys his evening, but at the same time, not tarnish his good name," Ahzya mused. "So, may I request your wise advice on a hypothetical situation?"

Hill and Uran looked at each other and then nodded.

"So, if he were to ask me to marry him tomorrow, should I say yes, because if I say no, it would make him disappointed?" Ahzya asked in a serious tone. "Or should I refuse him, damaging his pride but not dragging him down by being associated with a wretch like me?"

This made both women pause, and Ahzya blinked innocently.

"Of course not, a marriage between the two of you would be totally out of the question," Uran said, after a moment.

"That's what I thought. If you insist, I will attend with Master Dryen," Ahzya said, pushing past them. "Even though, if I choose not to, he'll survive a little disappointment. I doubt he's serious in his threats not to attend. Good evening, ladies."

Ahzya curtsied and left the room, carefully closing the door behind her.

# CHAPTER NINETEEN

MAIN ENTRANCE, CASTLE PRYNESSE, ALPANIA

Jonathan looked up at Ahzya from the bottom of the half spiral staircase and smiled approvingly. Meanwhile, Ahzya was too focused on walking in the high heeled boots Madam Hill had picked out for her. She had been tempted to replace them with her other boots; however, both Hill and Uran still watched over her with stern gazes as she descended the stairs. Ahzya couldn't quite understand why she needed to wear such ridiculous footwear, especially when they couldn't be seen under her long dress anyway.

The dress itself was different from anything else she had ever seen in her life. With draping pale blue silk fabric, it felt like she'd stepped into a swirling sea of soft clouds. The skirt dropped straight down from her waist and flattered her thin hips and legs. A few inches of the skirt dragged on the ground as it had initially been paired with a thick underskirt; however, Ahzya's short stature made it look somewhat strange, so they'd removed it. The bodice of the dress cinched tightly around her form so she barely had any room to breathe. The sleeves started at her biceps instead of the shoulder, leaving her tanned skin exposed at her neck and top of the shoulders. The sleeves themselves were long and flowing; the hem embroidered with black threaded designs. Merida practically forced Ahzya to borrow a thin silver necklace that now hung around her neck.

Getting into and wearing the dress had only been part of her transformation for the evening. Noelle and Merida attended to her in the bath, setting a selection of bottles by its side. Ahzya ignored their gasps as best she could as she stepped out of a robe and into the hot water. Though both maids had almost been bouncing with excitement about attending to her as a lady's maid would, they lost a lot of their spark on viewing her bare skin.

Burn scars marring her thighs disappeared under the surface of the water, and long marks made a hideous pattern on her back. Ahzya chose to act as if these wounds weren't visible and scooped water with her hands to wet her upper body. Merida and Noelle composed themselves and helped her wash, their touches tender over the scars.

Her hair received a whole treatment, from being washed thoroughly in the bath, to being massaged with a bit of oil. Ahzya couldn't deny the fact that she smelt divine from the perfume and oils, so at least she wouldn't have to be embarrassed by her scent. Her short hair was twisted into tight curls and left to set. Her attendants muttered about how to best style her short hair, which, while convenient for everyday life, was hell for formal occasions. They settled for pulling the top half into a small bun, made mostly of hair pins. The rest of the curls, they brushed out to rest on the nape of her neck with loose strands framing her face softly. Several flowers were picked from the garden and tastefully pinned into her hair.

Her makeup took almost as long as her hair, and the other maids were having so much fun that Madam Hill had to hurry them along. They used dark black pencil to line her eyes and dusted her eyelids with a soft crimson colour. Ahzya's skin looked flawless and her eyes an even brighter green by the end. Strawberry-orange tinted lipstick stained her lips, and Ahzya could hardly recognise her own reflection in the mirror.

Ahzya arrived at the end of the stairs; she curtsied to Jonathan as she had been told to do by Madam Hill. She looked up to find Jonathan looking at her with a strange look in his eye. There were only so many leers one could witness in the underworld before one learnt to recognise the lustful desire that burned in the eyes of some men. Fortunately for

Jonathan, though the look was similar to those she sometimes drew in the taverns, his gaze was that of admiration rather than oppressive desire. If it had been anything less pure, Ahzya would have turned tail and damned the consequences.

Jonathan offered his arm and Ahzya accepted it, reluctantly grateful for the support while walking in the boots.

"You look divine," Jonathan complimented as she joined him.

"I have been tortured with knives and fire, but none of those came close to this. I may be so bold as to say that a beauty treatment is the worst torture any girl has ever gone through. I swear I revealed all my darkest secrets in the first three minutes," Ahzya replied earnestly.

"I'm flattered that you would go through such for the likes of me," Jonathan drawled.

"Oh, believe me, if I had a choice, I wouldn't have. But like all other forms of torture, my personal welfare and wishes were not considered," Ahzya whispered back.

Jonathan just chuckled at her declaration and led her through the corridors towards the ballroom. It felt strange to be attending the very ball she had been helping prepare for earlier that day. She had never imagined herself in this kind of situation. Ahzya used to dream of one day getting married; however, even in her dreams, it had never been quite as extravagant as all of this. It all suddenly became very daunting, as they continued towards the giant engraved doors that led to the ballroom. Other couples and finely dressed women and men were mulling around in the hall, and there was a queue to enter.

"Don't be nervous," Jonathan whispered into her ear. "I'll be with you the whole time, and if you embarrass yourself accidentally, I'll come and sweep you away into the night."

"I think that would embarrass me more than anything else," Ahzya stated nervously. "How will I be introduced?"

"Don't worry, I'll handle all of that for you," Jonathan said, smiling down at her.

"If you make it something weird, I promise I'll turn and leave as swiftly as the words leave the announcer's lips," Ahzya replied, tilting her chin up.

Jonathan chuckled again, and Ahzya couldn't help but notice that he was enjoying himself more than usual. His eyes hadn't stopped sparkling since she'd joined him at the stairs. His right hand rested on her hand that hooked under his left arm.

"So, you wouldn't appreciate being introduced as Her Majesty the Queen Catherine Torpay, queen of the dishes and draperies?" Jonathan asked in a low whisper.

Ahzya chuckled half-heartedly and noticed that several of the younger officials were watching her. Whenever she met their gazes, they suddenly looked away with disinterest. Ahzya gave a shrug, they were probably just wondering who the hell she was.

"It seems we are attracting quite a lot of attention," Jonathan stated, guiding her slowly through the crowd. "It must be my partner and the gown I picked out for her. They're both exquisite. I must admit, I don't usually get this much attention on my arrival."

"If you are fishing for an 'oh, you must be joking, people can't help but notice you because you are so handsome' then you should look elsewhere," Ahzya stated, looking up at him.

"You still said it. Do you think I'm handsome?" Jonathan laughed, stepping back to lean forward, drawing level to meet her gaze.

Ahzya rolled her eyes and then sighed. It seemed the night air had changed the tone and feeling between them. Jonathan had continuously flirted with her and drew attention all week; however, his gentle hold and gaze were different. His smile appeared truly genuine. Even his eyes were bright, devoid of their usual scheming darkness.

Perhaps the clothes she wore merely put her under a spell. She wouldn't have been especially surprised when it came to Madam Hill and her strange ways.

They finally made it to the ballroom door, and Ahzya noticed that two guards held them open for the crowd. Ahzya detected utter boredom on the guards' faces as they came to a pause at the door behind several other couples.

"You two appear to be having a thrilling evening," Ahzya spoke up with a friendly tone.

"I must admit, I do feel very much like a glorified doorstop right now, miss," one of the guards answered with a chuckle.

"I would tell everyone to hurry up and stop dawdling; however, I don't think they'd take very kindly to my suggestion," Ahzya stated, her eyes dancing with untamed mischief.

"And while I'd find that very amusing, I would hate for people to think of you badly," the guard answered with a lopsided grin.

"I think you talk too much, soldier," Jonathan said, his tone flat. "Please consider where you are stationed and act accordingly."

Ahzya flashed him a glare and went to remove her hand from his arm. Jonathan's eyes widened a fraction at her sudden recoil. Then his lids lowered, one brow dipped, and he snaked his arm around her waist instead.

"I'm sure Jonathan apologises for his rude attitude," Ahzya said to the guard. "After all, he was once a soldier the same as you, and I am a lowly maid. So according to his words, I should detach myself from him as soon as possible, perhaps I should even bow to you."

Ahzya did a flourished bow and the guards smiled. Jonathan chuckled, the sound vibrating from his chest to her shoulder. Ahzya glanced up at him with raised eyebrows.

"I'm sorry," Jonathan addressed the guard with a now friendly tone. "I'm guilty of jealousy just like the best of men, so you must excuse me if I was rude."

"Not at all," the guard answered, no longer looking the least bit bored. "You'll have to forgive our disappointment that Miss Torpay decided to attend with you despite her refusal yesterday."

"Higher powers were at play," Ahzya sighed in frustration.

She leant to the side and lifted a hand to block the side of her mouth closest to Jonathan. She then continued to whisper loud enough for both guards and Jonathan to hear her.

"I'm actually planning a speedy escape early in the evening, followed by a revenge plan of the sweetest humiliation," Ahzya assured.

"Pardon?" Jonathan interjected.

The guards burst out laughing, and Ahzya saw it as a job well done.

"If you require any co-conspirators, let us know," the guard replied. "For now, we'll allow you entrance to enjoy your evening."

The couples in front of them moved forward, and Ahzya offered a final curtsy to the two guards, who smiled back. Jonathan left his hand resting around her waist as they walked ahead to where a middle-aged man was dressed in over-the-top robes. As the noise volume increased upon entering, Jonathan leant over and said something in the man's ear.

Not only was there lively chatter amongst the multitude of finely dressed individuals but a large group of musicians were also playing a tune in the background. The violins hummed through the air and Ahzya closed her eyes momentarily at the long notes. Ahzya had always been fascinated with the instrument after arriving in Alpania. In Ulkadasa the majority of instruments were used by breathing into them, like flutes and trumpets.

Above the melodic flow of the other instruments, Ahzya heard a particular melody line being played by a single violin. She opened her eyes, trying to pinpoint where the sound was coming from. It took her a moment to see a lone violinist on the balcony above, almost blending in with the curtains. She played as the flow of her body sent her midnight black hair dancing loosely around her form. Her gown was simple, but even with its simplicity, it couldn't reduce the enchanting aura.

"Her Royal Highness, Princess Cleo Erinth," Jonathan said by Ahzya's ear.

Jonathan joined Ahzya in watching the princess on the balcony. The information surprised Ahzya, as she would have expected a royal to entertain the crowds while front and centre.

"Why is she hidden way up there instead of playing with the band?" Ahzya asked. "Her playing is magnificent; I've never heard something so beautiful."

"She's not playing for us. Watch her, she's in a world of her own," Jonathan said.

Cleo's eyes closed as if she were the only one in the room. As the melody picked up a more jovial rhythm, she bounced and spun. A smile lit up her face and her bow slid across the strings smoothly.

"Cleo isn't the kind of person who enjoys drawing attention. She's much like you in that aspect," Jonathan continued. "Some people think she is strange and weird, but I know that she's just not the type to prattle on like the rest of the nobility."

"I'd say you're leading the way of the prattling nobility," Ahzya ribbed.

"My prattle is tactical, theirs is nonsensical," Jonathan defended.

"Still, she must truly love her family. She travelled far for her mother's birthday."

"It would be strange if the princesses didn't show up for such an important celebration," Jonathan explained, before moving forward.

"Come, I think the attendant wishes to announce us."

Sure enough, moments later the attendant called out with a booming voice.

"Introducing Sir Jonathan Dryen and Miss Catherine Torpay," the attendant called.

Several people in the room turned to look at them, and Ahzya gripped onto Jonathan's arm without thinking. Jonathan just smiled at the crowd and Ahzya followed his lead.

"I see you refrained from an unusual introduction," Ahzya said, trying to ease her nerves with conversation. "I'm a little disappointed by how simple it was."

"I was going to have him announce you and me as a couple, but I thought you'd leave me for sure," Jonathan explained. "Something along the lines of 'Jonathan Dryen and his beautiful, sophisticated partner, Miss Catherine Torpay' would sound pleasant to my ears."

"That wouldn't be so bad," Ahzya stated calmly. "They can already see that I am your date, and as for the beautiful and sophisticated part, they can clearly see that's true."

"I can go and tell him to reintroduce us in that manner if you wish," Jonathan said, grinning.

"I think I'll pass on that offer."

It took only a moment for them to be surrounded by people when they reached the bottom of the stairs. Ahzya was introduced to so many people at once that it was impossible from the very beginning to remember them all. It was only when they parted to allow a beautiful blonde into the circle that Ahzya had a moment to process any of what was happening.

The blonde had hair curled and pinned up onto her head, and her blue eyes danced below long lashes. With the blonde's richly designed dress, Ahzya could tell that a large sum of money had been invested in the outfit. From sparkling gems along the bodice to the jewellery hanging from her neck, wrists and ears, everything was lavish.

"Sir Jonathan Dryen, you should be more aware next time and ensure your partner isn't swamped," the blonde stated cheerfully. "I'm sure she is quite bewildered by your popularity."

"Your Royal Highness, believe me, it was not my intention to overwhelm her," Jonathan answered, bowing deeply to the blonde. "Had I realised such, I would have kept her to myself all evening."

"Saying such things! Mind your manners," the blonde said, slapping him gently on the shoulder. "Your partner seems just as surprised by your actions."

Well past being surprised by any of Jonathan's flirtatious lines, Ahzya offered a resigned smile.

"Now, won't you introduce us?" the blonde urged, smiling back at her pleasantly.

"After your harsh comments, I'm not sure I want to," Jonathan said reluctantly, before he promptly continued with their introduction. "Your Royal Highness, this is Catherine Torpay, Catherine, meet Her Royal Highness, Princess Anna Erinth."

"It's a pleasure to meet you, I've heard so much about you from my handmaid and mother," Anna said immediately. "You must come and meet my sister."

Jonathan cleared his throat, but Anna hooked her arm into Ahzya's.

"I'll be borrowing her for a while," Anna practically sang to Jonathan. "You have plenty of other people who wish to speak with you."

Jonathan looked down at Ahzya with a look that was a mix of sympathy and something else Ahzya again couldn't quite decipher. He released Ahzya's arm as Anna began to drag her away.

"I'm sorry if I seem rude interrupting and then dragging you away," Anna apologised while sticking close as they zigzagged through the masses. "Jonathan does get a lot of attention at these things, and you looked a little bit bewildered."

"I must admit, I was feeling a little claustrophobic," Ahzya offered in response.

"I love him, but that daft man should have respected your refusal at the market," Anna stated, tsking her tongue in disapproval. "I'm glad you've come though. When Cleo and I heard about the tale, we wanted to meet you and cheer you on."

Anna guided her almost in a dance through the crowd, and finally, they arrived at a platform where King Mark and Queen Maria were both sitting and talking with other people. Ahzya spotted Princess Cleo standing at the back of the platform. She was in the middle of a conversation with Commander Ray, and both looked up as Anna stood beside them.

"Ray, I believe you have met Catherine?" Anna stated with a genuine, yet ever-constant, smile.

"Indeed, but it's a pleasure to see you here tonight, Miss Torpay," Ray said with a bow. "Now, ladies, I must go, people to see and all that sort of business."

The three women smiled at him and curtsied as he turned and walked away.

"I'm Cleo, Catherine, it's a pleasure to meet you," Cleo said, introducing herself.

"Cleo, I'm supposed to introduce you!" Anna said, pouting.

"And what would the difference be other than the words coming from your mouth instead of my own?" Cleo answered, her voice soft like velvet.

"Argh, fine," Anna sighed. "Do either of you want a drink?"

"I'm fine, thank you," Cleo answered her sister quietly.

"I wouldn't mind a drink if you are going to get one yourself," Ahzya answered.

"Alright, two drinks coming right up. Wish me luck in my journey through the swamp to the drinks table," Anna joked with a bubbly laugh.

"May your journey be swift and blessed, and may no giant stomp on your feet," Cleo stated, making a random symbol in the air with her hands.

Ahzya and Cleo were left alone as Anna disappeared into the crowd. Cleo remained silent for a moment, and Ahzya didn't know whether to say something or to stay quiet. Ahzya didn't mind being silent for a bit, but she didn't know whether it would be considered rude to do so.

Up close, Cleo held as much regal charm as she had from the balcony. Her eyes were a strange dark blue, appearing indigo in light, with a dark ring around them that made the colour pop. A ring on her right hand connected by a chain to a bracelet on her wrist and a pair of diamond studs twinkled in her ears, but otherwise her skin was free of jewellery.

"I apologise if we both seem peculiar," Cleo stated suddenly. "I dragged her into another country for a couple of months, and I guess she caught my weirdness during that time. Though I don't feel truly sorry, because I do enjoy the results of my corruption. She'd begun to fade under the spotlights the nobility aimed at her here, but she got her spark back."

"The most joyful memories in life are those ridiculous moments spent with someone you love," Ahzya reassured quickly. "I had a friend who I used to joke around with all the time. People could hardly take us seriously and thought we were mad half the time."

Cleo laughed softly and crossed her arms in a relaxed position across her chest.

"I guess we will get along then," Cleo stated with a smile. "Some people are prone to misunderstand things that they don't experience themselves, but if embracing differences is enough to class us as mad, then mad I'll be."

Cleo chuckled and motioned for Ahzya to take a seat. Ahzya was glad for the rest, as the heels of the boots were killer on her feet, and she wasn't sure if she could survive the whole night without removing them.

"My sister seems to have been interrupted in her mission by a group of visiting friends," Cleo stated. "I guess my blessings failed this time."

Ahzya gazed towards where Anna had disappeared and noticed that several young men and women surrounded her. She also spotted Lesley moving through the crowd, a tray of drinks held above her head. Guests reached up and took glasses as she passed by them. Suddenly a man stepped back and the tray, which luckily only had one drink left on it, toppled over. The drink spilt all over a young man's shoulder, and Lesley looked horrified. Lesley frantically tried to mop up the liquid, even while she curtsied continuously in apology.

"Oh, the poor girl," Cleo exclaimed beside her. "Fortunately, that's my cousin, and he's just laughing it off."

"I should go and see if she is alright," Ahzya said, standing up. "I'll be back later, though, if you don't mind my company."

"Not at all, if you don't return, I'll personally head a search party to retrieve you from the masses."

"Even though I'm only pretending to be a lady, and I'll be serving you breakfast tomorrow?"

"We may live in a classist society, Catherine, but I have never allowed mere class to dictate how I treat the people around me," Cleo stated seriously. "As a maid you may experience the dark side of elitism, but that doesn't define who you are. You have probably worked harder in your life than any of the nobility in this room. I choose who I interact with, not ridiculous rules."

Ahzya began to understand why all the soldiers and maids respected Cleo and the buzz that had followed the news of her arrival at the castle that morning. Cleo wasn't as forward as others in the royal family, but she had a maturity and warmth of character that Ahzya didn't see in many people.

Ahzya curtsied, and Cleo nodded a goodbye before turning to watch the first official dance of the evening begin. Ahzya pushed past people but was going against the natural flow of the crowd. She managed to squeeze through, the bodice of her dress causing her to take short breaths in recovery.

Ahzya slipped out of the ballroom, following in the direction Lesley had disappeared. The door of a small office was ajar nearby, and Ahzya heard several voices drifting from the doorway.

"I'm sorry, Madam Uran. It was an accident," Lesley's sweet voice said apologetically.

"How could you be so careless?" Madam Uran's voice said accusingly. "I wouldn't be surprised if we receive a complaint about it."

"I would like to see you manoeuvre between that horde without spilling something," Ahzya interrupted, stepping through the door.

Lesley tried to warn her off with a shake of her head and an urgent glance. Ahzya was still seething from the treatment to Noelle the week she'd arrived and also the evidence of mistreatment she'd spied on the other maids. If no-one dared to stand up, then Lesley would be the next person to be beaten.

"Pardon me?" Uran asked in a shocked tone.

"People are bumping and moving around constantly out there," Ahzya stated. "I'm surprised an accident didn't happen earlier. You are being unfair in your criticism of Lesley."

"You should watch your tongue or I'll—" Uran said, temper flaring.

"You'll beat me like you did the other maids?" Ahzya finished, her tone cold as ice. "Go ahead!"

"Lesley you may leave, just make sure it doesn't happen again," Uran stated, pointing towards the door. "Catherine wishes to speak with me alone."

Lesley shot Ahzya a sympathetic look, but Ahzya smiled back with a wink. Lesley's gaze switched to that of guilt as she realised what Ahzya was purposely doing, but the door slammed shut the moment she was out. Uran locked the door with a noticeable click and turned back to face Ahzya.

"You think you are quite the hero, don't you?" Uran stated with a sneer. "Let me tell you now. Your goody two-shoes act won't last very long once I'm done with you."

Ahzya had already braced herself for the impact, but the slap left her ear ringing nonetheless. Another blow was dealt to her jaw, this time with a clenched fist. Ahzya's sight blurred slightly, but she straightened after the strike.

"You should realise now that the only person you should be concerned about is yourself," Uran said, punching Ahzya in the face once again. "No-one else is going to stand up for you, or defend your actions, or even care one jot what you are feeling."

"Is that what you tell all the girls?" Ahzya stated evenly. "Do you tell them all that so they stop standing by each other? Because I'm sorry, but you could break all my bones and yet I would still use my last breaths to defend those women."

Uran slapped her again, and her eyes were boiling with rage by that point. The temptation to turn on Uran and choke her was strong. However, Ahzya didn't need a body to deal with, and everyone would guess it had been her anyway.

"No-one ever stood by me," Uran stated fiercely. "We are all selfish beings, and only the most selfish will survive."

"Perhaps you should stop passing your own demons onto others," Ahzya stated firmly.

Ahzya met Uran's gaze evenly and didn't blink as a minute ticked by.

"Excuse me, little miss popular," Uran spat. "I have work to do."

Uran unlocked the door and exit the room, slamming the door shut behind her. Ahzya's face stung, but nothing seemed broken, and no blood was drawn. All in all, it had all been worth it, and Lesley escaped without harm. With a roaring headache, Ahzya didn't feel like returning to the party, and a lady's powder room was close by, so escaping there was her best bet.

# CHAPTER TWENTY

MAIN BALLROOM, CASTLE PRYNESSE, ALPANIA

The moment Ahzya returned to the ballroom, her hand was claimed for a dance by an official. Ahzya spent most of the dance looking up at his chin, which he kept at an upward angle. The official had quirked his brow and pranced around with his ears pricked in an air of self-importance. Ahzya politely listened to the official talk about his status and where he worked and how he knew King Mark personally. She wasn't surprised when it was revealed he was the nephew of the adviser who'd prattled on to King Mark in the royal courtyard.

Then along came Jae Kim, cousin of Cleo and Anna on their mother's side, and still wearing the drink-stained shirt from Lesley's earlier accident. He neither spoke too much about himself nor expected her to talk about herself, instead he marvelled on the various characters at the celebration and the refreshments table he'd spotted at the far end of the room. Having found a common interest in the food served, they twirled and dipped their way across the room to the point of interest. They spent a few lovely minutes dining on the tiny morsels of food, before Jonathan appeared at her side.

With a bow, he invited her to dance and dance they did. Ahzya focused on Jonathan's movements, so she could easily follow how he led them in the dance. Jonathan seemed too focused on thoughts far away and his unusual silence made Ahzya somewhat curious. Any question that may have parted her lips was interrupted by Jae cutting in to claim the rest of the song. Jonathan was jolted from his daydream when Jae tapped him on the shoulder and actually looked reluctant to release Ahzya's hand. However, a bold lady quickly ducked in to claim Jonathan's arm.

"You appear to be quite the adept dancer, Miss Torpay," Anna commented as Ahzya and Jae joined a small circle of the royal cousins. "Your movements are graceful yet purposeful."

"You flatter me, I'm only quick to observe. I've never attended a ball, my feet are more accustomed to village jigs, so the whole notion is new to me, Your Royal Highness," Ahzya replied, snagging a drink from a passing tray.

"Having a great partner makes things easier," Jae commented.

"I see, and I assume you speak of yourself with that statement, thus why you stole her from Jonathan Dryen earlier?" Anna spoke up cheerily.

"I felt my cutting in would be welcomed, considering our Jonathan appeared tongue tied."

"Since you seem to have such high knowledge of ball customs, do you feel that conversation in a dance is highly necessary, Jae?" Cleo asked, her arms crossed comfortably in front of her.

"No, not necessarily, a lot can be said without words. However, in such situations, there is usually a requirement for a more intimate setting," Jae answered, receiving several raised eyebrows. "I've heard that those, specifically in a marital relationship, may leave conversation to the non-verbal cues: a sultry look, the brush of skin against skin, a kiss perhaps. I will refrain from saying more as that may be ungentlemanly. As I am a gentleman, I was unaware of a marriage between Miss Torpay and the Mister Dryen, therefore I felt it was my duty to save her from such an awkward dance. There was the chance that Jonathan was merely boring Miss Torpay, but I didn't want to take chances."

"You could have been a gentleman and saved me from Vincent, Jae," Yuna, a female cousin and Jae's sister, cried. "He took an interest in telling me about all his business in Luseo, and every one of the acquaintances he made there."

"Sounds like you had no shortage of conversation then, no need for me to interfere," Jae answered with a grin.

"It was a sermon, not a conversation," Yuna said, her shoulders drooping.

"Well, that's good, you could do with receiving a few more teachings on top of the church services we attend each week."

"You're a menace, brother," Yuna said, hitting his arm in frustration.

A young man approached the group, one hand sweeping back his hair and the other straightening his coat. With a deep bow, he offered a hand to Yuna and, at a pitch a little too loud even in a crowded ballroom, asked her to dance.

"I'd be honoured to," Yuna answered, taking the offered hand, her cheeks flushing.

"Just make sure you don't talk about your business or acquaintances, or she'll come gossip to us about you," Jae said, slapping the young man on the shoulder.

"I wasn't planning to," the young man answered directly. "Yuna is far too intelligent and accomplished to force the conversation onto such ridiculously mundane topics."

Jae chuckled as they watched the pair circle onto the dance floor and join the throng.

"Those two have liked each other for years," Jae said, leaning towards Ahzya. "Neither of them seems to have enough courage to actually move forward with those feelings though."

"They're still young, they'll figure it out," Ahzya said with a smile.

"Ooh, spoken like advice derived from knowledge and wisdom," Jae said, raising his eyebrows. "Is there a suitor for you, Miss Torpay? Surely not Jonathan Dryen?"

"Certainly not," Ahzya firmly replied, causing Jae to smile slyly. "My heart is a rather stubborn soul at the best of times and firmly attached elsewhere."

"Dare I pry?"

"Food," Ahzya answered with a grin. "It's all there is room for at the end of the day."

"Indeed, how understandable. It gives energy, it gives comfort and it's delicious…"

"Then shall we make it a party of three and raid the refreshments table?" Cleo queried.

Cleo, Ahzya and Jae made a curious group, spinning and ducking dancing couples. A glass of alcohol surging through her veins, Ahzya's mood felt bubbly as she let out a merry and genuine laugh.

SOUTHERN BALCONY, CASTLE PRYNESSE, ALPANIA

Ahzya sensed Jonathan's presence long before his footsteps alerted her to his approach to her side. Ahzya had escaped the crowds to get some fresh air and cool her flushed cheeks. Considering how late it was, the option of going back to her quarters was tempting.

Jonathan smelled of alcohol and perfume. Obviously, he'd been having an enjoyable evening after she had left him. Ahzya swore she even saw a smear of lipstick on the collar of his shirt.

"My date abandoned me for the night air of the balcony?" Jonathan drawled, resting his elbows on the railing. "Does my angel feel closer to the heavens by doing so?"

"I had to visit my brethren at some point. They miss me greatly," Ahzya said, waving her hand towards the starry night sky. "Besides, you didn't seem to miss my presence at your side. Some might say you came to life once I left."

"Jealous?" Jonathan said flirtatiously.

"Relieved actually," Ahzya said curtly. "For you can return to your admiring crowds, and I can retire to my room for a well-needed rest."

"Admit it," Jonathan said, mirth evident in his features, "you're enjoying yourself."

"I am," Ahzya admitted, but her brow furrowed. "It feels hypocritical somehow."

Jonathan didn't say anything in reply to that. He turned his back to the railing and tilted his head to survey her. He reached out to hold her shoulder, his eyes showing concern as she turned her face into the light. Jonathan stepped closer to study her face. His gaze rested on her jaw and cheek where Madam Uran struck her earlier. Ahzya didn't think it would have bruised so soon after and she still had makeup on.

"What happened to your cheek?" Jonathan asked, his sudden concern caught Ahzya off-guard.

"I ran into something," Ahzya replied, looking up at him nonchalantly.

Jonathan seemed thoroughly unconvinced. Ahzya winced as he ran his thumb over the bruise.

"Like you weren't aware that this could happen," Ahzya scoffed, weirdly annoyed by his reaction. "It's not right for common maids to befriend nobility or be invited to balls."

"I only thought you'd enjoy it," Jonathan replied.

"Enjoy what?" Ahzya hissed in an angry whisper. "Befriending the friends and family of a man I plan to kill? Even with my dulled conscience, that doesn't feel right."

"I meant the sense of freedom," Jonathan reasoned, with a shake of his head. "From what I know, you're always hiding and running. After you complete this job, you'll be pursued unceasingly. I wanted you to take this time to be pampered and have fun."

"Forgive me if I don't find it fun to be bullied and bashed by the head maids," Ahzya sassed.

"One of the head maids did this to you? Why?"

"It's not uncommon," Ahzya replied honestly. "The head maids are both accustomed to dealing punishment to those who don't please them. Uran is the worst one; I don't believe Hill would do it herself, though she definitely turns a blind eye."

"They beat you because of me?" Jonathan asked, his gaze darkening.

"Don't flatter yourself. They do hate me because they believe I'm the one seducing you, but I'm capable of earning my battle scars," Ahzya explained jovially. "I defended one of the maids from unfair criticism and received a slap or two instead."

Jonathan's aura had turned murderous. His jaw clenched shut and he glared at the bruise on her face as if it were a sworn nemesis. Ahzya grew uncomfortable, as her sass and light-hearted explanation only worsened his mood.

"Does it hurt?" Jonathan asked, his eyes softening as he met her gaze.

"Nah, really, I've been through much worse," Ahzya answered with a shrug.

This statement was true. The severe scars on her back and thighs were the obvious marks from her past of abuse. Even that didn't begin to explain the amount of physical strain and injuries she had endured in the past. Her experience didn't make the places on her cheek and jaw sting any less.

Jonathan's palm cupped her chin and tilted her head in several different directions. Ahzya raised an eyebrow, unimpressed by his strange assessing methods. He caressed her bruise again, the skin tender to his touch, and the pain caused her to flinch. Ahzya pulled away, wrenching her head out of his gentle grasp. Jonathan's eyes widened somewhat in surprise.

"You know, I don't usually get that kind of reaction," Jonathan pondered, letting his hand drop to his side.

"Oh really? So, you go around touching maids' bruised cheeks often then?" Ahzya said, drawing further away and wrapping her arms around herself in faux protection.

Jonathan didn't immediately respond with one of his usual quips. The pause drew out so long that Ahzya began to think that maybe he no longer wanted to talk. She wouldn't have minded it, but she noticed that Jonathan's expression had grown dark again. His eyes held such ferocious anger that Ahzya felt transfixed. It was a raw emotion, and a thrill ran up her spine at the familiarity.

"This is why he doesn't deserve to be king," Jonathan stated, his voice low and sharp.

"It's all done behind closed doors," Ahzya reasoned, looking away. "King Mark probably isn't even aware it's happening."

"How can he rule a country when he doesn't even know what goes on in his own castle behind closed doors? A king's whole role is to know and to act; serve justice. Instead, he's too busy employing advisers who can only advise him on how their wives are complaining about their spending money."

Ahzya snorted at how accurately it described several of the advisers around King Mark.

"So, you think he is unsuited to be king," Ahzya said pointedly. "Why not get rid of the advisers; become the counsel he needs? Instead, you want to pass the judgement into your own hands by having him killed?"

"Partially. I'm not asking you to understand my reasons," Jonathan warned, switching his glare directly at her. "Despite what you may think, there is more to it than you could ever imagine. I told you before not to dig any further; I suggest you take the hint and stop."

"Calm down, Jonathan," Ahzya said, brushing off his sudden hostility. "I'm not about to argue with you. I never insisted on you telling me. Besides, I understand your sentiment."

"You understand?" Jonathan asked, raising an eyebrow.

"Mm, I'm not merely in this for the money either," Ahzya stated, staring out at the night sky.

"Then why are you doing it?" Jonathan asked curiously.

"I can't say," Ahzya said slyly, before wagging a finger at him. "I warn you, JP, if you try to dig any further, I will not take kindly to it. Two can play at secrecy. Honestly, as long as our end games are the same, the individual rationalisation doesn't matter."

Jonathan suddenly chuckled, and the dark light to his eyes disappeared as quickly as it had appeared. He found her payback amusing, and Ahzya relaxed against the railing of the balcony.

"So, why did you become a portreeve over in Triox?" Ahzya asked, her tone casual.

"I thought I would enjoy the challenge that it promised," Jonathan replied, breathing out a stream of vapour into the night sky. "The castle was stifling; I felt I couldn't breathe."

"The officials, soldiers and even King Mark seem impressed by your efforts down there. Keeping the evil at bay, they say," Ahzya continued, rolling her shoulders.

"Yes, well I can say that I undoubtedly have more power over there than the last portreeve managed," Jonathan answered seriously. "Triox was in a terrible situation when I arrived there."

"If you can't beat them, join them?" Ahzya asked, her eyes narrowing as she glanced across at him. "Seems like that was your approach."

"I have had a lot of doubt thrown at my methods. However, the facts show that crime has improved even if it hasn't completely disappeared."

"Your methods of taking away the curfew and reducing soldiers on the streets mustn't have been a popular decision amongst the officials."

Jonathan glanced across at her with a look that was a mix of amusement and surprise.

"I didn't know you took such a keen interest in my work," Jonathan stated with a tilt of his head.

"Boredom makes people research the strangest things," Ahzya answered without a moment's hesitation. "You seem to forget that I live in Triox and have done so for a few years. Consider it the questions of a citizen of your province. The changes seemed crazy for a royal officer to establish, and I'm curious to know what your thought process behind that was."

"Once I removed the curfew and reduced the number of guards the level of thefts and violence slowly dropped," Jonathan stated.

"Seems crazy," Ahzya mused.

"Without the thrill of nearly getting caught, stealing becomes just an ordinary task," Jonathan stated. "Many of them are only thieves because they like the thrill of the steal and the attention that their near-misses give them."

"Really?"

"Triox is a wealthy port province and trade is incredibly successful, even with the crime rate. There isn't much to entertain and the thrill seekers increased. Illegal fights led to betting; betting led to fights over money; the domino effect was evident. It was an unpopular approach, and I'd probably get punished if they knew that I began to see the black market as something to be harnessed rather than something to be destroyed. Again, if I allow some leeway and enforce things secretly, many of the criminals just returned to everyday life."

"Is that the real reason you think I'd appreciate you drawing attention to me? Do you think I chase this thrill of being caught?" Ahzya asked, her eyes narrowing.

"I already told you my reason, so that's not the case," Jonathan drawled, his tone changing. "It's not bad attention. They just think you are a beautiful woman, who's caught my eye."

"Pfft. Well, just to be sure, I'm not simply in this for some thrill-seeking adventure. I'm one of the scary ones," Ahzya stated, and she saw Jonathan smirk. "I'm the type who steals to survive. I'll survive by biting, scraping and clawing my way through life."

"I don't think you are scary," Jonathan said, leaning over the railing of the balcony. "I find you charming. The only thing I find scary about you is that you hold so much of my heart."

Ahzya glanced across at him as his puppy dog eyes sparkled with conspicuous amusement. Her mind flashed back to the conversation with Madam Uran earlier. Ahzya was quite sure she wasn't disappointing him, especially when all he wanted from her was someone he could tease mercilessly.

"Your flirting skills are what I find scary," Ahzya replied coolly.

"Because they affect you in strange ways?" Jonathan asked, his voice deepening.

"No. It's scary because I fear for your future. How will you ever find a bride when your lines are so horrible it's like they are coming from an immature sixteen-year-old running high on testosterone?" Ahzya said, turning away from him with a purposeful flick of her hair.

"Ouch," Jonathan said with a fake wince.

"I think I'll retire to my room now," Ahzya said, the night breeze playing with loose strands of her hair. "An angel shouldn't have too much excitement in one night or they might begin to desire a permanent home on this earth, and that just cannot be."

# CHAPTER TWENTY-ONE

## Sephe 1407

maid's Quarters, castle prynesse, alpania

Noelle almost pounced on Ahzya the moment she walked through the door of their small quarters. Already dressed in her nightgown, Noelle's face was rosy red from recently scrubbing. Her eyes sparkled happily, and she hugged Ahzya tightly. Noelle only released her for a moment to admire Ahzya's dress with a long sweeping glance.

"You look so gorgeous, Cath!" Noelle cooed.

"Thank you, Noelle," Ahzya said, prying herself gently from Noelle's arms and dropping onto the cot with a sigh. "Did you get off early from the celebrations?"

"Early?" Noelle repeated incredulously. "I only escaped half an hour ago and it's around three in the morning! We've both been awake since three this morning—I mean yesterday morning!"

"I guess time flies when you're having fun," Ahzya said sarcastically.

Noelle didn't seem to notice the sarcastic note in her voice because she let out a short, excited squeal. She then started dancing with an invisible partner around the room, which meant taking a couple of steps towards the door and returning, making her nightgown swirl around her.

"The dances were all so sophisticated," Noelle stated. "I could barely keep up with what they were doing, but they moved as if it were their second nature. It is so much different from the country dances I've gone to. I'd be a complete fool if I had to try and remember all those dainty steps. I can barely handle grabbing a partner by the hand and spinning around aimlessly!"

"Believe me, I was completely out of my element," Ahzya stated, reaching to try to unbutton the back of her dress awkwardly. "I practically just held onto Jae for dear life."

Noelle giggled and approached Ahzya to help unbutton the dress.

"It didn't look that way, in fact, I heard the other ladies stating how jealous they were when you were dancing with Jonathan Dryen," Noelle said cheerfully.

"Jealous about my partner, not my dancing skills," Ahzya countered, allowing Noelle to help her out of the dress.

"Jonathan Dryen seems like an incredibly nice man," Noelle stated with a sly smile. "What do you think about him, Catherine?"

"Well, he is handsome…" Ahzya pondered, drawing out her answer.

"Mhmm," Noelle sighed, indicating for her to continue.

"He's well-liked by the king and nigh on everyone else."

"Great qualities in a man."

"He has a unique sense of humour and knows just what to say—"

"Sounds like heaven, it's rare to find men like him nowadays," Noelle stated, watching Ahzya closely. "The boys back home used to put grubs in my lunch pail and then had the nerve to say that they liked me."

"I hope one day you find a boy who puts flowers in your lunch pail instead."

"Or even better: jewels and gold," Noelle replied, a peal of laughter following her comment.

"I wouldn't rule out the possibility that Jonathan Dryen would put grubs in lunch pails too," Ahzya continued with her assessment. "He is a brilliant liar; an utter nuisance, and a complete—" Ahzya stopped herself from swearing. "I hate his annoying smile whenever someone compliments him. Ergh, I've never met someone who made me want to punch their face in so badly."

"Talk about full circle! I thought you were interested in him. He certainly seems to have taken quite a shine to you."

"He enjoys torturing me with his teasing and incessant company, that's for sure. Why is everyone taking his interest in me to be romantically inclined?" Ahzya said, pulling on her sleepwear with a swiftness due to the cold.

"Maybe because he invited you to a royal ball and bought you a gorgeous dress. Men don't invite women they're not interested in to royal balls. Besides, perhaps we see things about him that you haven't noticed?" Noelle offered, lifting her knees so that her chin rested on them. "Like when you are focused on working and he watches you with a concerned look on his face. Or when he glares down any other guy who looks like he is taking an interest in you. Oh, and his smiles whenever you offer to carry a heavy tray for one of the other maids. I even heard that one of the ladies this evening tried to seduce him and even kissed his neck!"

"I saw evidence of such a claim," Ahzya replied with a snort.

"But he pushed her away, saying she should return to the party and retain what was left of her dignity, because he wasn't interested in her," Noelle gossiped.

"Never!" Ahzya denied, with a shake of her head. "He must just be bored. I'd be bored if I had to hang out with annoying officials and doting ladies all day too."

"You're not being honest," Noelle chided softly.

"Even if he is in love with me, I can't return his feelings," Ahzya said firmly.

"Why not? Because you are a maid and he is an official?" Noelle asked. "Can't true love win in the end; become a happy love story between the classes. It usually turns into a scandal, where the one in the lower class is tossed aside. Imagine a marriage where both parties are dedicated and power through prejudices."

"I'm sure Jonathan would be able to do whatever he wanted. I doubt anyone would have the power to change his mind, or oppose him in his decisions," Ahzya said, slipping under the covers of her cot. "The madams would just have to put up with it, along with all the other nosy nobles."

"So, what's wrong with the attachment?" Noelle pressed.

"There's someone else," Ahzya admitted quietly.

"Oh? Ooh!" Noelle exclaimed. "Well, that makes sense then! Why didn't you just say so?"

Ahzya kept quiet and flopped her head down on the pillow. Hair pins stabbed into her scalp, and she bit down a yelp. She sat up to wrestle the weapons out of her hair, trying not to yank out her own hair while doing so.

"Is it a one-sided love?" Noelle continued with the questions. "Did they not return your affection, but you still hold onto the love you have for them? How tragically loyal, you poor thing!"

Ahzya could sense the tragic love tales swirling around in Noelle's mind, but she couldn't bring herself to brush off the sudden ache in her chest. Finally free of pins, Ahzya's hair splayed across the pillow as she lay down. Her hand snaked under the pillow.

"Did you confess your feelings? Perhaps he really does love you back after all," Noelle said, her voice becoming hopeful for Ahzya. "Sometimes men are so dense that they don't even realise our nuanced affections."

Noelle wasn't taking the hint Ahzya's silence to end the conversation, so Ahzya relented with a half-hearted laugh. "He returned the love. He even confessed his attraction first."

"Then what is his name? What does he do?" Noelle asked, her eyes brightening.

Ahzya rolled onto her side to face Noelle. The poor girl had been starved of any romantic conversation for the past few months and now that Ahzya had confessed a romance, Noelle was hooked. Ahzya understood that most girls craved such conversations now and then. The conversation wasn't going to end well if Noelle continued pressing for information.

"Come on, Ahzya, you are the first real friend I've had here. I want to learn more about you," Noelle begged. "Back home I have a large family. I miss the adventures and conversations with them. The other maids haven't a skerrick of romance, what with the ban by the madam monsters."

"What about your former roommate?" Ahzya asked, propping herself up. "Was it, Blaire?"

"Blaire? She didn't have a romantic bone in her body," Noelle said in confusion.

"Didn't she elope with a guard though? That's why they're so uptight about the rules?"

"That's what they say, but it doesn't make sense. Blaire was tense the day before she disappeared. She seemed more frightened than excited. Her disappearance did coincide with that of a castle guard, but I don't see how they'd be connected. The guard had grown up in Alpania and Blaire was originally from Liondel."

Noelle stated these things as if it were impossible for them to know each other when they grew up in different countries and weren't stationed in similar places in the castle.

"Anyhow," Noelle dismissed quickly. "Your lover?"

Ahzya closed her eyes and let out a deep sigh.

"He passed away," Ahzya stated, her heart suddenly aching.

Noelle tensed up as Ahzya watched her from across the room. Noelle opened her mouth a couple of times like a goldfish, but no sound came out. The realisation shocked Noelle into silence and Ahzya felt bad. She left her bed and wrapped her arms around Noelle.

"I probably should have said that from the beginning," Ahzya soothed. "I don't talk about it."

"I am deeply sorry," Noelle blurted out.

"It is fine. You didn't know," Ahzya answered quietly. "Now you know Jonathan will move on to another pretty woman or embrace his bachelor life of solitude, and I will stay as I am."

Noelle's arms encircled Ahzya, her hand patting her back. Ahzya rested her head against Noelle.

"Sometimes, I do want to talk about him, he was pretty cute," Ahzya recollected nostalgically. "It's just that I'm the only one around me who remembers him, so it feels like a precious secret I shouldn't utter aloud."

"You don't have to force yourself to talk about him, but don't silence your memories either," Noelle advised. "Sometimes, telling people who don't know, keeps the good memories alive."

"I'll consider it," Ahzya said, detaching herself gently and returning to her own bed. "Good night, Noelle."

"Good night, Cath," Noelle said.

Noelle finally settled down to sleep and Ahzya soon heard her soft breathing from the other side of the room. Sleep eluded Ahzya as she hugged the embroidered handkerchief from under her pillow. Pushing the handkerchief to her chest, her eyes ached to let tears slip down her cheeks.

## Five Years Earlier: Feybel 1402

### Kilerth, Northern Province, Alpania

Cole recognised her in the middle of a crowded marketplace, where she doubted even Peter would have noticed her. Curled in an alleyway, Ahzya wished that one of those sweet buns she saw people taking around would somehow make it into her possession. It should be easy to steal it, especially with that group of beautiful ladies attracting the store owner's attention.

Ahzya snuck forward and slipped unnoticed by some rather refined gentlemen. The crowd was thick, and several ladies sneered at her tattered clothing as she pushed past but paid little attention to her beyond that. It had been eight months since she had run away from Port Joonver, and her clothes were a little worse for wear. Street dust clung to her skin like a disease and every day Ahzya bathed in the creek nearby to rid herself of the brown layer.

Ahzya liked to hide her small pack of belongings at her makeshift camp before entering the town each morning. The street urchins had a habit of stealing from fellow children. Ahzya was older than the majority of them; however, that didn't deter any of them from trying to take her pack the moment she arrived. Ahzya couldn't blame them, it was difficult for them to survive and many of them starved or died due to illness.

Now, with the smell of sweet buns drifting into her senses, her stomach rumbled with hunger and anticipation. There was a certain thrill that came from stealing, but it was a sickening feeling for Ahzya. She didn't deserve to receive anything from the vendor. She, a mere orphan and immigrant, should have been happy and stayed at the orphanage in Ulkadasa.

The sweet bun owner flirtatiously spoke with a woman at one side of the stall and Ahzya casually reached for one of the paper bags which contained the buns. She tried to appear confident and innocent, so that her movements didn't catch anyone's attention. With the bag now in her clutches, Ahzya began to turn away, but the stall owner chose to look across at that moment. She froze as their eyes met, and the owner quickly frowned and reached out to grab hold of her.

"Oi, don't you dare try and steal from me!" the stall owner yelled.

His hand grabbed onto her wrist like a clamp and Ahzya gasped quietly. The crowd around the stall turned to look at her with sneers and frowns. They backed away from her, as if they thought they could contract a sickness. Her heart beat faster as she glanced around at the judging faces and back at the angry stall owner. Ahzya flinched as he lashed out at her, striking the side of her head with the palm of his hand multiple times.

"Excuse me, but what seems to be the matter here?" a male voice called from behind Ahzya.

The voice sounded oddly familiar and Ahzya didn't dare turn around lest it was someone who would recognise her. The crowd fell silent around the stall and Ahzya could hear her heart beating in her ears. Her face stung and grew heated from the impact from the vendor's hand.

"I just caught this rotten thief trying to take one of my buns," the stall owner answered, his voice filled with rage.

"I doubt this young lady would do such a thing," the male voice answered. "I'm her friend and I believe she was merely waiting for you so she could pay."

At this statement, Ahzya turned her head to peek over her shoulder. Standing with his arms crossed and ash-blonde hair peeking out of a soldier's cap, was Cole. His grey-green eyes were looking at the stall owner with a serious gleam to them. Despite the situation she found herself in, Ahzya couldn't help but feel relieved to see that he had no wounds, an improvement on when they'd met.

"I don't believe you! She was about to steal it!" the stall owner yelled, yanking on Ahzya's arm.

"Perhaps if you weren't so distracted flirting with women that aren't your wife, you could pay attention to customers trying to buy your products," Cole stated sternly. "What would your wife say if she knew? Now unhand the young lady or I'll make you."

The stall owner glanced over Cole's clean, plum-toned uniform and sheathed blade at his left hip and dropped Ahzya's arm. Cole rested a hand on her shoulder as she took a step back and arrived at his side.

"Now, how much is one of your sweet buns?" Cole asked, reaching into a pouch on his belt.

"Four copper pieces," the owner answered.

"Very well, I'll take two," Cole said, opening a leather bag and retrieving the coins.

Ahzya raised her hand to stop him, but Cole just smiled down at her in a friendly manner.

"I insist, especially after this man's rude behaviour," Cole stated. "I'll walk you home to your father's place, he invited me to dinner anyway."

Cole then retrieved the two buns from the stall owner and gripped Ahzya's hand. His hold was gentle but reassuring as he led her through the crowds and into a side street that was less busy. Cole then dropped one of the paper bags into her hands and slowed his walking.

"I don't think I've ever done something like that in all my life," Cole stated, grinning widely.

Ahzya remained quiet, with one hand holding the sweet bun and the other still tucked into Cole's own hand. Her eyes looked up to scan his face, but her stomach was already uneasy. Ahzya suddenly didn't want to eat the bun after all.

"Don't look so scared," Cole stated, his expression fading. "I'm here as a friend, so don't worry about anything else. Although, I'm honestly surprised to see you here."

Ahzya glanced around at the other people walking through the street. As her heart hammered in her chest, she felt as though their eyes followed her. Cole gave an audible sigh and began leading her through the streets until they exited the town. The creek soon provided some peace and quiet and they sat down on the grassy bank.

"The castle and *Moonstruck* crew are still looking for you," Cole said quietly. "I was actually sent to put up posters."

Ahzya's eyes widened and her head drooped forward. That meant she'd have to move on to another area. The last few towns she had lived in had soon received the posters about her disappearance and she'd left before anyone could recognise the similarity between the description and her.

"They've included a sketch this time, though it's not a very good likeness," Cole paused quietly. "You're far cuter."

Ahzya felt on edge, her posture tense and ready to bolt. Cole bent over to try and get a glance of her face. He then pointed his thumb towards his pack with a flick of his wrist.

"I can accidentally burn them as fire fuel?" Cole suggested, gauging her response.

Ahzya's head shot up at his suggestion and she turned to look directly in his eyes. She noticed they were filled with concern and also an underlying hurt.

"Why would you do that?" Ahzya spoke finally. "Wouldn't that be going against your orders?"

"Well, they didn't technically order me to put up the posters, just to travel to different towns *with* them," Cole answered. "Besides, we're friends. Covering for each other is what we're supposed to do. We are still friends, right?"

"You aren't trying to befriend me just to convince me to go back with you, are you?" Ahzya asked, hooking her arms under her knees.

Cole drew back at her words and winced before shaking his head.

"According to the rest of the world, I've spent today putting up posters and doing my duty for the kingdom," Cole answered. "You can rely on me."

Ahzya let a small smile touch her lips and started to relax. Cole continued to watch her closely. It was obvious that he had a lot more questions he wanted to ask her, but he chose to be quiet.

"When the search for me has quietened and I'm all but forgotten, I'll come and visit you," Ahzya whispered resolutely. "It's better for everyone if for now it appears that I've disappeared or never truly existed."

"Why?" Cole asked with confusion.

"I was stupid and stepped out of bounds," Ahzya answered. "My decisions have affected other lives and not in a good way."

"Then you can write to me," Cole stated. "We can even use different names. That way we don't have to lose touch. And if you ever need anything, just ask. I may not earn much with my soldier's pay, but I can afford to send you some money."

"Cole, while I appreciate the offer, I don't want you to be responsible for me like I'm your child or something," Ahzya said with a smile. "I'm sixteen now, I'm an adult who will deal with my problems myself. You've already lied for me; I can't make you go against your soldier's conduct. Your friendship is all I require. I'll take care of the rest."

"By stealing sweet buns?" Cole asked, raising an eyebrow.

Ahzya chuckled and Cole scowled.

"No, I can safely promise you that I'll never look at or eat a sweet bun ever again," Ahzya said, her eyes sparkling.

Cole smiled and leant back, falling to lie down in the long grass. Ahzya copied his movement and listened lazily to the cicadas singing to each other. The sun flashed through the leaves and branches performing a light show on her eyelids. Ahzya purposefully relaxed her tensed muscles and took a deep breath in and out. A tired buzz flowed through her body in a comforting way. For the first time in months, her racing mind stilled as she heard Cole's gentle breathing beside her.

Ahzya awoke hours later, and the cool air caused her to shiver as she came to. She glanced towards where Cole had been lying down and immediately realised that he was no longer there. Ahzya sat up quickly and glanced around. There was no sign of Cole, but beside her was a canvas bag with a note attached. Ahzya flipped the note over and over, her eyes studying the lines of ink. They looked like masses of squiggles and Ahzya urgently put it to the side so that she could open the bag. Inside the bag was a stack of posters, all similar to those she'd seen in previous towns. The only difference was a sketch of a healthier version of her, an almost innocent aura to it. Beside the posters was a small pouch which Ahzya slowly opened to reveal several shiny coins. Ahzya picked up the note and slung the bag over her head and shoulder. She began running towards town, her urgency only added to by the fact that the sun had almost disappeared over the horizon. There was only a gentle orange glow, and she stumbled over rocks in her path.

"Cole!" Ahzya called urgently as she entered into a street.

The street was illuminated by a lit lantern on a post and Ahzya bit her lip. She already knew that Cole had probably left. Ahzya cursed the fact that she had fallen asleep. They had barely spoken during that time, but Ahzya had felt so comfortable in his presence that now she missed it.

"What ya yellin' fo'?" a young girl's voice asked her suddenly.

Ahzya turned her head to see a child sitting against the building. They were wearing tattered clothing and their skin was covered in dirt and mud. Their platinum blonde hair was cut short, the sides shaved and the top a tangle of loose curls. Their figure was so lanky and clothes so loose-fitted that it was difficult to tell whether they were male or female, but their voice was decidedly feminine. Her cheeks were hollow, and her blue eyes watched Ahzya with an air of disinterest. Ahzya paused as a plan entered her mind, and she turned to face her directly.

"Can you read?" Ahzya asked bluntly.

"So what if I can?" the child answered, her tone sharp.

"I want to offer a trade," Ahzya offered, reaching into her pocket.

"Trade?" the child answered, their interest piqued.

Ahzya removed the sweet bun that was still wrapped in the paper bag from her pocket. The girl's eyes widened at the sight of the bag and Ahzya knew that she knew what it was.

"I'll offer this sweet bun in return for you reading a note I just received," Ahzya stated.

"Ya aren't joking, are ya?" the girl asked, crossing her arms.

"No, I swear you will receive the bun as payment."

"Fo' readin' a letta?" the girl asked doubtfully.

"I can't read," Ahzya replied, trying not to blush in embarrassment.

"Ya need to get betta at barterin'," the girl scoffed with a shake of her head. "I feel like I'm rippin' ya off. Give me the food an' the letta."

The girl held out her grubby hands expectantly.

"You read the letter first and then I'll give you the sweet bun," Ahzya said, her eyes narrowing.

"Ha, now ya gettin' it," the girl praised, flashing a toothy grin. "Give me the letta."

Ahzya handed over the note and the girl studied it for a moment before reading it aloud. Ahzya was listening so intently that she didn't even realise that the girl read it in a clear tone with none of her previous accent.

*I had to return to Prynesse by the end of the week, but you looked so peaceful that I didn't want to wake you up. You can burn the posters for warmth and please don't hesitate to write. I've written my address on the reverse. Perhaps it's best just to address it to 'Cole', I don't want my mother to be confused if a letter for a fake name arrives. Stay safe! I also consider that visit a promise, so I'll be expecting you.*

*Your friend, Cole*

The girl finished reading it and then flipped it over a few times before handing it back. Ahzya reached out for the letter while offering the sweet bun in the other hand. With the sweet bun safety in her grasp, the girl roughly tore the paper bag. Ahzya hugged the letter and bit her lip. There was a reason she hadn't promised to write.

Ahzya felt tears sting her eyes as she turned to walk back down the streets towards her small makeshift camp. The girl began to follow a few steps behind, when Ahzya paused, so did she.

"Do you need something?" Ahzya asked cautiously.

"Figure I still owe ya a letta or two," the girl answered with a shrug. "I can write too ya know."

"Because of one sweet bun?" Ahzya asked doubtfully.

"Ya really need to learn basic barterin'," the girl said, tsking her tongue. "If ya don't like it, I'll offer ya a partnership."

"You'll read and write letters for me, but what will you get in return?" Ahzya asked, secretly intrigued by the idea.

"A bodyguard. You're stronger than me," the girl stated, her accent slipping again. "Ever kill someone before? Wielded a weapon?"

"I've stabbed a pirate before, and I own a dagger," Ahzya offered.

"I knew you were an intriguing soul!" the girl exclaimed in awe. "My parents didn't bother naming me, so I rotate twelve different ones through the twelve months of a year. It will take a while to explain each one, but my friends call me Max, so you're qualified to just call me that."

The girl rubbed her palms on her clothes and reached out to shake hands.

"Ahzya," Ahzya said, shaking the offered hand.

"You gave me your real name?" Max asked, raising an eyebrow as Ahzya nodded. "Aw, you're cute. But from now on, never give your real name to anyone. On the street, always use a fake name."

Ahzya fell asleep that night with Max nestled next to her. They lay beside the fire she started with the posters, and she clung to the letter as if it were her most precious possession.

# CHAPTER TWENTY-TWO

### Present Day: Sephe 1407

EASTERN WALL, CASTLE PRYNESSE, ALPANIA

Ahzya had to hand it to Madam Uran, she could deliver one hell of a punch. Her cheek and jawline had truly bruised up overnight, leaving the area tender and painful. Even a layer of makeup did little to disguise it at first, but Noelle helped to mask it with an extra application. Ahzya felt ridiculous with such a thick layer of makeup coating her face and became aware of every look she received. She had never been one to feel self-conscious about how she looked, and the whole situation felt overly surreal.

In Triox, she could have just wandered around with the bruise on display like a proud badge of survival. A bruise meant that she'd survived and won. Usually fights in the Triox area only ended when one side was dead. Since their little confrontation that resulted in her bruises hadn't ended with Uran dead, there was little to be proud of.

Luckily the castle had been pretty quiet for the day, and sleepy inhabitants were only just beginning to exit their rooms late in the afternoon. Kola woke up earlier than the rest, but it quickly became apparent that she wasn't feeling well due to the lack of sleep and Ahzya sent her to bed for an afternoon nap.

Now Ahzya sat on the warm stone of the eastern inner castle wall, basking in the afternoon sun. Her eyes closed in a sleepy manner and the breeze played with the baby hairs around her face. Having met Cole in the exact same position, Ahzya daydreamed of her visits to Prynesse after the search for her came to a halt.

Two years of random appearances and planned holidays had brought the two of them closer. Cole, who wore his feelings on his sleeve, was quick to admire and love. Ahzya took a little longer to admit that her own feelings had grown from friendship to love.

Their relationship was innocent and sweet. It was never official; never known by anyone else other than his mother, who didn't know Ahzya's origins, and Max, who helped their correspondence. They held each other in high respect, barely ever fought and only ever looked to protect each other. They both had their demons, but the more time they spent together, the smaller those troubles seemed and the less they were affected, at least on an emotional level.

Both of them came covered in wounds and scars, beaten and exhausted, yet found an oasis to recharge whenever they were together. They didn't speak about their conditions, instead they revelled in childlike adventures and dreams. A personal sailboat with enough room for them, an eventual child and enough supplies to last them exploration trips to other lands. Cole was fascinated with other countries and their cultures, which was part of the reason why he'd initially been so interested in Ahzya. Though she'd managed to train herself out of it, back then her Ulkadasan accent had still revealed itself, especially when she was with Cole.

Even then, Ahzya had hidden her true employment, or at least she never spoke about it, and Cole never asked. They'd spent their last few months together as though each visit was their last. Only once he was in his last days, she'd found out that he'd known the whole time.

Ahzya had arrived on the porch of Cole's house, brushing snow from her jacket. Cole's mother rushed her inside, wordlessly leading her to Cole's room. Wrapped in a pile of blankets, the fire from the blazing hearth warming the room, Cole had lain on his bed, his frame rattling with each breath. Cole's mum sat down in a chair by the bed, her head bowing, eyes squeezed shut, and hands clasped in front of her face.

As Ahzya took Cole's hand in hers and placed a gentle kiss on his knuckles, his eyes had flickered open. He'd clung to her hand with a desperation that scared her. He pleaded with her to take up a different path, as if he'd known he was about to die, leaving her to face her demons alone once more. Even in his fitful sleep, he begged, tears streaking his cheeks. He'd wake with feverish horror and Ahzya soothed him with words of reassurance before he drifted off again.

Ahzya had stayed by his side until his health improved. She only felt satisfied when he stood in his uniform, a reassuring smile revealing his teeth. As she kissed him goodbye, he stroked her cheek, gazing over her face as if to capture it in his mind. Ahzya had assured him that she'd be back shortly, that he'd barely notice she was gone, but there was no next time, when she returned, he was gone.

Cole's passing made Ahzya feel vulnerable, angry and alone, and instead of turning from the life of crime, she'd delved further. What did it matter; what was the point? Cole wasn't there to witness it either way.

Caught in a gang war, tortured for the amusement of a corrupt lord, stealing for anyone that offered any small reward, it almost turned her into an emotionless shell. Ahzya couldn't tell how she managed to get out of it all alive, nor could she say when she'd become less reckless and more professional in her art. There was no sudden realisation, no turn, just a slow withdrawal.

Of course, the only way to truly rid oneself of the underworld would be to outwit every connection, every ally and foe you'd ever come in contact with. The easiest way to do so would be to fake your own death. Even then, you'd have to have somewhere to escape to and a means to start a new life, somewhere no-one would ever recognise you. Crime was a difficult network to truly rid yourself of, its barbs dug deep and its reach was wide. Too often, faked deaths became actual bodies.

Ahzya had considered faking her death once or twice. She even had her talented con-artist friend, Max, who had been there to patch her wounds and coax her to eat after Cole died, so she felt she could truly trust her to help. However, in the end, she still didn't have anywhere to go; no plan past her supposed death. Her ship fund had been dug into too often and wasn't looking healthy enough for her to buy a good boat equipped for the high seas.

While she said money was no motivation for her anymore, if Jonathan could fork over enough money for her boat at the end of her mission, she'd be quite content. After his recent interference, Ahzya might even ask for extra compensation.

Ahzya sat up straight and reached her arms towards the sky, stretching her fingers by flexing them into a fist and then out again.

"See how my sunflower stretches her petals towards the sun, her beauty surpassing all," Jonathan's poetic voice interrupted her stretch.

"JP Dry, I was just thinking about you," Ahzya spoke casually, not even checking if Jonathan was alone.

"My, my. And what exactly was I doing in this daydream of yours?" Jonathan queried, his head appearing above her in her line of view.

"Nothing, it was more I was thinking of asking something of you."

"Whatever thou wisheth, my lady, please allow my ears to hear your sweet request."

Ahzya rolled her eyes at him and patted the stone wall next to her. As prompted, Jonathan took a seat, sighing as he too stretched his long limbs and then turned his attention to her.

"Jonathan, would you honour me by..." Ahzya trailed off, looking down at her hands as if contemplating her next words carefully.

Jonathan's face grew serious, waiting for her question earnestly.

"Honour me by providing compensation," Ahzya continued, meeting his eyes. "My heart..."

Jonathan's eyebrows raised just a fraction and eyes dropped to her chest as she placed a hand over her heart. Then he anxiously gazed over her face, as Ahzya decided to quickly continue.

"My heart cringes every time I see you; it's like it's allergic or something. I can't think of any way for you to compensate, so a monetary retribution will have to do."

Jonathan drew in a deep breath and then turned his back to her.

"Tsk, you shouldn't tempt my heart like that, what if I'd assumed your question was more romantically inclined and just kissed you passionately right here and now? You play with my feelings," Jonathan stated after a moment, crossing his arms.

"Sorry. My heart is a kingdom of its own; I do not rule it," Ahzya replied with a chuckle.

"If it's a kingdom, then all I have to do is conquer it, and I believe I'm somewhat capable," Jonathan replied, a slight confidence in his voice.

On that note, he slid back and his head landed perfectly in Ahzya's lap, a cheeky grin flashed up at her as he landed.

"How old are you?" Ahzya asked incredulously.

"Where are your manners? You shouldn't ask a man his age. If you do, you must first share your own. I'm extremely shocked by your conduct today," Jonathan pouted.

"Ugh, sit up!" Ahzya said, pushing his shoulder.

"Fine, I'll tell you," Jonathan said, remaining resting on her lap. "I'm a mature and handsome thirty-two years of age. Now you can reply with your own."

"I'm twenty-one, now get lost, old man."

"Hey, I'm in my prime!"

Ahzya pushed him once more and he rolled over once before promptly rocking back into position.

"Ah, it's nice up here," Jonathan breathed. "Now I know why my brother liked it up here."

Ahzya frowned.

"I even believe his tales about meeting a guardian angel, now that I've met my own guardian angel here. He was always so giddily happy when he spoke about her. Ah, he was such a dork," Jonathan continued with a chuckle, watching the clouds overhead lazily.

"What is your brother's name?" Ahzya asked, waiting for the answer.

"Cole."

"I take it from the past tense, he passed away?"

"You're not very subtle or comforting, are you? But no matter. He passed away roughly two years ago, a short while before I became portreeve over Triox," Jonathan answered, his tone changing.

"Must still be pretty raw for you then," Ahzya said quietly.

"People say that some days are better than others, but I've never felt that; every day is the same as the one before. But maybe that's because of the nature of his death."

"Nature of his death?"

"He was murdered. Beaten and left to die," Jonathan said, his voice turning gruff.

"And his attackers?"

"Ignored. Left to wander this earth as if they'd done nothing."

Ahzya looked down at Jonathan, studying his features closely from the wrinkles at his furrowed brows to his jawline tense from gritted teeth. Her gaze softened even when Jonathan switched his piercing hazel eyes, which looked more golden in the sunlight, to meet her own.

"What's that look for? Is that pity? Because I have no need for it," Jonathan asked, quirking one of his eyebrows. "My revenge is going to be sweet."

"I have no pity for you, just understanding. Consider it a look of comradeship."

"Comradeship sounds too much like war brothers, and I was hoping for something a little more romantic, still starts with 'c' and ends with 'ship'."

"We both already have lives that throw us into a courtship with death, and I don't two-time."

"Ah, I don't plan to settle down with death. Now that I've somehow left myself open to you again, you are obliged to tell me one of your weak points or perhaps your sad backstory."

"Our stories are scarily similar, if I tell you what I've discovered today, both our revenge plans may become distorted. The situation is already warped enough as it is."

"This mess could hardly be hurt any further, so you may as well confess your secrets."

"Cole probably wouldn't agree with our revenge plan," Ahzya mused, looking up at the sun.

"And what would you know of my brother's wishes, may I ask?"

"For one, he was always far too forgiving. He had no sense of justice in regards to his own situation. I wish I was more like him, but my blood is too poisoned by the hunt for justice, even if that's seen as a sin in everyone else's eyes."

"What are you talking about?" Jonathan sat up.

"We have a connection, after all. One that's stronger than any romance or friendship. Turns out we are avenging the same person."

"What was my brother to you?" Jonathan asked pointedly.

"Allow me to reintroduce myself. I'm the guardian angel of your brother Cole," Ahzya said with a crooked smile, extending a hand towards a wide-eyed Jonathan.

## Maid's Quarters, Castle Prynesse, Alpania

Ahzya fell onto her bed out of exhaustion and let out a long sigh. A headache made her head feel weighted and her eyes were dry and hot. The realisation they'd come to on the eastern wall had caused a long conversation to occur between Ahzya and Jonathan. Jonathan hadn't pulled any more jokes or flirtatious remarks during that time, and instead earnestly asked for a full explanation. Ahzya had given him one as best she could. Of course, a few falsehoods had been thrown in to cover her true origin and any other part of her life before and after Cole. She had been honest about her feelings for Cole, however, as she figured Jonathan was owed at least that much truth.

Considering their newfound connection, Jonathan asked about her plans for the assassination. While he stated he still didn't care how it was done, he was curious about how Ahzya would avenge Cole. Ahzya briefly explained the plan, which she'd finalised overnight. The guests would soon leave the castle and the king's patterns would quickly return to what they had been. The overnight patrol had let slip as much, stating tonight would be the last of his rounds before the king returned to his duties. The guard was so enthusiastic about returning to his usual guard post instead of walking the perimeter of the castle, Ahzya almost felt bad that his slip of information would end with tragedy.

Jonathan found no fault in her plan, wishing her luck with her endeavour, though he was less excited than Ahzya had expected him to be at the final steps of his plans unfolding. Ahzya could almost see the gears turning behind his eyes, he spent several minutes, brow furrowed, watching the lazy sun set on the horizon. She did not force him into further conversation; she revelled in the silence brought on by his musings. Ahzya excused herself without a word as it got darker and retreated to her quarters.

Noelle was out for dinner duty and, though early, Ahzya considered climbing into bed immediately. However, her moment alone left her with a chance to look over her gear one last time and sharpen her weapons. Then she should consider having something to eat, she'd barely had anything at the ball and she'd been too preoccupied to eat much more than a few pieces of fruit for breakfast in the morning.

Sitting up with a swift movement, Ahzya let out a low groan at the inevitable few hours until she'd be able to return to such a restful position. She reached under the low-sitting bed and pulled out a flat package she'd stowed under there with several other packs. She unbuttoned the flap on top and folded it back, revealing a plaid scarf. She removed the scarf, which revealed carefully folded pitch-black garments. The material was non-reflective, finely woven woollen fabric, cut and sewn into breaches and a long-sleeved shirt, designed to fit her form perfectly.

Next was a pair of custom gloves which had firm leather on the palm with stretchable fine-mesh covering the fingers and leather pads on the non-nailed side of the tips of the fingers. The leather patches allowed for grip and protection, but the mesh provided more freedom of movement than all-leather gloves could provide. Two short bandages, which had tiny hooks on one of the ends, would be wound over the wrist and up the arms, hooking into itself, and serving as extra support for the wrist. It also served as an extra layer for a pair of leather gauntlets which lay over the bandage and the sleeve of the shirt. Soft leather black boots would serve her well as footwear, already worn in with a year of thievery work.

Finally were her weapons, four throwing darts that had hidden positions in the gauntlets, and two daggers, both sheathed at her hips. One was of simple design but perfectly weighted, while the other sported a familiar handle of twisted green and blue leather.

A whetstone and small vial of oil made quick work of tending to them, more out of reassurance than an actual requirement of sharpening, as Ahzya was frequent in her weapon care.

With her equipment checked, Ahzya slid it back under the bed and went in search of some sustenance for her body, closely followed by a light workout and stretching.

Mid-routine, Ahzya noticed a bounding head of brown curls approaching and Kola pounced onto her back. Ahzya completed several push-ups with Kola on her back before standing and galloping across the courtyard. Kola giggled as she bounced, and her arms held on tightly around Ahzya's neck.

"Good evening, little rebel," Ahzya greeted, as she breathlessly sat down minutes later.

"Good evening, Cath," Kola replied with a curtsy. "Today, I showed Cleo, Anna, Jae and Yuna how I learnt to cartwheel. Jae said I could become an acrobat in the future!"

Kola proudly told Ahzya about her afternoon adventures with her cousins. She went on to say that she didn't know if she could really become an acrobat, since she didn't have wings and the dark really scared her. Ahzya didn't correct her misunderstanding of what an acrobat was and just chuckled.

Kola gasped and suddenly ushered Ahzya to hide against the wall darkened by shadows. Curious to find what spooked the young girl, Ahzya noticed Jonathan and a soldier talking in the opposite corner of the courtyard. The soldier wore the plum-toned uniform of a general castle guard.

"That's the time-stealing monster I told you about before," Kola whispered, clinging to Ahzya's hand. "Isn't he scary?"

Ahzya watched Jonathan and the guard's conversation unfold. It grew heated, the guard annoyed, and Ahzya couldn't help but notice he seemed familiar. While talking to Jonathan, the guard's face scrunched in a scowl. Ahzya realised he was a guard she'd noticed giving her sneered looks as he passed when she was on maid's duty. At the time, Ahzya had just summed it up as someone who didn't approve of her association with the royals and their esteemed guest. There was quite a split between disapproving and supportive parties by this point.

"He doesn't look like a joyful fellow," Ahzya whispered back to Kola finally. "Besides, I believe he's part of the anti-Catherine faction."

"Oh," Kola whispered, her eyes quickly squinting narrowly at the guard. "The enemy."

"Gosh, I really am out here starting a war," Ahzya said, laughing at the way Kola clenched her fists. "Good to know my little rebel is on my side."

On the other side of the courtyard, Jonathan stepped closer to the guard. The guard sized up with Jonathan for a moment before throwing his hands up in surrender and walking away. Jonathan ran a hand through his hair. Ahzya shrugged it off and turned away. Her only duty to relieve any stress Jonathan was experiencing was to complete her job, anything else was stuff he'd handle himself.

# CHAPTER TWENTY-THREE

NORTH-WESTERN INNER WALL, CASTLE PRYNESSE, ALPANIA

A new day dawned, which consisted of a steady stream of royals and nobles leaving the castle. Kisses and waves were exchanged, a promise to meet again soon and to write often. Ahzya parted with a teary-eyed Kola who insisted that Ahzya should go home with her and be her new governess full-time. As a parting gift and some sort of consolation, Ahzya slipped a tiny bundle into Kola's hand before lifting her into the carriage and stepping away. Kola's excited head of curls immediately popped up and grinned at her, dimples and all.

"I'm going to name her Rin, after you!" Kola called, holding up the bundle of grey fur.

It was only fair that having killed Jonny, the rat, Ahzya should replace the pet with another, this time a baby rabbit, all fluffy and cute.

Ahzya curtsied as a thank-you and didn't bother explaining that the bunny was male. Nor did Ahzya wish to mention how she'd acquired said bunny after killing its parents while hunting that morning. In fairness, it hadn't been on purpose, it was awfully early in the season for kits.

"Goodbye, little rebel," Ahzya said, waving.

Kola's lip quivered again, but she raised her small hand in a salute. Like that, Ahzya's charge and source of chaotic energy trundled away.

The royal cousins left shortly after, including Jae, who took so long saying goodbye that the rest of his travelling party was halfway towards the gate by the time he finally began running after the group of carriages, his horse being tethered to the back of one.

Anna and Cleo planned to stay a few days longer, considering they'd arrived fairly late. If Ahzya succeeded in the assassination, then they'd be staying a lot longer than a few days, and many of the leaving parties would return. Ahzya was not invested in the politics of what happened after King Mark died, merely that she would not be around to witness it. However, while Jonathan supported the ascension of Cleo, it seemed that both sisters would be equally worthy rulers, from what Ahzya had witnessed. They had difference of character, but to pick between the two, Ahzya would have to study them in varying situations, and she neither had the time nor position to witness that. Her own duty would be ending very shortly, after that, this was neither her country nor point of care.

Night fell the following evening; lights moved around the castle as the staff and guards carried torches and lanterns to illuminate their paths. Ahzya heard rather than saw the evening's happenings, her breathing regulated and eyes closed. Down the corridor in a courtyard, a conversation between ladies-in-waiting covered several rumours from the ball.

Like a metronome, Ahzya focused on the beat of seconds to minutes as she bided her time. She'd gotten into position shortly after the last patrol went past, knowing the next would be the royal patrol. Her boots slotted into grooves between two of the large stone slabs of the corridor wall, which she'd prepared earlier in the day. Her body was just long enough to cover the gap between the wall and a central beam that ran vertically down the middle of the roof of the hallway. Her elbows to her interwoven hands were pushed into the gap above her head, between the wooden vertical beam and the roof. Another thick wooden beam protected her body from sight from anyone approaching from the south side. Her body arched into the roof, every muscle in her body strained as she waited in the darkness of the roof cavity.

Ahzya had planned the mission down to the minute, and lucky for her, the castle patrol performed their movements strict to the minute. Ahzya had to hand it to King Mark, even with his blindness to the injustice happening in his own castle, his soldiers were meticulous. Each soldier had their duty and their position; each member working to ensure there was no delay or mistake in the system. However, perhaps it was too regimented, and it was the only weakness that Ahzya had found. It could all be timed so it allowed just enough gap for an enemy, in this case, Ahzya, to infiltrate. It was like she'd pierced her way into the bloodstream, now she waited for the main cell to approach, to poison and destroy.

Ahzya ignored her painfully dry throat and mouth, her arms and shoulder burned, but she focused on that rhythm. Her ears listened to every audible sound, but one eyebrow twitched down.

*Nothing's stirring. It's too quiet.*

A patrol should have passed the end of the hall; only for a brief moment, an easily missed moment. However, Ahzya waited thirty seconds, still no sound.

*The patrol is late.*

The patrol always passed by five minutes before the king's patrol entered the corridor on their sweep. Even when the king hadn't been part of the king's patrol route, it had run the same. First patrol would march through the corridor, ten minutes would pass and the second patrol group would merely pass by the end of the corridor, finally the third patrol, usually escorting King Mark, would approach. Fifteen minutes was the window of opportunity, Ahzya had timed it, watched and noted it down.

Ahzya allowed two more minutes to pass, the king's patrol would approach soon, and the second patrol still hadn't appeared. Ahzya felt uneasy but retained her measured breathing and strong ambush position.

A minute and a half and still she remained in silence, every second hammering a nail of doubt into Ahzya's mind. Then came a grouping of footsteps. Ahzya quickly assessed the sound, searching for any irregularity. The group size was correct and the amount of conversation seemed normal, though perhaps a little more energetic than usual. They were on time, to the dot, despite the mysterious disappearance of the second patrol. Something still felt off.

Ahzya had to make a decision to either commit to her plan or escape from her spot. She listened a moment longer and her final decision was made. The footsteps, though correct in their size, the pacing was offbeat. It was a fractional difference, but Ahzya could tell they were slowing their approach. They were being cautious, as if preparing themselves for something.

Ahzya switched her grip on the beam above her head and kicked her feet from their grooves. She swung and let go, landing with her feet on the sill of a skinny, arched, glassless window. Gripping the smoothed stone, she steadied herself and squeezed through the gap. She bent down and dropped herself down from the window, now hanging on the outside wall. Ahzya released her left hand to try and grip onto a ledge below the window. She quickly followed it with her right, causing her hands to disappear from the line of sight from the corridor.

The group approached and Ahzya felt the tug in the tendon of her upper arms from the sudden change of tension direction. She forced her breathing to stay steady, but the beat of adrenaline heated her neck in an almost sickening fashion. The night air gave her some comfort as it cooled the skin on her back, but her neck and arms still burned. Ahzya knew she couldn't climb down or move anywhere in fear of making any minute sound which would alert the King's Guard, who were seemingly on the lookout for something amiss. The King's Guard passed in the same semi-out-of-sync manner Ahzya had heard them approach in.

Ahzya hoped that they would be so tense that they wouldn't bother checking outside the arched paneless window and thus discover her, looking guilty as all hell decked in dark clothes and armed with blades. However, the party didn't seem to consider that anyone would be foolish enough to hang outside a wall window, dangling precariously three stories above the courtyard below.

According to the tactical process of her mind, climbing down the wall would be easier, rather than expending energy pulling herself up. However, Ahzya considered that the way down was twenty times the distance of going up and a wrong footing or hold would end with plunging to her death. Pushing through the pain and returning to the corridor above seemed her best option in regards to that risk factor.

The footsteps of the King's Guard receded and an opportunity to climb was open, but a second of hesitation and a concentrated audio sweep, caused her to release her tensed arms. At the end of the corridor, two footsteps, confident and sturdy, passed by… the second patrol.

Switching up the patrol times, re-rigging the whole system, except for the king's patrol, which had been perfectly on time, all part of a quickly implemented defence system.

Ahzya's adrenaline caused every cell to vibrate, a pitfall feeling in her chest, and her mind raced overtime. If she climbed down, crossed the courtyard and rounded a few towers, she could get back to her own quarters in reasonable time. Ahzya also brought into consideration that the guard's rounds would have changed.

Her left arm started the movement; she couldn't just sit there hanging from the wall forever. The climb down felt like an eternity, several slips of grip and footing scared her, but her thieving garb protected her from any friction burn. Ahzya felt like a rock when she finally hit the ground and sat prone but hidden in the bushes. A cold shiver immediately coursed through her as the wet ground mixed with exhaustion.

A couple of stumbled and precarious moments dodging a weird new patrol pattern and Ahzya made it back to her room. She slid through the door and found Noelle on her knees saying her nightly prayer. Noelle began to turn in her direction and Ahzya stepped forward. Picking up a blanket from her bed, she tossed it over Noelle and began to get changed with as much enthusiasm as her cooling sore muscles could handle. Noelle chuckled before continuing her prayers in silence under her veil of woollen blanket. Tumbling her discarded daggers and clothes all together, Ahzya threw it under her bed and sat down, relaxing finally. Massaging her muscles, she waited as Noelle quickly completed her night routine and spun around to greet her.

"Catherine! Did you have a long shift today? I didn't even see you in passing," Noelle said, with a cheery and bright smile.

Ahzya offered a tight smile, her throat too parched to reply and her body already heading into aftershock from the adrenaline.

"You look pale. Lie down and get some rest," Noelle stated after explaining her day shortly. "Water? I'm sure some water will help."

Rather than lie down, Ahzya forced herself into a post-workout cooldown routine, her muscles already seizing. She sipped on the cup of water and Noelle fetched her a refill when the glass sat empty.

"I should start working out too, though maybe not to your point of effort," Noelle mused, as she sat lazily watching from under her bed covers.

"I've inspired you to greatness, have I?" Ahzya asked, stretching her arms across her chest.

"You make a girl not want to work out at all, arriving here all dehydrated and pale. However, with all the weird things happening with the castle, I want to be able to defend myself if some assassin tries to hold me hostage," Noelle replied, shaking her head.

"Assassin?"

"Yeah, that's why we were all suddenly told to stay where we were and not to roam the halls tonight. One of my friends is part of the night patrol and he said a warning letter arrived stating specifics on an assassination attempt."

"A warning letter?" Ahzya breathed, settling down on her bed. "It's a comfort that someone is looking out for His Majesty, but everything appeared calm out there when I was coming back tonight."

"I'm surprised you weren't told to return to here earlier like the rest of us," Noelle said, yawning.

"I was exercising somewhere secluded; they didn't know I was there," Ahzya dismissed casually. "Besides, they probably thought I could take on any assassin."

At this, Ahzya flexed her arms outside the blankets but winced at the stiffness. Noelle tsked at Ahzya, letting out a soft laugh and burying into her blankets.

# CHAPTER TWENTY-FOUR

DINING HALL, CASTLE PRYNESSE, ALPANIA

"Although it would be more comforting to know who exactly was sending through the information, we should be thankful for that secretive informant," Jonathan mused, herding his peas around his plate like a flock of sheep.

"Which one?" Commander Ray asked, his fork clinking on his plate.

Jonathan paused and looked across the table at Ray, before smiling with a look of curiosity.

"What do you mean? Of course, I'm talking about the informant who is writing all those warning letters," Jonathan replied, raising a glass of wine to his lips.

"If you were up with information, Jonathan, you'd know that the latest warning was written by a different informant than the first few," Ray explained, as if it were a usual dinner conversation. "The latest letter was written by someone who wanted us to believe it was written by the same person; however, any trained eye could tell the difference between them."

"I admit, they looked the same to me," Jonathan mused.

"Something didn't sit right, so I was suspicious, but we had experts make a closer examination and they quickly came to the same conclusion. The writing, ink and even the parchment had major differences from the first warnings," Ray explained further.

"Well, they could be working together still. Either way, we can be grateful for their concerns for Mark's safety."

"They've all proven to be unsubstantiated claims so far. Other than the letters there is no proof of any actual assassin or assassination plot.

We aren't to know if the authors of these letters are sending them to warn us or as a terrible joke."

"And yet, you are the one that insisted on raising protection and following precautions for in case both letters were telling the truth. Why, when you have such a strong opinion on the truth of the letters, would you go against Mark's wishes to keep things quiet and as normal?"

"If a mere branch sits in our king's path, we remove it, just in case it is covered in thorns. The letters, though seemingly insignificant and none of which seem true, have to be treated as thorned branches, and the king protected no matter what," Ray answered, laying down his fork.

"Even so, you are a commander of the King's Fleet, not his personal guard or even the castle protection, we have other commanders for such tasks." Jonathan paused for a moment before continuing. "What makes you think you should make that call over those Mark has explicitly selected for such tasks?"

"They have the duty of protection as loyal subjects, I have that duty and care as a friend, a friend that has been by his side for the majority of his life. I will do whatever it takes to ensure his safety from whomever or whatever threatens him."

"Don't think of yourself so highly, we have all been here by Mark's side."

King Mark let out a heavy sigh and raised an eyebrow as he looked between the two men. His cutlery had been laid on his plate shortly into the discussion, and even the queen paused her eating to purse her lips in silent disapproval.

"Are you both unaware that I am right here?" Mark spoke up. "You speak as if you're at a war meeting without me, rather than a dinner gathering between my family and two best friends."

Ray bent his head in apology and Jonathan glanced along the table as if only now registering the presence of the four members of royalty.

Princess Anna smiled sheepishly back at Jonathan while Princess Cleo appeared to ignore the entire conversation and reached for another fresh bread roll.

"Ray has been giving me counsel on the subject for a while now, specifically because I requested his opinion. However, I have been making the final decisions under my own conclusions, so please do not suspect the commander of stepping out of line," Mark spoke clearly. "I am treating the threat seriously, especially considering the recent assassination of Prince Ivan in Lavania."

Queen Maria hushed her husband harshly from the other end of the table, and their gazes turned to Cleo. Cleo stuttered her tear of the bread roll on hearing Prince Ivan's name, her mouth pushing into a thin line. Jonathan bowed his head for the first time and King Mark shifted in his seat. Cleo quickly recovered her composure as if nothing had happened.

"What are your thoughts about the letters then?" Cleo asked, her tone casual.

"Well, as for the letters, I've been mulling over the subject also—" Mark began.

"I thought you were going to revert things back to a pleasant dinner occasion," Maria interjected, her eyes almost begging her husband to change the subject.

"I think it's a little late for that, Mother. The mood has already changed, we may as well allow them to discuss it, otherwise things will just fall into an awkward silence," Cleo said, offering her mother a sympathetic smile.

"You are no better, I know you'd much rather discuss such subjects, Cleo," Maria replied. "Anna, my love, let's leave these business-minded fools to their discussions. Noelle, fetch us some tea and something sweet, and bring them to my personal sitting room."

"Right away, Your Majesty," Noelle answered with a curtsy from her position next to Ahzya.

Anna escorted her mother through the doors with Noelle close behind, and the room was silent for a moment before Cleo leant back with crossed arms and spoke.

"Is there any chance that last night's warning was sent as a distraction?" Cleo asked. "Perhaps the real intention was to put us on guard and thus create a diversion."

"We did consider that, so, while we focused our efforts in the area the letter warned, guards were also sent to protect the rooms in which the royal family were staying," Ray answered, turning towards Cleo to continue the discussion.

"But what if this isn't about an assassination at all?" Cleo mused. "What if we're talking about a theft instead or an infiltration—"

"It's highly unlikely, considering it would be easier to infiltrate the castle without the warnings. During Maria's birthday there was an increase of traffic, and we'd pay less attention to seeing strangers around the castle," Mark interrupted with a thoughtful shake of his head.

"The error of multiple authors can't be overlooked. Do we know how many people saw the original letters on our end?"

"What are you suggesting?" Jonathan asked, sipping on his drink.

"I'm not suggesting anything really. You all seem lost on ideas, so I figure going over all possible lines of questioning will either rule out or bring up options for what is going on," Cleo answered with a half shrug.

"The only three people that have seen the letter are in this room, and it's not like we discussed the details of the letter around other people," Mark stated, interlocking his hands in front of him.

"Until today. I'm sorry, I get bugged by things I don't know," Jonathan said, bowing his head.

Jonathan and Mark continued their conversation, but Ahzya was aware that Ray's focus had shifted. She was already painfully conscious of the elephant in the room; it was no wonder Ray's mind had turned to the same point as hers. That day in Ray's room, where that inconspicuous note should have held no importance. Clear and concise lettering would have been easier for any reading lesson, not the scrawling of a child.

"Ray, I've become aware of some changes they've made to the south-east tower. Will you make time to go on an inspection with me?" Cleo asked, standing up from the table suddenly.

"They've made changes to your corner of the castle?" Ray asked, reaching for his hat and settling it onto his head with a grin.

"They wouldn't dare," Cleo stated with a chuckle. "I'd kill anyone who dared to touch my slice of paradise. I may not be living here currently, but I don't intend on giving the head maids any reign over my castle. They are prone to try and design it into some regal... thing."

"Madams Hill and Uran have decorated and designed the rest of the castle. They are mighty fine at what they do. Haven't you taken a chance to look around during your visit?" Mark interjected, raising his eyebrows at his daughter.

"Ray, they've added a rooftop garden on part of the wall, a great spot for stargazing. I was wondering if you'd give me a lesson like old times," Cleo continued, ignoring her father. "It's beautiful and it will be a welcomed distraction from the hideous décor around here."

"Cleo!"

"Run, Ray." Cleo jumped over her chair and bounded towards the door like a kid.

Ray followed, turning only to tip his hat towards the two men left at the table. Mark let out a low hiss, as if he'd just drank a shot of strong alcohol, and crossed his arms.

"Did my own daughter just steal my best friend for the evening?" Mark asked, shaking his head as the door closed. "What do you say, friend, have a drink with me in my study?"

"Why should I? I'm not your *best* friend," Jonathan sneered and looked King Mark up and down. "I'm afraid I have other plans... with Miss Catherine."

Mark looked at Jonathan incredulously and then glanced at Ahzya.

"He may have plans with me, Your Majesty," Ahzya spoke with a smile. "But I've made no such plans with him. I'll have that drink with you. Besides, with a possible assassin roaming around, it'd be unpatriotic of me to allow you to return to your study alone."

"Don't be too concerned for him, he has bodyguards to help him back safely," Jonathan said, standing from his seat.

Mark, with his arms still crossed, looked between friend and maid for a moment before straightening and bringing his hands down on the table.

"You know what, Miss Torpay, I accept," Mark said, crossing over to Ahzya and offering her his arm. "How good are you at holding your liquor?"

"On a tray or in my stomach, Your Majesty?" Ahzya returned.

"A fascinating comeback," Mark said with a chuckle. "Let's go with both. The former has always left me intrigued. How do you all manage to carry so many things around on one hand without dropping things constantly?"

"Funny fact, most of us were circus performers in our former lives."

NORTHERN HALLS, CASTLE PRYNESSE, ALPANIA

"Did you kill him?" Jonathan's voice, clear and concise, confronted Ahzya.

Ahzya squinted slightly and rubbed her own forearm. Her heart was oddly fluttery and her head fuzzy. The last person she wanted to meet right now was Jonathan. Alcohol had a weird effect on her and she felt sick. Ahzya sighed. She hadn't even drunk that much.

"No," Ahzya replied simply.

Ahzya kept walking, intent on passing Jonathan without extending the conversation.

"Isn't that why you went? A perfect opportunity," Jonathan asked.

"Pfft, what kind of idiot would I be, to be seen entering the king's study with him and end up being the only one exiting alive?" Ahzya replied, before pausing and looking directly at Jonathan. "Or perhaps that's exactly what you want. This could just be one of your weird Triox plots to dispose of criminals. Fake an assassination job and get us caught in the process."

Jonathan didn't move, he remained leaning against the wall, his arms crossed. A sickening shiver skipped across Ahzya's spine, and she sighed, taking a deep breath to rid of her lightheadedness.

"Who else knew of your plans last night?" Jonathan asked, his tone even.

"No-one, I didn't utter a word of it," Ahzya responded, crossing her own arms. "Except to you."

"Well, it's safe to say you're compromised."

"The plan may have been compromised, but I don't believe my identity was."

"They may have no proof, but they'll have suspicions."

"Why do you think I drank with King Mark? He doesn't suspect a thing," Ahzya answered bluntly. "Do you think he would have gone alone into a room with a suspected assassin and then poured himself alcohol? It's unlikely."

"I recall you saying you don't drink."

"I don't."

"So that scent on your breath is natural and not the work of the spirits?"

"Wine. We had wine. And I don't drink as a rule while working, but when a man, abandoned by his friends, wants a drinking partner and fixes you with puppy dog eyes, one's rules can be set aside for an hour or two."

"So, if he flashes his royal puppy dog eyes while you assassinate him, you'll give up the whole thing?"

"Maybe! His baby blues are mighty convincing."

"Don't get sarcastic with me," Jonathan threatened.

"Sorry, I thought I'd speak a language you're fluent in, since it appears we don't see eye to eye when I use plain ol' Alpanian."

"You should go home." Jonathan spoke quickly.

"That's where I was headed before you interrupted me," Ahzya said, rolling her eyes.

"I don't mean your quarters in the castle," Jonathan answered, his gaze firm. "I mean Triox, or wherever the hell it is you call home."

Ahzya froze, cursing her buzzing head and low alcohol tolerance. Something was wrong with Jonathan, but for the life of her, she couldn't seem to focus. A bucket of icy water was what she needed and there didn't seem to be one on hand.

"I know the plan failed, but I won't give up so easily. I know you don't want to be the plans guy, so I've already come up with another approach. You'll have to forgive me though, because I don't feel like sharing it with you this time," Ahzya explained, offering a forced grin.

"Don't you get it?" Jonathan said, moving towards her with a swift movement. "You're fired. I don't need you, or any of your plans. I'll reimburse you for the work you—"

A slap sound interrupted anything else Jonathan was going to say and instead he looked at Ahzya as if she was crazed. Ahzya's cheek stung, and she shook her head before slapping herself on the other cheek. She had to sober up and surprisingly the slaps actually helped.

"Wow, phew," Ahzya sighed as she shook her head one more time. "Okay! If you're going to pick a fight with me, Jonathan Dryen, at least have the decency to do so when I'm sober."

"I was hoping you would be more reasonable this way," Jonathan said, with a soft snort. "Cath, take this opportunity and leave. This is no longer your duty."

"Whether you believe it's my duty or not, doesn't matter," Ahzya replied evenly. "I told you. I accepted it as a job for you, but it's personal for me too."

"I'm giving you the chance to get out of this alive and well. You're a thief, not an assassin. Go fix your life. I won't offer this again, so pack and leave, while I'm feeling generous."

"What? You've suddenly grown a conscience? Or is it because of your brother?"

"Go home," Jonathan ordered, his voice flat and his eyes going dull.

"You'll just have to kill me," Ahzya replied, her eyes narrowing. "'Cause I'm not going until I've finished what I came here to do."

"Believe me, I will kill you if you don't leave," Jonathan said swiftly. "I'm not the kind of person who can forgive failure and disobedience."

"Why let me walk away?" Ahzya asked. "Surely you don't need any loose ends floating around."

"Perhaps I don't want the trouble of dealing with your body," Jonathan said angrily. "Perhaps I decided to let you go and live the rest of your life. You are young and it's not like I go around killing everyone for the thrill of it."

"Or perhaps you've changed your mind knowing that your brother and I are connected," Ahzya said, her voice sharpening. "I get it, I remind you of him. You don't really want to see me killed or captured trying to take revenge because you think it would break your brother's heart if he knew."

"You may have been *his* 'guardian angel'," Jonathan said, his eyes darkening. "However, to me, you are just a tool. A tool that doesn't work and needs to be thrown away."

"What if I hadn't told you about my relationship with your brother?" Ahzya asked. "I doubt we'd even be having this discussion."

"If you had never met my brother..." Jonathan paused, taking a step forward.

Jonathan was so close that Ahzya was reminded of that moment in the tavern. His breath had an alcoholic scent and, with his height, he still towered over her. However, she didn't feel intimidated like the first time. Ahzya knew his secrets; knew what made him tick.

"I'd still be asking you to leave," Jonathan continued slowly. "My revenge plot is only on those who had a role in wronging my brother. I've come too far with this revenge plot to let an incompetent thief mess this up, whether she's related to my brother or not."

Ahzya and Jonathan stared at each other, a mixture of anger and stubbornness set in both their eyes. The tipsy heart fluttering was replaced with adrenaline-fuelled pumps and she didn't feel the least bit cloudy anymore.

"I can see why Cole never introduced us," Ahzya said darkly.

"Pitiful," Jonathan scoffed.

"Am I really that pitiful, do you think?" Ahzya asked.

"Of course," Jonathan answered, breaking into a lopsided grin. "What kind of girl ruins her life because of a teenage crush? You've got to be pretty pitiful to let your childish heartbreak turn you into a murderer."

"You're right," Ahzya said, turning away with a clenched jaw. "I've got to be crazy. Thank you for being so thoughtful, *JP Dry*. Consider our contract null and void."

"I'm glad you're finally seeing sense," Jonathan answered, holding an equally icy tone. "Sleep well, you'll have quite the journey tomorrow."

"I don't think I'll be able to sleep, I'm far too excited by the fact I won't have to deal with you anymore," Ahzya bantered back. "I wish you the sweetest of dreams, Jonathan."

Ahzya stalked away, removing the maid's headband from her head in a huff.

"You're cute when you're angry," Jonathan called out, just as she rounded the corner. "Goodbye, Cath. I'll miss you."

*Sarcastic ass!*

# CHAPTER TWENTY-FIVE

MAID'S QUARTERS, CASTLE PRYNESSE, ALPANIA

Noelle was still awake, flicking through a book and smiling to herself. She looked up when Ahzya entered and flashed her a kind smile.

"You're back early. No big exercise routine tonight?" Noelle asked, flexing one of her arms in a teasing manner.

Ahzya crossed over to Noelle and threw her arms around her neck. Noelle was so taken aback that she just let Ahzya stay like that for a minute without saying anything.

"Noelle, I drank too much," Ahzya finally admitted, with a throaty chuckle.

"Are you really drunk? Why?" Noelle asked in confusion as Ahzya pulled away.

"I was dumped," Ahzya said with a victorious grin.

"Dumped? Jonathan Dryen dumped you?" Noelle asked, tossing the book aside.

"Yup," Ahzya said with a nod. "That means I'm free. Maybe I should take a trip to the ocean. I've been so stressed because of that jerk; I haven't even been sleeping. Should I just quit and travel?"

"You should!" Noelle replied enthusiastically. "I thought he was better than that! Though I guess since you weren't going to fall for him, it's for the best. He seemed so sincere though. He shouldn't have even tried if he was going to be cruel in the end. Yes, I think it's for the best you go."

Ahzya frowned across at her roommate and pouted, acting drunk, although the alcohol had already lost all its effect on her.

"Do you hate me? You want a room to yourself, don't you?" Ahzya whined.

"Of course not, I adore you," Noelle said, tilting her head at Ahzya affectionately. "But you're like a caged bird here. You can't stand the injustice from the head maids, you're always out exercising, you love hunting and sneaking off to see your horse. Someone like you was never meant to remain in the cold stone walls of a palace. Just one look at you and I know you're always mulling something over in that pretty head of yours. You'll go crazy if you stay here too much longer."

"You can tell that much from just being around me?" Ahzya asked, blinking in confusion.

"I told you, I come from a large family, you get used to noticing the small hints from those around you, because not everyone gets a chance to speak in such chaos," Noelle answered with a warm laugh. "I could be totally confused, but I haven't seen you give one purely genuine smile the entire time you've been here."

Ahzya wasn't quite sure how to respond.

"So, if you have something you need to do, to ease that weight on your shoulders, then take courage and do it," Noelle said, reaching to pat Ahzya on the head. "Even if it means leaving the castle without saying goodbye, I'll cover for you and say a relative died or something like that."

"What if it's all just a lie? What if none of what I portray is genuinely real?" Ahzya asked. "You've already managed to see through to my true nature as a free spirit. What if working here is truly just a stepping block, and I'm only acting nice?"

"We all lie, some more than others, but you can't fake the impact your words and actions make on those you encounter. What may feel like falsified interactions to you, can become moments of change, both positive and negative, for your audience," Noelle reasoned. "Because of your presence, Mrs Youn, Lesley, Merida and I have formed a camaraderie that wasn't there before. We've been inspired to have each other's backs and protect what we can. We had all been dreading the hell that would be unleashed over Her Majesty's birthday celebrations, but, while it was hectic and brutal, we actually had moments of fun. I laughed so much with those beautiful souls and, without you, I never would have believed that Mrs Youn has a comical side! These results can't be faked, Cath."

"How are you so nice?" Ahzya asked genuinely.

Noelle chuckled and shook her head.

"I just read too much," Noelle said. "I just quote things from my favourite books. I delivered the ideals well, though, didn't I?"

"Yeah, you should be a theatre performer instead of a maid," Ahzya answered. "Perhaps you should be the one quitting instead."

"I'm content with you and my family as my fans. Work as a maid is a bit more reliable than a travelling theatre performer," Noelle answered. "Besides, theatre means late nights, and I'm already ready for bed and it isn't that late."

Noelle yawned as if to prove her point and put her book away properly. She then snuggled into her bedding but peeked out momentarily and clicked her tongue at Ahzya.

"Since you've been drinking, make sure you get to bed soon as well," Noelle instructed.

"Good night, Noelle," Ahzya said, waving.

"Go—" Noelle yawned, and lifted the covers over her head "—ight, Cath."

Ahzya sat in silence, allowing a gentle smile to settle on her lips as she waited, listening to Noelle's breathing even out. Only when she was sure Noelle was fast asleep did she begin packing her belongings. Ahzya had little to pack, she'd always been ready for escape at any moment anyway. She folded her maid's uniform one last time and laid it on top of the folded blankets and sheet of her bed. Ahzya didn't get changed into her normal clothes, instead she pulled on her thief uniform from the previous night. Luckily her muscles hadn't seized up too much due to her exertion, but she certainly didn't feel like hanging from the ceiling again any time soon.

The night air left her breath hanging in a wispy white cloud just beyond her lips whenever she breathed out. Other than the mist from her breath, there wasn't a cloud to be seen, and the stars glimmered in the velvet black sky. Ahzya could understand why Ray and Cleo had chosen such a night to use the garden rooftop to stargaze. Even if she found herself in a puddle of blood, she hoped she'd at least be able to die looking up at them, it would make it almost romantic.

Ahzya paused and chuckled.

Through everything she'd faced, not once did she feel like forfeiting her life. The challenges almost made her too stubborn to die. Ahzya felt like she'd lived her life so far hurt and selfish, and she was unsure whether she had no pride or too much.

The thought scared her a little. The dangers of her job had always been high, but she never went into a job believing that she may die from it. If she were to be executed under the moon, she'd pass with no regrets. Reggad was the only thing of value to her and the mare would be well looked after by Noah. Yet still a dreadful knot settled in her chest as she took steps through the night.

Her target destination was an enclosed walkway situated in the north-western sector of the castle. It was a serene place, secluded from the rest of the castle by its unique design.

The design of the walkway was most intriguing, as it was not set at ground level but instead was carved into the ground. When they began building the area, testing the soil revealed that the earthy layer wasn't deep and instead turned into stone. This meant rather than digging, the job was mostly carving and hauling away chunks of stone which were used to build the exterior office. Designs of each former king were carved into the stone slab walls and the northern wall had a waterfall. The waterfall sourced water from the river that ran through the northern castle grounds. It gathered in a pool at the bottom before draining through a system to the underground stream that was discovered under the castle during the building process.

It wasn't all rock and water, as earth had been rearranged and flowers planted throughout. Even a tall holm oak sat as a focal point in the centre of the walkway, the path circling it out of respect. Considering the first floor surrounding the space consisted of plain walls and no way into or to overlook the area, it was often covered in shadow. It was a miracle the oak had grown so strong considering both the shade and stony soil. It had become the secret pride of the royal family.

The walkway with all its beauty ran between the main castle offices and King Mark's personal office, which he frequented in the evening, where he could tend to paperwork in relative isolation. The walkway was the only entry and exit to the king's office, though Ahzya suspected there was another secret passageway. With such a serene main walkway, heading to a late-night work session would almost be pleasant.

Ahzya paused near the entryway of the castle offices. Considering the late hour, it was unlikely that any officials were still up attending to paperwork. A couple of soldiers went by on their rounds, but they weren't on high alert, and Ahzya easily avoided detection by slinking into a small gap between pillars.

Ahzya couldn't be certain that King Mark hadn't already entered his night office; however, if that were the case, she'd already set her mind on staying there until he appeared from his office again.

Ahzya eventually found herself in the walkway, the waterfalls and faint moonlight making the area look and sound almost enchanted. Ahzya eyed the holm oak, finding it looked far too ordinary for the value that the royal family put on it; however, as an ambush spot, it would work well enough.

The lower branches of the oak had been removed as the tree grew, allowing for a spacious circling walkway. It made climbing into the tree difficult which, in hindsight, was a great move to prevent adventurous castle children from turning it into their climbing tree and secret base.

Ahzya's thigh grip strength turned into her best asset as she shuffled up the trunk, her legs straddling the tree to keep her progress up. She reached the lowest branches fairly quickly and disappeared gratefully into the protection of the thick maze of the canopy. It wouldn't be a bad way to pass the night, but it also possessed Ahzya with a veil of sleepiness. Of this strange phenomenon, Ahzya could only blame wolves, undignified men and other creatures that roamed the night. Her years of roaming across Alpania had taught her that a tree could offer a safe haven for sleep, lifted off the ground and out of the normal view of any passersby, unless of course they looked up. So, as she now found herself in the comforting arms of the holm oak, the wide branches of which were easy to balance upon, her trained survival instincts recognised it as perfect conditions for an evening of sleep.

Ahzya quickly found a way to pass time, her dagger cutting into the bark of the precious family oak. Ripping up the darker skin to reveal pale wood underneath, Ahzya began carving into the trunk. She caught the bark cuttings in her lap and shuffled them into a pocket ever so often to avoid any build-up, lest it fall and give away her position. A crudely carved horse head began to appear, and Ahzya removed a bottle from her pocket which had a refined carving on its front. Using the bottle for reference, the tree soon sported a non-sanded or polished version of the stallion head.

Content with her artistic endeavours of the night, Ahzya pulled out a rag and then popped the cork stopper of the bottle she'd been using for reference. The bottle held a sweet-smelling chemical, although Ahzya tried to avoid getting too close. Pouring a generous amount on the rag, the bottle was recapped and returned into her pocket. She cupped the rag in the palm of her right hand. It would soon be dawn, it would either be go time or she'd have to go on the attack. Her eyes stayed fixed on the corridor leading into the tower to the king's office, awaiting her opponent's next move.

KING'S PERSONAL OFFICE, CASTLE PRYNESSE, ALPANIA

Sleep. Sleep was finally the last call of business King Mark had for the evening. As he closed the last ledger for the night, Commander Ray also closed the report set in front of him with vigour.

"Your reports all up to date?" Mark asked, leaning back in his chair and feeling the leather back for the first time in hours.

"As up to date as they'll get tonight," Ray answered with a shrug. "Besides, you don't want me to finish it now, you've just managed to complete your own pile of work. I'd hate to add one more piece of paper for you to review."

"Your thoughtfulness is overwhelming, Commander," Mark thanked with a chuckle. "Considering the sun will wake up everyone else in an hour or two, let's leave and try to get to sleep before the early risers make too much noise."

"At least you have a warm bed and wife to help settle you, I have an over-fluffed bed and no ocean lullaby. My chances of beating the castle's featherless roosters are extremely low." Ray stood and rolled his shoulders.

"Oh contraire, I have a bitter tea, which my delightful wife insists I have before bed on late work nights, and a lonely bed, for my love is one of those early risers we've been speaking about."

"The position of king can be a lonely task." Ray shook his head.

"I sometimes am able to convince my queen that she requires further beauty sleep; however, it depends on her mood whether she takes that as an insult or a touching display of care."

"As a bachelor of many a year, I must admit I do not face such trials."

They left the office via a spiralling staircase, one soldier leading the way with a lantern and two others following closely behind them, extinguishing all the lights in the office as they left. The group was quiet, the early morning stillness casting a calming spell on them. The sound of the waterfalls in the courtyard became louder as they walked down the corridor at the end of the stairs. The recent rain caused the river through the castle grounds to flow quickly and it affected the grandiose chorus of the waterfalls.

"Although it's a different kind of water sound, I may just climb into the ol' holm oak and settle down for the night. Might feel more at home there than my room," Ray mused aloud.

"Commander, that tree represents the royal ancestors and this country's past and present accomplishments. Do you really think it's an appropriate place to sleep?" Mark replied.

"I'm sure it's the most reliable tree around."

The waterfalls resounded as they made their way across the courtyard and started passing under the grand holm oak. Ray tried to stretch out his neck by rolling his head while looking up at the branching canopy above. He must have moved too quickly, because he winced and his right hand flew to his neck to massage out the cramp.

"A man really shouldn't stay looking down at tiny pieces of paper for long periods of time," Ray mused, slowing his stride as he continued to ease the pain in his neck.

One of the soldiers following behind them let out a slight grunt, as if agreeing with him, and King Mark laughed. Ray's eyes came back into focus when one of the branches bent under a weight too great to simply be a squirrel or movement of the wind.

Though subtle, under the sound of the cascading water near them came a muffled strangling grunt. Ray spun, his left hand falling to his right side, where usually his cutlass would sit sheathed. One of the soldiers hovered on his knees mid-slump, his eyes glazed and mouth agape. The other had fallen unnaturally backwards, his helmet knocked over his eyes as he'd fallen to the ground. The only other sign of movement was the bending branch overhead, the leaves shaking as a shadow moved quickly towards Ray from above. Ray braced himself, knowing it was too late to back away, as a black clad figure dropped through the canopy. A sharp blow connected with his chin, the knee of his attacker knocking him back a pace. The attacker didn't fall to the ground but dangled from the branch like a gymnast.

"Get out of—" Ray began to say, remembering his royal friend.

His warning was cut off as the attacker swung their legs and wrapped them around his neck and shoulders. The full weight of the shadow fell onto him and Ray grabbed a firm hold of a thigh. A clothed hand clamped over his mouth, sweet droplets filled his nose and mouth as he attempted to breathe in. Ray struggled, tightening his grip in an attempt to loosen the constrictor-style attack on his neck and shoulders.

Relieved, Ray noticed that the soldier that had been leading the way had dropped the lantern and was in the process of putting himself between Mark and the attacker. The soldier was armed with a sword, and he was already reaching to draw the weapon.

Given the situation, procedure called for the soldier to draw Mark out of the area. By keeping his sword in front of him and walking backwards, he'd be able to defend any direct attack. The movement of the soldier had cut off an advancement by Mark who seemed ready to run to defend his friend. However, seeing his own soldier step in, Mark began backing away too.

"ATTA—" the soldier yelled, bringing up his sword.

The weight on Ray's shoulders shifted and an object flew in a flash at the alert soldier. The soldier's sword fell slightly, and a thin black dagger sunk into the right side of his chest just below the collar bone. The blade must have found a gap in his rib cage as it sunk deep and the soldier's breathing immediately became short and quick. Unable to breathe or talk in any helpful manner, the soldier waved his arm at Mark to run, as the pain forced him onto his knee.

Whatever chemical was covering his mouth, Ray could feel its effects setting in. In a last-ditch attempt, Ray switched his weight and suddenly threw himself forward in a somersault motion. The move could have ended with his own broken neck, but if it earnt Mark a few more seconds then Ray had to try. Either way, whether it was the chemical or the blow to his own head, Ray blacked out in a second.

# CHAPTER TWENTY-SIX

ROYAL COURTYARD, CASTLE PRYNESSE, ALPANIA

Weakened by the chemical, Ray's vice-like grip on her thigh loosened. Ahzya assessed her situation again, from where King Mark was moving, to the soldier who was breathlessly struggling with a collapsed lung. Just as Ahzya relaxed her attention on Ray, he plunged himself forward awkwardly bringing her own body down with him. Ahzya put out her hands and tried her best to detach her legs from around Ray's shoulders. Having already started to relax her legs to jump off, Ahzya rolled with Ray's movement, somersaulting as she hit the ground.

Ahzya lifted herself to a crouch and glanced back at Ray, but he didn't move. Getting to her feet, she paused momentarily as the stabbed soldier weakly lifted his sword at her, his teeth gritted and a desperate determination in his eyes. Ahzya clicked her tongue and, considering the soldier was already on one knee, she brought a quick upwards roundhouse kick into his sword hand. Ahzya stepped close and, with one hand reaching to block any counter measure the soldier put in place, brought her knee into his jawline with her full weight.

Ahzya place a steady hand on the soldier's shoulder and pushed him to the side, she couldn't take any care for them, unfortunately they were all on shift at the wrong time. Finally, she could focus on her main prey.

King Mark still faced towards her, but anger was in his eyes as he glanced over the scene of his fallen soldiers and friend. He should have called out by now; there were enough soldiers patrolling the castle that one of them could arrive on the scene quickly enough. He now stood in the stone corridor to the offices, any sound or call he wished to make would echo.

Ahzya stepped over the now unconscious soldier and started running towards the king. King Mark brought two daggers into view, which he'd drawn from their hidden position in the back of his belt. Ahzya could hear her own footsteps, her breathing even. Her blood felt like it was boiling through her veins and her skin burned under her fitted clothing.

Collateral was all that those soldiers and Ray were, yet attacking the black and purple uniforms left a bitter taste in her mouth. All because King Mark couldn't do his job properly. He complained of paperwork; spent hours on paperwork. But it wasn't paperwork that ran a country, it wasn't going to be paperwork that could save a life. Ahzya forced her own uneasiness to aide her mind into a rage.

The handle of twisted green and blue leather slipped into her hand from her sleeve. She didn't reveal the blade fully though, and she continued to run at full speed towards King Mark. King Mark steadied his footing, his left foot forward so he was side on, and his blades snaked into a defensive hold.

Drawing just out of reach of Mark, still running, Ahzya suddenly threw her own feet forward, leaning back, but remaining balanced upright. The gravel path, which led through the garden, ran part of the way into the corridor before seamlessly fading into a stone flooring. On the loose ground, Ahzya skidded and her blade lashed out as she slid past on the right of Mark's legs. Mark tried to take a swing at her as she passed, but the surprising slide technique meant he was trying to attack behind him.

Ahzya's attack landed at the back of his left knee, slashing into the muscle causing it to buckle, putting him off balance. Ahzya couldn't attack immediately, but she stopped skidding and found she was on the firmer stone flooring. Thus, getting back to her feet without any loss of grip, Ahzya dashed back. Mark crossed his blades to stop Ahzya's dagger in its downward strike. However, Ahzya swivelled and kicked one leg into the wall, pushing into Mark with as much strength as she could muster.

A sturdy male frame was difficult to knock over, and Ahzya knew it would take more than a wall push to completely unbalance Mark. Mark slid on the gravel but used their interlocked blades to push back. He followed it up with two swift slashes of his daggers, the steel singing as they detached from Ahzya's own blade.

Wanting to get a bit more space between them again, Ahzya used this chance to shuffle back a step. She countered a follow up downward strike with the slim dagger and caught Mark's second blade with the reinforced leather greave on her left arm. Ahzya followed through with a left-handed strike at Mark's chest and stepped close again, planting her left foot on the ground towards his own. As her punch landed, Ahzya brought her dagger wielding hand in a cross attack. Ahzya didn't aim for the head, instead she purposely missed any contact and brought it across his body. In one swift movement, Ahzya swung her right leg in a sweep kick. The kick struck the back of both his legs, including the one she'd sliced moments before. As she sweep kicked, she forced her right arm against Mark's chest.

Finally, King Mark was knocked off balance. He stumbled backwards awkwardly, falling onto his back heavily. Ahzya allowed her sweep kick to spin on the gravel. Without hesitation, Ahzya jumped and brought all her weight down onto Mark's chest, her knees leading the way. Several of his ribs cracked audibly, a chill coursing its way through Ahzya's body at the sound and feel. Ahzya's own gaze twitched for the first time as, with the breath knocked out of him, Mark let out a wheezing groan.

Aware that their fight on the gravel path and the sound of their battle may have already caught the attention of someone nearby, Ahzya gripped the dagger tightly in her fist. She took in a quick breath before bringing the dagger down in several sharp precise hits.

Ahzya stumbled to her feet and stood above Mark's motionless body as his eyes glazed and blood swelled at the wounds. Ahzya let her hands drop to her side and breathed out shakily. Her eyes had cleared of their earlier fiery rage, and to her own horror Ahzya released a breathy chuckle.

Fearfully, Ahzya snapped out of her dazed state and scanned the castle grounds. Ray and the soldiers lay still where she'd attacked them. Ahzya rose onto the balls of her feet and stepped over the Alpanian king.

EASTERN CENTRAL TOWER, CASTLE PRYNESSE, ALPANIA

Ahzya's hand grabbed onto the leather handle of her travel bag and yanked it out of the nook she'd stashed it in earlier. Ahzya had made a detour on her way to the courtyard earlier, placing her belongings in a hide hole in the eastern wall, so she could avoid returning to the maid's quarters.

The travel bag was between where the ceiling rafters and round wall of the eastern central tower met. Unlike the outer wall, guards weren't stationed at every tower. This meant the tower was left abandoned most of the time, especially on the top floor which served only as an outlook point. This particular tower had a pointed cone roof, and therefore there was no access to the roof. From the eastern wall, Ahzya could make her way to the outer wall. Of course, if the alarm was raised, then the gates would all be on high alert and locked down immediately.

Luckily, having been friends with Cole, he'd shown her another entrance, a tunnel that only soldiers and officials used. It would be under watch as well, but less strictly, leaving more opportunity for escape. These routes were often used by trainee soldiers who wanted to sneak back in after curfew, although Cole always denied ever using the tunnel for such exploits.

Ahzya knew she didn't have enough time to get changed completely, but she pulled off her black, hooded, stretch-cotton scarf, which also had a built-in face mask. Blood shimmered on her gloves in the low dawn light that streamed in through one of the tower's windows. She pulled them off roughly and tossed them into her bag. She wiped her hands on the top of her pant legs and went to reach into her bag for a green tunic that she could throw over the top of her current outfit with a belt.

Ahzya instead grabbed onto the leather handles and spun, bringing the bag up defensively. The bag ripped open as a sharp, curved blade sliced through the cotton threads. Ahzya threw the bag away from her, directly at her attacker, and rose to a defensive stance.

"You know it would have been a lot less painful if you'd just taken that blow," a male voice spoke as the two of them started to circle each other.

"You only say that because you want an easier job, but there isn't much fun in that," Ahzya replied, trying not to glance at her dagger that still lay on the floor where she'd been kneeling.

"Ah, but you've become quite the nuisance, I simply can't allow you to see the morning through," the man spoke again.

Ahzya could clearly see the man in the dawn light, and her eyebrows dipped.

The man was wearing a plum-toned uniform, right down to the beret on his head. He was the same guard Ahzya had seen speaking heatedly to Jonathan a few days previously. However, this time Ahzya saw him for who he truly was. The twin curved daggers, dragon carvings showing as he flipped the blades with apparent ease, was enough warning for her.

"I have to wonder what I've done to be hunted by the infamous Rimak," Ahzya replied, continuing to circle. "I thought you went after princes, not maids."

"You know of me?" the man replied, his teeth flashing in a grin.

"Eh, I know of your blades. Well, the crown prince of Lavania's blades," Ahzya mused, jutting out her chin towards his daggers.

"Let's just say, the prince didn't require them anymore," Rimak said, shrugging.

"So I heard."

Rimak stepped forward with an attack, and Ahzya dashed forward, ducking under his right arm. Rimak twisted his blade and brought the flat of the blade into her back as she passed. Rimak chuckled as she spun to face him again.

"You said I should have some fun with this," Rimak stated slyly.

"You know, if you allow me a second to arm myself, I could up the fun even further," Ahzya replied through her teeth, her back smarting from the blow.

"I wouldn't want you to embarrass yourself. It's not like you're actually a killer. Just a petty thief if I've heard correctly. Compared to me, you may as well be a toddler holding a spoon," Rimak jeered. "You won't be the first maid to go missing recently. It's really such a waste that such young women have to die due to sticking their noses in business that shouldn't concern them."

"And what exactly does a seasoned assassin such as yourself have to gain from killing maids?"

"I know everything, you see. I know you're trying to dip your toes in the assassin business for JP Dry. Honestly didn't think you'd last this long without getting caught. We were actually relying on it."

Ahzya's eyes flashed in angry confusion and her gaze dropped to her dagger.

"However, JP actually seems to have grown attached to you. After you failed your assassination and escaped the other night, instead of being captured, I tried to convince him of another route, but he told me to wait." Rimak took a step and kicked the blade towards Ahzya, but she'd be diving into his blade's reach if she went for it.

"This is your idea of waiting?" Ahzya asked, taking a step back.

"I'm not a patient man, I also don't take orders very well," Rimak replied. "So, I decided I'll go ahead with my plans, and he'll just have to thank me and, more importantly, pay me later."

Ahzya couldn't say she hadn't been expecting some sort of betrayal, after all, she was dealing with the criminal world; these things weren't exactly uncommon. Collecting her payment would be made more difficult though, since it appeared Jonathan never intended on paying her a cent. However, there were other ways of collecting on the promised amount and more, if only she could get out of her current situation.

"A poisoned drink and a maid's disappearance, especially when the maid was only recently hired, make for a wonderful set up," Rimak continued, taking another step and kicking the dagger closer again.

"Poison?"

"I'm actually surprised you didn't start with the poison path rather than a direct attack. Most new killers aren't confident enough to actually get their hands dirty," Rimak said, almost sounding impressed. "It's a pity you didn't have enough guts to go through with it, *then* I would have been impressed."

"You fool," Ahzya muttered, her head tilted forward, looking up at him.

"Anyway... when your bloated rotting corpse appears in the moat a few weeks from now, they'll all consider it a closed case. They won't really do a proper investigation anyway, they never do in the chaos of a monarch's death, no matter how much they think they do. People just want answers, regardless of how thrown together they are," Rimak said. "Fascinating really, every country, it's always the same."

"Speaking from direct witness, I take it?" Ahzya asked, trying to prolong the conversation.

The ripped travel bag lay strewn on the floor just to Ahzya's right. Although she made sure she only looked at the green and blue leather blade in front of Rimak, in the corner of her eye she spotted a black pouch peeking out of the tear of the bag.

"Of course," Rimak replied, taking two steps this time.

Ahzya made her move, dropping to her right and grabbing onto the black pouch. She continued the movement, the song of a blade swinging just behind her. Four strides and she was at a paneless window of the tower; a jump brought her onto the sill. Ahzya didn't hesitate for a moment as she leapt from the tower. Having already planned the escape, Ahzya relaxed her body and made sure her knees weren't locked straight. She landed on the balls of her feet on the stone wall below and immediately rolled forward.

Ahzya ripped at the ties of the black pouch she'd grabbed, and it unfolded to reveal a double-bladed knuckle duster. Two blades were fused on the opposite ends of a fitted knuckle grip and a blade sheened on the outer edge. Ahzya fit her right-hand fingers into the grips and felt the weighted movement.

Rimak landed on the wall behind her and rolled, bringing him close behind her. Ahzya twisted, her weapon colliding with Rimak's curved blade. With a fluid movement, Ahzya reversed her swing's direction to parry the second dagger.

Rimak raised his eyebrows at the appearance of the strange new weapon and a smile played on his lips.

"That doesn't look like a child's toy," Rimak stated, following up with two more attacks.

"No doubt you think it would make a lovely addition to your collection," Ahzya seethed.

"You're not wrong."

Ahzya had received the weapon from the only trip she ever made outside of Alpania since she'd arrived on shore the six years earlier. She'd been hired and accompanied by a man, Jetti, who was a bodyguard for an influential family from the eastern country of Liondel.

Jetti was a master of close combat, specifically wrestling. Ahzya hated wrestling ever since, but she had to admit she learnt a lot under Jetti. Ahzya couldn't rid herself from her small frame, but Jetti was only amused by this fact, as he set her to practice against guards twice and three times her own size. Only when she'd managed to defeat these guards did Jetti gift her and train her with this strange weapon. Ahzya had left the party shortly after and returned to Alpania without a word, but with her bag full of Liondel riches and the weapon.

Now, having blocked Rimak's attacks, Ahzya felt her body move into the proper stance, as if Jetti was sitting there giving her amused instructions again. Her left arm and leg moved forward; the arm held out to the front. She left her hand open rather than clenched. The right arm gripped the weapon firmly down her right side next to the waist. Ahzya should have set her right foot turned to the side for an anchoring stance, instead she stayed light on her feet.

Rimak led with his right blade, and Ahzya stepped into the swing but went to the left. The swing came down in front of her chest. With her open left hand and arm she latched onto his right arm. Ahzya swung her weapon upwards close to Rimak's hand. The handle of his right dagger caught between the knuckle and the blade of Ahzya's weapon. While she did this blow, Ahzya twisted her own body weight into Rimak's elbow that was already locked by her left arm.

Rimak's right dagger clattered to the stone wall. Despite having his right arm in a latch, Rimak still had his left blade, and he moved to stab her.

Ahzya didn't intend to stay stationary though. Since she'd already been pushing her body weight into his right arm, as she twisted to the right around his body, Ahzya just followed through. Her own back brushed against Rimak's, and she swung the right blade of her weapon blindly into his body. Her blade landed just below his armpit, stabbing into the flesh of his pecs and skidding along the ribs.

Ahzya removed her blade, trying to let it slide along his side, as she moved away from him. Despite the pain he must have been in, Rimak swung his elbow back, collecting Ahzya's head as she tried to step away. Ahzya's eyesight blanked for a second and she stumbled forward. The solid merlon of the wall's crenellation met her left hand as she sought balance. Ahzya stumbled further when she found that she was right near an embrasure, a space between each merlon of the battlement.

Rimak approached her, the sound of his shoes only slight on the stone wall. Ahzya sighed, she was exhausted by this point. It had been a long couple of days. She trod into the embrasure and turned to Rimak.

"I'll make it easy for you," Ahzya said with a tired tone.

Ahzya tossed her special weapon onto the battlement and gave a salute, causing Rimak to pause his approach.

"Maid leaps from castle wall after poisoning the King of Alpania. A senseless closing to a dark secret of abuse faced by castle staff daily," Ahzya said, smiling gently.

"What a noble death," Rimak scoffed.

Ahzya took one more step closer to the edge, totally unarmed and prone. Rimak let his left arm fall loosely by his side and his right hand pressed into his wound.

Then Ahzya jumped.

Ahzya planted her hands onto Rimak's shoulders as she leapt forward and firmly planted her knee into his left-side right where she'd sliced him. Rimak fell backwards, Ahzya following him down. Rimak cushioned Ahzya's own fall and then she sat up. She clenched her hands and began striking as steadily as she could. Rimak's dagger had been knocked from his hand during the fall, so he was now unarmed too. However, he was a fully grown male and Ahzya, both tired and light, still made for an easy target.

Rimak grabbed her waist and rolled them over, switching their positions. He landed a hefty blow on her jaw once but reached for his dagger with his right hand and stood up. Ahzya's chest heaved, and she knew she only had one chance before she'd really be bathing in her own blood pool.

Ahzya lifted her knees to her chest, keeping her back on the ground. With a strength summoned from pure necessity, Ahzya kicked both legs at once. She aimed for his stomach, right under the ribs. Rimak took the blow heavily and stumbled back, his height meaning that the embrasure behind him struck mid-thigh. His own body weight worked against him as he toppled back, while Ahzya got to her feet. Rimak wavered for a moment, but the embrasure was tilted towards the outside of the wall.

Moments from a headfirst fall to the grounds below, Ahzya leapt forward and grabbed onto his left arm. Rimak let out a yell of pain as the rest of his body fell and put all the weight on his injured arm.

"I knew you wouldn't be able to kill me," Rimak said, his eyes watching her haughtily. "You don't have enough guts."

Ahzya gripped his hand and winced as the castle wall dug into her abdomen. His eyes were so proud, but she began pulling him up. Only a tiny bit further and he would be able to pull himself up. Ahzya saw a glint in his other hand in the torchlight.

"You may be a thief, but you are so weakhearted you wouldn't be able to do anything for yourself," Rimak said, reaching for the ledge.

"You're seriously doing this right now?" Ahzya groaned.

Ahzya gritted her teeth, and a sudden decision had to be made. She would have to start pulling Rimak up, otherwise she would start slipping over the edge too.

Ahzya didn't know why she'd grabbed onto the assassin in the first place. Something about seeing the castle uniform topple over the edge of the wall made her scared. As Ahzya met the assassin's gaze, her eyes narrowed. This man wasn't Cole; she owed him nothing. Ahzya's lips twisted into a smile at her own foolish movements. There she paused, allowing the ledge to be just out of Rimak's reach.

"Perhaps you are right," Ahzya said. "If that's the case, I'm not sure I can lift you up. Like you said, I don't think I'm strong enough. Really wasn't wise to taunt someone while your life hangs in the balance... literally."

Rimak's eyes widened, and he began to clutch at the ledge, but Ahzya's gaze went cold. Ahzya held no sympathy for a man who had just tried to kill her. She had no grace for a man who was going to try and cut her down the moment he was back on stable ground.

Ahzya then let go, her hands loosened their grip and Rimak slipped. He switched his focus onto latching his hand onto one of her arms, but without her added support he wasn't going to be able to hold on. With the realisation that he would most likely fall, his other arm lashed out. A dagger shot through the air. Ahzya was prepared and she reacted quickly.

Ahzya rolled to the side, the stone wall digging into her ribs and causing her breath to be forced from her lungs. An audible pop reached her ears as she bit into the flesh of her inner lip to keep herself from screaming in pain. Iron-tasting blood spread across her palate, her shoulder ached and continued to send shoots of pain into her body. Ahzya needed to get the assassin off her arm before she lost all strength to keep them on the wall.

It didn't take long. At the twist of her arm and the added pull of throwing his dagger, Rimak's grip faltered. His piercing yell abruptly fell silent as his body hit the ground below. Ahzya felt a shiver go up her spine as she heard the thump. Her heart pounded with adrenaline. She gazed down and could see the outline of his body in the morning light below.

Ahzya became aware of the sound of soldiers moving around the grounds. Enough time had been wasted. Without another moment's hesitation, she disappeared from the scene.

# CHAPTER TWENTY-SEVEN

ROYAL COURTYARD, CASTLE PRYNESSE, ALPANIA

Cleo Erinth stood under the holm oak in the royal courtyard, her hands absent-mindedly playing with the tassels of a black scarf that wrapped around her shoulders. It was late afternoon by the time she'd managed to steal away and start her investigation. Cleo felt exhausted, although she wasn't unused to the feeling. Being around crowds of people did that to her, but this time it had been the hushed voices and her mother's tear-stained face that sapped her energy. Anna had moved around quietly, chatting with close advisers and gently consoling their mother. Anna was always good at those sorts of things. Cleo, however, was distracted by two short questions: How and why?

"I kept the scene clear of people for you. Enough curious noses tried to poke their way in. You'd think they'd have better things to do with their time," a stern voice broke into Cleo's musings.

Cleo glanced up as a broad-shouldered man joined her side. There was nothing extraordinary in the features of the man. He was muscular, but so were many of the castle soldiers. His outfit was simple enough, but in the grey hairs and heavy-set eyebrows, Cleo found the face of a friend, Royal Inspector Galien.

"I guess we shouldn't be surprised, I'm sure word will be released soon. I'm glad the castle lockdown will keep those curious noses from spreading any rumours to the rest of the country. Until we have a plan of attack, I don't need to be called to any meetings with lords or advisers," Cleo answered, lowering into a crouch.

"The assassin took out the rear guards first over there, then moved on to Commander Ray. The front guard only became aware of the attack at that point and moved to engage. The assassin threw a blade, causing the front guard to halt his advancement due to the severity of the wound. Commander Ray toppled forward, and the assassin incapacitated the front guard," Inspector Galien explained simply, guiding the account with hand movements.

Cleo envisioned the scene, and her gaze lingered on the blood-stained gravel where the front guard had fallen.

"His Majesty engaged the assassin in the hallway entrance. There's no way to know the specific details, the gravel indicated a lot of movement and His Majesty's wounds—" Galien continued, indicating the entrance Cleo had just entered through.

"So, the assassin approached from behind?" Cleo cut Galien off and stood up. "They must have hidden somewhere near the office entrance."

Galien bowed his head, before standing up as well.

"Ten seems to have found evidence that suggests a different approach," Galien stated, interlocking his fingers. "Boost?"

Galien leant and placed his hands at a height that was easy to step on to. Cleo looked up into the holm oak canopy and took a few paces back. With a speedy run-up, Cleo stepped into Galien's interlocked fingers. Combined with the boost of Galien lifting her and her own leap, Cleo almost flew into the canopy, her feet landing steadily on one of the more reliable branches.

A small face with pointed features, almost resembling those of a sprite, right down to the pointed ear tips, greeted Cleo as she arrived. Wide green eyes closed as the deceptively girlish head dipped in greeting. Pulled loosely away from their face was wavy hair, which was such a mix of black, green and navy highlights and lowlights, that it was impossible to know where one colour ended and the next started.

Despite her mystical features, Ten was neither fey nor magician. She wore a pitch black and aqua coloured uniform, with silver buttons and clasps and a black belt. A soft hood was an optional addition to the uniform with buttons securing it to the collar. The uniform indicated Ten as a member of the Umbra Lance, a group Cleo had founded. The Umbra Lance was a small group, lance fournie, of skilled individuals, hand-picked by Cleo, and under her direct command.

"You arrived quickly," Cleo stated with no hint of surprise.

"Galien sent Pig," Ten answered in a voice like sweet honey drops.

Pig was one of the many homing pigeons Ten had trained. If there was anything that Ten loved more than anything else in the world, it was birds. If left to her own devices, Ten would happily sit and bird watch all day.

"It wasn't too difficult for you to enter the castle because of the lockdown?"

Cleo asked this with a slight smile and Ten just clicked her tongue.

"Your assassin is quite the carver," Ten stated.

"Of human flesh?" Cleo asked, her expression darkening again.

"Wood," Ten answered, shuffling along the branch to reveal the tree's trunk. "They must have been camped up here for a while waiting for the ambush."

"Any assassins have a horse head as their mark?" Cleo asked, gazing over the skilful carving.

"None I've heard of," Ten answered. "But the assassin was acrobatic; they hung from the tree when they attacked the two rear guards. They then returned to the canopy before dropping on Ray."

"Did they leave a mark on the branches?" Cleo asked.

"Other than their carving? No, but there were no tracks from the rear guards to Ray. The assassin swiftly took out the rear guard, so they didn't really witness the attack, and the front guard only became aware after the assassin was on Ray."

"And Ray? How is he?"

"Still unconscious. I heard that he received quite the blow to the head. He should recover, but we'll just have to wait until he wakes up to see how much he remembers," Ten answered, her face scrunching in concern.

"You're not calling him Mandy Ray anymore?" Cleo asked.

"Oh, he's still Mandy Ray, but considering the situation, I thought it'd be best for me to remain professional," Ten answered quickly.

Ever since his promotion to Commander, Ten had called Ray 'Mandy Ray'. To Ray's face Ten reverted back to just Ray. However, Ten was endlessly fond of her nickname for him, the portmanteau of Commander and Ray sounded similar to manta ray, which was the bird of the deep sea. Since Ray was one of her favourite people, Ten felt it fit perfectly.

"If you're finished with the report up there, we should move on to the scene at the eastern wall," Galien called from below their canopy.

"I'd brace yourself. I hear he fell from the top of the castle wall; it's not pretty," Ten mused.

Cleo sighed and with a short wave, dropped down through the canopy and landed with a crunch on the gravel path.

"So, the victim is a castle guard? Was he on patrol on the eastern wall? Alone?"

Cleo was doubtful as they began walking to the north-east corner of the castle where an exit would allow entrance to the outside of the wall.

"That's how it appeared in the beginning, but, while he's wearing the uniform, he definitely is not one of our soldiers," Galien answered, remaining one pace length behind Cleo.

"An impostor? Amongst the castle guard?" Cleo asked.

"With the other royal family members visiting the castle, he could have slipped in with one of those groups. I've already sent messengers to ask, but they aren't missing any of their security detail."

Cleo didn't question any further, and so Galien also fell silent. Their passage through the castle went smoothly, castle soldiers saluted or bowed deeply as they passed. Usually, the castle soldiers were more casual when it came to greeting Cleo, since she almost demanded it, but the general feeling around the castle was gloomy and stiff. Cleo hated it.

"Do you suspect he's the assassin?" Cleo asked, breaking the silence as they exited through the inner castle wall.

"That is a possibility, I suppose, but I'm not convinced. Plus, why would he end up crushed at the bottom of the wall? I doubt it was out of guilt," Galien replied, shaking his head.

"I highly doubt that after stabbing my father, he simply tripped and fell to his death. Not after the stunts he pulled," Cleo said as they approached the body.

"He received a non-fatal wound to his abdomen under his left arm before he fell, so definitely not self-inflicted. We also found twin curved daggers not far from the body, I think they were thrown down after his fall," Galien explained, nodding to one of the soldiers standing guard at the scene.

"Well, the wound couldn't have been sustained at the courtyard, my father's blades were clean and the others didn't have enough time to react," Cleo agreed, coming to a standstill at the body.

The body was covered in a cotton blanket, but as Cleo arrived, a soldier stepped forward to draw it back. The crumpled form of a man was revealed, several of his limbs distorted at weird angles. Brown eyes stared unseeing, and his neck lolled to the side. Bone tore through his left pant leg and blood covered patches of the plum-toned uniform.

"His stature is also far too heavy for those acrobatics at the oak, it wouldn't have been able to hold his weight, at least not well enough for a sneak attack," Cleo mused aloud.

Galien simply nodded, his arms crossed over his chest. He'd already investigated the body earlier to check pockets for any further identification.

"We found blood splatter up on the wall, so I suspect he received the wound up there and then was pushed to his death. Although, with his weight, it would take someone quite strong to simply drop him over the edge, which doesn't match up with our assessment of the courtyard assassin either."

"There's a possibility these two incidents might not be connected. While it's convenient to suspect that it was a deal gone wrong between the assassin and their employer, there's absolutely no way of knowing for sure," Cleo said, her brow creased. "I'd have been inclined to suggest it was just someone cleaning up loose ends, had this guy matched the courtyard assassin's profile."

Cleo sighed and motioned for the body to be covered again.

"We'll let the coroner take a closer look to see if he can find anything else. I'm surprised he's not here already…" Cleo allowed her statement to trail off and she glanced at Galien.

"He will be here as soon as possible, Your Royal Highness."

"As soon as he's sobered up?" Cleo asked with a raised eyebrow.

Galien looked uncomfortable and averted his gaze.

"I know your younger brother is an adult, Inspector Galien, but it might be an idea to keep him in check sometimes," Cleo stated seriously, before changing topics. "Let me see the twin blades, since it's obvious he's not one of our soldiers, they might give us a clue as to who he is."

Galien brought forward the weapons wrapped in a piece of cloth and laid them on the ground before Cleo. Cleo squatted and folded back the cloth. A dark expression settled on her face as soon as she saw the blades' design. Cleo's jaw worked as she took a moment to run her hand over the blades and handles. Her tongue clicked on the back of her mouth, and she carefully wrapped them again.

"Make sure the blades are sharpened and polished; put them in a safe carry box too. I'll have to return them to their rightful family as soon as I am able to," Cleo stated solemnly.

"I take it the blades gave us an answer," Galien asked cautiously.

"The impostor is Rimak. He must have entered the palace after killing Prince Ivan. Right under my nose the whole time," Cleo said venomously. "Whoever killed him, whether out of greed, survival, or another purpose, did the world a favour. Murderous scum like him deserve every tongue of fiery hell that awaits them."

Understanding the weight of the moment, Galien sensed Cleo needed a moment to think, and he stood by her in silence. A castle soldier carefully picked up the blades on the ground and went to fulfil Cleo's orders. Cleo crossed her arms and glared at the corpse of the assassin. Several minutes passed and Cleo's form slowly relaxed with deep breaths and became neutral.

"Was he carrying anything else?" Cleo asked.

"Only a small vial half full of an unknown liquid. I've sent it to the alchemist team to figure out what it is this morning. They said they'd send someone with the results as soon as possible."

"I thought your brother would be the person to look into it, given he's our poisons expert," Cleo said, more annoyed than the previous time she'd mentioned him.

"I'll reprimand him, Your Royal Highness," Galien said, grimacing. "The alchemist team should have the results shortly."

As if summoned by their conversation, a light grey figure exited the castle gate and began approaching them. They were running at full speed, their alchemist cloak flapping around them as they ran. The red satin trim collar of their cloak shimmered in the sun, and above the collar was a flushed female face, holding an expression of urgency and exhaustion. The junior alchemist slowed to a jog and finally stopped and stooped into a low curtsy.

"Your majesty... the vial... *Aqua toffana*," the alchemist puffed.

"Take a moment, we can wait a minute," Cleo stated, slightly concerned about the gasps of air the alchemist was taking.

The alchemist shook her head, her now messy head of blonde hair flitting about her face.

"It's highly poisonous, a few drops... a few drops can prove fatal. It also has no taste, and the vial... it was—"

"Half full," Cleo finished for the exhausted alchemist.

"So, it's likely Rimak already planted the poison," Galien stated, his brow furrowing. "But surely we'd know if a poisoning had taken effect."

Cleo made the alchemist sit on the grass and waved at a soldier to bring across a water flask. Having delivered her message, the alchemist gratefully accepted the steps to recovery. As she watched the alchemist drink urgently from the flask, Cleo's brow dipped in thought.

"Does my mother still mix that potion for my father when he works late?" Cleo asked gently.

"I wouldn't know," Galien replied.

"She prepared one last night, I believe, Your Royal Highness," the young alchemist spoke again. "She even consulted with our alchemy team on what new combination of ingredients could be better."

"Has anyone been to my parents' bedroom since the attack?" Cleo asked, her brow furrowing.

"Her Majesty the Queen was taken straight to the stronghold residence when the castle went into lockdown. I don't believe anyone has investigated the royal suite, since she left the room before the attack," Galien answered.

"My mother would have locked the door when she left in the morning," Cleo said. "We'll have to drop by the stronghold and get my mother's key. I think it's best to immediately investigate my parents' private room. Let's call it a gut feeling."

### STRONGHOLD RESIDENCE, CASTLE PRYNESSE, ALPANIA

When Cleo arrived at the stronghold residence, Queen Maria was sitting stiffly in her chair. Maria's posture was straight as she listened to the solemn words of an adviser. Anna was similarly employed a few metres away, with a lady bawling her eyes out.

"Everyone leave! My family has endured you all for the morning. You've been insensitive enough to pester my mother with unanswerable questions. We thank you for your sympathies, however, now having received your thanks, I think it's well time you left," Cleo ordered them in her even tone.

Anna ran over to comfort Maria, as tears broke the barrier of her mother's eyelids, and gave her a handkerchief. Cleo knelt down in front of the chair and gave a small smile.

"You're a queen, Mother. You don't have to burn yourself out over that gang in order to prove your loyalty or dedication to this country," Cleo assured, resting a hand on her knee.

"Being a queen is more restricting than you'd think," Maria answered, tears still forming and falling from her eyes.

"Speaking of restricting," Cleo continued, without pause. "Since you're being kept here for the moment, I need to borrow your bedroom key. Do you have it on you?"

Maria lifted a ribbon loop from around her neck and pulled the end from her bodice, displaying a silver key hanging from it. She lifted it over her head and placed it in Cleo's hand.

"Why do you need to access our bedroom?" Maria asked curiously.

"Just following leads," Cleo answered, standing.

"Don't you think it's best to not roam the castle?" Maria said in concern as the idea of her daughter being attacked entered her mind. "I've been so distracted. Stay here and allow—"

"Mother, let me do this for Father's sake," Cleo interrupted.

Cleo then left them, with Anna also wiping away tears.

Several hours passed and Maria paced the sitting room, her face tense and her red-rimmed eyes unfocused. She'd managed to remain strong for the seemingly incessant stream of officials with the help of her eldest twin daughter, Anna. However, when Cleo had waltzed in and sent them all packing, she'd broken down. She'd never been more grateful for her no-nonsense, undiplomatic daughter. Now she just wanted Cleo to return safely, still fearful that the assassin could strike again.

"I'm sure she'll return at any moment, Mum," Anna spoke softly, drawing Maria from her daze.

"Cleo's been away from us so long that I can barely recognise her these days," Maria recalled. "She was always adventurous and somewhat distant, but now she's a woman of confidence, so sure in her ways. It's still difficult for me to understand how to connect to her as her mother. She's self-reliant, but I still worry about her. When she asked you to join her in her studies in other countries last year, I admit I was hesitant. However, with you here now, I see you haven't changed too much."

"I don't think I will ever be much different from what I am now, Mum, but I'm beginning to see glimpses of the world Cleo lives in. I begin to see that high-class relationships and dinner diplomacy aren't the only things that affect a country," Anna said quietly, before adding quickly, "Of course, those things are still important, and I do feel most at ease in those situations…"

Maria pursed her lips and tears swelled again as Anna trailed off.

"I just wish we'd taken the time to have these conversations without this horrendous att—" Maria sobbed into her hands.

Cleo entered through the doors into the room at that moment, making Maria jump. Cleo awkwardly hesitated at the sight of her mother and sister but eventually approached cautiously.

"I know you've had a tough day, but since Father...well, you need to be aware of our discoveries."

"Excuse me for a moment," Anna said quickly, scrunching a handkerchief in her hands.

Cleo waited for Anna to exit the room and for her mother to calm herself. Cleo prepared a glass of water and handed it to Maria gently.

"Your Majesty," Cleo began formally. "From our investigations today, we've concluded that two assassins had entered the castle last night, if not weeks ago. Last night, there were two attempts made to assassinate King Mark. The first, as you know, involved an ambush in the royal courtyard, and the second was by poisoning."

"Poison?" Maria murmured, her eyes scanning Cleo's in confusion.

"We believe the second assassin snuck into your bedroom and poisoned the sleeping draught you prepared for King Mark. The second assassin then made their way to the inner eastern wall and after a fight, with an unconfirmed party, was stabbed and fell to his death," Cleo explained simply. "However, before King Mark made it to your room to drink the poisoned sleeping draught, the first assassin attacked His Majesty and his party in the courtyard. The poisoned draught was therefore left until we investigated this afternoon, and discovered it was the same poison found on the dead assassin at the inner eastern wall."

"I thought one of our guards had died at the wall? And why are there two assassins, how many people wanted my husband dead?" Maria's breathing shortened as she asked question after question.

"Your Majesty, take deep breaths and remain calm, and I'll explain everything you wish me to," Cleo said quietly, remaining even and calm. "The second assassin seems to have disguised himself as a castle soldier, and it was fairly simple to realise he didn't belong in the royal army. I'm still trying to figure out why there were two assassins and two separate attacks planned, but I'm pretty sure they aren't working together. That doesn't mean I've ruled out the possibility that the first assassin killed the second one at the inner eastern wall, but…"

"You're making my head spin," Maria groaned, massaging her temple.

At that moment, Anna burst through the door she'd exited through. Her eyes and cheeks were damp with tears, but a smile spread across her lips.

"He's awake. Mum, he's finally awake," Anna burst forth.

A healer appeared behind Anna with a starch-white coat and he bowed low to Maria.

"He's conscious and asking to see you, Your Majesty. He may fall unconscious again shortly, but that's merely because he'll need further rest, so don't be too alarmed," the healer said, his wrinkled face lifting in a comforting smile.

Maria leapt from her chair and crossed the room quickly. She sidled past Anna and the healer and stepped into the next room. Lying in the middle of a large bed in the centre of the room, was her pale husband.

"My love, I'm here," Maria called, rushing to sit on the side of the bed.

Maria brushed her husband's brow with her hand, with the gentlest of touches, avoiding the bandage-covered wounds, and awaited his reply. A quiet groan emanated from King Mark's mouth before he sighed.

"I really don't like that black dress on you," Mark stated, with a small smile.

Maria chuckled through relieved tears and rolled her eyes.

"Shall I change into that green gown you always say I looked pretty in?" Maria asked, her hand brushing the fabric of the coarse black dress she wore.

"I'd like that," King Mark sighed. "You'd think I'd died with you all wearing black like this."

"You almost did," Maria scolded immediately.

"Don't worry, Your Majesty," Cleo said, appearing on the other side of the bed quietly. "I've always worn black. I'll probably wear something colourful to your funeral."

Maria's wide eyes and frown should have warned Cleo off any further comments, but Cleo, on seeing her father relatively well and joking, didn't take the hint.

"You should thank your assassin, Father. They saved you from death, though I doubt they knew that," Cleo said with a sly smile.

King Mark looked confused and closed his eyes with a pained look. In a moment, his breathing evened out and his face relaxed in an unconscious sleep.

"Cleo Erinth, why did you go and say that?" Maria scolded, her hand still holding her husband's.

"I figured if he had to be bedridden for a few weeks with those wounds, he might as well have something to think about," Cleo answered with an apologetic smile. "But perhaps I overdid it."

# CHAPTER TWENTY-EIGHT

CASTLE PRYNESSE, ALPANIA

The castle hadn't seen such a hive of news and gossip since the death of the previous king and the coronation of King Mark. Those events had taken place a good fifteen years prior and compared to the current buzz, the past had been fairly calm.

What began with the attack on King Mark in the courtyard, turned into a multifaceted assassination attempt and murder. The death of the assassin who had fallen from the castle wall, Rimak, was somewhat celebrated, considering he was infamous in his line of work. The question as to who could have bested the skilled killer was highly debated on, though, by all the gossip circles.

Two days after the failed assassination, necklaces appeared in the private rooms of Mrs Youn and all the maids. The necklaces had agate pendants hanging from thin braided cord. Agate was symbolically said to give victory, strength and protection to the wearer. At first, the Madams Uran and Hill attempted to confiscate the jewellery, having received none of their own. However, Queen Maria saw Noelle wearing hers and the story quickly spread. The unexpected, kind gift impressed Maria, so she gave permission for them to wear them with their uniforms.

The inner castle wasn't the only area affected by the weird events. The next day, the trainee soldiers in the barracks of the outer grounds, received dried borage flowers tied together with a ribbon of mulberry silk. Quite the gift, considering the expensive silk. Again, the gift appeared to send a message, with the mulberry silk known for being durable, and the symbolism of the borage flowers being courage and strength. Only the trainee soldiers received the gift and the statement, though somewhat obscure, didn't go unnoticed.

Then were the haunting nightly serenades, starting the night after the attack on King Mark, taking place in different areas of the castle each night. When the guards investigated the sound, they found no sign of the night bird. The serenade was always the same tune, whistled low and sweet before rising into an eerie high melody, echoing along the stone walls. The song wasn't a tune recognised by anyone, although it was confirmed to be the same each night.

Then came a break of three days, the night song wasn't heard and no more gifts were given. The castle inhabitants had almost calmed down when the body of Madam Uran was found, weirdly staged in her own bedroom.

Madam Hill found the scene early in the morning, alerting the closest guard, and Cleo appeared from the shadows shortly after. With Cleo in charge of the scene, the room remained untouched, and thanks to the obvious staging, Hill hadn't even touched the body.

Uran's body sat at a desk, which had drag marks showing it had been moved from its position against the wall to the centre of the room. Uran sat facing the door, and behind her on the wall was a message written shakily in blood.

*Justice dealt for crimes committed.*
*An eye for an eye, a life for a life.*

The body itself wasn't murdered in a bloody fashion; however, Uran's fingertips were covered in a red stain, though no wound was evident. Madam Hill confirmed that the message of blood was written in Uran's handwriting, or as close to her style of writing that could be achieved with only dipping her fingertips in blood.

The cause of death, as ascertained by the coroner, was strangulation. A blow to the skull and other factors did indicate that she was first rendered unconscious before her demise.

As for the staging of her body, other than her seated position, she was wearing a full face of makeup, and her hair was neatly organised. She wore a bright red lipstick, which Hill stated was strange, considering such an eye-catching colour was unprofessional for castle staff. The body was taken from the room and the removal of the thick makeup, upon closer inspection, revealed bruises. They were predominantly on her face; however, there was also bruising from blows to her arms and body, all concealed under the uniform she was wearing.

Laid out on the bedside table was a journal written in Madam Uran's hand. The contents contained detailed recordings of the mistakes and shortcomings of all the maids that had ever been under her instruction. Beside each entry was an exact description of the punishments she'd dealt, written in a self-satisfied and almost cheery tone.

The journal was open to a specific page under the heading 'Maid Merida'. The entry was dated neatly and the following report so detailed that it could pass as that of a scholar. First listed was the 'crime' Merida had committed on that date, which was as simple as being overcome by sickness in the presence of King Mark and Queen Maria. Uran reprimanded Merida in her notes, using decorum and professionalism as an excuse to paint Merida in an almost obscene light. She noted the exact number of strikes she herself had administered in way of discipline, but bemoaned the fact that Merida tripped and fell down a set of stairs before the full number was inflicted. Uran's steady handwriting then described an isolating rest period, the details of which were worse than what a criminal would face in prison. To end the hideous account, Uran congratulated herself and celebrated the fact that: "There will be no child running underfoot while chores are undertaken."

Cleo closed the journal with a snap when she finished reading a couple of different pages and she stood with her arms crossed.

Commander Ray approached her, knowing that the scene had been thoroughly investigated and had moved into a clean-up phase. He patted Cleo's dark hair affectionately and she turned, smiling genuinely.

"Feeling better?" Cleo asked, looking at a bandage wrapped around Ray's head.

"Never felt better," Ray answered. "I've never had so much approved time away from paperwork. I'm thinking of getting knocked out more often."

"I won't report you; I'll back you up if you say your head hurts for a couple more weeks."

"So, was it really justice, or just some twisted murderer?" Ray asked, nodding his head towards the message on the wall.

"Evidence points to an act of vengeance on behalf of some maids that Uran had been abusing in the name of discipline. Whether you class vengeance as justice or plain murder, I'm sure there's arguments for both. Uran's journal was enough to show her nature. The fact we only found out at her murder scene is concerning. Of course, this will call for a full investigation and rearrangement of staff and line of authority depending on the results," Cleo said, frowning at her own thoughts. "Many of the girls must have been keeping quiet over this, the fact they may have thought this was just how things worked, appals me."

"Do you think one of them took revenge into their own hands?"

"I'd be lying if I said I didn't have my suspicions, but there's no evidence and the job was too purposeful and well executed. Whoever did this had to have experience." Cleo sighed and clicked her tongue on the back of her mouth.

Ray gave an affectionate smile, recognising the habit Cleo did when she had a lot on her mind.

"Come on, kid, you've been in here too long. How about a drink?" Ray asked gently.

"Water?" Cleo offered with a smirk.

"Only the best for you. I've been sworn off alcohol due to my injuries, so a round of the Lord's best beverage is the most tempting drink on offer."

Thus, the pair left Uran's room with a cheerier tone, although Ray noticed a shadow of a frown crease Cleo's brow one last time as she closed the door behind them.

All those events took place over the course of a week. The royal family were advised to stay in the stronghold's royal rooms, which they followed, to the most part. Cleo couldn't be convinced to stay still and was allowed investigation time, although a team of elite royal guards also followed on high alert. With the first assassin still unknown, and possibly still in the castle, staff and soldiers alike were questioned and their employment and identities confirmed. Rooms were searched and the storehouses thoroughly recorded with what they contained and checked daily.

The last event to happen took place at dinner the day Uran's body was found, when bowls of hot soup were brought to the royal rooms. The soup's journey began in the kitchens, where it was tested for poison and then covered. The soup then journeyed on a heated tray, under the escort of two guards, to make sure the domed metal covers were not removed and the food untampered. The journey passed successfully, and the soups were placed at the dining table. However, upon the removal of the metal domes, the soup was revealed with splotches of red staining the broth. It was like blood had been dropped into the soup and began to mix with the broth with the movement of the tray.

Her Majesty, Maria Erinth, screeched in alarm, one of the maids that had carried it in fainted. Cleo scooped up a spoonful and watched, intrigued, as the stained content dripped off the sides. The alchemist report that evening just caused an intrigued confusion rather than disgust.

"The mixture proved to be quite harmless, Your Majesties, you could have safely consumed your meal. The blood effect was created by a cochineal mix encased in thin sugar capsules. When the capsules came in contact with the soup, the sugar melted releasing the dye into your soups and giving the blood-like visuals," the lead alchemist explained, in a tone of academic excitement.

"Though harmless, it's still a horrible prank or warning. The soup was inspected at the kitchen, how and when did the culprit put it in the soup?" King Mark asked.

"Ah, that part of their plan was equally as well thought out. The capsules must have been dropped into the soup on the journey to the stronghold. Which brings up the question of how. The trays were watched constantly, and the bowls were covered with the metal dome covering. And there is your answer," the alchemist continued, picking up one of the dome coverings. "The capsules were stuck to the inside of the domes and as they travelled, the steam of the soup, kept hot on the heated trays, loosened the capsules, and that is when the contamination occurred."

At that moment, Commander Ray entered the stronghold, a piece of parchment in his hand.

"I thought you ought to know that I've just received a new letter from our informant." Ray stated his business immediately.

"What do they say?" Mark asked, even as he took the parchment into his own hand.

As with the original warning letters, the parchment was covered in a childlike scrawl. This one confirmed to be the same hand, rather than the imitation.

"The impostor assassin is dead, infection disposed of, and the trickster's final performance come to a close," Ray quoted, as King Mark read silently.

"Kind of cryptic, isn't it?" Mark sighed, dropping the letter onto the table.

"I think the message is fairly clear," Cleo disagreed, propping herself onto the edge of the table. "The impostor assassin obviously refers to Rimak, who fell to his death dressed in a guard's uniform. Infection, though you may see it as a somewhat warped sense of justice, refers to Madam Uran. And the trickster seems accurate to the culprit of the gifts, night song, dinner fiasco, and, though I doubt you'll agree, to an extent the attempted assassination in the courtyard."

"I agree, I believe the letter is informing us we'll have no more events happening within the castle. I advise we proceed with caution, since a majority of our questions aren't answered, but in some sense, I'm inclined to trust our cryptic informant," Ray agreed, crossing his arms.

# CHAPTER TWENTY-NINE

ROYAL COURTYARD, CASTLE PRYNESSE, ALPANIA

"They say to face your demons head-on," King Mark said, leaning heavily on a crutch on his left side as he took several steps into the courtyard, "but this place seems a whole lot different during the day than that night. As long as I don't work into the night, I should be fine. The plus side of that idea, my wife will be pleased with the thought of evenings actually spent in each other's company."

His walking partner was unusually quiet, and Mark turned to look into his companion's face. Jonathan Dryen's face remained neutral, but he was watching Mark silently, so their eyes met immediately. He gave a thin smile.

"Don't worry, Jon. I'm fine. With the castle opening up again and yourself, Ray, and the twins looking to leave us shortly, I'm sure my quiet days will return. This will all become just a nightmarishly warped memory," Mark assured his friend with a smile.

"Do you truly believe all this has been wrapped up?" Jonathan asked.

"We can't be sure, but everything is going smoothly so far," Mark replied assuredly. "We've put extra measures in place for castle security."

It had been almost two weeks since the letter arrived indicating the end of the threat to the castle. The castle gates were finally reopened and staff and soldiers reunited with concerned family outside the castle. Only vague information had been passed on to Prynesse residents and general public during the lockdown. Even those inside the castle didn't know what was happening.

When retelling the story, which had been warped and enlivened with gossip, there were three characters: the assassin, the trickster and the informant. Many believed that the trickster and the informant were the same person. Others, more mystical minded, thought the informant was the ghost of a past prince, Prince Daniel, who was still a child when he was assassinated. They speculated that he was warning his family's descendants of a similar danger. As far at the citizens of Alpania were concerned, due to the limited information, it allowed the answers to be speculated on as much as they wished.

"What about the murder of the head maid?" Jonathan asked, continuing with his line of questioning. "How are you dealing with that situation?"

"There's no evidence," Mark replied, shrugging one shoulder. "Cleo said it would be impossible to pin down the true culprit. The claims of abuse have been proven true though. With Uran gone, many of the maids felt empowered to speak about it. Madam Hill has decided to step down. When she realised that Madam Uran had been killed because of her treatment of the maids under them, she decided to leave. She claims she never raised a hand against them herself, which is confirmed by the maids, but nevertheless she turned a blind eye. Considering her senior role, I'm glad she decided to take responsibility for her part in it."

"How do you plan to prevent such things in the future?"

"Maria will work together with the senior maids to find replacements, and there will be measures put in place to encourage staff to report any bullying or abusive behaviour. Things like this can't be changed overnight, but now that we are aware, I'm assured we can improve the environment."

Jonathan was silent, and Mark looked truly concerned.

"Is there something bothering you? You're usually quite vocal if there's something you don't approve of. This last week, you've been the most distant I've ever seen you," Mark approached the topic head-on.

"Were you going to take any responsibility for the problem?" Jonathan replied almost instantly.

"I understand my position as leader and I'm taking steps to—" Mark began to answer the question carefully, acknowledging the sincerity of the question posed.

"This isn't the first time this sort of thing has happened, Mark," Jonathan interrupted, his speech short and jaw clenched.

"If there's been something I've been missing, I'd appreciate it if you explained it to me."

"You're the king, you should already know what is going on. Instead, you don't even know what's happening inside your own castle walls." Jonathan's eyes narrowed.

"I don't claim to be omnipresent and all-knowing, Jon. I'm a human, limited to what I see and hear, with my own eyes and ears and those of my advisers. You have no idea how much I, as a leader, want to support and relate to those around me, but I can't..." Mark paused to take a deep breath. "I rely on information from others more than I ought, but I beg you, if you know of something that I ought to be aware of, tell me."

"You had all the information you needed when my own brother—" Jonathan's voice broke.

Mark's eyes softened with sympathy, but his eyebrow dipped in confusion. He waited patiently for Jonathan to continue. Jonathan clenched his jaw; when he spoke again, raw emotion still affecting his tone.

"You were there as my brother was lowered into the cold earth. As I had to lose—"

"Your brother's death hit home for us all, but I can only sympathise with you and your mother and the constant pain you must experience from your loss."

"He was found stone cold at your own castle steps, your own front door, and all you have to say is that you sympathise? My mother had to see her son hovering at death's door. Had to watch as he stopped breathing..." Jonathan stopped again, clenching his fist over and over again to stop it from shaking.

"You don't know how many people came up to my mother and I after the funeral and offered their condolences. They said that they were shocked that such a dreadful accident could happen to such a lovely boy. You call being beaten to a pulp by soldiers a mere tragedy and accident?" Jonathan growled. "It was murder. My brother stepped on duty happy and honoured to serve you, and that same day, other soldiers, who you praise for courage and honour, beat his body till his skin tore and bruises formed."

Mark chose not to interrupt his friend. Jonathan had never spoken about the death of his brother before and he needed to vent. He needed to mourn.

"You all say he was a lovely boy. But he wasn't a boy, he was a man. And a far better man than you or I could ever hope to become."

Mark watched as watery eyes turned harsh with anger, a rage that he'd never witnessed. Jonathan got angry, but never like this. He was the kind of man to glare daggers into a man but turn them into a joke. He'd always acted light-hearted after his brother's death, never seeming to care greatly about anything. He'd undertaken his work to a high standard nonetheless.

"You should have known about the abuse in your ranks. You could have prevented it. At the least, you should have punished them, the men who killed my brother. If I could have brought them to justice like someone brought Uran to justice, I would have done it. Instead, they hid in the ranks and vowed for their honour. Sometimes, I wonder if I'm standing right next to my brother's murderers and don't even know it."

Jonathan suddenly stepped forward and lashed out, knocking into Mark with force. Mark stumbled backwards, wincing harshly as he put weight on his injured leg. Feeling the situation was being ripped out of his control, Mark glanced towards where his royal guard were stationed. To his horror, they were absent from their post; no-one else was in sight.

"The only thing I know, is that I stood next to a man who was as responsible as those who murdered him. I stood by a man I called a friend, no matter our rank and title, and he betrayed me."

Jonathan shouldered Mark again and his injured leg buckled. Mark fell to the ground, a fear gripping him as he lay prone and unarmed.

"He betrayed my family and his subjects that put their trust in him as king. Only one more person has to die, only one, for this cycle of abuse and ignorance to end," Jonathan said, his vocal tone evening; he even looked calm.

Jonathan drew the sword attached to his hip and held it for the sun to gleam off the polished blade. His breathing regulated and his blade held steady.

"I should have always planned to do this myself," Jonathan said, with a slight grimace. "In some aspects, I really do respect you. The least I can do is promise that the future of your country is a bright one, I'll make sure of it."

Mark couldn't even utter an answer, he felt he could only offer a prayer. As Jonathan raised his sword to quickly strike him down, Mark's only thought was to how he hated this wretched courtyard.

ROYAL COURTYARD, CASTLE PRYNESSE, ALPANIA

The sharp blade bit into her left hand through her leather glove, but Ahzya held firmly onto the sword just below the cross-guard.

The journey from the holm oak to where Jonathan had inconveniently decided to clash with King Mark, was difficult to undertake without being seen. Ahzya had dashed across the last few metres the moment Jonathan lifted his sword to strike. Now grappling with Jonathan, she felt relief.

Since killing Rimak, stalking Jonathan proved a challenging task. The increased security didn't help her quest to impede Jonathan's goal, but she'd had help. So, when Jonathan and Mark left on their stroll together, Ahzya followed via the rooftops. In the courtyard, the holm oak's branches almost connected to the roof at one spot. For convenience and cover, she'd returned to her ambush spot from weeks before.

"What the hell are you doing here?" Jonathan seethed in surprise, as he recognised who now stood between him and his target.

"I'm enjoying the royal courtyard's peaceful ambience. Yourself?" Ahzya answered, keeping her tone light-hearted. "Some sort of sparring match by the looks of things. I would have thought you'd prefer a partner who was equally armed: for the challenge of it."

Jonathan landed a sudden kick to Ahzya's stomach, causing her grip on the blade to slip. This time the steel sliced through the leather, drawing blood. She released the sword's blade, but made sure to position herself between Jonathan and Mark.

"You need to stop this, Jonathan," Ahzya said seriously, her light-hearted act dropping.

"No, you're the one that needs to stop. I told you that night, I won't hesitate to cut you down."

"I get it," Ahzya stated firmly. "You need justice, but this is far enough."

Jonathan didn't answer, instead his sword flashed and snaked down to hit Ahzya across her body. Metal resounded as Ahzya let her braided blue and green dagger drop into her left hand from her sleeve and deflected the blow.

"Stay where you are, Your Majesty," Ahzya warned, as she sensed King Mark move behind her. "Keep your eyes on us."

Jonathan growled and descended another flurry of blows towards her. His swings were strong and assured, but Ahzya's dagger answered with a song of confidently parried metal.

Ahzya circled to her right, making sure to throw in some counter-attacks to keep Jonathan's focus on her. The last thing she needed was for Jonathan to throw a sudden attack at Mark and make her interruption completely useless.

"While Jonathan here is too deafened by rage to allow you your response, I wish to hear your thoughts. Depending on your reply, however, I may just kill you myself," Ahzya continued to address King Mark as though she and Jonathan weren't exchanging blows.

"Nothing he has to say—" Jonathan's complaint was cut short.

Ahzya pounced forward dealing a small cut to Jonathan's throat, so small it almost looked like Jonathan had nicked himself while shaving. With her dagger switched to a reverse grip, she dealt her warning attack and brought the hilt back towards her chest. Her footwork danced her a few further steps to the right.

"I can kill you quite easily and then hear his reply if you prefer, Jonathan," Ahzya offered, as Jonathan's left hand lifted to ascertain how much damage had been dealt.

"Cole's death wasn't considered murder; there was no reason to investigate or order disciplinary actions. As far as we were aware, his injuries were sustained by a one-off tussle with some of his fellow soldiers." Mark spoke with control, although his injury left him prone on the ground.

"A one-off tussle?" Ahzya scoffed, the comment irking her and triggering Jonathan to hiss. "His death wasn't classified as murder, but there was abuse. There's evidence of it everywhere, but the culture is encouraged in the training grounds. Trainees must become strong, otherwise they'll be crushed. To complain would be to admit weakness; speaking up just isn't a team-player move. Those who derive power from ganging up on isolated soldiers and pleasure from beating down those who don't bow, end up thriving. The victims are told to work harder and toughen up."

Ahzya paused long enough to rein in the fiery rage flickering through her nerves. How often had she watched Cole train while he thought she slept? He desperately sought to be stronger, as if he believed that if he was unable to protect himself, how could he expect to defend anyone else? Since he couldn't rid himself of his oppressors, he believed he had to change the only thing that was within his realm of control and power: himself. The more resilient he became, the worse the tormentors became, which meant the stronger he had to train.

"It should have been dealt with," Ahzya replied seriously. "Which is why at this moment you need to seriously focus on Jonathan. From what I've heard, you've been friends for years. You've got to face the realisation that your failure to even acknowledge the issue, has slowly turned your close friend into your enemy."

Mark took her advice and looked to Jonathan; to the blade in his hand still at the ready. Jonathan, however, kept his eyes on Ahzya, watching her movements in a wary and evaluating way.

"Revenge, especially for a seemingly noble quest, in this case justice for a brother, is like a soul-devouring bug. The more you dwell on it, the thirstier you become, to the point that everything in your being becomes connected to it," Ahzya continued, wishing to force Mark further into his realisation of what kind of predicament he found himself in.

Ahzya could already see Mark's mind scrambling to form a reply, an explanation so that he wouldn't worsen the tense situation.

Unfortunately, the fact was Jonathan had already set him as the bad guy, and that was unlikely to change. As for Ahzya, she was hoping for a straightforward response, but not expecting it. Kings were trained for different confrontations and exchanges, but even training couldn't prepare for an attack of a more personal kind, especially from a close friend.

"You didn't go unscathed from your tussle with Rimak that night, did you?" Jonathan asked suddenly, a slight smile touching the corners of his mouth.

*So, he's noticed.*

Ahzya glanced momentarily down at her right arm. Part of her outfit consisted of a thick belt of fabric wrapped around her waist and rising to rest underneath her bosom. Her forearm sat in a pocket of this belt, acting as a subtle sling. This meant that her arm remained fairly stable even as she attacked with her dagger in her left hand.

Despite several weeks passing since Rimak's fall from the castle wall had torn and dislocated her shoulder, recovery was proceeding slowly. Unfortunately, Ahzya had to make use of the arm on several occasions and had undone any recovery she'd begun to give the injury. She could push through the pain, that was no problem for her, but if she continued, she knew she could eventually lose all function over it. Her arm already felt numb, a sign of extended nerve damage.

"Why overuse a limb if your job can be achieved with just one?" Ahzya replied, lifting her left shoulder in a lopsided shrug.

Jonathan went on the attack again, landing heavy blows to her left arm as she parried them with her dagger. His movements included a calculation for the extra length that he could achieve with his sword. Jonathan appeared cautious to decrease the distance, considering Ahzya could make a quick attack if he drew too close during combat. Jonathan focused on force rather than speed, so, while Ahzya could easily parry the blows, it became tiring with the continued jarringly weighted motions. His plan seemed to be to tire her and then take her down.

Ahzya's only advantage with this plan was that with dual-blade training, she had drilled her non-dominant left hand to equal dexterity as her right. The hours of strength training meant that her left arm wouldn't falter quickly.

However, as Jonathan delivered a downward slash, Ahzya gritted her teeth and felt the dagger handle slip in her grip. Her wound from grasping Jonathan's sword at the beginning of their altercation left a painful pressure point and, as blood seeped through the glove, it made the leather grip less secure. All Ahzya required was a little more time, but Jonathan noticed her momentary slip of control and delivered a lightning follow-up move. Her dagger was jarred from her grasp and slid onto the gravel path. Ahzya shuffled back a couple of paces warily and glanced back to Mark.

"You're stubbornly fighting against me, aren't you?" Jonathan asked, even as he confidently stepped forward after her. "Do you crave death?"

Ahzya felt the sword slash just above her head, as she dropped her body weight and slammed her right shoulder into his stomach. As soon as she hit, she dashed out to the left, so that she once again stood between Jonathan and Mark. Jonathan had the wind knocked out of him, but he didn't double over, instead Ahzya felt his blade slash the back of her tunic, slicing through skin. Considering the presumed cowardice of dying to a stab in the back, Ahzya spun to face Jonathan. There was a glinting fury settled in Jonathan's eyes, and Ahzya felt a tightness settle in her throat.

A screeching chime rang out. A black arrow ricocheted off Jonathan's sword, causing Jonathan to freeze before a clear female voice projected across the courtyard.

"Dryen, that's enough," Cleo Erinth ordered, her bow drawn and aimed. "Drop the sword and face me, before I let fly another arrow."

Jonathan weighed up his options, but considering Ahzya stood in front of his true target and Cleo would fire before he could remove Ahzya, the sword dropped. Cleo eased the tension on the bow string, but left it raised at the ready.

"Are you injured, Father?" Cleo asked, keeping her focus on Jonathan and Ahzya.

"Not physically," Mark answered. "My orders are to apprehend Jonathan Dryen."

# CHAPTER THIRTY

ROYAL COURTYARD, CASTLE PRYNESSE, ALPANIA

Cleo Erinth didn't arrive alone, and several of the King's Guard, in their violet uniforms, stepped forward on Mark's order. They set Jonathan on his knees and set to binding his arms behind his back. Only once he'd been bound did Cleo lower her bow and approach. She offered a hand in lifting her father from the ground, her eyes scanning his form for any fresh wounds.

Ahzya stood loose-limbed, her left arm hanging by her side and her right still in its sling. Her concentration remained on the group at the entrance. Two king's guardsmen stood with their arms bound and their heads downcast, an escort guard keeping a watchful eye on them. No doubt, they were the guards who had abandoned their post. However, the main focus of Ahzya's attention fixed on the figure of Commander Ray. After a visual sweep of the courtyard, Ray's own eyes trained on Ahzya, a glimmer of recognition settling in his features.

The courtyard was a sight to behold, a scene that confused those who had just joined. Jonathan struggled against his restraints, his eyes glaring threateningly at anyone who approached. Then there stood 'Catherine', the sweet former maid, who was said to have quit according to the other maids during the staff census. Yet here she was, not wearing her uniform and bleeding from gashes on her palm and back.

"So much for being my brother's guardian angel," Jonathan growled low, his nose crinkling in disgust as he looked at Ahzya. "If you truly wanted revenge for my brother, you wouldn't have interfered. I thought I saw the same rage burning in your eyes when we talked about him, but I must have been wrong. If that were true, you would have done what was required. Turns out you haven't got the guts to execute justice."

Ahzya knelt to the ground, and let out a long sigh, purposefully meeting Jonathan's gaze.

"It's not so simple," Ahzya whispered more to herself than anyone else, before replying to Jonathan with more confidence. "I loved your brother, but getting revenge for Cole doesn't even begin to scratch at the number of grievances I have against King Mark."

Jonathan continued to glare and winced as the tight ropes pinched the skin of his wrists.

"My grudge goes further back than Cole's death. Six years' worth of anger is too much time to be fixed by merely killing him. I wanted to hurt him; make him regret it," Ahzya said, her eyes flashing with a spark of rebellion.

"You should have just taken the opportunity, because it's over now," Jonathan said, his rage melting away with chilling speed and a sly smile appearing instead. "You didn't think I'd just allow you to walk away freely as some kind of heroine, did you?"

Ahzya controlled her reaction, if Jonathan wanted to drag her down with him, he'd have to be ready for a storm. Even if his assassination plot had been discovered, his other sins and dealings in Triox were currently hidden.

"Mark and Ray," Jonathan called out, "don't you recognise her? Your attacker."

King Mark now stood composed by Cleo, his aura of control back. He assessed Ahzya with a refreshed viewpoint, but his memory of the event remained clouded and unsure.

"You know, you get to hear a lot of things being a portreeve, especially over a crime city like Triox," Jonathan spoke loudly, so that all around could hear. "I'm sure you're all curious about this mysterious woman. I hear your silent question: Who exactly is she?"

Mark didn't interrupt Jonathan, instead he calmly glanced between Ahzya and Jonathan. Ray, who had moved up to the group, held a mysterious look in his eyes as he watched Ahzya.

Ahzya took a breath and hung her head, in a way of avoiding the enquiring eyes of the others watching. Ahzya remained silent, making no immediate attempt to defend herself.

"Catherine Torpay is an alias, of course. Filthy street rats like her are bound to have one or two by her age. She's not so different from all the other orphaned outcasts out there; she started the same way, loaves of bread no doubt." Jonathan's voice was lively, like the many times he'd told tales at the royal's dinner table before. "However, this girl's amazing abilities are quite renowned in the world of thievery and corruption. Not a lock too difficult or situation too dangerous."

Ahzya spoke not a word in defence, her silence indicating an admittance to the crimes being laid against her.

"She has a name in the underworld: one you may recognise," Jonathan continued, his confidence growing every second that Ahzya remained unmoving. "*Trickster*. Coincidentally or not, it seems the gossips were right on the money with their nickname for the prankster that's been playing with all of you like pieces on a chess board."

Quite a crowd had gathered at the entrance to the royal courtyard, and a murmur rippled through the group. Those who had arrived late to the scene were trying to get a rundown, and those who were trying to listen kept hushing the rest.

"You might as well tie her up too. If you don't, you'll just be falling into the web of lies, trickery and treachery that this devil has woven for you all. At the very least, she's equally as guilty as me, for the courtyard attack. I'm sure there'll be backlash if you allow a notorious thief to slip from your grasp."

Suddenly a sound, like a sarcastic snort, erupted from the unmoving figure of Ahzya Xion. King Mark tensed at this interruption and Ray's brow furrowed in uncertainty. The royal guards looked curious, but Ahzya fell silent again. This time her shoulders were shaking. It wasn't an especially noticeable movement, but her chin tilted and her shoulders straightened. Ahzya began to lift her downcast head slowly, a low chuckle escaping its captivity in her throat. Her slender left hand covered her mouth and Ahzya's eyes shimmered with tears of mirth and amusement.

"Oh, stop it, Master Dryen, you're making me blush. You're right, it's true," Ahzya admitted, a wide grin spreading across her face. "I'm one of the best around."

This statement shocked the crowd to silence and Jonathan frowned. He should have been happy, she'd practically just signed her arrest warrant; locked her own shackles, but there was something in her manner that scared him. Fear gripped him as she sat in front of him, her eyes flashing and the grin showing nothing but—confidence. Jonathan shied away from her eye contact for the first time.

"The nickname, Trickster, always felt a little cliché, but having you describe me in that manner, Master Dryen, I'm starting to warm up to it. You've heard the tales, no doubt, or seen the reports. They say I'm a silent mover, I sneak unseen into any building," Ahzya stated casually. "That, and knowing the market for what items are of higher value, are the basics. I also maintain my considerable dagger skills."

The King's Guard were watching for Mark's orders, as Ahzya continued to admit to everything and even boast about her skills. Mark held up a hand to tell them to wait, he had reservations about where Ahzya was going with her speech.

"I don't really care what the rumour mills say about me. I get such a rush from stealing things; it's pretty addictive. Nothing is safe from my clutches. I find a way in and steal every single belonging that's being protected, they rarely know I've been there till I'm long gone."

Ray now stood beside Mark, seemingly calm, but even he shook his head in uncertainty. From all points of view, it appeared that Ahzya had gone crazy. Her body language was that of an insane woman, shaking with barely contained laughter. The huge grin on her face was smeared with blood from her injured hand and her eyes were wide.

"It's an intriguing story, an orphan with the will to live and the dedication to train, becoming a symbol of envy in the criminal underworld. I'm quite inspiring, actually, aren't I?"

Ahzya directed this question at Jonathan, who was looking wary. Ahzya giggled, swaying slightly as she reached her left hand out to lay it on his shoulder. Ahzya's tongue flicked across her dry lips, pausing for a moment, her hand gripping Jonathan's shoulder tightly. Jonathan looked like a ghost had gripped him, unsure if the effect was from Ahzya's hands or the wild gleam of her grey-green eyes.

Suddenly Ahzya's eyes changed their expression and, in a second, all amusement left them, and they held only a hostile glare. Ahzya's crazed grin disappeared from her face and her mouth was set in a determined line as her body ceased its shaking.

"Of course, all good tales do have an underlying basis in truth, which is why I had no doubt JP Dry would be convinced," Ahzya delivered this with an assured and even voice. "As he sought the perfect person for his quest to infiltrate Castle Prynesse, who would come to mind, but the silent thief whose story kept being fed to his handsome ears."

This latest instalment again bewildered all listening. It was as though a spell had been cast to turn everyone to stone and there was a moment of dead silence as everyone tried to collect their thoughts. No-one moved until at last Jonathan spoke, his hazel eyes staring blankly.

"All this time, I thought I was the one who approached you, but you're saying that you purposefully brought yourself to my attention?" Jonathan asked carefully.

"A good trickster doesn't work alone," Ahzya said, pausing and stretching her shoulder muscles. "I had some help from my contacts, but the gossip tree helped a great deal for free."

"But why?" Jonathan asked, and the others could tell by his tone that he had given up.

"'A good thief never gets caught; like a breeze, their acts are seen but they remain invisible.' I lived by that code. However, it truly was revenge that caused me to build my reputation and approach you. I'd heard of a man who may have been seeking a thief to aid in a heist at Castle Prynesse. It sounded like a dream job. I could exact revenge and gain a pay cheque that would allow me to finally rid myself of this pathetic lifestyle." Ahzya spoke with a reflective tone. "When I finally met with you, you raised the stakes. Rather than stealing something, you sought to assassinate King Mark. In the first instance, I was shocked, but I pushed it aside, convincing myself that it worked with my own agenda."

Ahzya stood and turned her attention to Mark, clenching her injured hand.

"Leading into the night I attacked him, I didn't care about his position as the leader of a country, but our own interactions from the past. I didn't want to face my past; I just wanted it gone. By facing him as my enemy, it embodied the unrealistic wishes I'd held as a teenager. If I defeated him, I'd be able to move on and be free from it all," Ahzya said, pausing as she let out a soft chuckle.

"When I was finally in that moment, the rage-filled adrenaline coursing through my veins, King Mark just lay there. You don't understand the agony of realising the person that you've held responsible for taking everything you ever truly cared about... is just a mere man. He isn't an evil beast. He isn't some tyrannical conductor. He's just a flawed human that made a mistake of judgement," Ahzya said, sounding exhausted. "Realistically, I was guilty of the same crime."

Silence finally fell. Ahzya seemed confronted by her outpour of honesty and clenched her jaw shut. Cleo was the first to move, ordering the guards to take Jonathan away. King Mark motioned for Ray to stay with him and then dismissed the rest of the crowd.

"So, you're—" King Mark began to address Ahzya.

"Peter Lant's adopted Ulkadasan sister, Ahzya Xion. This blade was the final puzzle piece I needed to put things together," Ray interrupted, holding up Ahzya's green and blue braided dagger.

Ray had picked it up shortly after arriving at the scene and, after looking at her closely and listening to her somewhat vague story, he'd come to his conclusion.

"You're alive?" Mark asked in surprise, looking at Ahzya with newfound curiosity. "We'd searched everywhere to try and find you."

"She's grown into quite a powerhouse," Ray commented admirably.

"Escaping deportment just to grasp onto survival while living on the streets will do that to you," Ahzya answered, her brow furrowed at the memory. "Peter Lant didn't deserve to be reprimanded or punished for merely trying to help an abandoned orphan. So, I disappeared. You didn't find me because I didn't want to be found."

"Deportment? Punishment?" King Mark looked seriously confused.

"I was eavesdropping on your conversation at the house that night. If a smuggled person is discovered in the sailor's care or household, then punishment must be taken out upon the sailor. The smuggled person would be shipped back to their country of origin—"

"That is true, in most situations," King Mark interrupted. "It's true that I was reprimanding Private Lant for blatantly trying to deceive me.

However, my final decision was based on the fact that you were a minor and an orphan. It would have been counterintuitive to send you back, especially considering Private Lant tried to follow procedures and smuggled you out only as a last resort. As a humanitarian issue, the orphanage was not taking its duty of care seriously. I was there that night to inform Lant that you could stay, but that I expected to be consulted and trusted if anything like it happened in the future."

Ahzya felt tears sting her dry eyes and her throat went dry. She exhaled an exhausted huff of a laugh, which took the last of her energy with it.

"I guess it's as I said, I'm also guilty of mistaken judgement. I was fifteen years old and scared to death. I could stand returning to Ulkadasa, but Peter..." Ahzya trailed off, she was tired of talking.

It didn't help that Ray was looking at Ahzya affectionately, a sympathetic smile on his face. He turned to face King Mark, who was massaging his temples in a soft rhythm.

"So, what's your call, Mark? Do we lock her up?" Ray asked, crossing his arms. "While she's a notorious thief and an attempted assassin, she did save your life twice now."

King Mark glanced at his friend with exasperation.

"Unfortunately, it's out of my hands, her actions will have to be judged by the law," King Mark answered with a sigh. "Besides, there are still far too many questions she has to answer."

Ahzya offered up a thin smile but said nothing. Some tricks must never be revealed, and some truths best left undiscovered.

A blur of purple approached Ahzya from the corner of her sight, but she slumped in the other direction. The wound to her back caused her tunic to stick to her, damp with blood. Everything around her buzzed and additional pain shot through her body as she hit the ground hard.

# CHAPTER THIRTY-ONE

MEDICAL ROOM, CASTLE PRYNESSE, ALPANIA

Ahzya blinked her eyes against the light and swallowed a groan as her whole body ached. She lay on her stomach, arms by her sides and head turned to the right. Ahzya tried to swallow but there was no moisture in her mouth, only a thick phlegm that coated her throat. For a moment, she felt like she couldn't breathe and struggled to sit up.

"Calm, Zah," a familiar voice soothed. "I'll help you."

Through a set of complicated movements, someone helped her sit up and brought a cup of water to her lips. Ahzya closed her eyes as she sipped on the water. Her body leant against that of her helper, and they stroked her lower back comfortingly.

"What happened?" Ahzya asked, her voice little more than a croak.

"You nearly got yourself killed, that's what," the voice rebuked her in a whisper. "Now hush, I don't want them to know you've woken up yet."

"How'd you get in here?" Ahzya asked, after another few sips.

"Castle Prynesse has some gorgeous inhabitants; so helpful," her companion's awe-filled voice replied.

Ahzya smiled softly and attempted to open her eyes again. This time she succeeded and when her eyes grew accustomed to her surrounds, she tilted her head to look up.

"You look good in glasses, Max," Ahzya commented.

Max, Ahzya's co-conspirator and best friend, grinned at the compliment, feeling the thin metal frame of her glasses. Compared to when they'd met five years earlier, Max was unrecognisable. To outsiders, she barely ever was recognisable, as she changed her appearance like one would normally change clothes. Currently she had her own hair on display, with its short curls combed into a male style. Max had dyed her hair brown this time, and even her eyebrows were dark over her blue eyes. She'd grown taller and lost her stick-thin stature.

"Where'd you get the outfit?" Ahzya whispered suspiciously.

Max glanced down at her outfit and kicked one leg over the other. The apothecary's uniform sat almost too perfectly: a green vest buttoned over a white, collared shirt, and brown pants met similar coloured boots just below the knees. The bottom of the long white jacket splayed itself over the bed where she sat.

"Oh, the cutest apothecary," Max answered with a dreamy sigh. "I'll have to return it to him before he wakes up. I do make a rather dashing imitation of him, don't you think?

"Scarily so," Ahzya returned with a shake of her head.

Similar to when they'd first met, Max's features were rather androgynous; therefore, she could easily manipulate her features to imitate the opposite sex when a disguise required it.

"So, what's the plan, Zah?" Max asked, resting her chin on Ahzya's shoulder gently. "When should I help you get out of here? I think they'll transfer you to the dungeons as soon as your health is more stable."

"Mmm," Ahzya pondered. "About that..."

"I don't like that tone," Max answered, stiffening.

*You definitely aren't going to like it.*

"I think it's time, Max," Ahzya said tiredly. "I don't want to be running my whole life. Now I've been caught, I'll just take my punishment... I'm so exhausted."

Max let out a pent-up sigh. She got up and eased Ahzya back to a relaxed position on the pillows.

"I know you are," Max finally said. "So...no elaborate prison break required?"

"No." Ahzya shook her head.

"Okay," Max said in resignation.

A minute passed and Max glanced towards the door of the room.

"I need to go," Max said, moving away.

"Thanks, Max," Ahzya said, chewing her lip to prevent tears from forming. "For everything."

Max swung her head back around and resolutely pointed at Ahzya.

"This isn't goodbye, Zah," Max said, with a grin. "You'll get so sick of me sneaking in to visit you. If they ship you off to anywhere else, I'll haunt those grounds too. Once you've rested up and are satisfied that you've atoned for your crimes, I'll be waiting at the gates when you're released. If you change your mind, and decide that atonement isn't for you, I'll break you out. Either way, when it's over, we'll buy that boat and chase freedom on the endless seas."

Max saluted and exited the room, her voice perfectly imitating her apothecary identity as she briefly spoke to the guards outside the door. Ahzya chuckled and relaxed her head on the pillow. Her wounds still ached, but now that she'd decided to face her punishment head-on, it felt like a weight had been taken off her soul.

DUNGEON, CASTLE PRYNESSE, ALPANIA

Jonathan Dryen sat on the small cot in his cell below the castle grounds. He leant against the bars, his face relaxed and eyes staring unseeing at the stone wall opposite. Shadows flickered due to the light thrown by wooden torches against the bars of the cell, but otherwise nothing moved.

The two king's guards who aided in the betrayal of King Mark shared his cell, but they also rested on their cots. They didn't show any sign of anger towards Jonathan and appeared to have easily accepted their circumstances. It wasn't like they didn't know the risks when agreeing to the plan, and Jonathan had chosen them specifically. Cole wasn't the only soldier who had gone through hellish abuse in the ranks of the king's army. If Jonathan could have brought about revenge or change, they'd volunteer for the role.

The silence amplified the sound of boots on the stone floor and the rattle of the gate to the cells. The gate clicked as it unlocked, and a palace guard entered. Someone entered behind the guard, identified as a prisoner by the leather cuffs that encircled the person's wrists. The newcomer wore a jacket, with a hood shadowing their face. There were already two guards inside near the entrance, and the new prisoner didn't move a muscle as the guards discussed something in a hushed tone.

The rattle of keys indicated the unlocking of the door to the cell next to Jonathan's. The new prisoner held out their arms obediently so the guard could release them from the cuffs. When released, the newcomer stepped into their cell and went to sit on the single cot which sat against the far wall of the cell. The door locked behind the prisoner, and the guard spared a quick look towards the other cells before turning to leave.

"You'll all receive a meal in a couple of hours, no doubt you're hungry," the guard said.

Jonathan and his cell mates didn't respond, but the newcomer nodded their head before lying down on the cot, their left arm folded beneath their neck for support. A quiet sigh was heard from the new prisoner, and then silence filled the quarters as the guard left them alone.

Jonathan moved so he could comfortably look over his shoulder, through the bars, to study his neighbour. The newcomer's figure was spread over the small cot but still fit comfortably within the sides. If the small frame hadn't given it away, the bandaged left hand and the immobilised right arm gave away the identity quick enough.

Jonathan continued to watch Ahzya silently, more out of boredom than anything else. Ahzya seemed relaxed enough, and, after giving a yawn a couple of minutes later, sat up to roll her neck.

"Do you regret it?" Ahzya asked simply, her gaze set to Jonathan.

"Not for a second," Jonathan answered confidently. "Cliché as it is, I'd do it all again."

Ahzya nodded her head slowly as though what Jonathan said made sense or at least that she had expected it. She looked tired, her eyes were glazed and in the low light her features were solemn.

"Do you regret it?" Jonathan asked Ahzya back.

"I'll probably regret it," Ahzya answered, after a hesitation.

"Many prisoners regret their crimes when they lose their freedom," Jonathan accepted. "You're young—"

Ahzya softly chuckled and shook her head.

"I've lived far too long in one lifestyle to develop a conscience to regret most of my crimes," Ahzya countered, massaging her right shoulder with the knuckles of her left. "I suspect I'll wake up on some days filled with rage at King Mark and wish I took that chance. Revenge and the idea of revenge is an almost sweet relief as an idea."

"You obviously believe that Mark doesn't deserve death for his crimes in one sense. Why did Madam Uran face death for her crimes?"

"Uran took a life, by effect of her own hands, and gloated about it. Her abuse was constant and justified in her own mind. She didn't have excuses for it, she had reasoning," Ahzya replied, her gaze darkening.

"Since it seems you hold repentance as a saving factor, why then is Mark innocent despite his apparent reserve in making an apology?" Jonathan genuinely queried.

"What happened to Cole on a weekly basis is disgraceful and should mar the opinion on Mark's perfect leadership; however, his hands are innocent of Cole's death." Ahzya looked down and ran her thumb over the ridges of her bandaged hand. "Cole made sure to keep his failing health as secret as possible, but it weakened him by the day. He could barely breathe some days, and his heart wasn't functioning properly either. When I last saw him, he knew he was dying from it. The night he died, I suspect he collapsed, not from the beatings, but his illness."

Jonathan remained silent. Ahzya had a feeling that he already knew. Ahzya could only go from what she'd witnessed before Cole's death, Jonathan had received the coroner's report.

"What angers me the most is that no-one stood up to protect him. No-one made a stand to say that it was wrong. Cole was an upstanding soldier; there was no need for him to go through any disciplinary actions. He was beaten due to jealousy or mean-heartedness and no-one protected him. They didn't kill him, but they made his life a living hell."

Jonathan gazed through the bars at her and just sat watching her. He watched the emotions play out on her face with a strange look in his eyes. Ahzya began to feel like she was talking too much again and shrugged.

"We're all, by nature, wrathful and selfish beings. In the name of doing the just thing, I'm sure we've both committed offences against people who feel we deserve the flames of hell," Ahzya mused further and then chuckled. "No doubt that'll be the reason we're behind bars for a while to come."

"Do you think the reason we're here is partially due to this 'informant' character?" Jonathan broke his silence, crossing his arms. "After all, I assume you didn't clue Cleo and Ray in on your suspicions that I'd attack Mark myself. Also, the whole reason I hired you was to make it seem that they'd caught the assassin they kept being warned about. Then Rimak could have achieved his mission successfully."

Jonathan raised an eyebrow as Ahzya smirked. Due to her insane act that afternoon five days ago, Jonathan became wary when she gained that amused look in her eyes.

"So, that's what your big plan with using two assassins was," Ahzya sighed. "Seems we were both in the business of plotting against each other. It must have annoyed you when I was actually doing a decent job, considering you were trying to put me behind bars."

"You seemed to slink your way out of all the traps I set for you. You escaped from the ambush on the north-west wall, which I'd warned them about. With all the attention I was drawing to you, you still managed to be like a shadow the rest of your time in the castle. I was beginning to think you'd actually be able to complete the assassination on your own," Jonathan admitted with admiration.

"Yet, you still worked against me," Ahzya pointed out, but she didn't seem annoyed by it.

"Your competence didn't sit well with my previous hire. Rimak wasn't happy with my interest in you: saying it discredited his reputation. That's why I warned you off, even if you succeeded, I was convinced he'd attempt to get rid of his competition. I wasn't blinded to his bloodthirsty nature."

"You didn't intend on paying Rimak anyway, I'm surprised he fought me over it. No doubt, the way of justifying hiring him, you'd already planned a reward of death for him."

"As the portreeve of Triox, I would have to hunt him down and destroy the assassin rat when he was sighted in my city. I would do my duty, and that's what the castle would have believed," Jonathan shrugged. "Regardless of my plans, someone warned the castle."

"I'm not sure how they first caught onto your plotting before you contacted me, or who took the initial step. Well, not for certain," Ahzya said, trailing off, but Jonathan didn't respond so she continued. "You thought you'd dealt with the informant, and you probably did deal with the initial ones. I heard of a maid and soldier who suddenly, without warning, ran off with each other. The maid didn't even tell anyone else about her budding romance which she left everything to pursue. I found it strange. The maid hailed from Liondel, perhaps she recognised Rimak, and with the help of the soldier made sure a letter of warning was given to the king. That's when you contacted me, so I could take the fall as the assassin they'd been forewarned about."

"You came to that conclusion all through the fact you took over the position of a maid who suddenly eloped?" Jonathan almost laughed.

"Unfortunately, I missed a lot of things in my concentrated effort to start my identity afresh. I only realised the puzzle pieces after Rimak attacked me, and I withdrew into hiding. I should have escaped the castle that night, but the irregularities made me stay. I hated the fact that you'd tried to outwit and use me."

"I'm surprised you didn't just sneak into my room and kill me," Jonathan stated, raising his hand in a 'I did what I did' kind of manner.

"There are more effective ways of exacting revenge than actually killing the person," Ahzya said, her eyes gleaming.

"Aah, like life in a cell, for instance?" Jonathan said in a light tone, waving his hands at his cell.

"It's one method, though I think you chose that one for yourself," Ahzya said, shrugging back at Jonathan casually.

Jonathan squinted his eyes at her for a few minutes; Ahzya kept eye contact with a slight smile.

"So, that's the first informant, what about the child?" Jonathan eventually asked.

"Ah, unfortunately that was due to my own oversight. The childlike writing was that of a friend of mine, at least that's the handwriting she chose this time. She found out that you had another assassin in the castle and tried to warn me. I don't have the ability to read and write Alpanian, considering I can speak well enough, that surprises people, but I don't go around advertising it. She figured that I'd be eavesdropping as part of my planning. It was obvious, but it didn't click as a message from her. If I hadn't been so distracted…" Ahzya paused and glared at Jonathan pointedly, "I should have easily figured it out."

"And Cleo and Ray? Who informed them?" Jonathan continued his questioning.

"I don't claim to know all the happenings. I do know that there was someone investigating Rimak shortly after I left Triox, perhaps they found out the connection between he and you."

"What about the night song and gifts? Did you plan that too?"

"They helped keep the security in the castle high. You didn't make your move because of it. Unless the informant forced the trickster into a withdrawal and put the castle at ease, we knew you'd be unlikely to proceed with your next attack," Ahzya concluded, moving her position on the cot.

"If we weren't both such lone-wolf bastards, and hadn't spent our time plotting against each other, we may have actually made a good team," Jonathan mused, his eyes shifting as Ahzya moved.

"I'd say it's been great doing business with you, but we both know neither of us have attained the goal we initially set with this job," Ahzya replied, the mood lifting as they exchanged a light banter.

"We might not have achieved riches or a new age for our country, or our revenge, but we can still take something from this situation," Jonathan mused, a mischievous light entering his eyes.

"And what's that?" Ahzya asked obliviously, as she lay down on the cot and closed her eyes.

"Love. You're a beautiful woman, and my looks don't do me an injustice. Just think, with hours stuck here, who knows what we could achieve. I'm not suggesting we move too fast. Tomorrow we could try holding hands," Jonathan said dreamily, his old smirk touching his mouth for the first time in a while.

The only reply to his flirtatious line was a loud, obnoxious snore and he gave a relaxed chuckle.

# CHAPTER THIRTY-TWO

### OREC 1407

DUNGEON, CASTLE PRYNESSE, ALPANIA

Cleo Erinth looked up as a pair of guards escorted Ahzya Xion into the room, her hands in cuffs. As an interrogation office built underground alongside the dungeons, the room was windowless and small. A table sat in the centre of the room with two chairs facing off over the surface. Some papers were laid out by a quill and ink pot, and Cleo straightened the parchment as Ahzya took a seat opposite her.

"How are your injuries?" Cleo asked.

"With several weeks of rest and little else to focus on—other than recovering—I'm as good as new, Your Royal Highness," Ahzya answered formally, rolling her right shoulder as proof.

It had been a little over a month since Jonathan's attack on King Mark in the royal courtyard. Other than meals, nothing else really happened at the dungeons. Ahzya filled in time with slow and careful training of her shoulder along with other exercises.

Jonathan had offered a weird kind of company for the first two weeks, but he'd been moved to an offsite prison. The castle wasn't in the habit of holding a lot of prisoners in the dungeons and so, other than the changing guard, Ahzya was alone.

"I apologise for not conducting an investigation and judgement earlier. Your situation is a unique one, and I had crucial business to take care of out of the country, therefore it's taken a while to decide on a course of action," Cleo explained.

"I'm a criminal, you don't owe me any explanation or speedy outcome," Ahzya answered with a matter-of-fact tone. "I *am* curious why you are the one tasked with prosecuting me."

"I'm the most impartial person for the task," Cleo answered, shuffling the papers.

"Impartial? You're the king's daughter," Ahzya doubted, her eyebrows tensing.

"Yes, that's a relationship I can hardly deny. However, given the fact that most of our soldiers feel like you've taken a stab at their honour by running around the castle freely and causing havoc, I really think I'm your best option. Given the situation, the nobility are highly invested and wanted a higher-ranking officer to pursue the line of the questioning. Commander Ray was a top pick, but he was dismissed, considering his investment in your youth and your attack that rendered him unconscious. All I can do is assure you that I take my duty seriously, and I won't let any predetermined emotions—that you assume I have—cloud my judgement," Cleo spoke clearly.

Ahzya relaxed her expression and nodded her head, accepting her moment of judgement had arrived.

"How about we start with your name?" Cleo said, dipping the quill in the ink pot.

"Ahzya Xion, spelt A-h-z-y-a and X-i-o-n, spelt as A-s-s-a S-y-n in Ulkadasan," Ahzya explained specifically.

"State your age and place of birth," Cleo said, writing swiftly on the parchment.

"Guess I'd be twenty-two now," Ahzya said, almost as if the realisation surprised her. "I was born in Port Shanville, Ulkadasa."

Cleo inclined her head and continued to write on the parchment, although Ahzya couldn't see what she noted down.

"Now, Your Royal Highness, we needn't insult each other's intelligence by discussing things that have already been said. I'm sure King Mark and Commander Ray have stated what happened in the courtyard, and I'm smart enough to know that your soldiers were eavesdropping and making notes the week I was first brought to the dungeons," Ahzya stated, tilting her head to the side. "Therefore, I don't need to retell anything I said to Jonathan either. No doubt you have more than enough reports and paperwork outlining my movements and nature."

Cleo paused her quill in mid-air and leant back in her chair. Her face didn't betray any of her thoughts or emotions, as she surveyed Ahzya's own relaxed posture. Several minutes ticked by and neither of them spoke.

"You're right," Cleo said finally, placing the quill on the table. "I'm not as against paperwork as our Commander Ray, but with too many pieces of paper the important ones can get hidden."

"So, what's the verdict? What's to become of me?" Ahzya asked without hesitation.

"King Mark has handed control over your fate to my hands," Cleo answered. "He did make a few suggestions and offered advisory points for me to consider in my final decision. He was torn between the fact you saved his life on two occasions, and that you plotted and tried to kill him. There's also the accusation of you murdering a member of the castle staff, and the incident resulting in injuring Commander Ray and three other royal guards. That's only the crimes you're accused of committing in the castle, who knows how many illegal activities you've committed before then."

"I'm a mysterious commodity." Ahzya shrugged.

"King Mark suggested a few more years in a cell or prison might be enough to rehabilitate you. I had another idea, which he agreed to after a little convincing," Cleo continued, crossing her arms. "We have a system in place that allows prisoners to work through their imprisonment. Your hard labour can make your sentence less boring, as well as help our country gather resources, improve our infrastructure, and other benefits, depending on the form of labour."

"How long am I going to be free labour for the Alpanian royalty?" Ahzya asked, a shadow of a frown creasing her forehead.

"At least five years. We'll have meetings during that time, and I'll assess what risk you are to the royal family and the people of Alpania. If you show good behaviour and an improved mentality, we'll discuss your freedom. Keep in mind that my approval and that of your supervisor must be undeniably convinced in order for that to happen."

Ahzya intertwined her fingers, and her gaze shifted around the room. She doubted she had much choice in the matter, but on closer thought, being out working would be better than trying to fill in years stuck inside four walls.

"Understood, Your Royal Highness, I'll be in your care," Ahzya said, bowing her head.

"Good, I'll explain the rest of the conditions on the way."

"We're leaving now?" Ahzya asked, glancing at the door.

"Time is of the essence," Cleo said, standing up with purpose. "I'm leaving Alpania today and won't be returning for six months. I'll get ready and double check everything is prepared and then we'll leave. It's not like you have much to pack, I imagine."

Ahzya almost rolled her eyes at Cleo's sarcastic final comment.

"I do have one favour to ask," Ahzya said hesitantly.

"If it's about your mare, you shouldn't worry. Noah will continue to care for her, and I can guarantee you'll see her sooner than you think, but I'll explain that while we travel," Cleo said, nodding to the guard that stood at the entrance of the room. "Also, you have visitors."

"Visitors?" Ahzya asked, a subtle quirk in her left eyebrow.

"You may say you're a lone wolf," Cleo replied, sizing Ahzya up, "but I disagree."

Cleo stepped into the doorway as the guard opened it for her.

"From within the castle and outside, you don't know how many people made it their business to approach me in order to beg for a merciful conclusion. They were concerned for your well-being, even when I suggested it was all just an act on your side," Cleo said, shaking her head. "You draw people to you, whether it's a lie or not."

Cleo then left. Ahzya stood awkwardly, waiting to see who her visitors were, since Max wouldn't have bothered with such an official visit. She didn't have to wonder long, as four women hustled into the room, instantly making it feel smaller.

"Mrs Youn, you're out of the kitchen!" Ahzya exclaimed, her eyebrows shooting up.

"I do leave it on occasion," Mrs Youn huffed.

Mrs Youn stood in front, arms crossed, but her eyes scanned Ahzya's body in concern. Either side of her stood Lesley and Merida, with Noelle hidden behind, as if she couldn't bring herself to fully show herself to Ahzya.

"What have they been feeding you? You've grown gaunt!" Mrs Youn fussed, moving forward to place a warm hand on Ahzya's cool cheeks.

The castle's main kitchen didn't handle meals for prisoners—criminals didn't deserve such delicacy.

"I eat well enough," Ahzya assured, shrugging.

"Nonsense," Youn seethed, pursing her lips.

Ahzya looked past Youn, aiming to distract herself from the emotion welling in her chest. She finally locked eyes with Noelle, whose red eyes were still flooded with tears, lips pouted and nose sniffling. Noelle began to sob and she ran forward, pushing Youn to the side. She began to hit Ahzya on the chest with clenched fists, so gently Ahzya knew she meant no real harm.

"It hurts," Noelle sobbed. "Make it better."

Finally, the tears that previously only threatened to escape, brimmed her eyes. She tried to gulp down the knot in her throat.

"Sorry," Ahzya whispered. "I'm sorry."

Noelle threw her arms around Ahzya and squeezed tight.

"We know you killed— you did it for us, but why did you have to go through it alone?" Lesley spoke up, in tears too.

"What nonsense!" Youn rebuked. "She didn't want us all in prison together, that's what."

"We knew you were hiding a dark side when Noelle and I saw your scars," Merida said. "We couldn't imagine how that had happened to you. You faced the Madams without a hint of fear, as if nothing they could do would hurt you."

"It was our cowardice that led you to—" Lesley began.

"You hold no responsibility for my actions, I alone—" Ahzya interrupted vehemently.

"That's the point!" Lesley cut Ahzya off. "You made sure we weren't alone, but you were. You were the one left alone."

Lesley watched Ahzya shake her head in firm denial and moved to join Noelle in the hug.

"Because of you, I don't have to worry about putting my child in danger. I can enjoy this beautiful journey, surrounded by a caring family of friends," Merida spoke, gently joining too.

"Oh my, what am I going to do with you all?" Youn sighed.

Youn approached the hug pile and patted each head of hair affectionately. She twisted her neck to glance at the guard standing awkwardly at the door, watching the messy group of teary maids and prisoner.

"What are you gawking at?" Youn chided softly.

The guard threw up his hands in defence, as if to say that he hadn't said a thing, they could fill the room with tears if they so wished.

## ROYAL CARRIAGE, UNKNOWN, ALPANIA

The chains of Ahzya's cuffs rattled as the carriage trundled over uneven ground, and Cleo glanced up from where she was casually sharpening a dagger that slid into a sheath on her boot.

Cleo had changed since their interrogation and now she sat, comfortable yet sophisticated, in a black and aqua uniform. A black leather neck and shoulder piece had a short aqua cape hanging from the left shoulder. Ahzya assumed that this cape allowed for a quiver of arrows to sit on the right shoulder without contending with the cape. A fitted black overcoat buttoned up on the right side of her chest with silver buttons and had boned cotton side-panels of aqua. Her boots were practical, housing two sheaths for daggers and made of matt soft leather. Cleo also had a utility belt at her waist which had several pockets and two longer curved daggers, one at either side.

Ahzya supposed these finely crafted clothes and weapons were all perks to being the daughter of the king, but she also sensed the weapons Cleo carried weren't just for show.

"A gift," Cleo said suddenly, interrupting Ahzya's assessment.

Cleo placed a bag, which had been sitting beside her on the seat, onto Ahzya's lap. The bag was made of sturdy leather, and Ahzya had assumed it held Cleo's travel supplies.

"It's your uniform. Wear it when you're working with me. You aren't required to wear it elsewhere. You'll also find some of your previous belongings. Your weapons have been passed on to your supervisor," Cleo explained.

"Why would they need my weapons?" Ahzya asked.

"It's not for them, it's for you, if your supervisor deems it necessary," Cleo answered simply, before Ahzya's confused expression made her explain a little more. "Circumstances may require it. You'll understand soon enough."

"There seems an awful lot of stuff I'll understand 'soon enough' and not much I know for certain now," Ahzya said with a shake of her head.

"I guess I should explain," Cleo sighed. "The supervisor you'll be working with has certain seasons and time frames that you'll be assigned to them for. Outside of these times, you will be under my direct supervision and guidance. Since we may be travelling a lot together, I've ensured that your horse will be available for your use."

"What use might I be to a princess?" Ahzya asked.

"Considering your wit and skills, I'm sure I could think of multiple mundane tasks," Cleo teased, though the humour didn't reach her eyes or lips. "I know I'd receive multiple frowns if I said this around anyone else, but I'm impressed with the way you think and work. Well, except for the vengeful side which almost killed my father."

"Understandable," Ahzya said with a nod to Cleo's last statement.

Ahzya tentatively unclasped the bag on her lap, continuing when Cleo waved a hand to allow her further search. The first thing Ahzya spotted was an aqua and black garment lying across the top of the bag's contents.

"What exactly does this uniform stand for?" Ahzya asked, noticing its similarity to Cleo's.

"Consider it a job offer, with a trial period over your sentence of hard labour," Cleo said.

Ahzya waited but Cleo didn't explain further, instead she peeked out the curtains of the carriage and sheathed her boot dagger.

"It seems we are arriving. We don't need any curious eyes, so—" Cleo reached into a pocket on her belt and drew out a key.

Cleo made swift work of releasing Ahzya from her cuffs and threw them on the seat without a second thought. The princess shifted forward on the carriage bench and adjusted her clothes.

"I hate riding carriages, but since I could hardly have the renowned Ahzya Xion waltzing out of the castle on horseback, this was the only option," Cleo said, as the carriage finally trundled to a stop.

"Why do you seem to trust me?" Ahzya asked suspiciously, stretching her freed hands.

Cleo visibly tensed; her gaze dropped while thoughts unfurled in her mind. Ahzya could see a battle being warred, but Cleo subconsciously clicked her tongue and came back.

"I don't," Cleo replied. "I don't, but I want to...I need to."

Ahzya's brow dipped. Cleo looked at her as if she were a challenge to overcome, but at the same time, Ahzya felt she wasn't the reason behind it.

The door to the carriage opened quickly, interrupting the moment, and a surprising sight beheld Ahzya as she gazed out. A scattering of windswept cirrocumulus clouds drifted high in the sunshine-filled sky. Sea birds flitted across the backdrop calling out to each other with screeching voices. The smell of the air brought a light to Ahzya's eyes and, with the carriage now stopped, she heard the familiar whispers on the wind. If that hadn't been enough to give it away, a familiar figure blocked half the view. Ray offered a hand to Cleo, who ceremoniously shook it.

"I'm afraid I'm merely a delivery service today, Ray," Cleo said apologetically, as she leapt out of the carriage. "I'd love to stay, but the others are already waiting for me, and we want to make good time before nightfall."

"Consider your duty complete, your horse is all ready," Ray answered, with a soft smile. "Travel safely, and assure Ten that I'll record accurate and specific bird details for her."

"Come back safely, Mandy Ray," Cleo ordered.

Cleo pulled Ray into a hug, slapping him sturdily on the back several times.

"Behave yourself, Ahzya. Remember you are meant to be doing some self-reflection with this hard labour, so don't allow yourself to enjoy it too much," Cleo ordered, squinting menacingly.

Cleo then gave a two-finger salute to them both. She mounted a black stallion, which had been kept a short distance away by a hooded male figure wearing a similar uniform to Cleo. The attendant mounted their own horse, and the horses pranced a few steps before they trotted away together through the crowd of townspeople.

Ahzya watched but spun around with a surreal sense of mounting excitement when they'd disappeared in a natural bend of the streets.

Life in Port Joonver was as busy as it had been years ago when Ahzya had first stepped foot in Alpania. Fishmongers yelled competitive prices to the passing crowds and sailors unloaded various products. The breeze turned Ahzya's head into a gentle flurry of hair, slapping against her face. Ahzya couldn't help smiling at the sting, but pure joy came when she spotted the crown jewel.

Sitting at the main dock, its sails furled neatly and the sun gleaming off the polished deck, was the majestic *Moonstruck*. Her title as queen of ships was as accurate as six years prior.

"I don't like to waste time on long explanations, so we'll talk as we walk, and the moment we step foot on the gangplank the words end and the work starts," Ray interrupted Ahzya's awestruck survey of the scene.

"Yes, Commander," Ahzya said, grabbing the bag Cleo had given her and stepping one pace behind Ray as he began walking.

"First of all, as a prisoner of the crown, I am assigning a guard to keep an eye on you when we are near any ports. However, since I doubt you've the insanity to jump overboard miles from land, I don't care to waste the time of any of my men on being a babysitter," Ray spoke bluntly.

"Yes, Commander," Ahzya agreed, taking two steps for each of Ray's strides.

"Second of all, you'll be our rigging monkey on this expedition and when you're free you'll help in the galley. You were injured, but Princess Cleo assures me you'll be up to the task," Ray toned the last sentence almost as a question.

"I'll be able to work at full capacity, Commander," Ahzya answered.

"Thirdly, and most importantly..."

They were almost at the gangplank, and Ahzya strained to hear the last instruction.

"Don't address me as Commander. You'll address me as Captain or Ray, though if you follow the rest of the crew, it'll be just Cap," Ray finished, stepping onto the gangplank and turning around.

Ahzya hadn't stepped on the gangplank and she came to a halt. The adrenaline coursing through her veins was as prominent as any of the covert missions she'd gone on. Ahzya clicked her heels together and raised her hand in a salute.

"Permission to come on board, Captain," Ahzya requested, keeping her posture straight.

"Permission granted," Ray said, a sparkle in his eye.

Ray reached out his hand towards Ahzya in an offer.

"Welcome back, our little shipmate," Ray said affectionately.

Ahzya accepted Ray's outstretched hand and the moment she did, there was a roar of cheers from on board *Moonstruck*. It was then that Ahzya noticed multiple crew members hanging from the side of the ship, half of them familiar faces.

Ahzya felt a prickle of anxiety, an overlay of judgemental sneers seeping out of her subconscious. She became aware of the fear she'd harboured since taking up the garb of a thief, a member of the underworld. If her short-term family hated her, hated her wretched past, if they shunned her for her wickedness, she wouldn't blame them. Despite the temptation to lower her head, Ahzya pushed herself to look straight into their faces. Instead of disgust or animosity, smiles and enthusiastic waves greeted her. Relief surged through her veins as Ahzya sheepishly stepped onto the gangplank, but she'd barely taken two steps when she was nearly tackled in a hug.

"Your guard, Ahzya Xion. I figured he was the best person for the job, considering I've heard him swear to never let you out of his sight on countless occasions," Ray called out with a playful grin.

His face had matured, but the blond hair and bright blue eyes were enough to identify Peter Lant. Despite his reserved nature, he had waited long enough for his sister to return, and any embarrassment from the public display of affection was dismissed.

Peter didn't say anything, it seemed words escaped him, but when their eyes met, it felt like nothing had to be said for he and Ahzya to understand each other.

"At least let her step onto deck, Pete," a familiar voice jeered from the deck.

Two shocks of red hair indicated the presence of jolly Nate and his nephew, Ethan. Ray's First Mate, Johno, was as muscled and large as ever. Beside him, looking small and timid was the cook, JB, who offered up a small wave when Ahzya looked at him.

"You're all still here?" Ahzya asked with a raised eyebrow, as she stepped onto the deck.

"Wouldn't be anywhere else," Johno answered in his booming voice.

"Aren't any of you aspiring to have a ship and crew of your own?" Captain Ray queried.

"Nah, Cap, we're content where we are. Besides, there is one obvious setback to being a captain that none of us are especially keen on," Nate replied with a mischievous grin. "Too much paperwork."

"Smart choice," Ray muttered under his breath.

Ahzya looked across at him at this, but Ray was there to meet her eyes and winked.

"Hey, Cath—er, Ahzya." Ethan approached awkwardly. "Guess our meeting in Prynesse was fate."

"If meeting previous to today is considered enough to be fate, then I share my fate with about seventy-five percent of the crew," Ahzya replied, recognising the flirtatious undertone.

Ethan massaged the back of his neck and hung his head in a depressed manner. Nate, being the loving, encouraging uncle that he was, slapped Ethan on the back and tried to hide a grin behind his callused hand.

"Aww, poor little Ethan's pick-up line fell flat, like a stingray on a butcher's table," Nate teased.

Ethan looked up at his uncle with what was almost a glare and shook his head.

"That doesn't even make sense... Did you come up with that all on your own?" Ethan said, a confused look on his face.

"Obviously he made it up on his own. You probably just don't get it because you've never been poetical like your uncle here. Pure genius with words, he is," Johno said, grinning wildly.

"You can't fault Ethan on his courage though, approaching our shipmate while Sergeant Lant is standing like a mother bear over her," Nate said with a tone of admiration.

"All right, crew, there's something wrong with this picture, who wants to tell me what exactly that is?" Ray asked, suddenly taking on a serious tone.

"Well, first of all, that shock of red hair is way too bright, secondly that stature needs some work, he kinda looks like a stick with—" Nate began, his own red hair falling around his face.

"Not Ethan, Nate. I'm concerned about this picture of all you strong lads standing around like a gaggle of geese at a picnic; like a group of little old ladies doing knitting while talking about their latest quilting projects; like vultures around a dead rabbit; like earthworms after rain; like ants around a bread crumb; like bees on a—" Ray said, looking solemnly around the group.

"On it, Cap!" the crew interrupted in unison.

Ray trailed off and watched as his crew hurried to their stations and tasks. He adjusted his hat on his head and ascended the stairs to the helm.

"Make sure our supplies are balanced, tend the sails, and double check you have everything you need. Then kiss your loved ones goodbye and come ready for adventure. We set sail at dawn!" Ray ordered, his voice carrying across the whole ship.

Ahzya hung the leather bag over her shoulder and let a toothy grin rest on her face.

*I'm finally home.*

THE STORY CONTINUES IN BOOK TWO OF THE

SERIES

COMING IN LATE 2026

KEEP UPDATED ON FUTURE TALES AND ADVENTURES BY VISITING
WWW.HANNAHAFINCHWRITER.COM
AND CONSIDER SIGNING UP FOR THE AUTHOR'S NEWSLETTER.

# ACKNOWLEDGEMENTS

They say the writing process can be rather lonely—and it is—but I've been blessed to have worked with a team of individuals that made it equally as exciting.

I would like to thank my editor Kayleigh from Enchanted Edits for proofreading and giving me the peace of mind to finally share my story with the world. I don't know how I would have combated my problem with commas without her.

My cover artist Ellie deserves all the praise for bringing my vision for the illustration to life; bringing her own perspective to my ideas. Very few things can live up to my vivid imagination, but this piece of art crafted by Ellie's hands exceeded my expectation.

This book would never have been published if not for the kind words and support of my circle of friends and family that combated my infuriatingly perfectionist nature. More specifically Josh, Mum, and Ezra for giving me feedback at various stages and keeping me—mostly—emotionally sane throughout it all.

I would also like to thank you, the reader, for taking a chance with my debut novel and its new world and characters. I hope you were able to experience, even in a small portion, the joy, laughs, and emotions, I had while creating it. I am blessed and grateful for every pair of eyes, every heart, and every soul that took the time to delve into this book. You are part of the reason my dream of holding a book of my own creation in my hands came true.

This story wouldn't exist if God hadn't blessed me with a creative spark; therefore, finally, and most importantly, all glory be to the One True Creator.

# ABOUT THE AUTHOR

Hannah A. Finch began life as the only daughter of a family of seven in rural Victoria, Australia. Imaginative adventures with her siblings turned into a passion for writing them down. Now, from her love of good food, music, and nature, to her over-attachment to the subtlest of side-characters, not even chronic illness can keep her from exploring and chronicling the fantastical.

Being plagued by plots of kingdoms and intrigue, or by that one character that wants to cause chaos, may not be everyone's idea of fun, but for Hannah it's what makes life enchanting.

Apart from writing, Hannah likes recording her own reading adventures, snacking, watching TV shows and virtual boy bands, and listening to tunes. Above all else, she adores her family—now more extended than the original seven—and hopes to write books her nephews and nieces will be excited to read in the future.

You can find out about upcoming releases and news by following Hannah on social media and visiting her website:

www.hannahafinchwriter.com

www.ingramcontent.com/pod-product-compliance
Lightning Source LLC
LaVergne TN
LVHW091528060526
838200LV00036B/524